..DATE DUE

DEC 17 1991	

SPARTINA

SPARTINA

John Casey

 Alfred A. Knopf   New York   1989

Library of Congress Cataloging-in-Publication Data
Casey, John. Spartina.
    I. Title.
PS3553.A79334S64   1989   813'.54   88-45765
ISBN 0-394-50098-9

Manufactured in the United States of America

Published June 26. 1989
Reprinted Three Times
Fifth Printing, December 1989

I gratefully acknowledge the following institutional support:
the John Simon Guggenheim Foundation, the National Endowment for the Arts, the
MacDowell Colony, the University of Virginia Center for Advanced Studies, the
Virginia Center for Creative Arts, and the Pinchot Institute for Conservation Studies.
Special thanks for marine tutorial to:
William Tongue of Westport Point, Massachusetts, Lenny Chesney of Brockton,
Massachusetts, and Stephen Jones of West Mystic, Connecticut.

SPARTINA

*D*ick Pierce swung the bait barrel off his wharf into his work skiff. He cast off and began to scull down Pierce Creek. He built his skiffs with an oarlock socket on the transom. He had to tell most buyers what it was for. In fact sculling was a necessity for him—this far up the creek it was too narrow to row and, except at high water, too shallow to put the outboard down.

The tide was still dumping and he let her drift a bit. A spider's strand broke against his forehead. A light mist came off the water but dissolved as soon as it got above the black banks. Dick loved the salt marsh. Under the spartina there was black earth richer than any farmland, but useless to farmers on account of the salt. Only the spartinas thrived in the salt flood, shut themselves against the salt but drank the water. Smart grass. If he ever got his big boat built he might just call her *Spartina,* though he ought to call her after his wife.

He always started off these fair early-summer days in a mood as calm and bright as the surface of the water. Everything was lit up silver and rose—the dew, the spider's webs, the puffs of mist, even the damp backs of the dunes on the barrier beach that divided the salt ponds, the marsh, and the creeks from the sea.

Where Pierce Creek joined up with Sawtooth Creek he let the outboard down and cranked it up. He could see the breachway and through the breachway the horizon, a pale streak. The skiff climbed onto a plane with ease. Eighteen-foot, but she was as light as any sixteen-footer, and almost as narrow. She held as much as clunkier skiffs, he didn't clutter up the inside with knees or thwarts. She was extraordinarily high in the prow; he didn't mind taking her out in moderate seas. The only thing he couldn't do was run a deep trawl of pots way offshore. And that's where most of the lobster were in summer. He dared go twenty miles out, but it wouldn't do him any good without the heavy machinery to haul even a single trawl of heavy pots and heavy warp.

Dick throttled down as he went past Sawtooth Island to line up for the run through the breachway. He could see the line of surf on the sandbar just outside the mouth. He nipped through and turned hard to starboard to follow the tidal channel around the sand. He cut back to port, feeling the chine and the skegs catch and hold through the turn, and so out onto the glassy swell; for all his troubles, his skiff was sinless, and her sweetness sweetened him.

He soured a little after he'd pulled ten pots—trash in all but two—spider crabs and whelks. A fat two-pound tautog which he kept for bait. After he'd pulled a few more empty pots he began to think of the tautog as supper. Things looked up—three small keepers, one more questionable. He put the gauge on it and threw it back. Five for twenty. The kind of day he'd put up with in August but not in early June. He ate half of his cheese sandwich and drank half of his thermos of hot milk and coffee. He considered whether it would be worthwhile moving some pots to a deeper hole. It was a couple of miles away, might have someone's pots there already. And that hole was more frequented by sport fishermen who weren't above pulling a pot if the striped bass weren't biting.

Dick had caught a pair of them at it once. He'd come round the rock just in time to see them drop his pot overboard. A college kid and his girlfriend in a deluxe Boston Whaler, all white fiberglass, white vinyl rubrails, and chrome rodholders. Dick had come alongside, jumped into their boat with his six-pronged grapnel in his hand. He swung it against the kid's outboard casing, cracking the plastic.

Dick said, "I see you near one of my pots again, I'll put this through your goddamn hand."

The kid said, "I was just taking a look."

The girl said, "You're crazy."

Dick got back in his own boat. The girl wrote down Dick's boat number, cranked up her engine, and left.

It turned out it was the girl's boat. Her father sent Dick a bill for the engine casing. Dick sent it back with a note. "Your daughter and her boyfriend pulled one of my pots. That is stealing."

The father called him up. That was when Dick still had his phone.

"Mr. Pierce, my daughter tells me she and her boyfriend didn't take anything. Is that correct?"

Dick said, "They pulled my lobster pot."

"They may have pulled your pot, but they didn't take anything. You threatened them. You do that again, I'll have you charged with assault with a deadly weapon."

Dick said, "Go to hell."

The father was still talking when Dick hung up.

Some time later Dick went to Westerly on his annual round of banks. While he was waiting to see the loan officer, a man came up to him and said, "Mr. Pierce?"

Dick got to his feet and said, "Yes."

"Mr. Pierce," the man said, and Dick recognized the voice. "I've had a look at your loan application. If you'd care to step into my office . . ."

Dick thought of his application. The list of his jobs, the crews he'd quit, the crew he'd been fired from. His house. His mortgage. His wife's job as a piecework crab picker. His puny income from lobstering and quahogging. His pickup he was still paying for. His claim that his half-built big boat was worth forty thousand. His power tools . . .

Dick said, "Give me back the application."

The man said, "Are you saying you wish to withdraw your—"

Dick said, "Yes."

The man sent a secretary out with the form. Dick went around to the Hospital Trust, Old Stone Bank, Columbus. Nothing doing. At Rhode Island Federal Savings & Loan he got a woman loan officer. She suggested he get someone to cosign. Then they'd consider giving him half what he asked. At 17½ percent. On ten thousand dollars that was 1,750. Unless he built someone else a boat, he couldn't do it. If he built someone else a boat, then he wouldn't get his own boat built.

The woman said, "You're a family of four. If you depreciated your tools and your workplace—you work at home, right?—you could qualify for certain assistance programs for your family—"

Dick said, "Welfare?"

The woman took a breath and said, "Yes."

Dick didn't get angry with her. If she'd been slick, young, sure of herself, crossed her legs with a little scratch of nylon on nylon as she leaned forward, he might have blown up. But this woman wasn't sure of herself, was trying to be nice. Her cheap navy-blue jacket, the unevenly crushed ruffles of her blouse, the way she picked at the frayed leather corner of her desk blotter—were all awkward and nice. Dick said, "I know you're trying to help." The woman started to say something, Dick went ahead. "From what I've heard, welfare people come round to inspect your house. I've just told four banks more than I care to about my life. In the second place, I've got a half-built fishing boat in my backyard. I don't mean a little dinghy. She's over fifty foot long, eighteen-foot beam. She's damn near the size of my house. The welfare people could see she's worth thousands and thousands of dollars. The wood and hardware alone. Even half built she's worth more than welfare allows. But I can't get anyone from a bank to come look at her, I can't get you to ask someone who knows half a thing about boats to tell you she's already worth more than I'm asking to borrow. You could ask Joxer Goode, he owns the crab plant—"

The woman said, "I know about Mr. Goode...."

Dick said, "If I had a boat it wouldn't be a question of risk, I could sign up with Joxer Goode and haul red crabs. There are boats not much bigger than mine bring in twenty thousand dollars' worth of red crabs two and three times a summer. Joxer Goode has contracts in Providence and Boston, pretty soon he'll be shipping to New York City. His crabmeat sells at half the price of lobster, restaurants love his crabmeat, he's going to get rich. And the boats supplying him are going to make good money. He needs more boats, he can't get enough lobstermen to put out for crabs. They're stuck in their ways, and some of them are scared to go all the way out to the edge of the shelf. I'm ready to go. I need twenty thousand dollars and before next summer is over I could pay you your 17 1/2 percent. That's just on crabs. On the way out and on the way back I could stick a few swordfish. At four fifty, five dollars a pound, average size two hundred pounds, that's nearly a thousand dollars a fish. I'd have to be missing both arms if I couldn't bring in an extra ten thousand from swordfish."

Dick pulled out the glossy green-and-white flyer he'd picked up in the bank lobby. He turned to the page with green cartoons. There was a house, a kid in a cap and gown holding a diploma with dollar signs flying around his head, and there was a big motorboat. Dick pointed to the caption: "Let us help your dream come true."

The woman looked genuinely sad. Dick said, "Fishing-boat captains who own their own boats make around forty thousand a year. I've been on their crews, I've built two of their boats when I worked in the boatyard. I've been on the water my whole life. I could be making good money, and you tell me to go on welfare."

The woman said, "If it was up to me . . ."

"Yeah, okay, you don't hear me cussing you. It's the way it works—when I've got the money, the bank'll lend me the money."

The woman squared up her desk blotter with her fingers. Dick said, "Thank you."

The woman said, "Have you thought of asking Mr. Goode to help you finance your boat?"

"Oh yeah. One of these days he might get time to take a look." Dick thought he'd talked enough for that day. He said thank you again and left before he got into the story of his miscue with Joxer Goode. He got into his pickup and got out of Westerly. He felt a sludge of depression. The pickup backfired as he slowed down for a light, reminding him he'd have to put in a new muffler. At least he hadn't got mad at anyone this trip, not so he said anything drastic.

Now, drifting on the swell, he decided to leave his pots where they were. He'd spend the afternoon tonging until he had enough quahogs to make the trip to the shellfish store in Wickford worthwhile. The quahogs put him in mind of steamers—summer prices had begun, and he had a scheme for steamers that would bring him several satisfactions. The moon was right, the tides were right. There was a risk, but if he pulled it off it would make up for a lot.

*D*ick had had this plan ever since a Natural Resources officer had run him out of the bird sanctuary. Dick had dug steamers on the inside beach of Crescent Pond his whole life. When they set up the bird sanctuary Dick was all for it; it meant the salt marsh would be pretty well preserved, from Sawtooth Creek all the way to the Green Hill restaurant. Dick still owned the sliver of marsh between Pierce Creek and Sawtooth Creek and he could still shoot ducks and geese on that edge of the sanctuary. Clamming was allowed, but the Natural Resources officer had run him out of Crescent Pond because he'd come in with his skiff. No motors in the bird sanctuary. Dick said he'd row. The officer got stiff about it, impounded his peck of steamers. The only other way to get to Crescent Pond was to walk the mile-long trail from the state parking lot. Easy enough if you didn't have a basket of clams to carry.

Tonight Dick was going to satisfy himself. He'd borrowed Eddie Wormsley's tractor with its front scoop. At eleven at night he got his two sons to climb on back, drove the tractor out of his own driveway, down the shoulder of Route 1, and nipped into the bird sanctuary, where a tree had fallen across the woven-wire fence and pushed it down. There was an old causeway that the farmer who'd owned the marsh in the 1800's had put in for his wagons to come and get salt hay. It was probably a hundred years old, silted over and covered with grass and bushes, but firm enough to keep the tractor from bogging down. The boys clung to the fenders, their feet on the clevis bar, ducking as the branches of scrub whipped past. When they got to Crescent Pond, Dick lowered the front scoop. The beach was bare twenty yards out—a full-moon low tide. Just up from the waterline Dick stuck in a corner of the front scoop and drove, cutting a trench fifty yards long. The moon gave enough light so that the boys could pick up the clams and toss them into the fifty-five-gallon drum Dick had lashed to the clevis bar and the back of the driver's seat. By midnight they'd filled the drum. Dick thought he heard the Natural Resources jeep on the seaside beach. He raised the scoop, the boys climbed on back, and Dick notched the throttle up to get them up the slope of sand and over the crusted lip of earth where grass and scrub began. Dick kept up his speed back along the swath he'd cut on the way in, the boys clinging like limpets to the back of the tractor, ducking branches and vines. Dick shut the motor off when he got near Route 1 and sent the older boy out to the shoulder to make sure the coast was clear. Dick drove the few yards necessary to get past Sawtooth Creek, then turned into the tangle of brush that was his sliver of land between Pierce Creek and Sawtooth. When he got in a ways he stopped, and he and the boys loaded gunny sacks with the clams, tied the throats of the sacks, and lowered them into Pierce Creek. Dick left the boys to finish with the clams on their own. Dick got the tractor back to his yard, up onto the flatbed trailer, hitched the flatbed to his pickup, and drove as fast as he dared to Eddie Wormsley's. Dick told Eddie what he'd been up to. Eddie laughed, but he got worried too. Eddie had been caught killing a swan the year before. The Natural Resources officer let him go, but he didn't want more trouble. Dick hosed down the front scoop and the rear tires and scrubbed out the treads of the front tires with a wire brush. Eddie made him pick out the leaves and pieces of vine. Dick asked him if he wanted a cut when he sold the clams. Eddie wavered, finally said he'd better not. Eddie gave Dick a beer and then sent him home. Dick knew it must be late—Eddie was famous for his night hours.

Dick was up at dawn. He loaded the gunny sacks into his skiff and skipped past Westerly on the glassy morning sea. He sold the clams to a shellfish dealer in Connecticut for $112.

He set some more pots on the way home, and pulled and rebaited his others. He was pinching with hunger by the time he got back. The tide was just trickling in, so he had to scull the last bit to his dock. He made himself a sandwich in the kitchen, but his wife, May, heard him and lit into him before he could start eating. She was weepy with anger. She took him to the boys' room. They were lying on their beds with the covers back, their legs and arms puffed up like wormy logs.

"Look at that! Just look at that!" May almost never got mad at him, and when she did he always felt awful, but this was worse than usual. Dick saw what had happened—the ride through the brush had whipped some cuts across their arms and legs—their hands were okay since he'd made them wear gloves to pick up the clams. Poison ivy had got into the cuts and scratches and foamed up in wet blisters and raw spots. May wanted him to take them to the hospital. Low as he felt, Dick resisted that idea. Dick said he'd get them something from the drugstore if they would go lie in the salt creek till he got back. "It'll sting some, but salt water'll pull the juice right out. I swear, May, it's the best cure. When I got fish poisoning all up my arm I cured it with salt water." May wouldn't answer him, but the boys did what they were told. Dick felt bad enough so he spent more than twenty dollars on tubes of cortisone gel.

By evening the boys felt better, but May was still sullen. After supper, when he was smoking a cigarette on the porch before the mosquitoes came out, he found out why she was still so mad. "Parker stopped by to see you," she said. "He was here when the Natural Resources officers came by. He made it worse, his being here. Eddie Wormsley's one thing, but Larry Parker!"

"I should have told them to wear long pants. I am sorry about the boys, May."

Dick was amazed that didn't do it. He apologized to her once a month at most. May said, "I need some money to get the phone back."

Dick didn't say anything.

May said, "They want a fifty-dollar deposit."

Dick peeled it off the roll, let her settle back in her chair, and said, "I'm going down to the Neptune to see the ball game. Maybe I'll run into Parker."

He felt bad about that as he drove past Galilee, then he remembered he only had forty dollars left, and twelve hours before he'd had $112. He put a five-dollar bill in his left pocket and swore not to spend more than that even if he had to buy Eddie a drink. Of course, if he ran into Parker, Parker would buy.

*P*arker had always scared Dick a little. Parker would do anything, that was part of it. And Parker seemed to know things about Dick that Dick didn't. Parker said he'd never get Dick into anything that he himself wouldn't do. That didn't strike Dick as much of an assurance.

Dick had gone off on some wild-ass rides with Parker. One time a few years back, Parker got hold of a motor yacht that the owner wanted moved from Newport to the Caribbean. The owner gave Parker a credit card for fuel, berthing fees and food, and two plane tickets back to Boston. The guys at the Neptune who knew Dick and Parker were surprised the two of them got along. But with just the two of them running the fifty-foot yacht, they didn't see much of each other the first week. After four hours on, one of them would wake the other up, say a word about the weather, and that was it. Each had a cabin of his own the couple of times they tied up at night. Parker was eager to get south, so they usually ran all night. With the owner's credit card on board, fuel economy was not a big item, so they ran as fast as the seas would allow.

Dick had loved the trip south. The boat was good, even in a half-gale. He liked getting a look at Chesapeake Bay, Cape Hatteras, the islands off Georgia. It was there Parker took him on a side trip in the dinghy. They went up a salt creek that cut into Ossabaw Island. "Lookee there," Parker said, "I'll bet it's the first time you saw one wasn't on a shirt." Dick looked. He saw the eyes blink first and then took in the body floating in the muddy water. He'd always liked Parker for taking the time to show him an alligator.

Parker got less amiable when he started looking for fun in the islands. He railed at Dick for turning in early, for getting cold feet at padding the expenses. Parker thought Dick was having a case of social nerves, that Dick was intimidated by the fancy bar life. Dick had to admit he was thrown some by the accents of the West Indians, the English, let alone the foreigners. Parker got into the act, even dressed the part. A pale sweater woven so loose you could just about see through it, no shirt. Cream-colored topsiders, no socks. But Dick could tell him apart from the carriage trade. Parker leaned forward, his eyes moved fast, and his mouth, with his bad teeth and gray fillings, was held in small and tight, even when he was having a good time. Parker did have a good time. Dick saw that, envied him his nerve, and admired it.

It was funny—when Dick was with his friend Eddie Wormsley, Dick was the wild hair. When Dick was with Parker, Dick was the fuddy-duddy. But it wasn't just that, or the foreignness of the people or the sleekness of some of them, that put Dick at half-speed. It was the *place* that knocked him for a loop. The air, the sea, the islands. Dick had fished off Cape Cod, Maine, and Nova Scotia. All that was more or less the same, or at least understandably different. The West Indies was another planet. The air smelled different, touched his skin like silk. The water was the same salt water, but the colors were different, greens and blues he'd never seen. The movies and magazines hadn't prepared him. And it made him uneasy that he had very little idea what kind of bottom or what kind of deep the waters hid. The whole thing left Dick in a daze. They'd finally worked it out that Dick would put in the first part of the evening with Parker, then he'd turn in early and have the first part of the day to himself. Dick most often took the twelve-foot dinghy and just poked around, caught a few fish, turned them back.

Dick went along happily when Parker took on a couple of tourists he'd met in a bar. They paid five hundred bucks for two days and a night of fishing and gunk holing. Parker gave Dick 40 percent. That was fine with Dick, Parker was the ace at dealing with strangers. Dick did the work of keeping things shipshape, set up the fishing rods. Parker did the patter.

Parker and he finally delivered the boat to the manager of a yacht club. A day late, no problem. But then Parker cashed in the plane tickets, got them passage to Florida with another guy he met in a bar. Parker showed Dick the bus station in Miami and split. But Dick had four hundred cash in his pocket and all he had to worry about was May being sore at him because he got back a week late.

Though there *was* that one other little detail. A month passed and Parker had showed up on Dick's front porch. Dick knew what Parker wanted. Dick said, "I threw those old boots out, if that's what you're here for." Dick had discovered them in the bottom of his sea bag, the name *Jimenez, J.* stenciled in ink on the canvas lining.

Parker laughed and said, "No, you didn't."

"I tried them on, they didn't fit, I chucked them."

Parker nodded and smiled.

Dick said, "Besides, the heels had broke off."

Parker said, "There you go, you got the right idea but you came out wrong. Bring the boots, I'll show you."

Dick got the boots and Parker slit the canvas lining and fished out a handful of flat plastic pouches.

Dick said, "What is that? Because if that's heroin—"

"Dickey-bird. Never go near it. This is just a little toot, is all this is. If anyone had've looked, these here boots belong to Jimenez, I'd've spoken up. As it is, we're still sixty-forty, and I'm here to pay my debt."

Dick said, "No thank you."

Parker thought a while. He said, "Look, one out of three, maybe one out of two crews has someone doing coke when they're out there pulling pots ten, twenty hours straight. You know that. I'm not hanging around some schoolyard with this stuff. So that couldn't be the problem. Now, I did use you a little, you've got a fair gripe about that, but on the other hand I know what I'm doing and you were being what I'd have to call real slow. So I used your rugged good looks, you know, your grim Yankee manner. But I'll tell you, I'm not crazy and I'm not greedy. Keep it simple, keep it small." He pulled out a roll of twenties and counted out ten of them. Dick did the math in his head. "Five hundred bucks for that?"

Parker said, "Roughly. I don't sell on the street. You want to come along when I—"

"No. I wasn't doubting you."

"Oh, I get you. Yes, it is amazing. That's what does people in, it's so goddamn amazing. That's why I don't do more. This little, even if someone mentioned it to someone, it could be just a little recreational use. Now, *dealers,* dealers get eat up, and not just by the Coast Guard. They eat each other. Users are small fry. So we'll stay small."

That "we" set off a caution light. Dick hadn't gone south again. He'd helped Parker move boats—motor yachts, sailboats—anywhere along the Northeast coast. Parker knew the damnedest people, he seemed to specialize in careless rich people. One guy called him up from Nova Scotia. He'd got his ketch down there and run out of vacation. Parker and Dick brought her back up to New York. On the way Parker got up to his game again, picked up a family off the dock in Rockland, Maine, made a quick deal with the father, took the whole family including the three kids out for a long afternoon. Parker had just walked up to their recreational vehicle and started chatting. He let the kids haul the sails, take the wheel, gave them certificates saying they'd passed their offshore crew rating, signed it "Lawrence Parker, Capt." It didn't seem to be the money, though Parker had picked up a couple hundred bucks. It was just that he needed to be up to something.

Parker had actually owned boats of his own. Dick didn't understand how Parker got the first one. Somewhere along the line Parker got one boat that was barely afloat and worked it a whole summer with two green college kids. First week in September her engine caught fire, she burned and sank. Parker and the two college kids came in in the dory. Ran the outboard until it was out of gas and then took turns rowing all night. Parker collected the insurance, a good amount, but no more than a sound boat of that same size would have been insured for. Sensible Parker. Don't get greedy.

Dick couldn't explain to himself why he went along with some

of the stuff Parker got up to. Most of the time Dick didn't like
people who were slippery. Parker wasn't just slippery, though Dick
had heard him slither around until Dick didn't know how Parker
himself knew which way he was headed. Dick didn't think it was
the fun of being in on it that made the difference, but maybe that
was part of it. It was Parker's light touch too, made it seem he'd
never do any real harm.

May said Parker was a bad influence on him. True enough. But
in another way Parker kept him straight, Parker was the channel-
marker, shoal water on the other side of him.

Dick stuck up for Parker when May complained, or when someone at the Neptune made a crack, but Dick wouldn't have called
him a friend, not in the sense that Eddie Wormsley was a friend.
Eddie would cut off his hand for Dick and Dick would do the same
for Eddie. Eddie and he saw eye to eye on most things. Eddie once
had some words with Miss Perry but, that aside, Dick felt Eddie
and he were dumb the same way, capable the same way, set the
same way. Parker, now, Parker liked to change his skin and, what
was more, tried to get you to change your skin. One night in the
Bahamas Parker had come back with a girl, an English girl. Dick
was still on deck smoking a cigarette. Dick went up to the bridge to
leave them alone on the afterdeck. Parker and the girl went below.
Dick stayed on the bridge. Dick was startled to hear the intercom
come on. He and Parker hadn't ever used it, so it took Dick a while
to find the cutoff switch. He heard enough to get that the girl was
English, enough to get prickly. Dick didn't go below until they left.

Next day, after they put to sea, Parker laughed about it. So it
hadn't been an accident. "Those English girls love to chat, don't
they? No matter what, they'll just chat along. . . ."

Dick said, "Jesus, Parker."

"It's a whole different way they have—"

"You do what you want, but don't do that again."

"Okay. But it's all part of seeing the world, Dickey-bird."

On the whole they got along. Parker was a good cook, deferred to Dick's edge in boat handling and navigation. Parker knew a lot about the islands—who lived there, what they did, what was in the sea. If you didn't let him tip you off balance, you could have a pretty good time. Once a year was about right, enough to run your engine fast, shake out the sludge.

When he got to the Neptune, Dick found Parker at a table. The first thing Dick noticed was that Parker's right forearm was in a cast. Otherwise he looked healthier than before, relaxed, all spruced up. New shirt, red and white checks, the collar still stiff.

They had a beer, watched the Sox go ahead, hold on, put it away on a pop-up to Yaz. Parker collected a five-dollar bet at the bar, bought the loser a beer, and brought back two more for Dick and him.

"I got a boat," Parker said. "I got a college kid. I could use someone else. The kid don't know much. And my arm's not right yet."

"You going to be around here or you on your way somewhere?"

"I'll be around a while."

Dick didn't press just yet. He was thinking he didn't like Parker's boats when Parker had college boys along. Parker played with them a little too hard, worked them too near the edge when they weren't used to it. Halfway through a night of hauling pots Parker would say in a TV announcer's voice, "It's time for . . . Captain Parker's Pep Pills for Sleepy Sailors!"

Some of Parker's college boys didn't get to sleep for a day or two after they got ashore. You could see them at the Neptune or the Game Room playing Space Invaders till closing, zombies with ten bucks' worth of quarters.

Parker said, "I could use some more pots."

Dick said, "I can find you some pots. I got a few heavy-gauge ones myself. Your college kid's likely to bust up wood ones."

"I got a few days. The boat needs a little work. You want to help out? Maybe make a run when we get her back in the water? Stick some swordfish. I hear there's some around."

"Can you handle the wheel with your arm? No use trying to nose up on a swordfish if you got your college boy at the wheel."

Parker smiled. Dick saw that Parker's front teeth looked good— all square and white. Dick said, "You been making some money?"

"Here and there. I could use some more. I want to get a boat, not the one I got, a good-looking boat I can use for charters. Winter down in the islands. Spring, work out of Virginia Beach. Come up here summers for the tuna derby. Take out some sportsmen. You know what a charter boat gets for a three-day run from Virginia Beach to the Gulf Stream? Twelve hundred dollars. The mate works for tips. Minus fuel, that's three hundred a day. The sports pay whether you get fish or not. 'Course it's better if you've got a reputation for finding fish. That and good food, some good stories. An all-around good time."

Dick laughed. "Sounds like your sort of deal."

"But it's got to be a class boat. Fast. Maybe twenty, twenty-five knots. Loran, sonar. All that good stuff. Going to cost, though. That boat I got in the yard'll only pay for a fraction."

Parker spun his beer glass in his fingers. "I got friends in the islands. I got a real good friend in Virginia Beach. But my crystal ball tells me this is the place for this summer. Haul some pots— I got a barge load set a week or so ago. But mainly get some swordfish. I know some about that, but I figure you know even more. You're undervalued around here. You ever hear rich people talk about stocks and bonds? That's always what they're looking for, is something undervalued. I could make something out of you. You could make something."

Dick changed the subject for a while. Told Parker about how he'd dug clams with a tractor, made a few quick bucks.

Parker was amused by the story, but came back around to his boat in the yard. "Tell you what, Dick. You take a look at her. I'll pay you to fix one or two things on her. Pay you two bucks an hour under yard prices, that's more than you'd make if you did it working for the yard."

"What's wrong with her?"

"The yard fixed her up some, a plate or two was loose. . . ."

"What's wrong with her now?"

"I ought to take a look at the stuffing box."

Dick said, "Damn. I hate messing with that. That's a real shitty job."

"Uh huh, a real shitty job."

"Okay, I'll take a look at her."

Parker said, "Only thing is, I can't have an outside worker. You know the rule. I'll have to sign you on as crew for you to work."

Dick said, "You going to use a spotter plane? I don't want to go out and wallow around in the swordfish grounds, just me and you."

"Maybe a spotter plane. Got to make some money, I owe the yard. Maybe second time out. You go down, take a look at her, and consult your horoscope. I'll be here."

*D*ick ran his skiff out with a half-dozen pots he'd repaired. He pulled his pots, rebaited a few. Brought in all the heavy-duty ones. He probably would go with Parker. He sold his basket of lobster, fifteen bucks. Groceries, nothing to put by. If he went with Parker, the boys could pull these few pots he'd left in less than an hour. May didn't much like the boys' going out alone if there was any sea running. She got a little bit grim if Dick took them out when it was blowing hard or foggy.

Dick checked the water temperature. Sixty-six degrees. Might be sixty-five out on the swordfish grounds. Sixty-five to sixty-eight was what they favored, and mighty picky they were about it. Dick wished Parker would hire a spotter plane. The rate was fifty bucks an hour plus a bonus of a hundred dollars per fish, no matter what size. The price at the wharf for swordfish was $3.50 a pound. Probably going up as the summer people came in. If Parker and him got just one 150-pound fish they'd pay for the spotter plane and his bonus. With a good fish, two hundred pounds, they'd start to make some real money. With a plane they'd spot the fish ten, fifteen feet down, not just the ones finning. Two, three fish wasn't out of the question. And if they stuck a real good fish the first day, they could keep the spotter plane working for a couple more days. Parker was generous about shares—of course he did have a busted arm. Dick was supplying the pots for lobster—or red crab if Joxer

Goode's price was good—and Dick was bringing the harpoons, a little more experience, good eyes.

Dick got to the yard early enough so he didn't have to argue with the yard manager about whether he was working on Parker's boat or just looking at her. He got down inside to the stuffing box. Rotten wood and the stuffing all clumped up. Tear it all out. One of the few decent things about the boat was easy access to the stuffing box. And the propeller shaft was true. The hull was fair to poor. Not a design he'd seen around—shallow draft, hard lines. Parker must have bought her down on the Gulf Coast. The half-dory on board was local, but not much good. Dick lined up a couple more strings of heavy pots, one in Westerly, one in North Kingstown, dropped them off alongside Parker's boat. *Mamzelle.* Dick wasn't sure the right way to spell it, but he knew it wasn't Mamzelle.

Dick stopped by Joxer Goode's crab-processing plant to check the price. The wells on Parker's boat were pretty big. The price for crab was about half that of lobster, but if they got to the right spot they might get twice as many. Dick asked if Joxer was there. Joxer had few enough boats going out for crab that he might just give a tip about where to set the pots. One thing Dick knew was even the nearest crabs were way out, on the edge of the continental shelf, took a day or more just to get out to the grounds.

The secretary told him Joxer was out on his motorboat showing some friends around the salt ponds and then picnicking on Sawtooth Island.

Dick went home and headed down the creek in his skiff. He took his quahog tongs. He didn't want to seem to be looking too hard for Joxer. When he got into the pond past Sawtooth he saw Joxer's boat pulled up on the tiny beach on the southwest of the island. Sleek little water-jet with padded seats, like the inside of a new car. Two couples standing on the beach. Joxer and his wife, both of them great big folks, played lots of sports. Tennis, water-skiing. Joxer had a little single shell. He'd been a single-sculler in college, Dick had seen the engraved cups in Joxer's office, and a picture of Joxer with a lot of Japs on board a fishing vessel. But Joxer knew his stuff. Dick had heard how Joxer had gone into the water with his scuba gear to cut loose a propeller fouled with a stray piece of polypropylene. The boat had tied up at Joxer's dock to unload crabs and got fouled as she was pulling away. Joxer had another boat standing by to unload and didn't want to wait around. So in he jumped.

Dick understood that. What he held against Joxer was his paying his crab workers piecework instead of an hourly wage. And then breezing through the plant jollying up the pickers, patting the women on the back. "That's the ticket, ladies!" As though it was a little-league game and a lot of fun. And his Jap foreman who never talked but just reached over the picker's shoulder and showed her how to do it faster.

Joxer was out to make his million. Didn't have time to come look at the boat Dick was building.

Joxer's wife. You couldn't tell she'd had two kids. Striding around in a tennis outfit or a bikini with a beach robe that just came to the tops of her yard-long thighs. Dick saw her waterskiing around the salt ponds and out on the ocean on calm days. She and Joxer were good at things like that.

The other couple were smaller versions of the Goodes. Same healthy good looks, but scaled down, and more willowy too—the pair of them.

Dick began to work his tongs.

The couples were in a huddle, pointing to parts of Sawtooth Island and back up to Sawtooth Point. Dick had heard there was some buying and selling going on. Dick wouldn't mind having Joxer Goode as a neighbor, that would give Dick a bit of a claim on

Joxer. Dick had always been a handy neighbor during snow, flood, power outage. But the only landowners left on Sawtooth Point were one old couple—every other house was now a summer rental—even the Wedding Cake, completed in 1911 by Dick's great-uncle. Dick's part of the family had never lived in it. When his great-uncle died, his son, who'd moved away, sold it, along with a narrow right-of-way from the Post Road. Dick's grandfather got the rest of the point, Dick's father sold off two house lots—the Buttricks' and the Bigelows'. Then Dick's father had sold off his house and the rest of the point, except for the acre Dick now owned, when he went to the hospital. He thought he'd leave Dick some money after his bills were paid. There was so little left, Dick had to use up his own savings from his Coast Guard tour to build his little house. Dick had tried to shut his mind to all the ifs. If his father had held on a little longer, the land prices would have doubled, tripled. If the old man had had health insurance. If the old man had deeded over some of the land to Dick. If, if, if. The old man had paid his debts. He probably held the record at South County Hospital for biggest bill ever paid by an uninsured patient. Dick had been away at sea, helicoptered off his cutter when his father died, was buried. Dick's hitch was up eight months later and he was back in time for the final accounting after probate. He'd figured there might not be a lot, but he hadn't been prepared for next-to-nothing. He'd thought of using the money—he'd hoped there would be ten thousand at the very worst—to send himself to the Merchant Marine Academy. He'd had a plan: by age forty he would be master of a ship. Here he was at age forty-plus in an eighteen-foot skiff. Here he was tonging quahogs. Here he was watching four beautiful people in swimsuits so small that all four of them wouldn't make a single shirt.

There was a small part of Dick that recognized that his dream of working his way up to master wouldn't have been a piece of cake.

He hadn't done so good in the Coast Guard, and that was before he could blame his bad temper on his bad luck. Even his friend Eddie Wormsley told him he wasn't good at taking advice, let alone taking orders. When Dick crewed on fishing boats, the various captains and shipmates had been glad to see the last of him. When he worked in the boatyard, even though the yard owner let him do his work his own way at his own pace, Dick drove boat owners up the wall. There was a pretty strong tradition at most New England boatyards of rich boat owners' putting up with blunt talk from grumpy workmen. The New England bankers and lawyers who owned boats didn't expect well-mannered servants —they even liked being roughed up a little by an old salt when they handled their boats badly, or came in to get a dumb mistake fixed. "Of course you broke your mast. There was whitecaps on the *pond,* and you tried to take her to Block Island." Dick's mistake was adding a little barb. Like "You're a real piss-to-windward sailor."

The yard owner let him go, but still called him in for a job now and again. And when someone asked at the yard to have a beetlecat built of wood, he referred him to Dick.

The beetlecat was a beauty. Cost four thousand dollars. Dick's profit was less than a thousand, and the pay rate finally came to less than three dollars an hour, including driving around for the right wood and fittings. You could buy an okay used beetlecat for a quarter of that. A new plastic knockabout for only a little more.

He built a couple of skiffs to sell, and then the one for himself. A smaller one for the boys. Thought he would just see if a man with a good skiff could make do. The answer was yes. Barely. But the *yes* gave him less and less satisfaction as the seasons went by. Then, three years ago, he started his big boat. He saw the plans in the *National Fisherman* and fell for her. That was the main part of it—he just fell in love. Later on he felt other motives, felt the jump this would give him. No one expecting it, he'd pop her into Great

Salt Pond at high water and chug past the rest of the fleet to the town wharf. The harbormaster would ask him if the owner was a resident. "You can't tie up here unless the owner's a resident. You know that, Dick." Dick wouldn't answer. Just stroll back and look at the lettering across the stern, as though he was checking where the boat was from. Dick wasn't sure of the name—maybe *May,* maybe *Spartina*—but underneath it would say "Galilee, R.I." The harbormaster would come back and look. Dick would show the papers. "Owner: Richard D. Pierce."

The harbormaster would say "Jesus! Jesus, Dick." The town-wharf crowd would see something was up then. They'd all come over, even Captain Texeira. They'd all say, "Jesus, Dick." Maybe Captain Texeira wouldn't say "Jesus," but he'd damn well think it.

"Where'd you get her?"

"She's not the one the yard's been building . . . ?"

They'd figure it out. One of them would pretend to just be strolling the length of her along the dockside, but he'd be counting the paces. He wouldn't be able to keep it to himself. "Fifty-four feet!"

Dick might say something then. He might say, "Near enough." The harbormaster would have seen it written down. He'd say "Fifty-four feet, eight inches." He was always setting people straight.

Dick had a couple of other scenes he couldn't help playing in his imagination no matter how he tried not to. Miss Perry, Captain Texeira, and the harbormaster were recurring characters. So was Joxer Goode. Joxer Goode with a sweet contract. "Dick, I need you and your boat. Here's the deal. . . ."

Joxer briefing the skippers of the red-crab fleet, pointing out likely spots near the edge of the continental shelf.

"And by the way, men, the *Spartina* was this month's bonus winner. Some of you sixty-footers better stay out longer."

Dick took a bite of the bottom with his tongs. He could feel the good crunch of sand. He was working in about eight feet of water, not far in from the gut. Farther back in the pond it was mud and black silt—with eel grass and wrack to get fouled in the tongs. Too much current near the gut for that stuff. Dick closed the tongs and flipped up the business end, using the padded gunwale as a fulcrum. He shook a bit of ooze and muddy sand loose from the basket. Bingo! Look what the Easter Bunny left. He pulled the tongs in and picked up the quahog. He used to say that to Charlie and Tom when they were little. So little they had to use both hands to pick up a good quahog. Look what the Easter Bunny left. Dick held the quahog in his hand, ran a fingertip over the fine grooves of the shell.

He reached in with the tongs again. It was a good patch in here. Hard to get to except by boat. Didn't get weekend quahoggers wading in with their forks, pulling their inner tubes on a string with bushel baskets riding in the doughnut hole.

The effort of tonging calmed him. The mild southwest wind blew toward him from the scrub at the back of the barrier beach. Beach plums, bayberry, beach peas, poison ivy. He caught a whiff of beach-rose blossoms.

He was bringing up a quahog or two with every try. Better than he'd expected. If he topped off a bushel he'd run them over to Mary Scanlon's Green Hill restaurant, just west of the salt-marsh bird sanctuary. The tide was running in—he could get up the salt creek right to the restaurant porch. He'd come away with a few bucks for May. Sweeten up the fact that he was going out with Parker. Mary usually threw in a pie or a cake that hadn't turned out just right—that would sweeten up May and the boys.

It came through to Dick that Joxer Goode was calling to him. Dick looked up. Joxer waved both arms and yelled again, "Ahoy! Dick Pierce!"

Dick finished sifting the basket, dropped another quahog on the pile, and waved back. Joxer beckoned to him. Dick saw that Joxer's boat was pulled up pretty high on the beach. Dick yanked his anchor up, but didn't crank the motor. He caught a little curl of the incoming tide that took him the first fifty feet, then he fitted his sculling oar and stroked across the current. Joxer waded in and caught the prow.

"Hello there, Dick. Sorry to bother you, but you haven't by any chance got a bottle opener on board?"

Dick shook his head, not meaning so much "no" as "goddamn."

The smaller man put down a big movie camera that rode on his shoulder on a padded stock. He said, "We have all this cold beer, but it's in nontwist bottles."

Joxer's wife said hello and introduced Dick to the other two, Marie and Schuyler van der something. Dick saw a look on Marie's face that was familiar to him. It was a little bit puzzled, a little bit vacant. Dick knew it from May. It meant "I'm not saying anything, but I'm not having as much fun as everyone else."

Dick said to Joxer, "You got a screwdriver—or a marlin spike?" Dick pulled his own rigging knife from his pocket and opened the spike. He took the bottle of Heineken Schuyler was holding and gave a little pry to several of the crimped furrows of the bottle cap with the tip of the spike. There was a satisfying hiss and a little foam leaked down the neck. Dick popped the cap off and handed the bottle back. Schuyler toasted him with the bottle and took a swig. Schuyler's wife said, "Would you like one, Mr. Pierce?"

Dick said, "No thanks."

Dick was having a little trouble with the bareness of the four bodies, particularly the two van der somethings. They looked barer than the Goodes. All four of them had early-summer pink-brown tans. Dick looked away and thought it might be the fact that both the van der somethings had perfect sets of tight blond ringlets.

Joxer had the knack of prying open the beer now. "Would you like a sandwich, Dick?" Dick hesitated. Joxer's wife handed him one and he couldn't resist. It was fancy egg salad with bacon strips in it. He wished he'd taken a beer.

Joxer said, "Come on ashore. I'm glad I ran into you—I've got a favor to ask."

Dick didn't want to scrape the bottom of his skiff on the sand. He tossed the stern anchor out, rolled up his boots, and waded ashore with the bow anchor. The skiff rode in a foot of clear water. Joxer looked at the boat. "She really is a beauty." He turned to the others. "She's not typical—Dick puts a higher prow on his boats. And a little more sheer—is that right, Dick?"

Dick nodded. He was uncomfortable, but pleased. Joxer said, "And all you need is that little twenty-horse there . . . and she flies along."

Joxer pried open another beer. "Dick's family used to own Sawtooth Island, Schuyler. You and the Pierce family are going to be neighbors in a way. Dick lives up that creek." Joxer pointed out the creek and then turned back to Dick. "Schuyler and Marie bought the Wedding Cake house last year. That used to be your grandfather's —or was it your great-uncle's?"

Joxer handed Dick the beer he'd just opened and sat down on a flat rock. The others sat on their towels in the sand. Dick leaned back against a round boulder. Barbara Goode said, "I love your boots. Don't you, Marie? I love the way all those folds gather under the knee. They go all the way up the thigh, don't they, when they're unrolled? How do they stay up?"

Dick finished chewing a bite of sandwich.

"They hook on to the belt."

"For when you have to go wading, is it?"

"That, and when you're working in a cockpit just got a wave dumped in her."

Dick wondered that Mrs. Goode didn't know all this. Or maybe she was just trying to draw the other woman out. If the other woman was like May, Mrs. Goode was wasting her breath. And making a fool out of him in his boots. When it was the two ladies that were barely covered.

Schuyler sang, " 'I am a pirate king! I am a pirate king! It is, it is a glorious thing to be a pirate king!' "

Marie had pulled a spare towel over her shoulders like a shawl.

Dick envied people who could just open up and sing. Parker would do that in bars every once in a while, just as if he was a guinea, knew some guinea songs too, he'd puff up his chest like a bird on a twig and let go. He'd do guinea opera songs, Elvis Presley, Roy Orbison.

Joxer and Barbara Goode smiled at Schuyler's singing. Dick recognized himself in Marie now—when Parker started singing, Dick slouched down in his chair.

Dick finished his beer and stood up. Barbara Goode said, "Dick, before you go, we've got a couple of favors to ask. Joxer and Schuyler are doing a clambake here on the island and they need some help from someone. Could we get you to help? I mean, if we could buy the clams, and maybe some lobsters from you. And if you could show them how to dig the pit. And where to put the fire and the stones and the seaweed. Joxer *thinks* he knows, but I know you know. We're going to have thirty people and I don't dare let the two of them get it wrong."

Dick said, "I'm going out in a couple of days, I'm going to be fixing up a boat for a friend of mine."

Schuyler cocked his head. "You're going out on the ocean in a fishing boat?"

"Yup."

"I'm doing a little film—that's what I do, is make films. You don't suppose I could go along? Me and my camerawoman?"

Dick was taken aback. "I don't know. It's for four, five days. It's not like it's . . . I suppose I could ask Parker."

Mrs. Goode said, "Well, let's get the clambake settled first. Joxer, you and Dick have a little talk."

Joxer walked Dick over to Dick's skiff. Joxer said, "This would be a big help. You can see how it is. Barbara's getting worried, this is her shindig, along with Schuyler and Marie. Barbara wants them to get off on the right foot now that they're moving in. So let's say five hundred dollars to cover the raw materials. You know the stuff—steamers, quahogs, potatoes, corn—I don't suppose there's any corn this early. Can you get thirty lobsters?"

Dick didn't know what to make of this. Even for thirty people, lobster, quahogs, steamers, and potatoes would come to less than two hundred dollars. Dick thought with regret of the barrel of steamer clams he'd just sold to the dealer. He didn't dare go back to the bird sanctuary with the tractor, but he might send the boys back. Drop them off in their boat with a couple of baskets. But Dick couldn't figure the five hundred. He said, "That's a lot of money."

Joxer said, "Well, Barbara figures it's a lot of work. And she's right. What with digging the pit, gathering the driftwood, the seaweed. And I think she hopes you'd give me a hand ferrying people from the point to the island, so there's the use of your boat."

Dick began to see. He couldn't see it all, but he began to get the picture. A lot of the independent lobstermen he knew had made deals with families who had summer houses. They drained the pipes in the fall, fixed the screens in spring. It started that way. Then they'd get a call that the family wanted to spend Christmas at the beach house if they could have the water turned back on, the heat, maybe a load of firewood. And if it wouldn't be too much trouble, get that Eddie what's-his-name to plow the driveway. And if there was a nice pine tree that would do for a Christmas tree, if it wasn't any trouble, just cut it and leave it on the porch. Half the lobstermen Dick knew got a nice Christmas check that way. And another nice check in the spring. He'd swore he'd never do it. But here it was. Five hundred bucks. Dick looked at the quahogs lying in his basket. He looked across the channel to the Wedding Cake. At least they weren't asking him to drain the pipes.

Joxer said, "Schuyler's an old school friend of mine. He's sort of a funny guy, but he might end up doing a lot of business in the area. He's talking about getting a boat built, I told him you were the one to see."

Dick said, "The only boat I'm building these days is my own." It occurred to Dick he'd better just say what he wanted. He said, "I'll do the clambake—"

Joxer said, "Terrific."

"If you'll do something."

"What's that?"

"You come over to my place and take a look at the boat I'm building."

Joxer said, "Sure. I'd love to see any boat you're building."

"This isn't any boat."

*Dick swore to himself not to take it out on the boys. He was bound to be in a foul mood what with fixing the clambake and working on Parker's boat. He'd bit off too much, and he was working for two different people. Dick dropped the boys off on the sea side of the bird-sanctuary beach. Charlie was nervous about going back there to dig steamers. When Dick tossed three peck baskets ashore, Charlie said, "The limit is a peck apiece."

Dick said, "I'm the third. I'll be back after I pull my pots. If the Natural Resources people come along asking you where you were the other night, you just say 'home.' You got a job to do and you can't stop to talk."

Halfway through the pots Dick remembered he wanted to take the boys' skiff on Parker's boat. That was the trouble with doing too much. But if he kept going at this rate he'd have enough for the engine by the 4th of July, enough to finish the boat by Labor Day. A good solid Cummins diesel. He'd decided to go first-class with the engine, first-class with the shaft and prop. He'd spent hours talking with the Cummins man in Providence, and at home measuring and remeasuring for the engine bed. The Cummins was the right size, the right weight. The Cummins rep had been as fair as Dick could ask. No financing, but he'd let Dick make a down payment of five hundred dollars to hold it at the old price. The Cummins price list had gone up 12 percent that spring. Dick had saved more than five hundred dollars right there. But he had to make another payment or the rep couldn't hold it for him.

Paying 12 percent more would be a burden, and Dick had sunk more than just money. He couldn't go with another engine without refiguring the size and weight, probably tearing out the bed. And what was as hard as the money or the work was the time he'd put in studying that engine. A diesel is a diesel, a pretty simple idea, but he knew this model inside out. He'd put one in when he worked at the yard, serviced it twice. And over the last year he'd read the manual so often he could close his eyes and see any page he wanted, words and diagrams both, down to every bolt, washer, and nut suspended magically in mid-air just the way they were in the manual.

He wasn't in love with it the way he was with his boat, but until he got the engine in her he couldn't feel good about her. There was some pleasure in looking at the line drawing in his mind's eye, and converting it to metallic, oily density, hoisting it, lowering it— a convergence of two daydreams here—into the boat, onto the preset bolts in the bed, jostling its huge weight on the hoist chain so that the eight holes in the thick-flanged base lined up, settled over the tips of the bolts, slid down, giving off a little ringing rasp, a steel whisper from the touched threads.

He'd do the clambake. He'd fix their boats, their docks, hell, he'd fix their toilets. He wasn't going to work for them because he wasn't good enough to make his living from the sea. He'd work for them to get himself out to sea.

*D*ick got all the clambake goodies onto Sawtooth Island. He made Charlie and Tom spend the night on the beach on Sawtooth to keep an eye on the lobster car and the steel baskets of clams he'd submerged alongside it.

He ran by the Neptune and left a message for Parker that the stuffing box was fixed, the bow pulpit was rigged, and they only had to wait their turn for the boatyard to put her back in the water.

He dug the pit on the beach. He had to get Charlie and Tom to collect a new set of rocks to line the pit. The boys had gathered their rocks from below the high-tide line, and Dick had heard that every once in a while these had pockets of moisture in them. Dick hadn't seen a low-tide rock explode, but he'd heard tell of some summer folks' blowing up their whole damn clambake, sandstone and granite shrapnel blowing holes through the tarp. It'd almost be worth it to do it on purpose—make them catch their hot lobsters on the fly. Of course things never went wrong when you wanted them to.

The boys had got a load of clean seaweed from the ocean side of the beach. When the fire burned out on the rocks, they dumped in the first layer of seaweed. There was a nice sizzle, and the air sacs on the seaweed began to pop. They got the whole wheelbarrow full of new potatoes in, and another layer of seaweed. A bit later the bigger quahogs, then the smaller ones and the steamers. Last of all the lobster. Resealed the tarp with wet sand and rocks.

Joxer had brought the first load of guests from the point to the island in his boat. Dick recognized some of them and nodded. A slice off the top of local South County and their summer guests.

Joxer brought him a beer and asked Charlie and Tom if they wanted Cokes. The boys had moved in behind Dick in a sheepish way that annoyed him, though he couldn't blame them—these first ten guests had come ashore and arranged themselves in a semicircle on the higher ground, as though the Pierce boys and their authentic South County clambake were on stage. Dick turned away toward the water.

Joxer and Schuyler were lucky with the weather. A perfect June evening, one of the first still summer evenings after an unsettled spring. Just enough movement in the air to bring the smell of beach roses in across the pond. The sky, the puffs of clouds, the flat water of the pond, the swell breaking on the bar at the mouth of the breachway, even the terns circling and fluttering over their nests in the marsh grass seemed suddenly less frantic as the afternoon glare began to soften, the air and water to carry more color.

Joxer said, "You boys want to go for a swim?"

"Go ahead," Dick said. "You got your swimsuits on. Then you won't have to wash up when you get home for supper."

"They're welcome to eat here," Joxer said. "I thought May and the boys would join us."

"They're used to early supper. Thank you just the same. Go on, boys, get wet and then go on home."

The boys looked around awkwardly, as though taking off their sneakers and T-shirts was like changing in front of a crowd.

Elsie Buttrick came down to join them. "Hi, Dick. Hi, Charlie, Tommy."

Dick said, "Hello, Officer Buttrick."

The boys smiled. Elsie was an old neighbor but also an officer in the Rhode Island Natural Resources Department, a sort of super-powered game-and-fish warden. This authority would have made any of Dick's friends more remote, but since Elsie started off as one of the Buttricks, a pretty rich family living on the Point, her official position brought her closer.

Dick was uneasy with her—closer wasn't easier—but he liked her for her way with Charlie and Tom. She sometimes gave lectures in the school system and called on Charlie and Tom by name. "Charlie Pierce, I know *you* know if snapping turtles live around here." Charlie said, "Yes, ma'am." She'd turned to the class. "He knows 'cause one took a snap at him right in Pierce Creek. Right, Charlie? And is Pierce Creek salt, brackish, or fresh water? That's too easy for you, Charlie. We'll ask one of the potato farmers."

Charlie reported all this, and more—the class trip to the Great Swamp, to Tuckertown to see potato planting. Elsie got Miss Perry to give a slide show on local birds, and—something that had puzzled Dick a lot—Eddie Wormsley to talk about trees. The only time Eddie ever got really pissed off at Dick was at the Neptune when Dick started to kid Eddie about his tree lecture.

Elsie said, "You boys going for a swim?" She kicked off her sandals and pulled off her jersey. She had on a faded red swimsuit. She flicked off her wrap-around skirt, and Dick saw Charlie look at her legs.

Elsie said, "Come on, you guys."

Dick was about to say something, tease Charlie about his girl-friend. He held back, puzzled by a sudden melancholy.

Charlie was sixteen. He wasn't as tough as Dick had been at sixteen. He was smaller, smarter, and nicer. Not a shitty kid. A scrawny, shy kid who took a look at Elsie Buttrick's legs. Dick knew he was too rough on him. From behind, Elsie still looked the way she had when *she* was sixteen. He remembered her walking up to him in her swimsuit that summer (at the town dock? at the boatyard?). He noticed her figure then. Little Elsie Buttrick all grown up. He watched her with pleasure as she came right up to him. She said she was sorry to hear about his father's death. Put an end to *his* looking at her legs.

The next thing he knew she was back in South County after college—*two* colleges. Brown and Yale Forestry School. In uniform. She was good-looking—not pretty all the time but often enough to throw you. And she was law. It was the combination that was shifty. And her being one of the rich kids. But she worked hard—she was like Joxer that way—you could see she put in a day's work.

Joxer said to him, "There's some more guests coming. If it's okay with you, here's the plan. I'll stay here with this bunch, and you get the next bunch. Schuyler and Marie are giving them a drink at the Wedding Cake and then sending them down to the wharf. You give them a lift. Then Schuyler'll wait for the late arrivals and bring them."

Dick said, "Okay. I'll just see the boys on their way."

"Right-o," Joxer said and went back to his guests at the top of the beach.

Dick called the boys. They gathered up their things and then argued over who got to row.

"Let Tom row," Dick said. When they were settled, Dick gave the boat a shove. "Don't run off tomorrow morning," he called after them. "I got some plans for you."

Elsie stood up in the water and waded ashore. "Aye, aye, Daddy," she said. She saluted and laughed.

Dick said, "You know a better way to raise kids?"

"Don't mind me. You might even be right. They still think you're pretty neat. After Ed Wormsley gave his talk on trees Charlie asked me if you could take the class on a tour of the salt ponds, up into the marsh."

"Jesus."

"It's a good idea. You know the marsh. In fact, I think you and I are the only two people left who know where the old causeway is. The one that runs into the bird sanctuary."

Dick was startled. He didn't say a word.

"Don't ever pull that again," Elsie said. "Once was funny. Twice would be a big fat fine."

Dick fixed his eyes on the breachway.

Elsie said, "There are two other Resources officers who have you in mind, but they can't prove it. They're puzzled because they know you don't own a tractor. That doesn't puzzle me. I know your pal Ed Wormsley. I'd hate to see Eddie in trouble again."

Dick rose to the bait, but didn't take it. He said, "Ah." Then said carefully, "I don't think Eddie had anything to do with it. If what you're talking about is whoever it was dug up the sanctuary beach. I thought I heard something that night. Could have been a tractor. Didn't sound like a tractor, but it could have been. But Eddie doesn't go in for clams. He doesn't like them, wouldn't know where to sell them. I got to go pick up some more guests. Now I guess you're going to put your uniform on."

Elsie laughed. "Nope. I'm out of uniform. Mind if I ride along?"

It wasn't worth starting the motor just to go a quarter-mile round the point to the Wedding Cake wharf.

Elsie said, "Don't mind me, don't mind me. Look. If you and Eddie don't do anything terrible, I'm on your side. Did Eddie tell you about the swan? Don't answer that. I'll tell you. I let him keep a swan he shot with his crossbow. I know you know about his crossbow. So long as you don't do anything worse than that. And so long as nobody finds out. I just want to keep this place from going to hell. Sometimes I think I should quit and go work for Save-the-Bay or the Clamshell Alliance. Lie down in front of the bulldozers when they start a nuclear-power plant."

"I heard that was all over with. They can't build it in Wickford and they can't build it in Charlestown."

"Yeah. That one's stopped. I don't know what I'm complaining about. And even the cottages my brother-in-law is putting up here aren't so bad. Have they showed you the architect's model?"

"What cottages?"

"I thought you knew. Here on Sawtooth Point."

"God Almighty." Dick stopped rowing.

Elsie said, "I'm surprised they didn't . . . I thought that was why they invited you."

Dick laughed once. "No. Who's this *they*?"

"Joxer, and Schuyler. And then there's my brother-in-law and Mr. Salviatti. I thought they invited all the neighbors. And then some of these people are ones they want to sell to. Maybe they're going to tell you later. Don't say I told you, okay? Look, it's not so bad. I hate to be the one. . . . I've seen the plans and it won't change much."

"How much do they figure to make?"

"Oh God, I don't know. Millions, zillions. You know what it's like around here."

The skiff turned a little as it drifted. Dick could see Elsie's face now that the sun wasn't in his eyes.

Someone yelled from the dock. Elsie waved and shouted, "We're coming!"

She leaned forward and touched his knee. "Look, Dick. I really am sympathetic. I was as horrified as you are. But everything west of Pierce Creek is still sanctuary. It's just a few more houses." She sat back and said, "Shit. Why am I saying this? I sound like them."

Dick felt bitterness about Sawtooth Point that he knew he could postpone. What he couldn't figure out now was Elsie. For a minute there, she'd been talking to him, and he'd been interested in how she opened up about her job, how she thrashed about. He'd always wondered about her and her job. Then, of course, he'd been stunned by this news, but even after that he'd felt she was telling it to him straight enough. When she said she was sympathetic he thought that was so too.

The change wasn't so much that she got sentimental about the bird sanctuary, whereas he was feeling the old barb of his father's hospital bill and the loss of Sawtooth Point. He could go her way—he had a soft spot for the sanctuary himself. Was it that she couldn't go his way and *think* about money? Not just that. There was her sudden change, her correcting herself, swearing, trying to get her feelings just right—pulling it all back to how *she* felt.

He began to row again. Her head swung back into the sun. Her face became dark. She said, "I've got to ..." She leaned back. "Fortunately, I have my month's leave now. I shouldn't have told Schuyler I'd help him with his movie. Did you know that's what he does? Makes short documentaries. He wanted to know if you could take us around some. You have any spare time?"

"Not these days. I got to make some money. And if I do make some money, I got to work on my boat."

"Well, maybe we could just come along when you pull your pots. I think Schuyler's got some money to pay."

"What's his movie about?"

"He's got a couple of them going. But one is about South County. He has an educational-TV contract, and he's got another one for the state tourism people. And part of his investment in the cottage project here is to make a film strip about what a great place it is."

"Busy fellow."

Elsie said, "He's pretty good at it. He's not just a pretty face." Elsie laughed at that.

Dick recognized one of the reasons Schuyler rubbed him the wrong way. He was a pretty boy all right. And he looked amused all the time. He looked at this, he looked at that, and was amused. Dick didn't mind Joxer's being hearty nearly so much as he minded Schuyler's looking amused. It figured Schuyler would look at a fishing village and a salt marsh and take pictures. Of what was amusing.

Dick pulled up to the dock, and guests clambered in. Dick got up and helped Miss Perry to the stern seat. As the boat filled up Elsie gave up her seat beside Miss Perry, sat down beside Dick, and took the starboard oar. Elsie's sister took Elsie's place and her husband handed her a baby.

"Sally, you remember Dick Pierce? And this is baby Jack—John Dudley Aldrich the third. Can you believe that little eggplant has all those names?"

Dick remembered Elsie at fourteen and fifteen. Sally was the beauty then, Elsie the loudmouth.

Sally ignored the part about her baby. "Yes, of course, Dick Pierce. You haven't changed at all."

Dick saw that Sally had. Not for the worse. Before, she could have been any pretty girl. Now, she was softer, she looked a little tired, but her face was her own.

Elsie shoved off and slid her oar out through the oarlock. She said, "All set? And a-one and a-two."

"This is a rowboat," Sally said, "not a dance band."

Dick and Elsie rowed with mild strokes, the boat sluggish with nine people aboard, too much weight forward. Elsie chattered away with Sally and Miss Perry. Old home week. The other guests, most of them newcomers, exclaimed to each other about the view: the Wedding Cake, the island, the pond, how nice, how very nice.

Dick and Elsie backed the skiff in to the little island beach. Joxer helped Miss Perry and Sally and the baby. The other guests took off their shoes and went over the sides, calling heartily to Joxer and Joxer's wife. They were as cheerful as Joxer. Amused too. Polite as Sally and Miss Perry, they called back, "Thanks for the ride," and, turning to each other, turning away from each other, they waded through the clear water, stirring the bright sand, a little school of nice-looking people in bright clothes and bare legs. How nice, how very nice. Was it as easy for them as it looked? To move so lightly, to begin sentences by saying with a smile, "Tell me. How was—" To smile back and say, "It was marvelous" or "It was ghastly," smiles and words as quick and simultaneous as a school of minnows.

Money. It wasn't just money. "Tell me about—" "Yes, I know all about it" or "You know, I don't know the first thing about it." It didn't seem to matter which. Either one was an amusing answer. The whole conversation was a school of minnows, zig, zag, zig. Up to break the surface, down and away.

Dick had come up to a tennis court once to tell a fellow his boat was ready. The fellow said to the other players, "Ah. Just a sec." Turned to Dick and said, "We'll just finish the game. You don't mind." Dick stood by. One lady cracked one, really pounded it past the guy's feet. She looked as good as a tennis player on TV. They all laughed. They were amused. Next time it bounced between the two of them on the same team. They both reared back but hung fire. They both said, "Yours!" All four of them laughed. Joxer and

Barbara Goode were playing on opposite teams. Maybe that was part of the fun. Dick waited and waited.

"Sorry, just wanted to finish the set."

Joxer sang out, "Hello there, Dick!"

Dick said, "Mr. Goode. Mr. White. Bill sent me, said you wanted to know the minute your boat was going in. Said you wanted to be there. It's going in now."

"Ah yes. You're from the boatyard." Dick had seen this guy every day for the last week. Mr. White added, "Tell Bill I'll be along."

Dismissed.

But Dick said, "It's up to you. If you want to see the splash, it'll be when I get back there." Mr. White's ketch was forty-five feet l.o.a., drew eight feet. She couldn't go in at low tide. The hoist, the marine railway didn't run themselves. It was the size of the boat, the size of the job that got to Dick. Even if you owned it for fun, you ought to know the difference between playing tennis and a forty-five-foot boat. Mr. White and Bill knew there was another size involved. It wasn't just money, but money was the length of it.

Time to check the clams. Dick tossed the bow anchor out, snubbed it, and waded in to set the stern anchor in the beach.

Schuyler and his wife, and Sally's husband and little girl came out in a canoe. An old canvas job, painted deep royal blue. The ribs and thwarts were dark with age but shiny with new varnish.

Sally and Elsie ran down to it. It turned out it was their family's old canoe. Mr. Aldrich had found her under the old Buttrick house. Fixed it up as a surprise. Had it hidden under a tarp at Schuyler's.

Everyone came down to it.

"That's your mum's old canoe, Jenny. I was just your age . . ."

The little girl didn't get it, but she was excited by the fuss.

Dick looked closer and saw some of the ribs were new. Stained to match the old ones. Someone had gone to an awful lot of trouble.

"Oh, Jack! This is wonderful!"

The new canvas looked tight as a drum. Dick saw the seats had been recaned too—old-style, row on row of little hexes.

Marie Van der Hoevel came over to him as he was fumbling under the edge of the tarp for a clam.

"May I help?"

He shooed her back with his gloved hand. "Careful. That steam'll burn you." He found a good-sized quahog. Open. He pulled off the tarp and stood back. "There she is!" Dick took a deep breath as the steam rose and blew slowly by him. Smelled right. He dug out a potato, dipped it in the water, and took a bite. "Good enough to eat," he said to Mrs. Van der Hoevel. "You want to try one?" Dick was pleased at how good it turned out. He dug out a potato and a small steamer, dipped them in the edge of the water, and held them out to her. "I'll put all this stuff in the washtubs," he said, "and you use that camp stove to melt butter. Smells pretty good. If this was August we'd have corn too, but this ain't too bad."

She touched the steamer and pulled her hand back. "Oh dear!" Dick put his glove between his knees and pulled the clam meat out for her with his finger, holding it by the tough neck. Schuyler and Elsie arrived in time to see her lean over and nibble on the clam. Dick pulled away the tough part of the neck. Mrs. Van der Hoevel reached for it. Schuyler said, "You don't eat the foreskin, dear." Mrs. Van der Hoevel blushed. She kept on chewing. She said "Good" out of the corner of her mouth. She reminded Dick of his wife again, though she was prettier. She was thin and jumpy—Dick could see Schuyler had her licked. But she kept herself together. Her white shorts had sharply creased pleats and a neat cuff, each leg a miniskirt flared around each narrow thigh—in the same way her hair flared out around her face made it seem even longer and narrower. At least Schuyler kept her in pretty clothes. Dick felt a pang of guilt about May.

Elsie got a pair of long vinyl gloves and high rubber boots and shuffled into the seaweed to help fill the tubs. She was about the same height as Mrs. Van der Hoevel, but a good bit sturdier and harder. The big black boots and gloves flippering around in the seaweed while she crouched down in her red swimsuit made her look like an agitated ladybug. Every so often Dick and Elsie had to take a few steps into the water to cool off the soles of the boots. Then back into the pile, digging for the potatoes and stray clams, flipping them so quick they were making the washtubs clank and ping like a dieseling engine. It was decent of Elsie to help out. He looked over at her as she bent over the hot seaweed. Her thighs between the boot tops and bathing suit were steamed pink, but had good hard lines. He could see what Charlie'd been looking at.

When they got through, Elsie shucked her gloves and boots, ran into the water, and dove out into a long glide. Dick was just wishing he'd brought a swimsuit when Joxer brought him another bottle of beer.

"If you're like most of the fishermen I know," Joxer said, "you'd rather get wet inside than out."

Dick said, agreeably, "If you spend enough time wet when you don't want to be, you don't swim so often." Dick scooped some water onto his face and neck. "The water's warm for June."

Joxer said, "Okay by me."

"Waterskiing season for you and Mrs. Goode."

Joxer laughed. "Nope. If lobsters thin out, my red-crab prices go up too. I'm about to buy a pair of refrigerator trucks, do my own hauling to New York and Boston."

"You got enough skippers going out for you?"

"Not yet." Joxer tilted his head back. "I hear Parker's got a boat."

Dick said, "Yup." He couldn't get himself to raise the subject of his own boat.

Joxer said, "She doesn't look like she could take much. Isn't she awfully flat-bottomed for around here?"

Dick nodded. "She won't be comfortable, but she'll do. For summer. We'll run a few pots. Might do red crabs if the price is good."

"If you and Parker go out, stop at my office. I'll tell you the price."

Dick said, "Can you guarantee—"

"I can't guarantee. But the price looks good—in fact, it's going up."

"I hear Captain Texeira—"

"Captain Texeira has two big boats and he's a senior skipper, and I can count on him. If you and Parker start hauling on a regular basis, I'd be happy to move on to that next subject."

Joxer looked away toward the guests filing by the food. Eyes back to Dick. Joxer said cheerily, "You certainly did the job here. This is first-rate."

Dismissed. Joxer wasn't a bad guy, but he was still an officer. Dick got some food and another beer, sat on a rock, and watched Elsie starting back from way across the pond, just a dark spot in the rippling light. The sun grew red and orange at the bottom; across the surface of the water and the land the near side of things turned blue and violet above their dark shadows. Dick felt his dry squint open up some, the rest of him ease up too—this violet half-light flooding the pond and marsh came into him like an easy tide.

When it got all the way dark, Joxer's and Schuyler's party began to light lamps—some candles in glass chimneys, some battery lamps, and a hissing gas lantern on the bow of Joxer's water-jet to light up the picnic-table bar.

The noise of the people talking was the same noise Dick used to hear coming back in on a fishing boat easing past the yacht-club porch. The engine would be thumping at quarter-speed, and suddenly they'd hear the voices over it—the whole clump of voices at once and then one or two breaking loose and blowing off toward the boat like milkweed floss.

Dick had always liked the sound. It was like spring peepers. Not so raucous, but more keyed up than ducks feeding in the shallows, chuckling to each other in between dabs. A silly sound, but a sign of a season.

You couldn't mind anything that came to its own place in a regular way. The seals went north in May, the terns came in, the striped bass came up the coast in schools. Real summer was bluefish, swordfish, tuna, sharks. When the water got to sixty-five degrees or so. And in the marsh, red-winged blackbirds, meadowlarks, and swallows. The spartina grew greener, everywhere there were new wicks of bright green.

By midsummer all the bright turned heavy and dark. In August the sky streaked with shooting stars, and next thing it was fall. The long mild fall, the clearest and best of Rhode Island seasons, with its own flurry of movement and ripeness. You could find stray cod all the way up the coves and creeks, broken off from the schools passing in deep water. Then the November gales blew through—things bent down, folded in place. The dead spartina broke, blew off, wrapped onto the next stalks, and sank under the rains down to the live roots, mixing into the blackness. It was useful death.

While Dick was thinking this, half-hearing the voices and the rustle of grasses stirred by light air across the pond, but still seeing a last glow of light in the sky and the sea out toward Block Island, he thought about his father's death. He got away from his feeling of bitterness that the old man's dying had stripped away the rest of the point, leaving his son and grandsons bare. Now he felt sorry for the old man, who must have felt his dying as a freak, not a regular gale but a tropical hurricane, too early, too destructive, tearing things away instead of bending them down and mixing them slowly into the dark marsh.

Then Dick tightened up again. Okay—he wouldn't get the point back. He'd get the goddamn boat built. It'd all go into the boat—

the little piece that the old man had left and whatever scraps and crumbs could still come off the point from the new owners. This clambake, for instance, went right into the engine. Five hundred dollars.

Joxer and Schuyler were good for some more. Parker would do for some too.

That was when Dick put Schuyler and Parker together in his mind. Slick and slick. He wasn't as slick as either of them, but the two of them would get to each other. Dick felt lucky. He was still a dumb swamp Yankee compared to them, but he had a clear will. He'd wanted his boat for a long time, but now it seemed a part of the way it was all going. As sure as finding fish when all the signs were right.

Dick took some of the party back to the point. Sally and her husband and kids. Miss Perry, who reminded him it was getting near to Charlie's birthday when Dick always took her and the boys out for her yearly fishing.

Back to the island. Dick gave the big white water-jet a wide berth. People were diving off her transom now that the tide was in.

He found Elsie. He said, "If you and your friend Schuyler want to take some pictures, I've got an idea for you. You and him bring your movie camera along when Parker and I go out for swordfish. We'll be out five, six days. We'll take you two along if Schuyler will pay for a spotter plane. The plane runs fifty bucks an hour. We'll leave at midnight, start our own watch at dawn. Use the plane after the sun's up. Take a two-hour break for when the tide's running strong. Use the plane another couple of hours in the afternoon if it's still calm. What do you think? If we use the plane it's pretty sure we'll get some fish."

Elsie said, "Parker's boat? I don't know about Parker."

"Parker's got his arm in a cast, so . . ."

"If Schuyler pays for the plane, who gets the fish?"

"Schuyler gets the pictures, we get the fish. The pilot gets his fifty an hour, but he gets a hundred bonus for each fish. What Parker and me'll do is pay the bonus out of the fish. That's as good as we can go."

Elsie laughed. "What's Parker going to say to this?"

"You talk to Schuyler. I'll talk to Parker. You won't likely get on any other boat. Right now the water's right. The weather's right. You can't find swordfish if there's overcast or too much chop. There's no guarantee it'll be this good again all summer."

Elsie said, "Okay. I'll bring Schuyler over now. But Dick—" She paused.

"What's that?"

"I don't know. I'm just worried when someone like you hangs around with Parker."

Dick said, "I have my doubts about your friend Schuyler. We're not getting married—we're going out for a few days to stick some fish and haul some pots."

Elsie went off. Dick knew what she was talking about. He would have worried the same as her if he wasn't so sure the tide was running his way.

The gas lamp was out now. Just the candle lamps were burning. By the waning moon Dick could see the partygoers were diving in naked. Let them have their summer fun. He'd send Charlie and Tom to clean up the island. This summer was going to see his boat. He could just make out heads bobbing in the water. They weren't so noisy now, just splashing and giggling. Some flood tide of money and fun had brought them to Sawtooth Point and Sawtooth Island. He wasn't going to back off. Just another fishery.

Dick had forgot how antsy he got the day before he put to sea. May had forgot too. She'd used to leave the house. Now he was barking at her, in between trips to the boat. He must have gone back and forth a half-dozen times.

Next to last time he found Schuyler, Elsie, and Parker on deck. Not doing anything, just gabbing. Once in a while either Schuyler or Elsie would lift up the camera each of them had strapped on. Dick muttered by them. Parker was bullshitting Schuyler. Tales of the high seas. Dick laid his harpoon up by the bow pulpit, but Schuyler wanted him to bring it over and talk about it. Schuyler and Elsie both raised their cameras. Dick pointed to the tufted wand sticking toward him from the camera pack. "That thing the microphone?"

"Yes," Elsie said. "What's that in your hand?"

"Jesus, Elsie, you've seen a harpoon. . . ."

"Explain how it works."

"You'll get to see how it works. That is, if we ever get going."

"Dick. Come on."

"When we're steaming somewhere with nothing much to do—"

Schuyler said, "Captain Parker tells me you got mad at the phone company once, you tore your phone off the wall and threw it out in the middle of Route One."

Dick said, "You worried about your camera?"

Elsie said, "Oh, for God's sakes!" Schuyler laughed.

Dick put his harpoon by the bow pulpit, pigeon-holed his charts and notes in the wheelhouse, then moved around checking the bait barrels and spare pots. Schuyler asked Parker what he thought of Rhode Island. Parker said, "Cute little state. First time I heard of it, I was running a charter boat in the Gulf, had a couple of Texans on board. One says to the other, 'I hear you picked up that land next to yours. You must have quite a spread now.' The other one says, 'Middling. Just over two and a half Rhode Islands.' "

Schuyler laughed. Elsie said, "They don't really."

Dick said to her, "He's only here summers with his bullshit."

"You mean Rhode Island gets bigger during the winter?" Schuyler said. He and Parker laughed.

"We're leaving before long," Dick said. "I'm going to pull a few pots and go to bed."

Schuyler and Elsie followed him to his house.

May was in her garden. Elsie waved and followed Dick toward the wharf. Schuyler went over to May and introduced himself. He got his camera going and pointed it at the ramshackle shed Dick had rigged. It had a wood roof, but the siding was mostly old sheets of canvas and vinyl.

Dick shouted to Schuyler, "Don't go in there!"

May yelled down to Dick, "When do you want your supper?"

"When I get back." Dick cranked the outboard and cast off. Elsie jumped in. "Can't you wait a second?" Dick started down the creek.

Elsie said, "Are you going to be like this the whole trip?"

Dick didn't answer. They got going faster when they passed Sawtooth Point. Dick couldn't believe Schuyler had made so much money just taking pictures that he could have bought the Wedding Cake.

Elsie got cheerful when Dick pulled a pot and a huge eel was curled up in it—made a big S from one corner of the parlor to the other. When Dick swung the pot up, the eel squeezed out between the slats. Three feet long and as thick as his forearm and it was flowing through a chink the width of his thumb. Elsie zoomed in on it with her camera. Dick turned the pot so the eel fell inside the boat. The eel wiggled between Elsie's feet as she filmed the rest of the junk in the pot—a large whelk, a starfish, and a spider crab. Dick turned the whelk so Elsie could film the single moist foot as it sucked itself into its shell.

"Fruits de mer," Elsie said. "Two of 'em, anyway."

Dick rebaited the pot. "The lobster have mostly gone from in here. Used to be you could make a living from within sight of land. Now you got to go way the hell out."

"But I get the feeling you like going to sea," Elsie said. "You like being way out there."

"That's right," Dick said. "I like the time out there. I hope having movie cameras along doesn't screw it up."

Elsie lowered her camera and looked hurt.

"I don't mean you," Dick said. "I mean that recording everything, having those things whirring like clocks . . . that might change the nature of time."

"Oh shit," Elsie said. "I wish I'd got that part. I suppose I shouldn't ask you to say it again."

"Schuyler have rules?" Dick said. He threw the pot over. He thought he'd better not let her get him talking again.

"There are rules," Elsie said. "I'm not sure what Schuyler's relation is to them."

When they got back, May was serving hamburgers and peas to the boys and Schuyler. Dick said, "Hope you didn't mind being left. Be sure you get to Parker's boat."

May served Elsie and Dick. Schuyler said, "We had a very pleasant time."

After Schuyler and Elsie left, Dick went into the bedroom and set his alarm for two. May came in and sat on the bed. "He seems nice," she said. Dick snorted. "I hope you'll get along with them," she said. "It certainly beats spending time with Parker and his crew."

"I am his crew," Dick said.

"I mean his pot-head college boys. That man and the Buttrick girl are just a nicer sort."

"Right this minute I'm not looking to improve my social life," Dick said.

"I wonder sometimes if you'll be able to fit in with anyone even after you have your own boat." She touched his head in a way that made her remark more sympathetic than nagging. Her touch also reminded him he was going to be at sea for the better part of a week. "Maybe you'd like to take a nap too," he said.

May stood up. "When you get back," she said. "Same as when you wanted your supper."

*T*hey left the dock just after 2:00 a.m. It was a late-June night that felt more like midsummer. As they slipped past the breakwater, Parker's boat began to work hard in the swell. Dick tried different speeds until he got her to move a little easier.

Dick had taken a nap. The others turned in. Dick could hear Elsie and Schuyler exclaiming and laughing over how grungy the bunks were.

She *was* a grungy boat, but Dick was content to be putting out to sea, slanting under the arc of the waning moon.

Elsie got up first. It was still dark.

She said, "It stinks of something in there. I can't tell what."

"If it stays calm you can air it out."

Ahead of them the sky was growing pale—at first just a smudge on the horizon and then, arc by arc, the stars were put out by light.

"It's calmer than it was," Elsie said. "But here we are in the middle of the ocean."

"Not in the middle," Dick said.

"Well—nothing but water. 'Water, water, everywhere, nor any drop to drink.' "

Dick turned on the radio-direction finder. "Here," he said to Elsie. "Get me a station in New York."

"You want music?"

"I want to show you how to find out where we are. It's easy now with just a few all-night stations on. Get New York, Boston, and one in Providence. Take a reading from each one, draw the line on the chart and where the lines meet, that's us."

Elsie said, "Like a back-azimuth with a compass."

"Yup," Dick said. "You got the idea. Here. You try it."

"Why not do just two lines?"

"You'll see. When you get that done, get some coffee and juice."

Elsie laughed at him.

Dick said, "After breakfast I'm going to tell you and Schuyler the name of everything on board."

Elsie said, "I don't want to know—"

"So you'll know what it is and where it is if I ask for it. You can laugh about it when we get home. You can take all the movies you want when there's not something else to do. It's not my way of being a son of a bitch. It's the way to run a boat. There are some things we can discuss, and there are some things we can't."

Elsie didn't say anything. She got her readings and drew them in. Dick looked at the chart. "Not bad," he said. "But it's a pretty big triangle you got. It'll do for now. You see why you do three? With two you can make yourself think you've got it. If you can make three agree, you know you're right. We got just enough time for you to do it again if you want."

Elsie did it again. Not an exact fix, but a smaller triangle. Dick turned on the depth finder. It flashed a reading. He said, "See if where you put us has that depth."

Elsie nodded.

Dick said, "Now flip that switch over there and get a reading from the loran."

Elsie read the numbers and found them on the chart. "Why didn't you just use the loran?"

Dick said, "Because things get broke. If the RDF breaks there's another way, but I don't have time to show you now. Get Parker to show you where the coffee's at. Ask Parker to take the wheel so I can go up and start looking. Bring my coffee on up. Lots of milk, no sugar."

*D*ick went up to the crow's nest. There was a long swell, which gave a good deal of motion to the crow's nest, but the sea was perfect, not a tear in the whole sheet of surface. Not yet six. They might get the plane by eight. He'd be tired by the end of it, but for the moment it felt good to let his gaze stretch out. The soft-seen sea was an ointment across the front of his brain. He looked far out and then wandered back, his eyes relaxed. He squinted and swept past the first rim of brightness.

After an hour Elsie came up. She had her camera on a padded U strapped over her shoulder. She took a shot of the bow pulpit with the harpoons lashed to it. She swung around and shot their wake, the only troubled water.

"What do you see when you see a swordfish? A fin?"

"Sometimes you see the fin. Sometimes just an inch or so of fin. Looks like a floating stick. If your eyes are good, you can spot a fish a couple of feet down just by the way it disturbs the surface. If it's choppy, you can't see 'em. If it's overcast, they don't fin."

"Why's that?"

"They come up so the sun'll kill worms that get in them. No sun, no fin. So you just hope for a day like this."

"And when you see one . . . ?"

"We nose up on him."

"You mean you sneak up on it?"

"You just come up on him. Sometimes he can even see the boat, he's not scared. A shadow scares him, so you come into the sun."

Elsie said, "And then what?"

"Then I get up in the pulpit. I stick him. The lily—that's the piece with the point and the barb—see it there. It comes right off the shaft. The lily has the line tied to it. The fish takes off, the line pays out. At the end of the line is a float. See there, the beer keg with the ring. If the line was fast to the boat, the fish could pull against the weight, tear the lily out. But when he pulls against the keg, the keg goes down some. When he eases off, the keg buoys back up. Same reason you use a fishing rod. It gives with the fish when the fish pulls, it pulls when he eases. Always tension, but no jerks."

"But if the keg is overboard, how do you pull the swordfish in?"

"You follow along after the keg. When the fish is dead, or just about dead, you can get the keg, and go right up and gaff the fish. We have a tail gaff. It's a wire noose that goes over the tail. Just forward of the tail even a big fish is no thicker than my arm. You get hold of that, you've got him. Pull him in and knock him on the head. Be sure you and Schuyler stand clear. The sword is as big as a baseball bat, and he can swing it. That's how they kill what they eat. They don't stick it. They swim into the school and whap that sword back and forth. Then they circle back and eat the fish they've whapped. The tail can knock you overboard too."

"Then what?"

"We kill him, gut him, put him on ice."

"How many do you think we'll get?"

"I've heard of a boat getting six in a day. And I've been out on a boat didn't get but one all summer. There's no guarantee. The plane helps. If the water temperature's right, the sea's smooth, the tide isn't running too hard, and you get a plane spotting, it'd be bad luck not to get one in four days. We'll be out past the sword-fish grounds to set some pots, but we'll do that early and get back around here for the daylight. Then, the third night, we'll go out to pull the pots, and keep looking on the way home. After three or four days you get so you can't see so good."

They stood quietly for a while, each in their hip-high steel hoop, Elsie with her left arm around the mast. Dick surprised himself by starting to talk again.

"There's a knack to how you look. You got to . . . unfocus your eyes. What you want to do is let as much come in as you can. You don't so much see a fish as you just get a feeling that something's different. You just feel a speck on your screen. Then you focus in. Most of the time it's a shadow of a wave, or seaweed, or flotsam. You'd be surprised how much junk there is out here."

"And you see sharks too, I imagine."

"Yup. And if you see one, you see fifty. If we stick a fish, it's likely there'll be sharks about by the time we pull him in."

"So they might eat the swordfish. And you get nothing?"

"Oh no. As long as he's got any life, they'll stay clear of his bill."

"How long does the swordfish live after you harpoon him?"

"Depends. If I buttonhole him, not long. Anywheres from a minute to a half-hour. If I just barely get the lily in, it could go on and on."

"But can't he swim faster than the boat?"

"Not for long—not towing a beer keg."

"Ah."

Dick liked this conversation, his eyes looking far and near, their voices coming in from some far-off station. He half-realized, half-remembered that when he was out for a long time in his skiff he talked to himself. Usually chewing on something bitter. When he felt good, he didn't say much. If he pulled a pot and got something worthwhile, he might say, "If they all came up like this, it wouldn't be so bad."

He almost missed it. For a while he couldn't find it again. He got a hint at the side of his eye and flicked toward it. Something. He yelled down to Parker and pointed. Parker headed the boat over.

Elsie said, "Where is it?" Dick was on his way down, keeping the dot in view, so he ignored her. When he got out on the bow pulpit, they were three or four hundred yards off. Another minute and he saw it was too black to be a swordfish. Dick rechecked the keg, the line, the lily, the knots. He motioned to Parker which way the fish's head lay. Parker swung the boat out in a curve, lined her up, and came ahead slow. It was a black marlin. Not too big. The aluminum shaft felt funny. Too late to get the wood one. He looked at the coiled line and keg, set his feet. Parker was letting the boat glide in. Dick felt the rail across his hips. He pressed into it. He raised up with the harpoon. The lily was way out front, a long way down, it seemed to be floating away from him. The bow came down off the swell. Dick lined up the lily and the thickest piece of fish. He jammed it in. The fish disappeared. Dick wasn't sure if he'd got it in until he saw the line pay out strong. He retrieved the shaft and got a grip on the rail in case he had to raise his feet. He got behind the keg and propped it up. The line peeled down to the last few coils. The keg went over, skipped twice, and then splashed through the top of a swell. Dick pointed to the keg in case Parker had missed it. Parker ground the engine into gear.

Dick looked back and saw that Elsie was filming from the crow's nest. Schuyler was leaning out over the side with his camera too.

Dick shouted to him, "If you go over, we pick the fish up first." Schuyler ignored him.

Dick thought, I didn't miss. I should have practiced some, but I didn't miss.

He said to Parker, "Skilley."

Parker didn't mind. Schuyler stopped shooting, made his way forward. "What did you say?"

"Skilley. Black marlin. Tastes as good as swordfish, but they don't buy 'em."

"What's the point, then? Just fun?"

"Good meat. If we get him, we'll cut some steaks. You'll see."

The keg dipped out of sight, came back up. Dipped again, popped up.

"See there," Dick said. "He's trying to get down."

Schuyler said, "Get down and boogie," his eye still glued to the viewfinder.

Dick hoped the lily was in good. It had felt right, but he couldn't remember. Dick pointed again and Parker nodded. Dick let Parker follow the fish. Dick went to check the gaff, make sure the wire noose ran smooth. They seemed to gain some on the keg. It was still pushing up water like a nun in a strong tide, but it was slowing, definitely slowing.

He took a deep breath and made fists to steady the flutter in his forearms. They were coming up on the keg. Dick got the boathook. He didn't want to pick up the keg if the fish had another run in him. The line was still taut, the yard or so he could see giving off a green shimmer through the top water.

Parker came up on the keg, kept it alongside. Dick saw the line go slack, tighten again, go slack. He waited until the line went really lazy. He put the hook under it, slowly raised an arc of it. He took in some line. Got the keg up. He glanced up at Parker to make sure he was with him. They slowly moved up the line, Dick coiling it in. And there was the fish. Dick saw the pale belly, then the bill, the mouth agape, the gills flaring slowly, the fins and tail still. No trouble slipping the noose over the tail and then tight. The fish tried to swim, but he was in air. Swung him right in. Felt like eighty, eighty-five pounds. Dick saw the lily, buttonholed in so he was amazed the fish had got as far as he did. A pretty fish, every line swept back for speed. The slender bill wasn't as long as Dick's arm. Dick got his foot on it, felt it stir under the sole of his boot, heard the tail slap once just before he clubbed the head. Once was enough.

He kept his foot on the bill anyway as he ran his knife from anus to throat. The stomach was full of bait fish. He gathered the innards in both hands and dumped them. Dipped the fish once to clean the blood out of the cavity. Took it below to put it on ice. Sloshed a bucket of water across the deck and scrubbed off the slick.

Parker slipped the two hoops of inner tube onto the wheel spokes and came aft to give him five. Then back to work.

The plane showed up, but didn't spot anything during the morning run. The plane went home for lunch when the tide began to run hard. Dick took a two-hour nap.

When he woke up, the boat was rolling more. The southwest

wind had picked up, and there was some sea running but not too much chop. In the crow's nest he could feel the motion amplified. She was not an easy boat. Two-foot seas and she was a goddamn barge. Elsie came up. Dick sent her back down when he saw she was holding on for dear life.

Dick could hear the plane, sneaked a look at it every so often. He climbed down at five. The plane could see better than him anyway.

He drowsed on deck. Parker had got Schuyler to take the wheel. Parker had left the channel open but the squelch up in case the spotter had anything to say; the crackle blended into Dick's nap.

They'd been moving east in slow zigzags. At seven-thirty the plane wagged his wings and left. Parker got Elsie to fix canned soup with hot dogs cut up in it.

They ate in silence, were through in a few minutes. Dick said, "Better juice it on out and pull some pots. We want to be back here by morning."

Parker said, "You want to look for a while longer? Just on the way."

The wind had dropped, so it was a bit more comfortable aloft. Elsie came up. She didn't say a word. After twenty minutes Dick looked at her. Even in the rich light of the late sun she looked green.

"You better go down," he said.

Elsie didn't say anything for a bit. Then, "On deck I can smell the bait."

Dick had to lean near to hear. He said, "Better lie down on your bunk."

Elsie made a face. Dick was watching her now, in between looks at the water. She suddenly leaned away from him, bent at the waist over the rail, and vomited. The pea soup and hot dogs carried on the wind, trailed across the windshield of the wheelhouse. Dick grabbed her as she retched again. She was bent over so far he was afraid she'd fall. He got his right hand on her right hip, groped for her belt. Got his other hand on her left shoulder.

She moaned weakly. He moved his left hand down onto her belt. "I got you," he said. "Go on, just let go."

"Oh no," she said. "Oh shit." She sounded terrible.

"You through?" he said. "If you're through, I'll get you down." She didn't say anything. He waited a bit, then got her onto the ladder. His feet a rung below hers, his hands on the ladder, his arms under her armpits.

When he got her down, she sagged back against him. He felt sharp tenderness for her, as though she was a little kid. He was also embarrassed by how aroused he was. He looked into the wheel-house. Parker was laughing his head off. Pointed at the streaks on the glass. Dick shook his head at him, and turned Elsie forward.

He sat her down on the foredeck. He got her duffel from the cabin and spread some clothes under her. She curled up against the low rail. Dick put a line around her and made the other end fast.

By the time he got a bucket of water and sloshed it across the window, got a life jacket under Elsie's head, and found her a Dramamine, the sun was too low to look anymore.

He turned in. Parker got him up at midnight. Dick woke Schuyler up, asked him how he felt. Schuyler said "Fine." Dick got him on deck to help bait the pots. Parker took a sounding and a fix. Dick put the first line of pots over. By 2:00 a.m. they'd set the pots and headed back. Schuyler and Parker turned in, and Dick took the wheel.

Dick could just make out Elsie, curled up on her side. The boat was rolling some, but not so bad. The moon came down off the starboard bow, made a long sheen across the easy swell. The light was always there, glistening, fading, glistening, no matter how fast it seemed to be racing past.

Dick thought of how *his* boat would feel, deeper and steadier. He thought of how she would sound, the engine lower, the creak of the timbers less abrupt than this set of nervous hummings and clanks.

He kept coming back to Elsie. He should have thought to get some of those new anti-seasick tapes. The Fishermen's Co-op had them—you stuck one behind your ear, instant sea-legs.

He saw her stir. Sit up. Discover the line on her belt. Rummage through her bag. She pulled on a sweater, stretched her arms. He could tell she felt better. She pulled her hands back through her hair and sank down again all in one motion, graceful as a passing wave. Her hand appeared and fumbled for the edge of her yellow slicker, found it, and pulled it over her shoulders.

He looked down at the compass and got back on course. There was a good reason for leaving women onshore. Being at sea opened you up. And if you wanted to do things right, you had to use all that opening up for what you were doing, for where you were, for what was going to happen.

Dick notched the engine up. He'd been lucky not to miss the skilley. He felt certain they'd see a fish tomorrow. He thought he should probably get Schuyler up to take the wheel the last hour before light, get himself a nap for an hour or so. He'd better use the wood shaft if the fish wasn't too deep. He'd been lucky.

After Schuyler took the wheel, Dick went forward and knelt beside Elsie. Watched her until she opened her eyes.

"You okay?"

She rubbed her hand across her eyes and cheek.

She said, "I feel stiff."

He brought a folded blanket and shifted her onto it.

She said, "I feel like such a jerk."

He said, "No. It happens. You'll feel good when you wake up." He tucked another slicker around her knees.

She said, "You're a good daddy," and laughed.

It annoyed him. "Officer Buttrick," he said, "Law-and-Order Buttrick. You looked about as green as your uniform."

She stared back at him and grinned.

Dick was surprised. Damn, he thought, she likes that stuff.

Maybe that was what it was about rich kids—everything was quick little laughs, everyone amused by who gets to who. Dick said, "I guess you're your old self again."

He went below, turned in, and thought of nothing but swordfish, 200, 250 pounds, swimming to meet *Mamzelle.*

*E*ven with six hours of the spotter plane, they came up empty.

They headed out beyond the swordfish grounds and hauled the pots just after sunset. Schuyler filmed by the floodlight on the wheelhouse. He said to Dick, "I thought fishing was the second most dangerous job in America." Dick kept an eye on the line coiling onto the winch, moved aside as a pot came into view. Schuyler called out, "Can't you work a little closer to the bull?" Parker laughed and said cheerfully to Schuyler, "You can be a real asshole."

They got a few okay lobster, a poor-to-fair haul of red crab. Dick guessed the whole haul wouldn't bring much more than three hundred dollars. They hadn't put out enough pots. The tender could have carried more, *Mamzelle* could have carried more herself. And they should have waited another day. Dick also wondered if they weren't too far out for lobster but not quite far enough out for red crab. He recalculated what he'd have to spend on new pots for his own boat, recalculated what he still had to find out.

They eased back into the swordfish grounds by sunup. The weather was holding. But nothing all morning. The plane wagged and headed back in. Dick heard the hum fade. Then hold steady. He thought it was a trick of the way noise carried. No. The plane came back, went into a tight circle. Kept circling. Dick went back up, couldn't see a thing. Parker got up to speed. When they got almost under the plane, Dick saw something. At first he thought it was the shadow of the plane. No fin, just a darkness. They got closer and he saw it was a fish. Not finning, just basking three or four feet under the surface. He'd have to use the metal pole.

He stayed up until he found which end of the fish was front, then slid down fast and got up in the pulpit. Parker came on too fast. Dick waved to him to slow down. Parker lurched into reverse. The fish was just out of reach when he heard the grinding. Dick leaned out. The fish gave one wag of his tail, veered off. Dick stuck. This time he saw the lily go in, too far back. Maybe behind the fin.

But the keg went over before he got to it, was bouncing away across the water. Then settled into a steady skimming, looked like a squat robot waterskiing.

Parker saw it, saw how fast it was going, jolted the engine into full forward.

The keg ducked under. Dick strained to see it. If it popped back up and jumped clear of the water, it meant the fish had pulled loose of it. Dick went up to the crow's nest, still looking. He saw the keg come up, then pull under again. Still on the hook. But if the fish could hold it down that long, he was in awful good health. It'd be a long run.

They followed for an hour or so. The fish would slow down, they'd get hopeful, then the fish'd go at it again. But the lily hadn't come loose, there was still a good chance.

The plane swept back and forth, a hum that was broken into dashes by the rise and fall of the bow, and wind across the rigging and wheelhouse. So it was a while before Dick heard that the plane wasn't sweeping, had tucked into another circle.

Dick came halfway down from the crow's nest to talk it over with Parker.

Standard practice was to put a crew member in the dory, let him follow the first fish. The bigger boat went after the second fish. When the second fish was lost or won, then they came back for the dory and the first fish, if it was still fast.

But if Dick went in the dory, Parker couldn't stick a fish, not with his arm in a cast. If Parker went, they still couldn't count on Elsie or Schuyler to ease the boat up on the second fish.

Parker said, "Elsie can go in the dory."

Dick said, "I don't know."

Schuyler had come up and joined in.

"If Elsie goes I don't want her on film. You know—a girl out there hauling a fish."

"She won't haul it," Parker said, "just keep it in sight."

Dick shook his head. If it died before the big boat got back to her, she'd have to haul it.

"How 'bout you, Schuyler?"

Schuyler said, "Elsie might miss something on board. She's okay with the camera but not as good as me." He brightened. "She could tuck her hair up in a cap. Look like a fisherman in a long shot."

Elsie came forward. Schuyler asked her if she could handle the dory.

"Sure."

Dick said, "Jesus, Elsie. This isn't a salt pond." He knew right off he shouldn't have put it that way.

Parker and Schuyler rigged the outboard and put the dory over the side. Before Elsie got in, Dick took her by the arm.

"Look. You just keep the keg in sight. That's it. If the fish dies, you may see some sharks. A lot of sharks. If you stay clear, there's no problem. If sharks start tearing up the fish, don't get in the middle of it."

Schuyler offered to help her strap the second camera on, but Dick made her put her life jacket on instead. He ran his eye over the dory—oars, oarlocks, gaff, flare gun, water bottle. Schuyler put the camera in. Elsie cranked the motor and eased away.

"Don't go too fast," Dick shouted. "And don't stand up!"

Parker veered off to head for the circling plane. Dick went aloft. He looked back. Elsie was an orange speck in the dory, the dory half hidden and indistinct in a trough. The keg blinked silver on top of a swell and disappeared on the other side.

Parker did better with the second fish. Crept up easy. Dick had a good shot, struck as hard as he could, trying for a quick kill. But the fish took off strong. Dick hoped it was just one good run. The keg kept plowing on.

When the fish slowed, it seemed to Dick it had been hours, but it was in fact only an hour since they'd put Elsie over.

Dick took in the keg and the line, got the tail gaff ready. Schuyler moved in close to him and was filming away. Dick glared at him. Schuyler said, "Don't look at the camera."

Dick looked at him again. "Fuck you, Schuyler."

Dick got the noose on and ran it up tight. The fish lunged. Dick braced a foot and leaned back, almost sitting against the weight. Dick lifted the tail out of the water so the fish couldn't swim, but he couldn't swing him on board, not with this much life in him. He got him half up, his bill dangling down, rapping on the hull now and again.

Parker came back. "Maybe I'll shoot him," Parker said.

"Get the gaff," Dick said.

Parker tried to set the gaff. The fish flipped himself in the air, almost horizontal. He swung back against the hull with a crack. Dick barely held on. The fish was half stunned.

Parker laughed and said, "I'll stick him again. He'll knock himself out for us."

Parker tried again, got the gaff hook in. The fish struggled, but not so hard.

"When I swing him in," Dick said, "you keep his head pinned. Okay—up!"

The barb of Parker's gaff tore loose. The fish landed on deck. Dick stepped back, pulled hard on the pole of the tail gaff, trying to keep the fish straight.

Parker stepped in fast and clubbed the fish's head with the side of the gaff. Parker tried to step on the bill, but it came up and cracked his shin. Parker said "Son of a bitch!" and shoved the gaff into the fish's mouth with his good arm. He gave it a twist and hooked the corner of the mouth when the fish swung his bill again.

Dick clubbed the fish and caved in the side of the head.

"I should have shot him," Parker said. He rolled up his pant leg. "It ain't broke. Son of a bitch."

Parker limped up to the wheel and got his ass up on the chair. Dick stowed the fish below, he'd gut him later.

Parker raised the plane, which they could see way back where they'd come from.

The pilot said the first fish seemed to be still going, still fast to the keg, the dory tagging along.

Dick said, "Maybe we should've took our chances, just let the spotter find the keg."

"The plane can't haul the fish," Parker said. "Maybe she'll scare off the sharks."

The boat was vibrating from the rpms and from smacking hard. Their wake was a ribbon of green and white.

When Dick saw the dory it was turning in an arc. Then it stopped. He couldn't figure out what had happened. He saw the keg floating in place. Elsie was breaking out the oars. As they got close, Dick saw a shark, then two more. Just gliding by the dory, still in wide circles. As Elsie rowed, the keg seemed to pull after her. Dick figured it out. She'd come in close and fouled the propeller on the line. That meant the swordfish was fast to the dory—unless Elsie thought to unclamp the outboard and chuck it. If a big enough shark started tearing at the swordfish, or if the swordfish gave a last run when it saw a shark, the stern of the dory would pull under.

"You see that," Dick said to Parker. "Pull up alongside the dory—we'll haul Elsie."

Dick got a line, put a big loop in the end. Parker swung the boat in. Dick threw the line to Elsie. She caught it, but the dory slid away on the front of a swell. Dick paid out the line. He shouted to Elsie, "Sit down! Sit down and hold on!"

Dick could see that part of the line to the swordfish was floating slack, but he couldn't see the swordfish. He hauled in the line to Elsie. He shouted to her, "Put the line around you!"

Elsie didn't move. She was holding on to the line with one hand, with the other she was gripping the thwart under her. She turned her head to watch a shark glide by the stern.

Parker shifted into reverse. The gap between the boat and the dory widened as the broad stern of the boat swung away. Dick didn't dare haul in hard, he was afraid he'd pull Elsie off balance.

"Elsie! Put the line around you!" She looked at him, and he shouted again, pantomiming putting his arm and head through a loop. Elsie looked puzzled. Dick put his end of the line around his chest. Elsie understood and pulled the loop over her head.

The dory bobbed down in the same trough as the boat. Dick pulled in, the dory nestled alongside, and Dick swung Elsie up hard. She twisted in the air, holding on to the line with both hands, pulling her feet clear of the dory, then flailing them as if she was trying to run in air onto the boat. Dick got a hand on the loop and hauled her in over the side. She scuttled toward the middle of the deck and held on to the hatch cover.

Dick looked for the line to the fish. The dory was floating away, but the keg was within reach. He leaned out with the boathook and got the line.

There was a sharp crack, then another. Dick looked around, puzzled. Parker had left the wheel and was shooting at the sharks, the fore-end of his rifle balanced across his cast. He levered in another round and fired. Then another.

"Parker, what the fuck . . ."

"Get the fish, asshole. Get the fish before they eat the goddamn thing."

Dick hauled the keg, pulled in the stern of the dory, found the line on the other side of the fouled propeller.

"Elsie, give me the tail gaff."

He hauled in the slack line. As the line came taut, he followed it with his eye and saw the swordfish. He saw the lily, the barb breaking back through the skin. Barely holding. Another fifty feet of line. He groped for the boathook with one hand and used it to shove the dory away.

"Elsie, give me the tail gaff." He turned around and saw her still huddled by the hatch cover. He looked around for the tail gaff, pointed to it. He got it himself. The swordfish came easily. Dick spread the noose, dipped it with one hand while he pulled the swordfish in the last ten feet.

As he leaned down to work the noose around the tail, Parker stepped up beside him and jabbed the long aluminum harpoon shaft in the water. Dick saw the shaft go by his face, traced the shine of it as the blunt end hit a shark on the cheek. The shark wheeled away.

Dick tightened the noose and pulled up with both hands. He couldn't do more than get the tail up over the gunwale.

"Hey, Parker." Parker had turned away to get his rifle again.

"Elsie, give me a hand." He turned his head. "Elsie." She looked up. "Hey Elsie, grab a hold."

She got to her feet and came over warily. He gave a heave and gained a foot and a half. He said, "Grab a hold of my belt and pull."

Dick hauled the fish, half-lifting it, half-sliding it over the gunwales. There was only one bite in it. A jagged piece of stomach and some shreds of intestine trailed out. There was a whole silvery baitfish sliding out of the torn stomach lining. The swordfish rapped his bill once on the deck, feebly. Dick finished him off. Looked the fish over. Two hundred pounds, two hundred pounds and then some. When he gutted it, he could tailor it so the shark bite wouldn't show.

Dick worked the lily out and hauled in the dory, got in it to fasten the lines to the davits. He got back on board. Schuyler was zooming in on the stomach of the swordfish.

Schuyler said, "Can you throw some of the guts over, get some of those sharks to come back?"

"You can if you want," Dick said. "Or you can help haul the dory. If I do it by myself, I may dump that camera."

Schuyler lent a hand, retrieved the camera. He said to Elsie, "Did you get any shots?"

Elsie laughed. "As a matter of fact, I did." Dick looked at her. She was still pale, on the verge of crying. She was sitting on the edge of the hatch cover, rocking lightly forward and backward.

Dick worked the fouled line off the propeller. It wasn't cut too bad, but it would have to be replaced. Deduct forty bucks. He looked at Elsie again. Her whole body was moving like grass in a very light wind, shimmering with fear.

He went over to her, put his arm around her shoulder. "I guess you saw some sharks," he said. She nodded.

"It's scary," he said, "but they weren't after you. Don't believe the movies. They weren't after you, they wanted the fish. If you get that right, you won't feel so nervous."

Elsie looked at him and nodded, her eyes still dilated and unfocused.

Dick said, "The first time I saw a shark alongside, I thought he wanted me. I thought his fin was some kind of radar, telling his evil brain that I was his meat. But that's just wrong. You understand?"

Elsie nodded. Dick could feel her still rocking slightly. He didn't think she knew she was rocking, it was just the light after-breeze of fear on her nerves and spine still stirring her a little, a silvery tip of spartina quivering.

He got up. She caught his arm. He said, "I got to put our fish away. You did good. Parker and me ought to cut you in."

When he finished with the fish, Dick was embarrassed. What in hell did he think he was up to?

Parker had brought out a bottle of bourbon. Schuyler had been looking for sharks where the entrails had drifted off, but they'd disappeared.

Elsie took a swig from Parker's bottle. Dick took a swig and got a beer for a chaser. He looked up. The plane was gone. The sun was showing orange along the bottom edge.

Dick tried to calculate the profit. The crabs would cover the fuel, and maybe the new line. Seven hundred for Elsie's fish, maybe five hundred and some for the others. Twelve hundred. His split, maybe four hundred. And marlin steaks twice a week for the family for six weeks.

It beat inshore lobstering and tonging. And he might have guessed light on the swordfish, maybe another thirty, forty bucks for his share. And Parker owed him a hundred for the stuffing box.

He took another swallow of beer. Parker swung the boat toward the sun, homeward bound. Dick felt good. He saw that, as he was getting closer to his boat, there seemed to be more ifs and maybes, more cross-currents. He saw all that, but he was up for it. He'd fought clear of how bad things had been. He was pulling toward his boat in August. He felt strong, and he felt lucky.

Dick took the wheel after supper. The other three sacked out. He throttled back to save fuel, rode easy across the long waves. By the time he saw land, the sun was down, the Matunuck Hills black against the sky. The water glistened jet and violet as he picked up the lights on the breakwater.

*D*ick slept twelve hours. At noon he picked up the engine in Providence. Got it onto its bed by suppertime. The next morning he borrowed Eddie Wormsley's flatbed and picked up another load of lumber. Worked from mid-morning till sunset. Eddie Wormsley and Charlie helped during the afternoon.

He put in another full day, and then it was time to see Parker about going out again.

If they had good runs every week, he'd have the boat finished by Labor Day. He'd have put in another ten thousand dollars. After that he needed another six or seven thousand for some more fittings, paint, RDF, loran. He decided to wait a bit before he got Joxer over and made his pitch to him.

Dick took ten bucks and headed for the Neptune.

The Sox were in the second half of a twi-night doubleheader at Fenway. Parker was at the bar.

Dick had a beer with him at the bar and then got him to sit

down when a table opened up back in the corner. Dick talked to Parker about his plans for his boat. Parker kept an eye on the game, but said enough so that Dick knew he was listening. During the seventh-inning stretch Parker said, "I may be around for the summer, I may not. If I'm around, we may make a few runs. But don't count on it to be regular. Right now it looks good—we'll go out tomorrow night. I'm not going to put out a lot of money for more pots. Maybe you should see if Joxer Goode will make us a deal—lend us some, rent us some. We'll promise him we'll go all the way to the edge of the shelf. I'm not so sure about a spotter plane. Six hours at fifty bucks. Maybe you want to split it?"

Dick said he couldn't.

Parker said, "Maybe you'll throw in your skiff. You're right about that dory."

"Then Charlie couldn't haul my pots."

"Forget your pots. Or better yet, bring them out with us."

"If I lend you the skiff, will that do for my half of the spotter?"

"Lend?" Parker said. "I meant a sale. I'll spring for two thousand dollars of spotter over the next month, you throw in the skiff."

Dick said, "Hell no." He was so mad he couldn't say any more.

"Get you another beer? Don't get all huffy, Dick. I been meaning to say something to you. You want that beer?"

Dick said no. Parker got up and went to the bar, brought back two beers anyway.

"Tell me if I'm wrong," Parker said. "You got laid off Texeira's boat 'cause you kept letting the mate and the crew know you're saltier than them. You didn't do too good in the Coast Guard for more or less the same play. You got fired from the boatyard for some miscues with a couple of owners. And one of your big days last year was when a big yacht pulled up on you in a fog and asked you how to find the harbor. You led his fifty-footer in your diddly-squat skiff with you rowing. Kept him putt-putting behind you, just to make him feel like an asshole. You laughed in his face when he tried to give you a tip.

"There's more, but that's the pattern. You spend a lot of time dividing up the world into the idle rich and the true-blue salts. The unworthy and the worthy. And what you do get out of all this? You get to feel pissed off. Am I leaving something out? You get to feel salty as hell, but mainly pissed off. You also get to be poor. Tonging quahogs in your eighteen-foot skiff."

Dick was mad as hell, but for some reason this anger made him cold and numb. Dick said, "Yeah, my skiff you just tried to cheat me out of."

Parker laughed. "I make you an offer. Instead of coming back and saying, 'No, but I'll take four thousand,' you get all indignant. You make everything a moral issue."

Dick said, "You want to make an offer on my kids?"

"There you go again," Parker said. "At least I got your attention. There are times I divide the world the way you do, the bad guys and good guys. And other times other ways, depending. Sexy, not sexy, tight and loose. But one way, one important way is this—players and nonplayers.

"What gets me is you could be a player. What you end up doing is what nonplayers do. Nonplayers drudge, and then bitch and moan about it, how bad it is, how unfair it is, and they drudge some more to make it even badder and even more unfair."

Dick said, "You ever hear me bitching and moaning?"

"Sometimes I can just look at you and feel it. Inside you're sucking on a lemon. You don't need to *say* it." Parker sipped his beer. "I want you to consider Schuyler. You look at him, and you despise him for being too rich and too cute and his house is too big. You'd like to show him he's not salty, not strong, not half the man you are. I'll tell you, you could do all that, and he would be amused.

"I look at him and I see some of what you see, but I also see he's a player. I don't know where he got his first chunk of dough, but I found out he's playing. He didn't pay much cash for the Wedding Cake—it was leveraged. Now he's in with Joxer Goode, and with Elsie's rich brother-in-law, and there's Salviatti too, who's even richer. When it came time to play, Schuyler threw in the Wedding Cake without blinking. If he'd have blinked, those other three would have known he was a nonplayer and they would've bought him out or left him alone. They would have finally offered for the Wedding Cake a lot less than what Schuyler's buying with it now. He was ready. And another thing is, he acted like any minute he was about to fly high with some other TV-movie deal. He didn't bitch and moan about how little money he got paid his last time out. He acted like things are moving, he's moving, and those guys got a sense that he's a player. When they said they're each raising a quarter of a million he didn't say, 'Jesus! That's all I've got!' He said, 'Will that be enough? Will that be enough to do it first-class?' And that got Elsie's brother-in-law talking about what kind of a place he had in mind, Schuyler got him on the defensive."

"How did you get to know all this?"

"A chat here, a chat there. I find out stuff, I put it together. There's a lot I don't know, but I got a sense of it. I don't know what Schuyler's worth, he may have a couple of hundred thousand somewhere. But I'm pretty sure that he's winging it on the Sawtooth Point deal. Flying right out in mid-air."

"You mean he just talked his way in?"

"No. No, you're missing the point. He held some cards. It's how he played them is the point. He got the Wedding Cake for a song. I looked up the asking price in the old ads. So I guess all he put down was a hundred grand, which I figure he got by selling his New York co-op. His wife told me they were living in her parents' house for six months. Before that, all he had of the Wedding Cake was an option for a year before he bought it. He went way out on a limb to get that card. He *was* going to play it by renting it to some guys to make a sleazo horror movie, get shares in the movie. But then this deal came along. Now, for him to play it, he had to pay off the mortgage. How did he do that? I don't know for sure, but I can tell you his wife is biting her nails. I think he went down to New York and raised money for the movie he's making, maybe for the horror movie too, and he used that money to pay off the mortgage. So now he's got to scramble to get the movie made. But look at him. He's having a good time. Then look at his wife. There's a nonplayer, a worried-sick, doing-nothing-about-it nonplayer."

"So Schuyler's hot shit in your book. So what?"

"It's a difference between you and me. You look for ways to put him down. I pay attention. You should pay attention. Apply what you pick up to your own situation. You're counting on me to take you out so we can bust our asses chasing red crabs and swordfish. If you want your money for your boat, you ought to be ready to play. One thing you got is your acre. The resort could make money putting another cottage in there."

"For Christ's sake, Parker! That's where I live—"

"Another thing you've got is Joxer."

"I got Joxer to say he'd come look at the boat."

"And I hear from Elsie that Miss Perry thinks you're a great guy. Get Miss Perry to invest. She's loaded."

Dick had made his mind up about that long ago. May had mentioned it when he started the boat. It just felt wrong. Dick looked at Parker and shook his head.

"Another thing you got is a way to make trouble. You're up Pierce Creek, the resort is going to screw up something for you. Pollute a clam bed. Get a lawyer and find some rights."

"I couldn't pay a lawyer."

"Do it on a contingency-fee basis. You don't really want to sue. You just want to have that on hand. Settle for peanuts, the lawyer gets some of the peanuts. But what you get is a noncash deal—a sweeter loan for your boat. A sweeter deal for your land. The lawyer gets snookered out of that. There's something in there, I can smell it. You could get hired as a consultant on what the currents are in the breachway and the salt pond, what'll happen if they dredge a channel. See, if they *don't* hire you, you could be a witness for the other side. If they hire you, you won't be called to testify, because you're their boy. It's worth something."

"Jesus, Parker."

Dick couldn't say more than that. He was numbed again, but not by anger. He felt as though Parker had picked up his life and squeezed it. His life, but what came out was foul. "Jesus," he said again. Dick felt he had to get clean. He said, "This is just beer talk."

Parker laughed. "Yeah. Maybe it is. Still, you go at your boat your way, the numbers don't work. No way you can make ten thousand dollars this summer just working. In terms of materials alone you got—what?—twenty thousand in your boat. More. Sitting there doing nothing. And God knows what you put in as labor. That's just like money sitting there doing nothing. You won't make it through the winter unless you get your boat working by the fall. You and May'll both be picking crabs come October. You think Joxer'll lend money to one of his crab pickers? What I'd do if I was him is wait till February, when you're really down, then offer you thirty thousand for your boat as is. Have the boatyard finish her, then sell her for triple that in the spring. If I couldn't sell her, then I'd put her to work with a hired skipper. It wouldn't be you. Joxer could trawl through New Bedford, get a pretty salty skipper, with ten, fifteen years at sea, doesn't have a reputation for being a sorehead."

Dick said, "I won't sell."

Parker shrugged. "Maybe you won't."

Dick said, "Look. You want to go out or not?"

Parker said, "Ah. Well. Sure. Nothing too strenuous."

*T*hey went out in the late afternoon so they could lay the pots at first light way out on the edge of the shelf and get back to the swordfish grounds for the better part of daylight.

Nothing doing for two days. They headed back out and hauled pots. This time they'd done that part right. They took it easy on the way home, zigzagging through the swordfish grounds. Still nothing.

Dick's share of the crabs was almost four hundred dollars.

Dick gave Eddie Wormsley half of what was left of the black marlin, and Eddie and he worked on the boat for two and half days, until there was nothing more to do without more money.

Joxer was away in Boston. Parker didn't want to go out again just yet. Just as well, it was Charlie's birthday. Miss Perry showed up in her beautifully varnished and polished station wagon—the wood trim as dark as the ribs of the old Buttrick canoe. She could have sold it for a fortune. It was almost thirty years old. It was one of the first cars the dealer in Wakefield had sold, and he'd made a point of keeping it going, pointed it out to customers, had a color photo of it in his showroom, which he took down when Miss Perry came in.

Miss Perry rarely drove herself anymore. On Sundays her driver was usually Phoebe Fitzgerald, Miss Perry's stone-cottage tenant, but when Dick bent down to open the passenger door for Miss Perry, he saw Elsie at the wheel.

Dick had known Miss Perry all his life, her father had had dealings with Dick's great-uncle and father. He couldn't remember when she hadn't seemed old. Miss Perry had called on May and Dick when Charlie was born to bring a present for the baby. And she came again on Charlie's first birthday, and then Charlie's second birthday, which was just a week after Tom was born. It became an annual occasion, and it always reminded Dick of the stiff black-and-white formality of his great-uncle Arthur and Pierce family gatherings at the Wedding Cake. There was the same awkwardness at first. May always treated it as an inspection and got the house clean. But the boys didn't have to dress up, since they always went out fishing in the skiff. Dick couldn't remember when they started doing that—he remembered Charlie and him and Miss Perry, the three of them, poor little Tom kept home with May that first time, so it must have been eleven years ago. They never went out far, just into one of the salt ponds, or, if it was very calm, just outside the gut. The initial awkwardness was eased by Miss Perry, not by informality, but by her unvarying ritual. She presented Charlie and Tom each with a gift, always a book, and each year she said the same thing. "This is for you, dear boy, it's a plain reader's copy and I hope you enjoy it. If you keep it nicely, if you don't tear the pages or scribble on them, I'll give you a brand-new book in its place when you're grown up."

Then she asked each boy if he'd liked the last book. They always said "Yes, ma'am." She asked each boy if he remembered any of it. "Yes, ma'am." And then each boy in turn would recite a little bit of poetry or prose.

Miss Perry would praise the recitation and the choice of the passage, and shake each boy's hand.

When the boys got older, this ritual became a joke between them and Miss Perry. One year Miss Perry forgot, or chose to forget, to ask them to recite, and the boys, then thirteen and eleven, brought it up. Now that Charlie was seventeen and Tom fifteen, it seemed to Dick that this rite was kind of silly, especially in front of Elsie Buttrick.

But Elsie kept herself well to the rear during the presentation and recitation. Charlie and Tom both laughed at "If you don't tear the pages or *scribble* on them," which Miss Perry said in a way that made fun of herself, and then both boys recited with good grace and an easy detachment.

Elsie stepped forward with her present for the boys, but stepped back when she saw that there was a final stage—opening the glass doors of the bookcase and admiring the collection as a progression of the boys' reading. Dick enjoyed this part—each book standing for a year in the boys' lives, marking transitions. May and sometimes Dick had read the books aloud to the boys until they were nine. And then the second, more subtle transition to full-fledged adult books. This year Charlie got Bowditch's *American Practical Navigator.*

It was a peculiar little library. All the books were by New Englanders, except some of the very early children's books such as *A Child's Garden of Verses* (Charlie's) and a complete set of Beatrix Potter (Tom's). Among the ten-to-fourteen-year-old books there were Thomas Bailey Aldrich's *Story of a Bad Boy,* Hawthorne's *Twice-Told Tales,* several books by Louisa May Alcott, John Greenleaf Whittier, Henry Wadsworth Longfellow, and a book by one of the boat-building Herreshofs about boys learning to sail.

And then, more recently, Thoreau, Melville, more Hawthorne, Sarah Orne Jewett, Francis Parkman's *History of the French in North America* (all nine titles for Charlie's fifteenth birthday), and Prescott's *Conquest of Mexico, Conquest of Peru,* and *Ferdinand and Isabella* (for Tom's fourteenth birthday). Joshua Slocum, although he hailed from the Maritime Provinces, had been included as a Rhode Islander, since he acquired the boat in which he sailed alone around the world here in Rhode Island, just on the other side of Narragansett Bay.

Miss Perry had said—not annually, only once or twice—that the collection was a history of New England thought and attitudes, but, given the enterprise of New England thought and of her whaling, fishing, and merchant fleets, that that history touched a great part of the world.

Miss Perry now repeated this to Elsie, as a way of bringing Elsie in. Elsie gave Tom and Charlie each a rigging knife, and Miss Perry said they should pay Elsie a penny, because a present of something sharp was unlucky and might cut the friendship.

The boys got the fishing poles out. Elsie asked Miss Perry when she should come back for her. Charlie said, "Aw, come on, Miss Buttrick. Be a sport."

Dick said, "Pretty tame stuff, after swordfishing. At least there's no sharks in the salt pond."

Dick found the flounder hole after some drifting around, getting their hooks cleaned by little scup. They started pulling in flounder, about a half-pound apiece. A couple of smaller dap.

They were alone in a deep cove. They could hear the rustle of the spartina. Tom had set the anchor and sat straddling the bow, dangling his bare feet over the water. Charlie was in the stern, Miss Perry in a folding chair in front of him, Dick and Elsie on the rowing thwart.

Miss Perry got a heavy strike. As she reeled in she chanted, " 'A minnow, a minnow! I have him by the nose!' " The boys had heard this line too. Elsie looked at Charlie. Charlie said, "It's from one of the books."

Dick leaned over past Elsie, caught Miss Perry's line, and swung the fish in. It was a sea robin, its pectoral fins spread like wings. Dick held the sea robin up to Miss Perry's ear so she could hear it croak. "My gracious," Miss Perry said. "It's prehistoric."

Tom looked back and said, " 'But what a horrible surprise! Instead of a smooth fat minnow Mr. Jeremy Fisher landed little Jack Sharp the stickleback, covered with spines!' " Miss Perry crowed with delight.

They had a pail full of fish. The fishing slowed. Dick said, "Time to go in?"

They all said no, and settled peacefully.

Miss Perry said, "We look like a daddy longlegs." She pointed at the poles jutting up and out all around, the lines running out and down into the still water.

"Missing a leg," Charlie said.

"Or three," Elsie said.

Miss Perry said, "No matter. We still give the *impression* of a daddy longlegs." She smiled at Dick, her face buttery with sunlight that filtered through the brim of her straw hat.

The skiff swayed a little as Elsie slid herself backward off the thwart and lay down. She nestled her head on a life jacket; her calves flattened out on the seat. She stuck the butt of her rod in her armpit, the first length of it across her thigh. Her hat was down to her nose. Her visible mouth yawned. She said, "This is nice. What's nice about flounder fishing is it's so dumb."

Charlie looked sharply at Elsie, a little bit hurt. Dick laughed. Charlie looked at Dick. Dick shrugged and tilted his head. Miss Perry put her pole on top of Elsie's and pushed down hard once. Elsie struggled to sit up, lost her hat, reeled in frantically until her bait showed. "Now, *that's* dumb," Elsie said to Dick. The boys laughed. Miss Perry confessed.

Everything was still again. Far off and aloft the wind was moving clouds across the sea, but around them the pond was so unruffled Dick could see green on the water near the bank, the sky on the middle of the cove. Dick was struck by love for Charlie. The skiff seemed to float in the center of his heart without a sound, holding Charlie.

This perfect stillness held for a minute. Dick's reflex of checking things rippled across it without spoiling it. Dick jigged his rod tip a couple of times. He narrowed his eyes against the bright water. He didn't want another fish; he ducked his head and said, "You want to run us home, Charlie? Get the anchor up, Tom. Make sure you wash the mud off."

Charlie cranked the engine and the skiff rose up, cut a long arc across the water. Dick swung round to face front, made room for Tom between him and Elsie's shins. He put his arm around Tom's shoulders. "When we get to the creek, you scull us up."

As they swung past Sawtooth Island, Dick saw that there was a ring of new-planted willow trees. They'd got the roofs on the first cottages on the point too. Dick thought of his boat, still not decked.

Tom broke out the sculling oar. Miss Perry came forward to take Tom's place. Charlie folded her chair and raised the motor in the well. "Now, watch this," Dick said to Elsie. "Not many people know the trick of it."

Tom worked the oar in neat pushes and pulls, and they nosed smoothly up the creek between the banks, a foot of perforated black mud at half-tide, topped by a mat of roots and stems and a shimmer of spartina.

Miss Perry chanted, " 'I scream, you scream, we all scream for ice cream!' " and Tom and Charlie chimed in.

As dumb as flounder fishing, Dick thought, but it seemed okay for Charlie and Tom to go along and get silly with Miss Perry. Somewhere they'd got goodhearted. It wasn't anything he'd taught them. Nor had Miss Perry, though he was grateful to Miss Perry for the way she seemed to draw it up out of them. For all her old-fashioned stiffness, she had the trick of that, as handy as Tom twitching his oar to and fro, moving the skiff up the creek smooth as silk.

*T*hey pulled up to the wharf. Charlie helped Miss Perry out, and they went on up to the house. Dick and Tom started gutting and filleting the flounder, tossing the heads into a bait barrel, the stomachs into the creek, where green crabs danced out to snatch them. He stripped the meat from the sea-robin tail and tossed it in with the flounder.

He carried the bucket of fillets up the path and into the kitchen. May put the skillet on the burner.

Dick got himself a beer, looked around for Elsie to see if she wanted one. He went out onto the kitchen porch. He didn't see Elsie or Tom. He called out. No answer. He looked down the path to the boat shed, only the front of which was visible among the trees. He'd built the shed when he first started work on the boat. It was huge and looked like hell—all it was was a framework of wood. The sides and the peaked roof were covered with heavy-gauge translucent vinyl which he'd fastened by nailing strips of lathing to the struts. There was no door, just curtains of old tarps he'd tied together. Once the weather had got warm, he'd torn away some of the siding to let the breeze in.

He'd built it so he could keep his tools and lumber dry. He'd also built it so he could keep people from seeing what he was up to.

He'd told the boys not to let anyone near it. He marched over to the front flap and pulled it back.

Elsie was just inside, under the prow, her back to him. Tom was off to one side, turned his head to look at Dick. He stepped back, opened his mouth, but didn't say anything.

Dick said, "Goddamn it, Tom. . . ."

Elsie turned and put her hand on his arm. "My God, Dick," she said, "this is beautiful. It is absolutely beautiful."

"Tom," Dick said.

"I told her," Tom said, "but she just came on in."

"Dick, this is just amazing. I've never seen anything like it." Elsie stretched her arms wide and ran her hands up either side of the sharp bow. "I've never seen a boat from this angle. I mean, such a big boat." She tilted her head back to look up at the prow. "It's so . . ." She broke off and walked around one side, trailing her hand along a seam. "It's like a sculpture. A real work of art." She looked at her palm, which was streaked with powdery red lead. She rubbed it on the seat of her shorts.

Tom slipped by Dick and out the front.

Elsie backed away from the side, pointed at the bow, and traced the line of the gunwale in the air. "And the way it slopes back on top too. I can see why boats are she." She laughed. "It sounds silly but it is just . . . so . . . sexy." She put her hands on her hips. "And the way the bow is so sharp and then fills out."

Dick said, "She's a workboat. She has to be sharp into the water but then carry a load. That's always the problem with boats—"

Dick was startled to hear May speak up behind him. "Don't start in on all that now. Supper's ready."

Elsie said, "I love the color too. Don't you, May? That sort of rose color."

Dick said, "That's just an undercoat to keep the wood from taking on moisture."

May sighed and stepped outside. Dick held the tarp for Elsie.

Dick said to Elsie, "I'll be obliged if you don't say anything about the boat."

"Oh. All right. When will she be ready?"

May, walking ahead, gave a short laugh.

Dick said, "When I get finished." He said to May, "You pick some tomatoes?"

May said, "It's all on the table." She stopped and said to Elsie, "That boat may look like a work of art to you. For us she's a hole in outer space."

"What do you know about holes in outer space?" Dick said. "*Star Wars*?"

"You mean a black hole?" Elsie said.

"You could call her that," May said, "Miss Black Hole."

"That'll do," Dick said. "It's been hard but it ain't that hard. No reason we can't eat a good meal this evening. You show Elsie where she can wash up."

Dick turned on the back stoop after they'd gone in. He wasn't as mad at May as he'd thought he would be.

He'd felt a real storm coming up in him, but it had moved through without breaking. He was hurt, though. He looked at the dusty backyard, torn up by the pickup going to and fro. The kitchen garden. The line of the treetops, dark green against the evening sky, like heavy seas from the cockpit of a small boat.

He would run the boys and May to the movie house in Wakefield on his way to see Parker at the Neptune. Pick them up on the way home.

The boat shed, with its torn sides, its pale sagging roof, looked like a scorched, cracked eggshell thrown out in the trash.

Through the screen door he could hear Charlie showing his collection of shells and fish skeletons to Miss Perry. Charlie had mounted them so the jaws worked. Tautog. Squeateague. Indian names. Names left over like bones. From half a mile away Dick heard the trucks leaving the building sites on Sawtooth Point. Narragansett. Matunuck. Words from before anyone had owned anything.

He thought, I'll get Joxer to take a look at the boat. Joxer said he'd come look. Then I'll tell May that one way or the other I'll have the boat out of here by Labor Day.

At supper Dick asked Miss Perry if the Narragansetts had really not owned land.

Miss Perry said they hadn't owned land individually; as tribes they'd had dominion over tribal lands.

"Then how come they had wampum? What did they buy?"

"Ah," Miss Perry said. "The chief use of wampum wasn't as money. A piece of shell embroidery, that is, wampum, was a symbolic depiction of events. It could be used as a chronicle within the tribe. Or it could be sent from one tribe to another to call a council, and then each side would make another bit of shell work recording the treaty, and the tribes would exchange them. The fact that wampum was *exchanged* may have led the English settlers to think it served as money. Commerce was, after all, very much on the minds of our ancestors. I think Everett told me that wampum as money may have been an English invention, like scalping, which the red Indians then adopted. Wampum is quite beautiful. Everett had a piece. It was made of the purple insides of quahog shells and pieces of porcupine quill, all strung into a mosaic. It had a meaning, which we can't decipher, but the design is a real work of art."

Dick thought of Parker. Indians were nonplayers. Elsie said the boat was "a real work of art." Where did that leave him? Were he and the rest of the swamp Yankees going to leave a name or two— Pierce Creek—and a relic or two—the silted-over causeway—and fade out? Get half remembered by bookish spinsters?

May brought in the first cake. She'd written "Charlie" in the middle. Around the name there were so many candles some of them were set at an angle, like pine trees growing out of a cliff. Miss Perry started them singing.

May, Miss Perry, and Elsie beamed at Charlie. Charlie sat up and puffed out his chest to blow out the candles. Dick felt a rush of irritation at Charlie that surprised him and embarrassed him. Not Charlie, anyone but Charlie, at least he'd been good with Charlie.

Charlie wasn't going to be a fisherman, he wasn't going to end up on the boat. Dick saw that. Dick knew he could talk him into it for a while, but Charlie had something else in him. Dick couldn't say what, but it shone in him from time to time. Dick was glad for it, but felt the separation already.

And there was May, sour about something, not just the boat, though calling it a black hole was as far as May'd ever gone in that direction. Elsie calling the boat a real work of art—she might have a job, but what a rich-kid thing to say. Even Miss Perry's queer old goodness shifted away from him, was once again just a reminder of how things had been when Sawtooth Point had been a hayfield, the Wedding Cake the product of the Pierce family's farming and fishing.

All three of these women now made him think of the flaws in his life, how it could check and split. Anger, envy, and regret. All of them bitter to his own taste. He didn't want them. Anger at home, regret toward the Point, envy up toward the hills where the big houses sat overlooking the hard little enterprises at sea level.

May brought in Tom's cake. "Hurray!" Miss Perry cried, to make up for Tom's cake coming in second, and then she started them singing again.

When Miss Perry and Elsie left and May and the boys went to the movies in Wakefield, Dick headed for the Neptune. It had been such a nice day for the women and children, he decided he'd better move away from them.

On the afternoon Dick was set to go out again with Parker, Joxer phoned. His voice on the phone was as big and booming as if he was shouting across the water.

Joxer had an hour to spare, thought it might be a good time to come look at Dick's boat. Dick held Joxer off a little, saying to Joxer that he was just loading bait barrels onto the pickup, but he supposed they might as well take the time now.

Joxer showed up in ten minutes. Dick popped a couple of beers for them and took Joxer to the shed.

Joxer walked around the boat once. Climbed the ladder over the side and lowered himself into the hold. Walked carefully along the keelson. Picked up a corner of the greasy tarp and looked at the diesel engine.

Put his glasses on to read the specs on the engine.

He and Dick climbed out, picked up their beers off the table saw.

Joxer said, "It's awfully hot in here. Let's step outside. Do you have the plans?"

Dick wiped his hands and gathered up the plans. His hands were shaking. Joxer held the front tarp for him, and they went to the front parlor and sat. Dick pointed to the lowest shelf of the bookcase. "I got an article on this type of boat, and the Cummins manual."

Joxer put his reading glasses on and skimmed the article from the *National Fisherman*. "Yes," he said, "I remember this. I thought of having the yard build one for my company. But then Captain Texeira said he'd go out for red crabs and . . ."

Dick said, "I hear Captain Texeira's retiring again."

"Semi-retiring," Joxer said, "but both his boats are still going out for me."

Dick took a sip of beer.

Joxer said, "This is going to be your boat, right? You're in alone, not partners with Larry Parker or anyone?"

"Just me," Dick said. "I've had some help from Eddie Wormsley and Charlie. I owe about half on the engine to the Cummins dealer. No bank loans. It's all my boat."

"No bank loans?" Joxer said. "You've tried a bank or two, have you?"

Dick thought, Here we go again. He felt an old anger run down its old tracks, and an odd momentary spurt of not giving a damn. The two cross feelings seemed to steady him. He said, "You know banks aren't interested in unfinished boats. Leastways if it's not a yacht. They don't want to know what I got out there. Could be a hole in the ground so far as they see. The point is, you've had a look at her."

Joxer tucked his reading glasses in his shirt pocket and stretched his legs out. "That's right, I've seen her. She's a little short, but she's deep and beamy. Good design, good materials. And your work is first-class. It is just plain first-rate."

Dick nodded and kept his mouth shut. He didn't want to get excited.

Joxer said, "There's still some work to do, and I guess you need a lot of equipment—hauling gear and whatnot. I don't want to presume, but could I ask . . . I mean, you don't need me to tell you what you've done so far is good work. So what *do* you want?"

Dick took his time. Joxer crossed his legs, folded his hands around his knee, and fixed his eyes on his thumbs. Dick was grateful for his keeping still.

Dick heard himself get it out. "What I want . . . is for you . . . to lend me enough money to finish her."

Joxer nodded and said, "Uh huh, and how much do you figure that will be?"

"Ten thousand dollars."

"Uh huh, and how would the loan be secured?"

Jesus, Dick thought, he didn't say no.

"The boat," Dick said. "She's worth at least ten times that right now."

"If it were up to me," Joxer said, "that might be okay. But I have some shareholders. An unfinished boat isn't readily marketable. What about your land?"

"It's already mortgaged. The second mortgage is how I got this far with the boat."

Joxer didn't say anything. Dick said, "My skiff and outboard are worth four thousand. There's half of it."

Joxer said, "We could only use half the value as collateral. It's a tough rule, but it's accepted practice."

Dick said, "There's the boys' twelve-foot skiff." He wished he'd kept his mouth shut.

Joxer said, "There is another way. If you could get someone with pretty ready assets to cosign."

Dick said, "Let me get this straight. I put up the boat, but if you want to foreclose, then you can get it from the cosigner if that's easier for you."

"Well, not quite. We have to make a good-faith attempt to sell the boat."

"So the cosigner could be anyone with something worth ten thousand dollars? Or would it be twenty thousand?"

Joxer said, "No. It would have to be someone of good standing with ready assets. A bank account, stocks, bonds. That sort of thing."

"So Parker's boat wouldn't do."

Joxer laughed. "Parker's boat may be here today, gone tomorrow. Just like Parker."

Dick said, "What about Eddie Wormsley? He's got equipment for his wood-and-lumber business, it's worth as much as his house. Tractor, portable sawmill, flatbed truck with a hydraulic arm."

Joxer said, "I don't think so. It has to be readily convertible assets. Look. I'll tell you what I *can* do. I'm—how shall I put this?—disposed to ask my company to lend you the money. There is an advantage to the company in getting another boat under contract to go out for crabs. Part of the deal, incidentally, will have to be that you undertake to make your best efforts to bring in red crab. We have a standard clause. It's usually a yearly agreement, but we'd have to make yours last until you pay off the loan, or, let's say, three years, whichever is longer."

"And that'll do it?" Dick said. "What about swordfishing on the way out and on the way home?"

Joxer held up his hand. "Yes, sure, you can look for swordfish. But no, that won't do it. You still need a cosignatory. What I'll do is see if I can find someone. Better yet—have you thought of Miss Perry?"

Dick shook his head. "Now, what puts you in mind of Miss Perry? I see her maybe three times a year. She likes my kids. I don't know what all you people keep saying 'Miss Perry' for. I don't mind dealing with Eddie Wormsley, we're in a lot of things together. Parker's an old wheeler-dealer from the word 'go.' I don't mind talking to you, you're in the business. I catch what you sell. You're out to make money." Dick shook his head. "It's hard to say. She's not . . . Look. It's like this. If you go to church and you see a fellow put a hundred bucks in the collection plate, what do you do? I don't suppose you go up and grab his arm and say, 'Hey, I could use some of that.'"

Joxer just sat there, let his chin sink onto his chest. Dick couldn't tell what Joxer was thinking. Dick felt worn out. He felt as though he'd opened a hole in his chest.

Dick said, "I got to get that bait on board." He got up. Joxer got up. Dick said, "Thank you for stopping by."

"I'm glad we had this talk," Joxer said. "I can't promise anything, but I'll give it a try. I want you to get that boat in the water. You're going out for a week now? You bring in some crabs, and we'll see what's up by then. Another thing in your favor is that you seem to be learning where to find those crabs."

Dick took in what Joxer said warily, but by the time he headed *Mamzelle* out past the breakwater, he let it bloom a little.

*T*hey didn't see a swordfish on the way out, but after they set the pots and came back into the swordfish grounds, Parker's college boy spotted one. Dick nipped up to the crow's nest alongside him. The kid pointed. "I'll be damned," Dick said, "I'll be damned."

A hundred and seventy-five pounds. Dick's share would go around three hundred bucks. The kid's share about seventy-five. He didn't look like he was in it for the money. Something to tell girls about, get the best tan he'd ever had.

They hauled more red crabs than last time. Didn't fill the wells, but respectable.

On the way back in, Parker asked Dick to check the kid out on dead reckoning and the RDF.

Parker let the kid take the wheel. Parker and Dick went aft to have a beer. Parker asked Dick if Dick could run his skiff in through the breachway to Little Salt Pond and from there up a creek to Mary Scanlon's restaurant. Dick said yes.

"Is there more than one way to go? Or is there just Sawtooth Creek?"

"There's another creek, but it's only good at the flood."

"Okay," Parker said. "Now, from the salt marsh in front of Mary Scanlon's, what's it like to get back to the sea—not going back through Little Salt Pond?"

"There's a whole maze of creeks in that part of the salt marsh."

"And all those creeks, they have enough water?"

"Some do, some don't. Those that do, it depends on the tide."

"But you know which ones do if the tide's in."

"Yup."

"And your little skiff'll get through the ones that do?"

"Depends on the tide."

"What about the dory?"

"That dory draws as much as my skiff."

"If you wanted to take a trip in the marsh from Mary Scanlon's restaurant as far west as you could go, how far could you get in your skiff? Without going back out to sea?"

"Not far. The next pond west is cut off. There's a high arm that connects to the beach, got a gravel road on it. There's a culvert, though. A small boat could get through. Depends on the tide."

"Then what?"

"Jesus, Parker. If you had a canoe you could carry over a few places, you could go right on up to New York City."

The kid sang out they were coming up on the breakwater. Dick took the wheel. He checked his watch. They'd still have an hour to unload the crabs. He'd see if Joxer had any news for him about a cosigner.

When they got to Joxer's dock, it looked like a Chinese fire drill. Captain Texeira's ninety-footer was tied up, but she wasn't unloading. The crew was just milling around. There was another, smaller boat, the *Marjorie,* and her skipper was standing by the bow rail yelling at Joxer. Joxer was talking to Captain Texeira.

Dick held *Mamzelle* off when he saw Captain Texeira get back on board his boat and cast off. He eased *Mamzelle* in when Captain Texeira was clear.

Joxer was now talking to *Marjorie's* skipper, who'd quit yelling. Joxer's Jap foreman came over to the *Mamzelle.*

"We can't buy crabs today."

Dick said, "What?"

"We can't buy crabs today. Our refrigeration plant is snafu."

"What the hell does that mean?" Dick said. "Speak English, goddamn it."

Parker said, "Take it easy, Dick."

Dick said, "Where's Joxer? We got a boatload of crabs, for Christ's sake."

Dick climbed onto the dockside and found Joxer on the other side of the hoist, still talking to the *Marjorie's* skipper, who'd come onto the dock and was now standing on his hat.

When Dick came up, the skipper took a step back. Joxer picked up the skipper's hat, brushed it off, and handed it to him. Joxer looked pale and caved in. Dick let his breath out. He said, "Aw shit, Joxer."

"Excuse me," Joxer said to the skipper. Joxer turned to Dick and recited, "We had a completely unforeseeable problem here. It is temporary, and I'm confident I can find a way to make it up to you. If you'll let Mr. Yamaguchi take a look, we'll keep a record of who's lost what. I can't—"

Parker came up and said, "Where's Texeira headed for? He's putting out to sea again."

Joxer said, "He's going to New Bedford."

Marjorie's skipper said to Joxer, "Why didn't you say so before?"

"Because they can't handle any more than what Captain Texeira's got. They're only buying half of it as it is. He's radioed his other boat to dump hers."

"What about your trucks?" Dick said.

"They're full. Believe me, I've tried everything."

Parker asked, "What the hell happened?"

Joxer took a long breath and let it out. "The old refrigeration plant broke down. That was okay, because the new one was on its way here. From Troy, New York. They got as far as Worcester and the company got in touch with the truck driver and called it back. As far as I can make out the check bounced, and the reason it bounced was that the refrigeration expert who was working for us had access to the account. It looks as if he cleaned it out and disappeared."

Nobody said anything after that. The skipper put his hat back on. Dick looked back at *Mamzelle*. He thought, At least we got the swordfish. He tried to figure what Joxer had to pay out to Captain Texeira. A ninety-footer coming in after a good run might have fifteen to twenty thousand dollars in her hold. Captain Texeira was saving Joxer at least seven thousand bucks by going to New Bedford. The crew probably weren't too happy about it, another half-day down there, work all evening, half-day back.

Mamzelle probably had three thousand dollars' worth in the wells. Dick's share, over a thousand bucks after fuel. He figured he'd take a bucket of crabs home, another bucket for Eddie.

When he swung past Eddie's house, he ended up giving them all to Eddie. He didn't want to taste the buggers.

Joxer had said there'd be an announcement in a week about when the red-crab plant would reopen. But if the refrigeration expert had all that money . . .

Dick thought he should try to figure where the offshore lobster were. The whole damn red-crab fleet would be trying too.

When he got to his house, he saw May's car was gone. He sat in his pickup. He'd given both buckets to Eddie, but he couldn't stop thinking about the red crabs. Maybe they could have put them in lobster cars, kept them alive in the pond. No. They were more fragile than lobster, lived deeper and colder. Had to be ice cold to stay alive, Joxer had to boil them live, pick them, flash-freeze the packaged meat so fast it was almost instant.

Joxer had spent two years trying to get the big lobster boats to go out the extra miles for red crab. When he got Captain Texeira on his side, he got not just Texeira's two boats but a couple more who tagged along. Joxer had given guarantees to four boats in all. Another four including *Mamzelle,* call it three and a half, went out on spec. Even if Joxer got the plant going, and even if Captain Texeira stuck by him, Joxer would be in trouble. The two other contract skippers and the three other skippers on spec might go back to lobstering. You could always sell lobster.

But Joxer's problem wasn't just a problem for seven boats. Half of Galilee rode on red crab by now. That's what shut them all up on the dock. They'd been mad as hell, had a right to be mad as hell. You don't spend hundreds of bucks on fuel, spend a week or two at sea, haul pots for ten hours straight, and have some Jap tell you so sorry, no buy red crab.

Invisible as Joxer's problem was, it would end up hitting Galilee as bad as a storm, undercutting something people had built on.

Dick didn't want to think this all through just now. He felt the general disaster enough to numb his sharper thought for himself: Joxer's company sure as hell wasn't going to lend him ten thousand dollars.

He looked up and saw May through the window. Charlie must have the car. Dick still wasn't used to the idea of Charlie driving.

May told him the boys had gone to a ball game. Dick took his shower, started fooling around with her. She stopped cleaning the kitchen. Afterward he told her about Joxer's problem. She didn't complain when he said he was going to the Neptune.

He put five bucks in his pocket and tried to think of something nice to say to May. "That garden work's getting you in shape some."

That didn't do it. May looked up and twisted her head as though she'd heard a mouse in her kitchen. Dick took another five. He said, "Tell Charlie I could use some help on the boat tomorrow."

*T*here was a ball game on the TV at the Neptune. Not the Sox, just a baseball game with Howard Cosell talking. Dick watched an inning, couldn't take Howard Cosell. Dick talked to a guy he knew off one of the big lobster boats, asked him how it was going. The guy laughed and said, "I guess all you crab boats are going to be tagging along now."

Dick said, "Fuck you," and looked around for Parker.

Parker came in an hour later. Dick had just bought his third shot of whiskey with a beer chaser.

"We got to go out tomorrow," Parker said. "Clean out the dead crab. Resources officer came by and told *Marjorie*'s skipper not to dump them so's they'll wash up around here."

"How far out you want to go? I got to work on my boat. Goddamn, let's go right now. I'm offering to go right now, not tomorrow."

"Dick, old buddy, don't get all cramped up about it. You got to take the bitter with the sweet. Plenty of time for your boat. You only got enough money for one coat of paint anyhow."

Dick didn't say anything.

Parker said, "I'll tell you what, though. I think we've had enough bad luck. Know what I mean? I think it just may be time for a little piece of good luck, just a small change of luck. We'll go out for a couple, three days. You bring your little skiff, not your big one. We'll put the dory's outboard on her. You're right about the dory, she's an abortion. I wouldn't want to have to depend on the dory."

"What the hell are you up to? You looking for the insurance on *Mamzelle*?"

Parker held up his hand. "Jesus, you get noisy on a couple of drinks. And wrong too. I'll talk to you tomorrow, after we clean out the hold. Let's not rush anything. Let's just get in the right mood and get synchronized."

*T*hey headed out for three hours and dumped the dead crabs before they began to stink. Bucket after bucket. Gulls swarmed in. A few of them dropped the crabs back on deck to break the shells. A few small sharks showed up at the end of the chum line, cruised through it, and went away.

Keith college-boy wanted to fish for tuna. Dick didn't care what they did. It was all a waste of time. He'd left Charlie and Eddie putting on a coat of paint. Parker was right about one thing, Dick didn't have enough money for more than a day's work on his big boat.

The kid had brought a boat rod with a reel full of hundred-pound test, a wire leader, and a lure made out of surgical tubing and lead head with glass eyes. He paid out line, clipped it with a clothespin to a stay. He strapped on a belt with a socket for the rod butt.

Dick said, "You ever catch a tuna?"

The kid said, "No, but I been out on a sport-fishing boat once during the tuna derby."

Parker was amused. He asked Dick if he'd go aloft and look for swordfish. Dick pointed out the tide was running hard. Parker asked him if he had any idea where the offshore lobster might be. Dick pointed out two places on the chart. He said, "But that was more than five years ago when I was last on a big lobster boat. They move around."

Parker said, "What about there?", and pointed to a spot.

"You know something?" Dick asked. "You talked to someone?"

Parker nodded.

"They'll tell you any damn thing. But if you want to work there, you're the skipper. I think we'd be better off spending money on a spotter plane for swordfish."

"I'll tell you what," Parker said. "We make any money this trip, I'll put it into a spotter plane."

Parker was in one of his hazy good moods. He was content to let the kid fish for a couple of hours at trolling speed, burn up fuel. Dick was restless, paced around the deck waiting for the tide to slack.

He heard the snap as the kid's line jumped out of the clothespin. He said, "Hey, kid, you awake?" The kid slid himself backward off the hatch cover and braced his feet against it. The line whirred out in spurts. The kid hoisted the rod tip up, then lowered it, cranking furiously. "Don't horse it," Dick said. He called to Parker, "The kid's got a fish." Parker pulled the throttle back, put the engine in neutral.

Dick looked at the line, followed it out. The big pull against the drag had been the boat. This fish wasn't going deep, it didn't act like a tuna. The kid was still working. Could be a marlin, Dick thought, that'd be something. The kid horsed the rod up, the fish broke the surface with a flurry, just twenty yards off the stern. Dick got the gaff, put a glove on his left hand to grab the wire. The kid kept cranking. Dick got the line in his left hand, saw the fish break again with a clatter. He swung it on board.

The kid said, "Oh."

Dick said, "It's a meal."

"I don't care much for bluefish," the kid said.

The bluefish thrashed across the deck. Dick knocked it out with the side of the gaff. He held it up by the wire leader. "It's big for a bluefish," Dick said. "Twenty pounds and some. At least you're not wasting time."

The kid was still embarrassed. All pumped up, feet braced, ready for two hundred, three hundred pounds.

Dick said, "I guess it takes more than dead crabs to chum tuna." The kid didn't say anything. Probably wasn't used to Dick being friendly.

Dick told Parker he was going up to look for swordfish. Parker said fine, but he was going to keep going slow enough for the kid to fish.

"It's your boat."

Up in the crow's nest, Dick calmed down. The wind blew up some, not hard enough to stop looking. He stretched and sniffed the wind, cool and salt up away from the diesel. Why not, he thought, I got no place to go, nothing to do. He looked down. The kid was filleting the fish, his rod butt in a rodholder. Not a cloud in the sky, a perfect July day on a gentle blue sea.

They went out and hauled their pots, threw away the crabs, kept a few lobster. They ate supper at dawn, Campbell's tomato soup with chunks of bluefish. Dick made a sandwich with a fried hunk of fillet in it, plenty of mayonnaise, and a cold beer.

Parker headed the boat farther out, spotted something, headed for it. It was a buoy marker with a double orange pennant. Parker came alongside and prepared to haul it.

"Jesus, Parker. This isn't ours."

"It's okay, Dick. It's all arranged. Lend a hand."

Parker only hauled to the third pot, opened it, and took out a package. He put the three pots and buoy marker back overboard.

Dick looked at the kid. The kid was in on it.

Parker headed back in. Dick went up alongside the wheel. "Parker, I told you a long time ago—"

"A long time ago," Parker said, "you swallowed hard and took a couple hundred bucks. Small. This is small. Small is the way to do it."

Dick didn't like it. It occurred to him that one thing he could do, when they got within a few miles of shore, was to get in the skiff and go home. That would be it with Parker and him. He wouldn't get on another boat. If he did get on another boat, he'd never get 40 percent sticking swordfish. The *Mamzelle* wasn't a good boat, but she was doing the job for him.

Parker asked him to take the wheel. Dick watched Parker and Keith get out some enormous whelk shells, big as he'd ever seen. They stuffed the whelk shells with sealed sandwich bags of coke. This wasn't quite so small as Parker said.

Parker broke out some plastic eggshells. Keith and Parker were laughing. Dick asked what that stuff was. Parker, still giggling to himself, brought one of the eggshells over to Dick. "It's slime," Parker said. "See." He pointed to the word SLIME written in dripping capital letters. "It's from a toy store. It's like Silly Putty, but it looks slimy."

Parker and Keith plugged the whelks with SLIME. It looked pretty much like the retracted foot of a whelk.

Just in sight of land Parker told Dick to stop. "Okay, here's the deal. Small and easy. You and I leave Keith on board. We go in with the skiff once it's dark. Get to where the creek goes by Mary Scanlon's parking lot. I go to the parking lot, meet a guy who has a truck. He's been in talking to Mary Scanlon about her buying specialty seafood like these *scungilli.*" Parker used the Italian word for "whelks." Parker said, "I drop the basket in the back of his truck, get back in the boat, we come back out a different way than we went in. We meet old Keith here, head back out for a bit. Small and easy. I pay you five thousand."

Dick shook his head.

Parker said, "This is easier than poaching clams." Dick wished he hadn't told Parker about that. Kid stuff, he looked silly. But it still set him up for Parker. You break a little law, you might as well break a big one. Parker said, "This is real money. This is half of the rest of your boat."

Dick looked off at the smudge of land. He said, "This five thousand. I don't suppose it's forty percent."

"No," Parker said. "It's a flat rate. I've taken most of the risk already. Your piece is five thousand. Very little risk. Anything goes wrong, I dump the whelks."

Dick liked that Parker didn't lie about the 40 percent. Dick didn't know what Parker was aiming to get, but he damn well knew it wasn't so small as—Dick took a bit to figure in his head—$12,500.

Parker said, "The beauty part is the deniability. See, your skipper said to you, 'Take me in to sell some whelks.' So you think to yourself it's kind of weird but what with no crabs and all . . . And maybe you've heard *scungilli* are aphrodisiacs. That's what they say. Turks and Greeks, someone like that. Better than oysters. So you think, What the hell."

Dick said, "What the hell. What about six thousand."

Parker said, "No."

Dick liked that Parker wasn't desperate.

"The only reason I want you," Parker said, "is for my peace of mind in a small skiff on open water. I don't want my fillings knocked loose, I don't want to get wet. I could use Keith, I could run the skiff myself with one hand. I just like the way you slide a small boat along."

Dick said, "You going to clear out after this? Go back to Virginia or North Carolina?"

"Hell no. I'll fish up here through August. Tell you what. We'll use spotter planes. Two days of spotter planes every week for a month. We'll get some fish, absolutely get some fish. We'll get five or six big fish."

"Suppose it blows too hard. Suppose the water gets too hot."

"Dickey-bird, we'll go round Cape Cod if need be. I'll do it. But you're thinking negative. This is all positive."

"Spotter plane," Dick said.

"That's right," Parker said. "We'll go first-class again. Hell, we'll take your girlfriend and Schuyler along to make more movies. We get two fish at once, we'll put Keith in the skiff. And you'll get your boat in by Labor Day, Captain Pierce."

Dick looked at the smudge of land again, felt *Mamzelle* roll in her awkward way.

"When you planning on going in?"

"After dark. Get in at ten p.m. In and out in an hour or so. No more than a dentist appointment." Parker tapped his new teeth. "Painless."

*I*t was high tide when they went in. No moon. Some gusts of wind from the southwest, and a patchy sky.

When they slipped through the gut, Parker, who was in the bow looking astern, said, "Oh shit."

Dick headed for Sawtooth Creek. "What's that?" he said.

"Thought I saw a boat out there. Maybe not." Parker started to come aft.

"Stay up there," Dick said. "This motor's too heavy on the stern as it is."

Up Sawtooth Creek, he took the west branch past the flounder hole. Then the long narrow creek that wound way up into the sanctuary salt marsh. Dick stood up to keep an eye out for debris in the creek. The water was so high he could see over the spartina. They were edging north of Trustom Pond. Dick could see the pole light at the corner of Mary Scanlon's parking lot. He hoped Parker would be quick—if the tide went out any, he couldn't get through the culvert under the Green Hill Beach Road.

Dick cut the motor a good ways short of the parking lot. After he broke out the oars, he cocked his head, thought he heard a motor far off. It stopped. He rowed up to the bend in the creek that came nearest to the corner of the restaurant parking lot. Parker scrabbled up onto the bank, pulling the clam basket full of whelks. He disappeared into the slope of bayberry and sumac.

Dick kept an oar on the bank to hold the skiff. He cupped his right hand around his watch to see the luminous hands. He waited a while. He spit in the creek. It floated away, the tide was going out faster. He looked at his watch again, maybe seven minutes had gone by. He heard the far-off motor again, then Parker sliding down the bank. Parker got in, pulled in the basket. It was still full. Parker hissed at him, "Go."

Dick rowed. Parker said, "What the fuck is that?" Dick heard the motor. He stood up. Over the top of the spartina he could make out the line of the creek they'd come up, not the channel itself but the dark break in the tall grass. Whatever was coming up was running without lights. The motor sounded high-pitched.

Dick cranked the outboard and got the skiff planing. If it was Natural Resources or Coast Guard, they'd have a Boston Whaler, probably a forty-horse. Dick figured he had a half-mile of creek to go before he got into the next pond. He could keep ahead of the whaler for that part. He wasn't so sure what next.

He got through the slit under the road, another quarter-mile to the top of the pond.

When he hit the pond he stood up. The upper part of the pond was full of hummocks, channels winding all over the place. Some of them went all the way to the open part of the pond, some of them dead-ended in little backwaters. He eased back on the throttle and heard the whine of the other boat.

He said to Parker, "Whoever they are, they're in our creek."

He headed west, took a turn into a backwater. Parker, crouched in the bow, said, "Oh shit. It's a dead end."

Dick said, "No, it's good. Get out. We'll pull her out." He tilted the outboard up, went forward past Parker and up over the bow. Parker climbed out, and they heaved the skiff's bow up, their boots pushing into the stiff mud. They slid her along on her skeg for twenty feet. Dick went back with an oar and pried loose the edge of the bank with the skeg mark running up it. It plopped into the water. He tried to prop up the spartina they'd flattened. He got some of it up, held some more up by pushing the length of the oar broadside against the base of the stems.

The motor whined by, went down a channel to the open pond. It banked sharply as it suddenly slowed, coughed, and took up a lower note. Picked up again, hummed around the pond.

Parker crept up beside Dick. Dick told him to push up some more grass.

They lay there. The humming moved up a note. Parker said, "How long you planning to stay here?"

Dick thought. He said, "There's a channel between this pond and Ninigret Pond. I was planning to go through to Ninigret and then out the Charlestown breachway. But there's a bridge over the channel. All they have to do is put one guy there to cover that, then they come back this way in their boat."

"What about we go back the way we came."

Dick thought about that. He said, "What did you see in Mary's parking lot? What made you come down?"

"There was this car," Parker said. "You know, looked too ordinary."

"If that's a cop, he heard our motor. He can just come down and stand by the creek. We ought to . . . Let me think."

In his mind, Dick could see the marshes—one marsh really, laced with creeks and dotted with ponds, divided by fingers of high ground. The whole marsh fringed by beach to the south. The chart of the problem was clear to him, but not the way out, not yet.

But what he saw more insistently, as he pictured the marsh from above, was the hummock where Parker and he lay beside the skiff. Himself dissolving. Not dissolving with fear, though he admitted that possibility. He could put that off for the moment. What was dissolving was something more important than nerve. It wasn't that there was that much wrong with bringing in some coke, Captain Parker's Pep Pills for Sleepy Sailors. But there was something wrong with how *he'd* got there. And something else in him was being leached into the mud. It wasn't Parker's fault. This stuff didn't do Parker any harm, it was part of Parker's way of cutting along through Parker's kind of life. But Dick saw himself leaking into the hummock.

He got to his knees and peered over the spartina. The whaler, or at least a white runabout, was in the middle of the pond, less than a half-mile away, scanning with a spotlight. The beam didn't reach the edges. The whaler cut toward the edge of the pond and swung in an arc. Dick ducked back down.

He said to Parker, "We'll go down the east side of the pond. There's no way out the southeast corner, so they'll be paying more attention to the creeks up here and the one into Ninigret. There's a couple of little islands we can keep behind. Then it gets real grassy just behind the beach. We duck in there and wait till we hear them up at this end, then we carry the skiff up the back of the beach and on down the front. Launch her off the beach."

"My arm's still kind of weak," Parker said. "How far we have to haul her?"

"Maybe thirty yards up to the top of the dunes. Across a gravel road. Then maybe two hundred yards to the water. You won't need your bad arm, we'll put a line around your shoulder. All you have to use your arm for is to dump them whelks."

Parker grunted. He got up and took a look down the pond. "What are we waiting for?"

"Let them go round the pond a couple of times," Dick said. "Let them get a little bored. If we're lucky, they'll wonder if we didn't get in to Ninigret. They'll have to take a look by the Charlestown breachway."

"Or they may come back in here," Parker said.

"It'd be good if they did that once before we start. Get it out of their system."

They lay still.

Dick said, "How we going to meet up with Keith?"

"He's just running her back and forth, half-hour southeast, half-hour northwest."

"Jesus," Dick said, "it ain't going to be easy finding him."

Dick turned on his side. The sky was cloudier. He was about to get up for another look when he heard the motor coming nearer. He did a little more housework on the spartina and lay down again. No point in even thinking of running off on foot—the skiff was in his name, registration number painted either side of the bow.

The whaler went by the mouth of the backwater at quarter-speed. Slowed down. Went into reverse with a clunk, gave a little dentist-drill whine as the prop pulled back and out of the water. The beam of light swung round. Dick put his face flat into the grass and mud. He was wet all down his front, thought he might have pissed himself. He listened for the shift to forward. His leg jumped once and he felt Parker's hand clamp on it. He listened. A shypoke called one hoarse note way off to the west.

A man's voice—"What the fuck's that?"

A woman's voice—"A bittern."

"A what?"

"A kind of little heron." It was Elsie. "They're also called shypokes. You just about never see them, but you can hear them a mile away." Elsie croaked like a shypoke.

"Yeah, great. You know where we are?"

The shypoke croaked back.

Another man laughed. Two men. And Elsie.

The first man said, "Cut it out, Buttrick. You know where we are?"

"Yes. Do you know where we want to go?"

"Go back to that bridge."

"The cut into Ninigret?"

"Yeah. Let's go."

Clunk into forward. The motor went slow ahead, sounded like a kid blowing into soda with a straw. Parker let go his leg. The whaler sped up, got up onto a plane, headed south into a clear channel to the pond.

They slid the skiff back into the water. Dick poled it out into the creek, rowed to the east bank of the pond. He could see the whaler's spotlight playing along the west bank. There were a couple of deep coves there would keep them busy for a bit. He leaned into the oars. They creaked, but the skiff was downwind of the whaler. There was a stretch of hard land that ran down the east bank for a quarter-mile, ended in a point with a little island off it to the south. He pulled as hard as he could without splashing. The skeg left a thin wake of phosphorescent plankton; each stroke of the oars left a pair of pale-green globes in the water.

Dick looked over his shoulder, picked out the gap between the point and the island, pulled into it and around to the lee of the island. Rested. The motor of the whaler was still humming low to the west.

It was only a hundred yards to the back of the beach. He rowed easy at the end, slid into the eel grass. There were some bushes along the shore. They pulled the skiff in among them. Above the bushes there was riprap laid along the steep bank. Dick climbed up to look up and down the gravel road along the crest of the dunes.

Dick rigged a loop of the bow line over Parker's shoulder. He hoisted the stern, one arm around the outboard. He couldn't see the cracks between the flat pieces of riprap, had to feel each step. The bow thudded onto a rock. Parker undid himself from the loop, turned backward, and hauled with one hand. He stopped to rest.

Dick picked up the stern and walked it uphill of the bow. He said, "Come up here. Drag her up."

They got the skiff to the gravel road, blowing hard. Dick felt exposed, kept on pulling across the gravel, down the beachside bank, rattling down the stones of the shoulder, then into the soft dry sand. He had to stop. He couldn't hear anything but his own panting and the sound of the surf. Parker caught up, grabbed the stern line, pulled it over his shoulder with his good hand, and hauled. Dick grabbed the outboard and scuttled backward, his boot heels digging holes.

The surf got louder, and they got going faster on the downslope. Dick felt the harder sand. Parker put a hand on his back. Dick stopped, turned around. A wave ran a tongue to Parker's feet. Dick looked up and down the beach. He could see the house lights from Green Hill, less than a half-mile east. If a jeep came from there without its lights, they wouldn't see it.

Dick pulled the bow round toward the surf and got the oarlocks in their sockets. He said to Parker, "When we get her out a ways I'll get in first. I'll start rowing. You come in over the stern."

When they got the skiff in knee-high, Dick saw a beam of light flash from offshore toward what Dick guessed was the Charlestown breachway. The light looked blue in the mist. If the light was just off the breachway, it was a mile and a half away. If it was the Coast Guard, say a small cutter, they could pick up the skiff on radar, be on her in three minutes.

Parker said, "Come on!" They waded in deeper. A wave rose up dark, chest-high. The skiff floated over their heads. She nearly pulled out of their hands as the wave spilled white around their waists.

Dick couldn't see if there was another big one following. He went in over the gunwale and got the oar blades in the water. He got enough of a stroke in so the skiff went over the top of the next wave before it broke. He pulled again. Parker was holding on to the transom with one hand.

A flare went off over the pond, waggled slowly down.

Parker got his stomach over the transom. Dick took another pull at the oars and then grabbed the back of Parker's collar.

Parker got his knee up over the side and spilled in, took a breath. "I lost my boot."

Dick rowed a few more strokes in case a bigger wave rolled in.

Parker said, "What's going on? Fucking Fourth of July."

Dick was glad there was some chop now they were beyond the surf. The skiff was so small she fit completely in the trough, wouldn't show up well on the radar screen, would look like sea clutter. So long as they didn't look too close. He angled away from the cutter so the skiff would present her narrow stern.

His arms were a little tired, but it was calming to keep pulling on the oars.

Parker said, "Hadn't we ought to crank her up?"

"Yeah. Get on up in the bow. You can't get any wetter."

The motor caught. Parker pulled out a piece of soggy chart and spread it on the rowing thwart. He cupped a hand around his flashlight and pointed to a smudged pencil line. "That's where our boy ought to be." Parker got the handbearing compass out of the bow locker. He switched the battery light on and wedged the handle into the rodholder.

Dick speeded up as much as he dared, angling the bow southeast across the waves from the south. The waves spread out some as they got offshore. Dick looked back. The beam of light was still shining toward the breachway.

Dick figured they were now a half-mile due south of Green Hill. He squinted at the compass dial lit up with a soft purple glow. He hefted the gas tank. Not too bad. Now just a five-mile sloppy run in the light chop.

Parker took his shirt off and wrung it out.

Dick leaned forward and said, "Your boot. I sure hope it didn't have your name written in it."

"Jimenez, J." Parker said. "Good old Jorge Jimenez."

As they got out farther the breeze was colder. Dick got Parker to steer while he wrung his clothes out, emptied his boots.

"What do you figure," Parker said, "another half-hour, forty-five minutes?"

Dick took over again. Parker settled down on a life jacket, his back against the bow thwart, his arms wrapped tight around his chest, hands in his armpits. Dick pulled his watch cap down over his forehead and ears.

Parker pointed out another flash of a spotlight. Dick looked back. Seemed like just outside the gut into Little Salt Pond.

Parker leaned toward Dick over the rowing thwart and said, "Busy, busy, busy. It makes you wonder. Is it all just for us? We're only little fish. Little, little fish. Maybe there was someone else going in. Maybe it was just bad luck we picked up that motorboat. Maybe the whole coast, you know, every little inlet was covered. I'd like to think it was bad luck. And that maybe that wasn't a cop in the parking lot."

Parker settled back and sang "Maybe, Baby" for a bit.

The breeze was steady, the waves regular. The skiff was doing okay. Dick put his watch near the compass light to see the time. If they missed *Mamzelle* they'd look mighty funny bobbing around out here once it got light. The Coast Guard might send up a helicopter. There was some mist but not a real fog.

Of course, if a real fog rolled in, they'd have a hell of a time picking up *Mamzelle*. Their problems weren't over.

When they'd run almost an hour Dick told Parker to start looking. Dick figured they'd been making just under five knots.

"I suppose your boy knows enough to keep the running lights on."

Parker said, "Oh yeah."

Dick said, "What's he do after he runs his half-hour out and his half-hour back in?"

"Back out a half-hour. In, out, in, out."

"So we could be chasing him out?"

"For a bit. Then he'll turn round."

Dick slipped the piece of pipe over the throttle and stood up. His sweatshirt was still pretty wet. The breeze flattened it against him.

Parker spun back around on the bow thwart. "Know what I think? I think they served us up. They've never been easy to deal with, I'd try to make a little deal, they'd be real aloof. This time— this time it wasn't quite so hard. Maybe I was wrong about being a little fish. Maybe they decided to serve up a little fish at Green Hill, you know, let the narcs get something for their arrest record. Big fish goes in somewhere else. Big fish has my money, what the fuck does he care. I'm no loss to him. I'm no harm to him." Parker spit over the side. "Maybe being a little fish cut the wrong way this time."

"Let's just find your damn boat."

Parker faced forward again. Dick heard him cackle. Parker looked over his shoulder. "You know what? Right now this little-bitty skiff with this little-bitty basket is worth more than *Mamzelle*."

Dick wondered if Parker understood the problem. Dick wondered if Parker might be crazy. Dick yelled up at him, "I'll tell *you* a know-what. There may not be enough gas to get back to shore. Then your goddamn basket is worth zero."

In the dark, with the skiff bobbing, Dick found it hard to tell the difference between sea and sky. There were some stars at the top of the sky, but just above the horizon it was pretty well clouded in. He also began to worry that, if he'd made one degree of compass error and Keith got off a degree or two the other way, they might have gone by each other. He started scanning all around, but he got a little sloppy about steering. He yelled to Parker to turn around and look astern.

Parker said, "Problem is, did we get served up by name or was it just a vague kind of thing? Hey, boys, somebody's coming in somewhere in South County. It makes a difference, you know. Makes a difference in what we do next."

Dick was afraid Parker really was crazy. He checked himself. *Mamzelle* making, say, six knots. Three miles out, three miles back. Even Keith couldn't get off a whole mile. Dick was pretty sure he'd be able to see a light up to a mile off. So where in hell was she?

"Hey, Parker. What exactly did you say to your college boy?"

"I told him go out southeast, do a one-eighty, go a half-hour at one-half throttle. Then do another one-eighty, and so on. Out and back."

"Did you tell him a number or did you say southeast?"

"I said both. Southeast, a hundred and thirty-five degrees."

It occurred to Dick that the kid might have subtracted 135 from 180 instead of adding 180 to 135. That's what Charlie did once when Dick was teaching him. So what would that give him? Forty-five. Northeast. Jesus. Then what would he do? If the kid caught himself would he be able to figure where he'd got to? And then would he be able to retrace his course and get back where he was supposed to be?

Dick could imagine the kid in the dark, with only the binnacle light on, just doing it by the numbers, by what he thought was the numbers. Not paying attention to which way the wind was blowing, which way the sea was running. On board the *Mamzelle,* inside the wheelhouse, it wouldn't be so damn obvious as it was in a skiff.

Dick imagined Keith steering, getting a little bored, checking his watch. Would he get bored enough to take a fix? Dick saw him drawing in the lines on the transparent overlay. Looking at the X. Goddamn, must be wrong. Do it again. Uh oh. Fucked up good.

"Hey, Parker. Did you draw in the line on the kid's chart? You know, the three-mile track he was supposed to keep his train on?"

Parker thought. "I believe I did. Yeah. Drew it on the overlay for him."

Dick checked his watch. Another twenty minutes at four and a half knots would take the skiff pretty near the southeast end of the three-mile track. Eight miles out to sea.

"Hey, Parker. I'm going to row for a while. Save a little gas. Get warm."

Dick rowed for ten minutes, felt better. He let Parker take a turn. Dick sat on the bow thwart, facing forward. After ten minutes they switched again. Dick figured they were making under three knots rowing. He was recalculating their position when he saw a white light way off to port, almost due north. The skiff rose on a wave, and under the white light he made out a red running light. Then the shaded white stern light.

Dick cranked up the motor and swung the skiff round. Parker looked back at him, Dick could just see his mouth open. Dick yelled, "Dead ahead." Parker's face disappeared as he swung forward to look. It reappeared. Parker said, "Suppose it ain't *Mamzelle*?"

Maybe Parker wasn't crazy.

"Better find out."

The problem was to catch the damn boat. The skiff now had a following sea on her port quarter. Dick had to take it easy going down the front of the waves to keep from plowing into the trough. He gave her more speed climbing the back of a wave, eased up as the skiff surfed a little past the crest, went skiing down the front.

It took them another twenty minutes to get near enough to get a close look at her. Dick peered at her. What he could see beneath the red running light looked like it might be the right color, dirty green. He let her pass by, and then he cut across her stern. *Mamzelle*.

Parker yelled, "Keith! Hey! Keith!" Dick ran the skiff under *Mamzelle*'s lee, was able to speed up enough to get past the wheelhouse. Parker blinked his flashlight and shouted. The kid must be deaf and blind. Then *Mamzelle's* engine cut back, clanked into neutral.

The kid came out. In the green-and-white glow from the running light and the masthead light, Dick saw the kid wave uncertainly. He looked dazed. Parker laughed. Dick was in a rage.

They got the basket of whelks and the skiff on board. The kid started to stow the basket in the hold. Dick said, "Better keep that right nearby. In case you have to dump it."

The kid looked at Parker. Parker said, "Yeah, okay. In the wheelhouse." He turned to Dick and said, "Well, well, here we are back on board *Mamzelle.* What say the captain orders grog for all hands. Give me a cigarette, Keith. The smoking lamp is lit." He pulled off his one boot. "Do me a favor, Dick. Throw that over-board." He held out the boot to Dick. "Then old Captain Parker'll make sure his crew get all warm and toasty." Dick took the boot and tossed it over the side.

Parker said, "Goodbye, Jorge. We commend your body to the deep." Keith laughed.

Dick said, "You take a little detour, kid? You take the scenic route?"

Keith stopped laughing. Looked at Parker again. Parker said to Dick, "I'll work that out. You go get some dry clothes. Keith'll fix some coffee. Then we'll look into my crystal ball."

Dick said, "Jesus, Parker."

"Yeah, that's right. I guess you don't have to call me Captain."

They didn't look into Parker's crystal ball that night or have a little talk. Dick sacked out. The kid got him up after four hours to take the wheel. A red smoky dawn. Headed at two-thirds speed for the lobster pots they'd set.

Parker got up a couple of hours later. The kid stayed in his bunk. Parker brought Dick some coffee but didn't offer to relieve him.

Dick waited.

Parker said, "Well, we can't stay out here forever."

Dick didn't say anything.

"But, then, we have certain problems about going in."

Dick said, "I'd like to get in. I got to work on my boat. Put my five thousand to work."

"Dick. Dick, old buddy. That run wasn't what you would call a complete run."

"I took you in. I goddamn saved your ass getting out."

"You saved my ass. You saved *your* ass. You saved our ass. We saved our ass. Our ass got saved."

"You said flat fee, Parker."

"Tell you what, Dick. Here's your five thousand right here." Parker held up one of the whelks, nudged Dick's elbow with it. "Here go, Dick." Dick looked down at it, looked ahead again.

Parker said, "See what I mean?"

After a while Dick said, "I see it's worth about as much as your word."

"You are an unreasonable son of a bitch. First you're all worried about your cherry, you say, 'Oh no, oh oh, I couldn't do that!' Next thing I know you want to get paid—before you've turned the trick. And what do we do with our little bundle? I just know what you'd like. 'Dump it.' But you still want your five thousand." Parker snorted.

Dick said, "Flat fee."

"For a completed run," Parker said. "I'm not going back on my word. We ain't through yet. It's real clear to *me*. You can see it my way, or you can go fuck yourself."

Dick thought again of getting in the skiff. Going in by himself. Not enough gas. He'd goddamn row in. And say what when he got stopped? No matter what he'd say, it would be the same as fingering Parker.

He wouldn't do that.

Dick could see the newspaper story. He'd seen stories like it, the Providence *Journal* was full of them. So-and-so, age such-and-such, stopped in his pickup on Route 1. Dick Pierce, age forty-three, of Matunuck; five to ten years. Next thing Dick imagined was Charlie pasting the newspaper story in his scrapbook. Parker was right about one thing. If it was up to him, he'd dump the whole basket.

By the time they got to the lobster pots it was blowing. A real smoky southwester. They spent so much time just holding on that it was well after dark before they got the pots hauled. It struck Parker as funny that they didn't do too bad, pretty near filled one well.

It was Keith who said, "Let's just go right in. Hose the whelks down so they're real slimy-looking. Play it straight up. Just do it."

All three of them were in the wheelhouse. Keith at the wheel,

Parker and Dick drinking soup with one hand, holding on with the other.

Dick didn't like it, but he didn't say anything. Parker finished his cup of soup and said, "I thought of that. I don't say no. My idea was maybe take the basket in the skiff at night, find an empty beach, bury the shells in a hole. Then just wait."

Keith laughed and said, " 'Yo ho ho and a bottle of rum.' "

Parker said, " 'Cute, real cute.' "

"There's a lot of problems," Dick said. "Where you going to find an empty beach this time of summer? A boat the size of *Mamzelle* laying offshore is a big radar blip. And there's no shovel."

Parker said, "Use the oars, use our hands. . . ."

"And we'd have a great big wet spot on the hole, a bunch of footprints. And on top of all that you'd have to go in and do it all over again to get the stuff back. And where are you? Right where we are now."

Keith said, "So what's your idea?"

Parker looked at Dick and said, "Yeah."

Dick said, "Let's put the whelks in lobster pots. Set them."

Parker laughed. "How many pots you lose a year?"

"It depends," Dick said.

"That's right," Parker said. "They work up against a rock, get the warp snagged. Storm works the buoy loose. Fishing boat runs over the line. I mean, I like that you're making a contribution, but this just sounds like a nicer way of saying dump them. We've lost pots this summer in flat calm." Parker pointed his thumb over his shoulder. "What's that out there? I wouldn't call it calm."

Keith said, "Look. This is all bullshit. Do it my way. It'll work. If you guys are nervous about it, I'll be the one carries them ashore. I'll put them in my car, drive off. If I get caught, I take the whole rap. If I don't, I get half."

Parker laughed. "Hoo boy! And a mighty hi-yo Silver! Away!"

Keith looked over his shoulder.

Parker said, "Don't talk that way, don't even think that way about my piggy bank, son. Not to mention Dick and me spent some time laying down in that swamp, spent some more time trying to find you wandering around out here. We don't want you doing any more wandering."

After a while Parker said, "We go in the way Keith says. If they've been told my name, then they're going to look and look until I'm gone. Maybe plant some if they can't find it. So it don't matter how long we wait. On the other hand, if all they got was just a date and a place, then we're just another boat and those whelks look pretty much like whelks. Tell you what though, Keith. You pour a bucket of old bait juice all over them. You know? In case they got a dog. Then we leave them sit right there on deck while we sell the lobster. I'll drive my station wagon up. No rush. Put in some stuff, you know—my sea bag, a couple of lobster, and my basket of *scungilli*. Be casual. If you can't be casual, be busy."

*A*s *Mamzelle* docked at the lobster wharf, Dick saw the green Natural Resources jeep. He kept busy.

It turned out it wasn't Natural Resources who came aboard. A plainclothes cop. Very polite. Showed Parker his ID. Asked permission to come aboard. Parker was just as polite. "You don't mind if my crew unloads the lobster?" The cop and his assistant watched the baskets come up. The assistant was the dog handler.

They went into the wheelhouse. Dick couldn't decide if he should watch them or not. Be busy. Dick got the lobster weighed in. When he came out with the money, the cop was just coming up from the hold. The dog handler struggled to lift the dog up from behind. The dog got his forepaws on deck, scrabbled up. Parker was smoking a cigarette, pointing with the hand with the cigarette to something he was telling Keith to take care of. Not a flicker. Keeping Keith busy. The basket of whelks on deck.

Parker said to the cop, "We got to hose down the deck, flush out the well. If you're all through down there..."

Keith swung the sea bags onto the dockside, swung the basket of whelks up alongside them. Then a bucket with three lobster in it, his foul-weather gear.

Dick went forward to check his harpoons, get a chance to take a deep breath. The cop strolled up behind him. Dick didn't think he could talk normal to him. He told himself the slow way this guy moved around was most likely boredom—a slow day on the docks stretching out in front of him.

The cop ran his hand along the metal harpoon shaft, gave it a rap. He said, "Thought they fired these things out of guns nowadays."

"You're thinking about whales," Dick said. "These are for sword-fish."

The cop wanted to hear about sticking swordfish. Dick told him. The cop took it in absentmindedly. When Dick got to the part about the beer keg, the cop gave the beer keg a tap. Looked it over.

The cop said, "Didn't get any this trip, huh?"

"No."

The cop yawned, ran his hand through his hair.

Keith got through hosing down the deck, and the cop made his way aft, stepping carefully. A bored little man in a suit and city shoes. He climbed back onto the dockside, looked around for his number-two man. Gave a start when he found the guy right next to him. The dog was back in the wired-off backseat of their car.

Parker started the engine. Keith cast off the stern line. Parker backed her, swinging the stern away from the dock while Dick held the bow line around a bollard. Parker nodded, and Dick let go, retrieved the line.

Parker headed *Mamzelle* out to her slip, between the last set of piles in the row. Dick looked back at the heap of gear, the basket of whelks, the two cops.

Parker backed her in. Dick made the two bow lines fast, Keith the stern lines. Parker and Keith climbed up onto the gray planking of the pier. Keith started off briskly. Parker stopped him, told him to set a spring line, and ambled off. Dick followed Parker, staying behind him, looking at his feet.

Keith passed him, picked up his sea bag, foul-weather gear, and the bucket of lobster, leaving two sea bags and the basket of whelks. The cop was still standing there. The dog handler was walking back to his car. Dick looked around for Parker, saw him starting his beat-up VW station wagon. Dick saw the dog handler was getting the dog out again.

Parker slowly backed toward the basket, stopped to let the guy with the dog get by. Dick leaned down to pick up the basket. The cop turned to him.

"What are those things? Conchs or something?"

"Whelks."

"Jesus, they stink."

Dick said, "Italians eat 'em."

Parker stopped. The dog rubbed her cheek and shoulder against the basket. The head cop said, "Hey. Keep her out of that shit, she'll stink up the car." The cop with the dog put his foot against her chest. The dog licked it and then sat.

Dick heard a boat coming up to the dock. The cop reached in

his coat pocket and took out his badge holder. Dick swung the basket of whelks in the VW, then Parker's sea bag and his. Parker slammed the back down. Dick got in the passenger seat and said, "Charlie's got my truck." Parker started the car and pulled off.

When they got onto the road Parker started laughing. " 'Italians eat 'em.' That's my boy, Dick. Says to Detective-Sergeant Russo, 'Italians eat 'em!' Italians eat that shit. I love it!"

"The cop was named Russo? Jesus."

"No, you don't get it. I love it. It was great." Parker did a bongo beat on the steering wheel with his fingers. "You know, one of those things you can't rehearse. If that dog had gone in nose first, instead of trying to roll in that shit. Where's a gas station around here? I got to make a phone call."

It began to rain again. Dick kept the window open while Parker phoned. The basket was stinking up the whole car.

*B*y the time they got to Route 1 the rain stopped. It was like that with a smoky southwester, on and off. Parker swung the VW into the Sawtooth Point gate. "It'll just take a minute. I got a real bright idea." Dick was too dazed to get worried over what Parker was up to.

There were a half-dozen new cottages visible from the drive. They looked nearly done, at least the roofs were shingled. A lot of planting going on too. They'd left all the old locust trees around the Buttrick house, but they'd torn up the drainage system. Between the Buttrick house and the Wedding Cake there was a pair of new bright-green tennis courts alongside the old clay one. Dick remembered when the Buttricks put it in. The chicken wire was torn off, and the old posts and the backboard were fresh-painted. The bushes around the outside were full of raspberries.

Parker drove right up to the Wedding Cake. The door was open. There were several crates and pieces of furniture on the porch, and a U–Haul truck was backed up to it with its tailgate down. No people.

Parker walked in and shouted, "Hey, Schuyler!" Schuyler appeared in the open doorway on the pond side. He'd just been for a swim. He had a towel round his neck and there were wet curls on his forehead. Otherwise he was naked.

"Hello there, Captain Parker. Want to go for a dip? Hello there, Dick, come in."

The hallway was empty. Through the open double doors Dick saw the main room was empty except for a record player and bottles and glasses.

Parker said, "What happened here?"

"We're moving to one of the cottages. And I had the cast and crew in for a little party. Finished up last Friday. Not our noble documentary, just a little quickie. College-kid cast. Nubile bodies in the water, on the grass, in mid-air . . . I told you about it, didn't I?" Schuyler dried his hair. "Bring the stuff into the kitchen. I'll be right down. I think there's something left for breakfast." He was halfway up the stairs by the time he finished speaking.

Parker went out to get the basket. Dick looked around. He hadn't been inside the Wedding Cake since he was a kid. He couldn't remember why he'd been there. His father, his mother. Great-Uncle Arthur. It was because Uncle Arthur's wife had died. Uncle Arthur was in black, there were flowers in vases. Miss Perry had been there. He'd gone onto the back porch with his mother and Miss Perry. He'd wanted to look through Uncle Arthur's telescope. It wasn't there. Because the war was over. It must have been late summer, the bushes along the seawall were filled with rosehips. Uncle Arthur had let him help look for submarines—that must have been the summer before. Twilight, no lights on. No light anywhere along the coast. But how bright the sea was long after his bedtime. How pale and still. The house, the sky, the sea.

Dick went onto the back porch. The lawn going down to the water seemed shorter. The porch still seemed vast and high. It ran the full length of the house, swelling into circular porches at both seaward corners. The wrought-iron table was still there, white, with a thick glass top. Maybe it wasn't the same one. The telescope had been there, but Uncle Arthur had moved it up to the widow's walk the evening Dick had stayed up to help Uncle Arthur watch for submarines. And it was from the widow's walk that they watched the sky rockets on V–J Day. Then Uncle Arthur's wife died.

Dick walked over to the circular porch where the table was. The planking was good, tongue-and-groove disappearing under the solid base of the rail. Above it came the fancy part, doily fretwork, a pattern repeated overhead at the angle of the posts and lintel. Looked like pieces of fan coral stuck in every top corner. And all that by hand, no skil-saws, no epoxy. He didn't remember it from the war, from his childhood; he'd noticed it from afar, from his skiff.

Uncle Arthur moved away. His father sold their house—later torn down to make room for the new Route 1. They'd still used the barn in the upper field, they'd gone on farming the Point even after the Bigelows bought a piece of land, and the Buttricks bought another piece. That money went into his father's boat, and probably the little house in Snug Harbor. That was after his mother went to the hospital. She died before the hurricane of '54. Maybe it went for her hospital bill too. His father's boat had gone down in the harbor in '54, the biggest boat in Galilee. Captain Texeira's boat had been at sea, didn't try to make port, heard the warning, and headed east. The hurricane hit the coast. Captain Texeira just rode out some heavy weather with plenty of sea room.

His father hadn't ever complained about the big things. Just old family quarrels, his new neighbors. Small complaints about small matters. He talked about another boat, never got one built, complained about the new boatyard, about rising prices. Then became quiet.

Dick had taken the old man's quiet to be disappointment in his son.

They'd been short with each other, that was certain.

When Dick told him he wanted to go to the Naval Academy his father had told him he doubted he'd get in. Dick was unsure of himself, took what his father said heavily and silently.

It turned out the old man had thought admission was only by congressional appointment, that it took a political connection. One of the old man's gripes was that Rhode Island was in the hands of Irish, and later Italian, politicians.

Dick spent his junior year in high school building a boat in the basement of the small house in Snug Harbor. His father complained of the noise. Dick spent most of his senior year on the water in his boat.

Here on this porch Dick saw another view. All this white fretwork, all the green lawn. Behind it the lush meadows, wet each morning with night mist. And the old man's careful hopes—marrying wisely and late, "good stock," he'd often said. "Your mother and I are both of good stock." Maybe he'd meant to reassure Dick. Dick had finished the thought with "And what went wrong with you?" The old man had expected a long, good marriage, he'd even expected that the Pierce boat would be saved, not the Texeira boat.

He hadn't been lazy in his expectations. He'd worked the farm. He'd worked his boat too. But he'd believed in his marriage, he'd believed in the natural order of the Pierces' owning land. And even after Uncle Arthur sold his portion and moved away, the old man had believed in a providence for the Pierces. It was as though he was able to fend off disappointment—not unhappiness, Dick knew he'd grieved for his wife—but he kept at bay his sense of being betrayed that loss gave rise to—loss of his wife, loss of half the Pierce land—by building a boat. When the boat was wrecked, all the bitterness came into him at once. He kept it in him the dozen years until he died.

And his petty snapping and griping had just been the leakage from his bitterness; the great mass of it he carried whole.

Dick tried to remember a time with his father when the old man had been easy. Some pleasure they'd had together. Every one seemed tinged. There was fishing, the old man had taken him fishing often enough, some of those times weren't so bad. Silent dim evenings casting for striped bass outside the gut on a strong ebb tide, the motion of their boat at anchor soothing both of them. The dark tide ran out under them, the calm swell lifted them gently on its way in to breaking on the sandbar, a hiss of white in the dusk. The little boat held just right between the running out of the tide and the slow roll of the sea.

To get them there Dick would row out the gut, take the channel around the sandbar, cut in behind it outside the breakers, and set the anchor. Pay out some line, cleat it. His father would sit for a minute, looking around. For a long time Dick thought he was checking to see if Dick had got it right. Years later, when Dick took his own sons out fishing, he realized it was just a pause. The old man did the same thing every time. He'd look to see how far down the sun was, look the other way to see if the moon was rising, then spit over the side to see how fast the tide was running. He'd nod to himself and pick up his rod.

They'd fish till the sky was as dark as the water and the tide slacked enough to let them go home.

Dick used to think that wasn't much. High-moon tides near dusk weren't all that frequent, striped bass were only around half the year at most.

Now, as he stood looking at the white fretwork on the porch of the Wedding Cake, it still seemed little enough—not for him, he was neither here nor there, but little enough balm for his father's bitterness.

Dick looked down from the fretwork toward the gut. The view was cut by new planting and a new piece of construction on Sawtooth Island, an open picnic shelter, no walls, just columns holding up a little roof. The new planting was willow trees. If they'd only put the willow trees in, they might have made good duck blinds.

Marie Van der Hoevel came up through the opening in the seawall. She'd been swimming too, her mass of hair was shrunk onto her narrow head. She was wearing a huge white robe which she held closed with both hands. She was walking with her head down, so she didn't see Dick till she got near the porch steps. She was surprised, didn't seem to place him. He tried to explain who he was.

"Oh, of course," she said, "Dick Pierce, out on the boat, the swordfish. Captain Parker. And out there." She turned to point to the island and then regathered the folds of her robe. "The clams, the clambake. Of course."

She dipped one foot and then the other in a bucket of water to wash the sand off. "I'll be back in a minute. Schuyler's around someplace."

Dick said, "I think Parker and him are doing some business."

She was gone. Parker and Schuyler appeared on the lawn beside the porch. Schuyler turned a hose on the basket of whelks. Parker was holding a shell in his hand, fitting the Silly Putty back in place.

Parker said to Dick, "We're off. Schuyler and I are off to New

York." He came onto the porch and gave Dick his car keys. "You think you could drop my car off at the Kingston station? I'll be back in two, three days. I've got another set of keys—just leave it in the parking lot." Parker went back down the side steps to Schuyler. Dick followed along, wanting to ask what was going on but feeling out of step.

Parker and Schuyler went around to the driveway and put the basket in the trunk of Schuyler's car. Parker started to get in. Schuyler said, "Let's eat here. We don't want to stop on the way."

Schuyler led them into the kitchen. Dick didn't recognize a thing. The pantry wall had been taken out, there was a new stove, refrigerator, the works. Schuyler got a frying pan out of a cardboard packing box, got plates and cups out of another.

Parker sat down at the kitchen table. Dick stood beside him and said, "You going to call this a complete run?"

"Getting close, Dickey-bird, getting close." Parker cocked his head at him. "Oh yeah. You want to get to your boat. Tell you what. You go on and use the lobster money. Keith took off so fast, he can wait for his share."

Dick said, "You got enough to go to New York?"

Parker said, "Yeah. I'll stop by my place."

Schuyler shut the refrigerator door and said, "Let's just go. I've got some change."

Parker pinched the front of his shirt with two fingers. "I'm a little ripe."

Schuyler took Parker upstairs to show him the shower and lend him some clothes. Schuyler came back with Marie, asked her what she'd like for breakfast.

"Just orange juice and coffee."

"Ah. As my friends in the business used to call it, the whore's breakfast. How about you, Dick? Everything?"

Dick nodded. He was startled by Schuyler's remark, he couldn't tell if there was a sting in it. He looked over at Marie, who turned her face toward him at the same time. Her eyes were wide open, a pale gray-blue. "Schuyler did a documentary on whores. He's fascinated by whores. He knows everything about them."

"That's not quite it," Schuyler said. "I had a favorite pair, they're retired now. They specialized in shy prep-school boys. They had pennants on the walls, St. Paul's, St. Mark's, Deerfield, especially Deerfield. They had a Yale banner too, the one that usually says 'For God, for country, and for Yale,' and they had added 'and for Sue and Sally.' What I wanted to do was film the testimonial dinner that some of their clients gave them, but they wouldn't agree. All I ended up with was pieces of interviews. You see, they really considered themselves educators. They'd explain things to the boys, you know, birth control, erogenous zones, postcoital tenderness. They had the most wonderful lecture on being nice to your girlfriend.

"The boys would come in from the Rough Rider Room drunk on rum and Coca-Cola, one of them would have the phone number, and they'd finally get up their nerve. And what they got was this gem of a talk. Sue and Sally would take two at a time into their bedrooms, sit them down, hold their hands, and explain it all. Then they'd give them a little sponge bath and administer the final exam. And then onto the next two. It was a perfect fifties institution."

Schuyler looked around from the cutting board full of scallions and cheese.

"I'll wait for Parker." He put slices of bread in the toaster but didn't lower them in. He started beating eggs and said, "Among other things, there was this element of latent homosexuality. I mean, the sexual links among the boys who were in on this, so to speak, together. But I never could get anything more than interviews. That was years ago." Schuyler sighed. "Maybe I should interview them *now*. They live together, someplace on Long Island. God!

A kind of counterpoint to *Grey Gardens*. Lido Beach instead of East Hampton."

Marie said, "Why don't you just finish what you're working on?"

"Ah. My darling," Schuyler said, "I forgot to tell you. It must have been the rush of trying to move and give a cast party....Elsie showed some footage of the documentary to the group in Providence and they loved it. Better still, they came up with more money."

"How much?"

"Twelve thousand. Of course they did say they expect the whole film completed on schedule. I mean that somewhat optimistic schedule I gave them at first. So I may have to..." Schuyler turned around and smiled at Dick. He said to Dick, "The secret of a light omelette is to beat the whites separately. I'm sorry this is taking so long and we've been boring you with...The film we're talking about is the one you and Parker are in. Do you get Channel Thirty-six?"

Dick was about to say he didn't have a TV. Marie said to Schuyler, "Luck is going to ruin you. Your good luck and charm are going to rot you from inside." Marie said this softly and lightly. Dick looked at her to see if she was angry. She looked slightly happier than usual, but otherwise neutral. She was as pretty as always. Her hair was dry now, and it fluffed up above a bright-blue hairband. She was wearing a white tennis dress with lots of little pleats in the skirt.

Schuyler said, "I should be embarrassed, shouldn't I? But, you know, good, earnest people seem to like to help cute little hippety-hoppers like me." Schuyler turned to Dick. "What Marie doesn't approve of is the way I get money out of thin air. Or so it appears to her."

"So it appears," Marie said. Her expression didn't change. Schuyler, on the other hand, furrowed his brows with puzzlement, then lifted them in surprise. Then smiled pleasantly at Dick. "Are you a cheerful sort of fellow?"

Dick said, "If there's something to be cheerful about."

Parker came in, wearing a blue seersucker suit. He still had on his white sneakers. Parker said, "Dick's a little on the negative side, but he gets the job done. You got to say that, he goes all the way. What do you think? A little tight, but I don't suppose I got to button it."

Schuyler poured the eggs into the omelette pan and shook it lightly. "Just right. What do you think, my darling?"

Marie turned her head. "Absolutely wonderful. Except for the shirt. I think just a nice white tennis shirt instead of all those stripes and buttons. Don't you, Captain Parker?"

Schuyler said, "I think she may be right. Especially with the sneakers. Try another shirt—they're in that blue duffel. . . ."

Schuyler scraped the scallions out of one frying pan onto the eggs in the other pan. "One thing I've always wished to be appreciated for is being cheerful. I mean, luck is just luck, but being *cheerful* . . . It's a regular Boy Scout virtue, isn't it? Part of the Boy Scout pledge—"

Marie said, "So you're going to New York today."

"Yes, my darling. I'm leaving now, because starting tomorrow I have lots of things to do with my luck and charm, among them a shitload of work in the editing room, that well-known sump of luck and charm. So if I'm going to help Captain Parker sell seashells by the seashore, it will have to be today. Those three guys are coming this afternoon to help you finish up moving. The only thing you have to do is tell them what goes where. I even leave it to you where they should put my piano."

Schuyler pushed the toast down, folded the omelette over, and got three plates out of a carton on the floor.

Without liking Schuyler any better, Dick was beginning to get on his side. Marie was like one of those fish who take the hook and just sulk on the bottom—no runs, no jumps, no play—takes forever to get them up without breaking the line.

Parker came back in. Marie was right, he looked better with the plain white shirt. Marie's face brightened up some for Parker. She sat up to take him in, her eyes getting wider as her head came up, like a china doll's. She was a knockout, no question about that, you could put her picture on a fashion-magazine cover right alongside any other model's—frame her face, which seemed to float, crystallize her widened eyes, her finely drawn sharp lips. Dick wondered if Schuyler ever figured he'd made a mistake, if Schuyler ever wanted more bounce. Or maybe he knew what he was getting, a shining ghost who made her clothes move right.

Schuyler, Parker, and Dick ate.

Dick said, "Good eggs."

"Wait'll you try the coffee," Parker said. "It'll set you right up. It's rocket fuel."

"Where do *you* want the piano?" Marie said.

"See if it'll get through the door into the back room. Did you know," he said to Parker and Dick, "I spent the year after I got out of college on a ship? I played the piano in the cocktail lounge. That's why I didn't get seasick on your boat. Maybe I should leave the piano here in the Wedding Cake and give myself my old job back. I don't know why I ever quit. The food was good, I had a cabin to myself, I got to play with the toys. They had a swimming pool and a gym, and you could shoot skeet from the top deck. And I didn't mind the work. Well, I did in the end—I refused to play 'Autumn Leaves' and I started telling jokes."

"I thought they caught you swimming nude with someone," Marie said.

"No, my darling, it was the jokes. 'Say, Tex, how come you bought that dachshund?'—'Well they told me "Get a long little doggie." ' And then I'd move right into the song. I did a lot of Texas jokes that cruise, we had lots of Texans. A Texan goes into a *pissoir* in Paris and while he's taking a leak he notices this Frenchman leaning over and staring at his shooting iron. The Texan says, 'Say, Bo—' The Frenchman says, *'C'est beau? Mais non, c'est magnifique!'* And I'd go right into 'The Yellow Rose of Texas.' I think it may have been that . . ."

Parker laughed.

Marie said, "Maybe that's where you learned to be so hippety-hoppity cheerful, when you were having such a good time playing cocktail piano."

Schuyler said, "Don't you move, my darling, we'll clean up. And then we're off to Gotham in the Batmobile. Tell Elsie . . . Never mind, I'll call her from New York."

Now Dick was completely for Schuyler against Marie. For his telling jokes, playing the piano, his playing money games with the rich partners, and taking Parker to New York. At the same time Dick knew that he himself was just as sullen as Marie, just as disapproving. As sullen as May had been when she burst out and said his boat was a black hole after Elsie had been saying it was a work of art.

Marie was Schuyler's May. Maybe Dick was Parker's May. What flavor you were depended on whether you had a wish or were being dragged after someone else's wish.

Dick wanted his boat, Parker wanted his fancy boat, Schuyler in his way wanted . . . might as well throw in Joxer Goode—they all wanted and wanted. Until this very minute Dick would have figured that all their wantings were different, that everything about all of them was so different they were each in their own shell. But now it was as if their wantings stretched out of themselves into each other, not just fighting it out with each other but conducting, backward and forward, some of Parker into Dick, some of Dick into Marie, Marie into May, Dick into Schuyler, Schuyler into Dick. . . .

Dick would have figured everyone was different the way everything was different. A lobster wasn't a crab, a blue crab wasn't a red crab. The old Pierces in the Wedding Cake. The Buttricks in the Buttrick house. Miss Perry in Miss Perry's house. Dick in the house he'd built on the last piece of the old Pierce place.

Now everything seemed to be leaking, percolating, flowing into everything else. Dick could turn around right this minute and be for Marie as easily as he'd been for Schuyler. He could go back another step and remember the Wedding Cake and Uncle Arthur . . . and be like Miss Perry. He could feel the way his father felt. He could stiffen up and wish to feel like Captain Texeira. He could let himself feel like Parker, he could try to back away and *not* feel like Parker.

He'd got onto an edge. Was it last night? No, the night before—he'd broke off the piece of black bank so it slid into the water, dissolved. Stopped being footprints and mud, slid into the salt creek.

It shouldn't take him by surprise, he'd always known both sides: that the salt marsh is the salt marsh, the sea is the sea, the sky is the sky . . . and that the land washes into the salt creek, the salt creek into the sea, the sea into every sea, and everything in the sea dissolves. Everything in the sea dissolves—the particulate matter into the deeps, then back into upwellings, into the chain whose first invisible links are animal-plants, plant-animals; and all the while the great fluid of the sea is drawn into the sky by the sun, takes passing shapes as cloud, and returns to the earth.

The cycle had always been a remote comfort. So long as it was out there—earth, water, air. Somewhere else. Now it was in this kitchen, suggesting dissolution, dissolving. His notion of *his*—his house, his boat, his difference.

He got up. He washed Schuyler's dishes. Took Parker's key and drove home in Parker's car. He didn't explain the car to May, he'd had enough of everything for the morning.

But May seemed genuinely glad to see him, didn't ask right off if he'd made enough to ante up the household money.

She said, "You want some breakfast?"

"We ate."

"Well, why don't you go ahead and take your shower. The boys are out for the morning. I was going to clean some, but I can get to it later."

This more than usually enthusiastic offer didn't please him as it usually would have. He still felt strange to his life, still as chilled and shriveled as he had felt hiding on the hummock in the salt marsh, still as constricted by nerves as on the foredeck of *Mamzelle* watching the cops search her, still as pierced as he'd been by his displaced boyhood when he'd stepped into the Wedding Cake.

He showered, came out in his towel, and took a hold of May's long waist. On the bed he slid her hairpins out the way she liked, even slower than usual, so it got to her more than usual, but all the while he couldn't get his mind off how he couldn't tell her what was going on on account of how right she'd been about Parker. He rubbed her slip on her skin the way she liked, feeling indecently competent as she breathed harder and got pink and hypnotized.

Later on she said that she'd forgotten how much she used to miss him when he'd been going out regular on a boat. It was a nice thing to say, but it didn't reach him. He looked up at a thin spattering of rain across the windowpane, the tired southwester dragging on.

*T*he next morning Dick dropped off Parker's car at the railroad station, got in the pickup with Charlie, dropped Charlie, then headed back up toward Wickford to a salvage-warehouse auction of Navy surplus.

He was still tired, still tense, still baffled by his unsettled sense of things.

The sight of all the material in the warehouse cheered him up at first. Jeeps, three-quarter-ton trucks, marine hardware, coils of steel cable, a half-dozen steel lifeboats, donkey engines, auxiliary generators . . .

When the bidding started he realized that the stuff was being sold in bulk in lots too expensive for him. He was about to leave when he ran into Eddie Wormsley, who also wanted some narrow-gauge steel cable. Together they managed to get a spool. Dick picked up some electrical wire and some defective porthole fittings no one wanted. The last of the lobster money went for steel davits.

Eddie said to give him a call after lunch and he'd come help with the wiring. Eddie was slower at wiring than Dick, but did a better job. Having Eddie around got Dick in a better mood, a better rhythm. Eddie's offer cheered Dick up, he'd been feeling uneasy and itchy about the wiring.

On the way home it began to rain again, not a steady clean rain, just more spitting and drizzling.

Several miles short of Wakefield Dick saw a bicyclist. It always annoyed him when bicyclists or joggers cluttered up a high-speed road, wavering along the shoulder. This one was actually on the edge of the right-hand lane, pedaling furiously. Dick recognized the uniform first, then saw it was Elsie. She recognized his truck, he saw her wave in his mirror. He pulled onto the shoulder a hundred yards ahead. He rolled down the passenger window, and when her face appeared, flushed and wet, he asked her if she wanted a ride. She said no, then yes. She hoisted her bike into the bed beside the spool of cable and climbed in beside him. She was in a raw mood too: the weather, having to leave her new Volvo at the dealer's for mysterious noises, but most of all having her leave canceled to spend two nights ferrying around two cops in a Natural Resources whaler.

"Alleged backup to the alleged alert for alleged smugglers. Three-state alert. From the Cape Cod Canal all the way to the Connecticut River. The state police and the Coast Guard must have used up a thousand man-hours, just racing around flashing their lights. The Coast Guard boat spent an hour zipping along the beaches, poking around with a searchlight. We chased a boat into the salt marsh, could have been kids poaching clams or even just fourteen-year-olds drinking beer." Elsie rolled down her right pant leg and flung herself back in the seat. "And I mouthed off to my boss about what a waste of time it is to use us as backup. The state police don't like having us along. Though the guys I was with would still be lost . . . We used up a tank of gas going up every salt creek. And my revolver got wet, so I'll have to clean it again."

It occurred to Dick that it was good news that the alert was such a big deal—it seemed less likely that Parker was the object of any special attention. But still, here was official Elsie right beside him in his truck.

Elsie told him where to turn. Up Miss Perry's driveway and into the woods. Another turn onto a narrow dirt road.

"This is the way to Quondam Pond," Dick said. "I didn't know your house was in here."

"Yes. Miss Perry sold me that little tip of her land."

The house was on the south side of a flat grassy clearing. From the clearing the house looked like nothing more than a big toolshed. A stretch of shingled roof and a dwarfed windowless wall. There was an open one-car garage at the side of the clearing, a covered passage from the side of the garage to the house. Elsie hung her bike on hooks inside it. She said, "Come on in. I'll show you the house."

The passageway was dark, but when Elsie opened the door to the house there was a glare of daylight. Elsie said, "Watch the steps, they go down."

There was one long main room, bright even on this gray day. The house was embedded into the slope, almost all window along the south side. The windows overlooked the small pond, an oval stillness except for the dappling of the light rain. On the far bank rhododendrons hung out over the water, their blossoms gone by. A few white petals floated where they'd fallen.

Elsie put water on in the kitchen, which was simply a back corner of the long main room. There was a freestanding stone fireplace and chimney two-thirds of the way to the kitchen.

Elsie walked past him, all the way to the opposite end, where the other back corner was curtained off by folds of shiny material. It seemed scarlet at first, but he saw it was changeable in the light, darker in the troughs of the folds, lighter, almost pink, on the crests.

Elsie came out wearing a terrycloth robe that was too big for her. It could have been the same one Marie was wearing the day before.

"You want to swim?" Elsie said. "I'm going for a quick dip, wash off this all-night grunginess."

Dick shook his head, watched Elsie as she went down a metal

spiral staircase into a small greenhouse that was built along the pond side of the house. The roof of the greenhouse slanted down from the bottom of the main-room windows. Below the greenhouse there was a grass slope and then the bank of the pond. Elsie jumped from the bank to a large rock two feet from shore. She let her robe fall and dove in all in one motion. She came up in the middle of the pond. It was all so quick Dick wasn't sure whether she was wearing a swimsuit.

He turned to look at the woodwork. It was simple but good. He remembered Eddie talking about doing the work a while back. The one really fancy bit was the steps down from the front door. Two concentric arcs, almost half-circles, nicely rounded at the lip. They somehow gave the impression of leading to water. The brown-and-gray fireplace and chimney stones were chinked with quartzite, and that pattern too reminded him of water, light reflected from water.

He thought of yesterday morning in the Wedding Cake—his undertow of thought then, started by the force of the Wedding Cake. . . . This house sure as hell didn't have anything to do with that old style, none of the ornament. And yet it was alike in a way. It looked as if Elsie was moving in or moving out. The squat back wall had built-in shelves, which were half bare, half a-clutter.

He looked around for the bathroom, found it behind the fireplace, on the pond side.

The toilet was humming. It was a huge plastic cube with a temperature gauge and a lot of wiring. The only normal part was the lid and the seat. There was a high footrest jutting out on the front, which made it awkward for a man to take a leak. Dick had to put one hand on the back wall to lean over the bowl. This struck him as funny. He started to laugh, had to bite his lip to keep steady.

He zipped up his fly and looked for the handle to flush. He found a handle but all it did was slide shut the lower level of the bowl. Maybe it was like a head on a boat, had a holding tank. He settled for shutting the lid.

He closed the door behind him and started laughing again. Elsie came up the spiral staircase from the well to the greenhouse, holding her robe wrapped around her. "What's so funny?"

Dick said, "That contraption in there."

Elsie went in behind the curtains at the far end. She called out from inside, "Oh. The *bio-let.*"

"The what?"

"It's like a *multrom.* Turns sewage into compost. No leach field. Keeps the pond clean."

She came out wearing shorts and a faded red sweatshirt. She pushed the sleeves above the elbow as she padded to the kitchen in bare feet. The stiff black shorts made her legs look particularly bare and harshly defined.

He was about to tell her about his odd morning at the Wedding Cake, Schuyler making breakfast for Parker and him. He caught himself. He thought of Marie coming up from the salt pond in *her* oversized robe, *her* chatter, *her* odd combination of boneless laziness and glass-edged attack. Maybe these rich girls all started conversations the same way, letting the fizz off the top of the bottle.

"I'm just going to have coffee and soup, that okay with you?"

While she was at the stove, Dick looked again at the shelves against the windowless wall. Quite a few books. One row of nothing but bird books. Boxes of loose photographs, a few more matted and propped up, a few in frames. Two cameras. There were three tennis trophies, two of them filled with pennies, straight pins, and odd buttons, the third a little statue of a girl serving. The arm with the racket had broken off.

Under the lowest shelf there were plastic-mesh baskets and a cardboard carton, all filled with stuff, as if Elsie were getting ready to have a yard sale. A pair of girl's ice skates, a skin-diving mask and snorkel, cans of tennis balls, a jump rope, a lot of bicycle inner tubes, a swim fin with a torn heel. That was the first basket. Dick shoved it back against the wall with his foot. It wouldn't go all the way. He picked up the handle of a butterfly net that blocked it, but the net was hung up on another carton. He gave up and wiped the dust off his hand.

Elsie was looking at him. "You're as bad as my sister," she said. "If you want to play with something, fine. But don't go around straightening up."

Dick reflexively stiffened against someone setting him straight. "Been here long?"

Elsie shrugged. "A year. Less. I've been fixing up the outside, putting in plants. I've got some furniture in storage but it doesn't really go here, and I can't afford new stuff. What's the rush? I kind of like it with just the minimum."

The one sofa by the fireplace and the one table by the window looked unrelated and forlorn. The sofa was a three-seater that had seen better days. The table was a rustic picnic table with benches, the cedar bark still on the legs.

The only other visible piece was a tall double-door wardrobe. It was carved and painted in some sort of old-time Italian or Portuguese way. It was faded, but still a beautifully made thing. Backed against the scarlet curtain, it made that corner of the room look like a side altar in a big Catholic church. It was a shame to have everything else so slack.

"It's all passive solar," Elsie said. "There's a pile of rocks at the back of the greenhouse, and the heat flows..." She gestured sweepingly. She stopped. "Did you know you have the most terrible expression on your face?"

Dick was embarrassed. "It's the benches and table. I like the wardrobe. I like the house and the pond."

"Well, good. That's the point. It's just a shelter by a pond." She put her hands deep in her shorts pockets. "I did a lot of the work, I mean hammering and sawing. Ask Eddie. And he and I worked on the plan. . . . I know it may look drab on a rainy day. . . ."

"No. It's . . ."

"But on a nice day you can float on the pond—we dredged it and fixed the little dam—you can lie there and—"

"I like your house. Eddie likes your house. He spoke to me about it. The air flow and everything."

"I just haven't gotten around to . . . I'm perfectly happy to get some advice. You have any ideas?"

"Nope." He had no idea what she wanted. But she could get him talking, he just couldn't keep his mouth shut around her. He said, "Well, maybe you could take the bark off your picnic table. Looks like a hippie girl with hairy legs."

Elsie laughed. "That's going outside. Eventually. Back to nature, where she belongs. And eventually I'll get some chests for all that equipment."

"Maybe you should put it out in your garage. Makes the house look like it ought to have hinges on the lid. Like a big toy box."

Elsie looked hurt, laughed, then looked hurt again.

"Aw, hell, Elsie, I'm just . . ."

"Did you know you used to terrify kids when you worked at the boatyard?"

"I was mean to kids? Naw. I may have explained things kind of briefly to one or two boat owners. I wasn't mean to any kids."

"I didn't say you were mean."

"First time I worked in the yard, I was just a kid myself. That was before the Coast Guard. Before I was on Captain Texeira's boat. I used to fall back on the boatyard when things didn't work out."

"That's funny. Even when I was a kid I admired the way you're good at things, the way you seemed to have worked out a good relation to things, I mean the physical world. I thought you and

Eddie—you around boats and Eddie back in the woods—I compared you with most of the men around. . . . You and Eddie seemed so real. And happy about . . . things."

Dick laughed. "You'd have to leave out a long list of real screwups. That goes for Eddie too."

"Oh, I know you and Eddie get into trouble. But that's because you have your own rules . . . or at least your own sense of things. I've always liked the way you and Eddie treated this part of South County as though . . . well, certainly not as if it *belonged* to you, but as though it were open to you, part of your natural territory."

"That's a pretty picture all right. Natural territory."

"Did you know the Indians—or, as Miss Perry says, the *red* Indians—didn't *own* anything?"

"Well, that's me and Eddie. But I'd like to have my natural territory so's it includes, say, banks. The way it is now, I'm not in what you might call the natural business flow."

Elsie didn't go on with the subject. She brought the soup over to the picnic table. She said, "I know you don't like this table with hairy legs, but it's all we've got."

Dick thought he'd spoken about money in some crude way. It irritated him. He said, "I see you got some tennis trophies. You going to join the tennis club when your brother-in-law gets it going on Sawtooth Point?"

Elsie smiled as though she saw through him. "Tennis used to be the way I punished boys. Now it's how I try to meet men. So maybe I will. Increase *my* natural territory." She got a picture from the shelf of herself and a man shaking hands over a tennis net. "That's me at seventeen. I just beat him. The old headmaster at Perryville— he still had a pretty good game." Elsie laughed. "Still! Old! He was only a few years older than I am now. He wasn't even forty."

"You got a long ways to go till forty," Dick said. "What are you—more than ten years younger than me?" He looked at the picture. "I remember you at that age there. You came down to the boatyard to tell me you were sorry my father died."

"I remember that," Elsie said. "It still makes me blush. I remember all the men in the yard staring at me, but by then you'd seen me, so I couldn't turn back. I'd thought I'd be . . . I thought because I was doing a good thing I'd be invisible and it wouldn't matter. I was just wearing my bathing suit. Sally wouldn't come, but, then, she knew men stared at her, and I still didn't quite believe they noticed me. . . . Well, I did sort of. . . ."

Dick said, "It was nice of you. No one else in your family ever said anything to me about my father. I appreciated it."

"Well, our whole family was falling apart that summer."

Dick nodded. "I remember all you Buttricks kind of disappeared for a while. But I saw you around some."

"I was going to the Perryville School. I stayed on as a boarder for two years. We'd sometimes go sailing. The school had two boats in the yard where you worked—do you remember those two pond boats? All the kids were scared of you. . . . You were a famous grouch."

"You were scared of me, were you?"

"Not me. But you *were* grouchy."

"I don't remember being grouchy to you school kids." Dick was embarrassed.

Elsie laughed and said, " '*School kids.*' Good God. I certainly didn't think of myself as a *school kid*. What a blow that would have been. I mean, maybe crackerjack sailor, or star rebel. But *school kid* . . ."

Elsie went off with the soup bowls and came back with coffee.

"Tell me," Elsie said. "What am I now? I mean, there I was then, little Elsie Buttrick, school kid. Now what? One of the Buttrick girls, not the pretty one. And maybe one of the Buttricks who had the nice house on the point. Or maybe—'Officer Buttrick,' as you sometimes say with a certain sneer. Or maybe I'm just one of the rich-kid crowd?" Elsie laughed. "I remember in college teaching myself to say tom*ay*to instead of tom*ah*to so the lefties wouldn't hate me." Elsie looked up. "So—is it A, B, C? None of the above? All of the above?"

He shook his head.

"Oh, come on. You can if you dare—where's your nerve?"

Dick took a while. "I'm not so concerned about what you think of my nerve that I'd go ahead and make you feel bad."

"Ooo. Well." Elsie sat up. "Schoolgirl gets taken down a peg."

"No," Dick said. "You pushed yourself into that one."

"In fencing that's called a stop thrust. You just hold your blade out there when the other guy jumps in, and there she is with a new button."

"You do fencing?"

"I did."

"I guess there's nothing you don't do."

"Just about."

"Except let other people get a word in—"

"Oh, for God's sakes! No one's stopping you! But I guess that's an answer in a way. What I think of as just my way of babbling engagingly, *you* think is obnoxious pushing."

"Yup."

Elsie said, " 'Yup.' 'Nope.' Now I've made you go all swamp-Yankee." Elsie smiled at him, started to say something else, didn't, left her mouth open.

It made Dick laugh.

"Well," Elsie said, "good. Now that we've got that all cleared up. Do you want a peach?"

Dick said yes.

Elsie went to get them, kept talking. "What I meant to get to somehow . . . I'll just skip right to it. I had an eerie feeling not long ago. It was about Miss Perry. I'm devoted to Miss Perry. I admire Miss Perry. What she's like is one of those eccentric eighteenth-century English vicars who knew *everything* about the place they lived. Crops, flora and fauna, local geology, social facts, *everything.*

"Miss Perry is pretty eighteenth-century in her formality too. You know how she's known Captain Texeira for ages, how she adores him? She still writes him little notes saying, 'May I call on you next Sunday?' She only sees him once a month. And you know how much she likes you, but she only sees you on your kids' birthdays. It's all so crystallized it might as well be in a glass case. And there's her one hour a week at the library reading aloud for children's hour. She likes that. But I remember asking her about her other good works, which she's not so fond of. She said she asked her father the same question when she was young and he said, 'Life is a series of minor duties, most of them unpleasant.' She said she was horrified at the time. I told her I was horrified now.

"Anyway, what happened was this. I started giving my ecology talks in the school, the ones Charlie and Tom came to. And I moved in here. One of the first days I was here, I came in, and I was just stopped cold—it was as if the house was haunted. . . . I thought, So this is what it feels like to be Miss Perry." Elsie put the peaches down on the table, her fingers lingering on them. "It wasn't so much a thought as a sensation. I felt her spirit, no, not her spirit. I felt the *form* of her life. I felt as though that form, that formal form, was hovering and it might suddenly crystallize the rest of my life."

Dick was startled. It wasn't the same thought he had yesterday, but it floated nearby.

Elsie said, "Of course it's ridiculous, there are so many ways Miss Perry and I are . . . not just different but miles apart. But at the time the feeling was absolutely terrifying. It went away fairly quickly, though my reaction to it didn't. I mean, every so often I find myself underlining differences between Miss Perry and me." Elsie laughed. "Which probably sounds pretty silly." Elsie leaned over her plate and chomped down on her peach.

Dick said, "I was thinking the other day...something like that. One thing I was thinking is how my father was, how he left me things I didn't even know about. For one thing, how hard it is not to be so..."

"Yes?"

"Not to be so goddamn gloomy."

"That does seem to be the local problem," Elsie said. "At least Miss Perry concentrates her melancholy all into one spell. That's sort of formal too, every year at the same time. I can't tell when I'm going to feel melancholy. It used to be whenever I went by our old house. Or smelled a certain smell, a sea-breeze-through-a-damp wooden-house smell...I used to blame everything on that house, on that one summer. That summer was the sun of my solar system. Now I don't know, I'm more in outer space....That was seventeen years ago. What were you doing seventeen years ago?"

Dick said, "That year. I remember that year. I got married in January, Charlie was born, my father died."

"But Charlie's birthday's in June," Elsie said.

"Yup."

"Oh, I'm sorry, I didn't mean to..."

"And I left the Coast Guard, went to work at the boatyard," Dick said. "Don't worry about it. Charlie came out nine pounds, so it was hard to call him premature with a straight face. I remember May's mother giving it a try."

Elsie laughed, then looked to see if it was okay.

Dick said, "And I built our house. May stayed with her parents in Wakefield while I was finishing it. I'd get off work at the yard, drive over, and keep going till after dark. Eddie Wormsley and me. Sometimes another couple of guys from the yard. That was just before Eddie's wife left him. He knew she was going, so he wasn't too cheerful."

Elsie said, "Ah. So it wasn't just my family. It was a bad year for all of you. Almost enough to make you believe in astrology."

"No," Dick said. "To tell the truth, that time wasn't bad for me. I liked all that work. I'd been bored in the Coast Guard. And I was glad I had at least that little piece of land left, and the house going up. And I had a son."

Elsie said, "Yes. There was baby Charlie. I don't envy my sister anymore except for her children. Last year I even went to an agency and asked about adopting." Elsie laughed. "Now, there was an odd scene. . . ."

Dick said, "You better talk to Eddie Wormsley about that. He got his son back from his ex-wife when the kid was ten. Practically grown up, or so Eddie thought. The kid was a good kid too. But, my God . . . you talk to Eddie about that."

Elsie said, "I talked to Mary Scanlon about it—"

Dick said, "Mary? Mary doesn't have a kid."

"No, no. She and I were joking about. . ." Elsie fluttered her hand and said, "Our spinsterhood. You see, she works evenings, I work days, so we were talking about sharing a daughter. Add a room for Mary out there." Elsie gestured to the side. "And I'd move my room over to that side. And we'd get Miss Perry to be the honorary grandmother. We might keep some slots open for male relatives. My brother-in-law for rich uncle." Elsie's hands flickered back and forth with each idea. "And a black-sheep uncle . . . You think you might like that one? Rogue uncle . . ."

Dick laughed. "Mary Scanlon and you. That'd be a pair all right."

"I don't know why you say that," Elsie said. "Mary speaks well of you. In fact she's very fond of you."

Dick said, "And I like Mary. I like Mary fine."

"Then, what?"

Dick shook his head.

Elsie said, "Then it's something about me!"

"No. I like you fine too. It's the pair of you. I was thinking of some poor guy walking in here, he'd get skinned on two sides at once."

"I don't know why you say that. Mary and I could very well be the two nicest people for miles around—"

"That's right. Could be."

"But just because we're independent women . . . Of course maybe you just feel threatened."

Dick laughed. "That's what I said—if the two of you got going, I surely would."

"Well," Elsie said. "So that's what you think. I suppose you prefer women to be like Marie Van der Hoevel, little whispering voices, and tiny narrow feet, pale noodle legs. You probably can't even tell she's meaner than Mary and me put together."

Dick checked himself. He didn't want to get into talking about Parker and him mixing with Schuyler and Marie. Dick said, "No. But, then, I don't know Marie. Just from the clambake. Didn't look like she was having much fun."

"Well, it's her own fault," Elsie said. "No, I shouldn't say that. Schuyler's impossible sometimes. But really I'm glad they're both going to stay here. And that is a measure of how few friends I have left around here. There's Mary Scanlon, but it's hard to see her, the hours she has to work. So really my best friend is Miss Perry. . . . I really do love her, but . . . I grew up here, and everyone I knew then has moved away. New York, Boston . . . Away. I see my sister, but now that she and Jack have two children, it's not the way it was. It's still nice, but . . . One thing I admire about Miss Perry is her friendships. Of course her best friend died, old Mr. Hazard. But she has Captain Texeira. . . ."

Elsie stopped short, sank onto her elbows, her fingers on her forehead. "I suppose I'm afraid of being here the way Miss Perry is here. But at the same time I admire the way she's here. And I want to stay here, I want to be here. I *believe* in staying here. It's just so hard sometimes. Of course it's my own fault. . . . I can be so difficult. I'm not really, I'm . . ." Elsie put her hands over her eyes, said "Oh shit," and began to cry.

Dick was alarmed. He felt a sharp sympathy for Elsie, as quick as a piece of paper being ripped down the middle. He had no idea what to do. It seemed like years since May had her crying fits. Or since he'd been nice to May when she did cry.

Dick held out his napkin to Elsie. When it touched her hand she made a noise so much like a growl that he pulled back.

"I'm fine," she said. "Give me that." She wiped her eyes and blew her nose and went right on. "One thing I was thinking is that we ought to be able to do anything. I mean, compared with plants and animals, we can see the whole world. But everyone seems to end up . . . shriveled into a corner. Have you ever seen a water shrew? They're little, smaller than my little finger. They're almost blind. They have to eat and eat. . . . When they make a new nest, they have to scout the fastest way from their nest to the water so birds won't catch them. They can only afford to feel out the path once. If there's a stone in the way, they run around it, if there's a twig, they hop over it. Then that's their path. If you take away the stone and the twig, they still run around the place where the stone was, they still give a little hop where the twig was. They're wonderful, but when they're in their preprogrammed mode they're just absurd. I *like* being an animal, but not that part. I mean, I'm grateful for being alive, I like having to do most of what I do, I just wish I wasn't so . . . caught by . . . I don't mind the real problems, the real rocks and twigs. It's being in a maze of things that aren't really there that makes me . . . it makes me sad for Miss Perry, it makes me sad about myself. When you live by yourself, you spend so much time going around rocks that aren't there. You spend lots of time making sure you're *not* something. That you're not afraid, that you're not lonely, that you're not absurd." Elsie looked up at him. She looked a little bewildered. She said, "Do you know what I mean?" She rolled her hand on the table so it touched his. The touch straightened his spine.

Tough little Elsie Buttrick. Far-off, fast-talking Elsie Buttrick, as quick and neat as a tern skimming the water. Dick had been alarmed to see her crumple, he was glad to see her rise again.

She stood up, picked up her coffee cup, put it back down, and shoved it aside. She took both his hands, and he floated to his feet. He bumped the corner of the table. When she touched his cheek, they were clear of the table, in the center of the room.

She said several things but he didn't take them in. He felt weightless, but when their bones touched he felt their weight against each other, as though they were small boats at sea rising on the same swell, jostling, fendered by their flesh.

He had one complete sting of conscience when they drifted apart for an instant. Elsie shoved aside the red curtain and they floated through.

Elsie said, "It's okay, it's all right." He didn't say anything. His mouth felt numb, his hands felt numb, even though he could feel her transmitted through them. She was transmitting her skin, her teeth, her breath, and her odd fit of tears for herself. And her sixteen-year-old self from seventeen years before—it came back to him now on a single beam of memory that as she'd walked up to him she'd pulled at her swimsuit. He saw it again—as she'd crossed the boatyard, she'd slipped her fingers under the edge of her red swimsuit ridden up on her haunch and slid it down with a neat inside-out twist of her hand. And said she was sorry about his father's death. Now she was only a step closer. She reached him now. He felt that everything that was happening and the sensations that were about to overcome him were as remote as that memory. Her sharper full-grown face was as remote as a star, light sent years ago reaching him now, fixing him on the surface of the sea.

*E*lsie shocked him. Not because they'd gone to bed, though that too put him in a state of shock. He understood that state of shock, felt the form of it, absorbed it. He knew that he was absorbing it willingly, that he was being bad, that he was going to come to Elsie's house again, that he would be harmed by what he was doing, that he was willing.

But in addition Elsie shocked him in a way that he hadn't foreseen: she didn't hide anything. It was more than that—she as much as said that now they could say anything to each other. What she looked forward to as much as making love was telling him things and giving him the run of her house and in the same way the run of her whole life. He wasn't sure about taking the invitation. What it turned out to feel like was that he was the one being opened up, that he was the one being penetrated by what she told him.

It was little things at first. The next afternoon he came to give her a ride to the Volvo dealer to pick up her car. When she climbed into his truck she laughed and said, "I certainly couldn't have ridden my bike today. I forgot how stiff I feel after, I mean when I haven't done it for a while." He must have looked startled. She added, "No, don't feel bad, it's nice, I hobbled around all morning thinking of how nice...."

He thought, Why shouldn't she say that? But that "haven't done it for a while" came from a distance.

Another time, several days later, they went swimming in her pond. They managed to squeeze the two of them into one large inner tube. They floated around, kept on floating even after it began to drizzle. She tucked his arms under her shoulders. The drizzle was a little warmer than the pond, it made his body feel oiled.

She said, "When I first slept with a boy—I was still at the Perryville School. My girlfriends who'd done it warned me I'd be disappointed. And I *was* in a way. But in another way I was amazed. I thought, What a wonderful way to get to know someone. I wanted to go to bed with all the men in the world." She laughed.

They drifted into the rhododendron branches. Elsie reached up and shoved against a branch. They spun slowly to mid-pond.

"I mean, it didn't take long at all to stop actually sleeping with everyone I liked. It was *why* it wasn't a good *idea* that puzzled me. And I'm still glad I thought that thought. And I'm glad that later on I thought, Why have sex at all? Almost the Catholic position. So to speak. Sex is just to have babies and the rest is a bad French novel. That was theoretical too. I still had my share of bad French novels."

Dick didn't feel he could complain. He just wished she wouldn't talk that way. He also felt ashamed that he wished she wouldn't, since he was doing what she was talking about. And he was equally ashamed that he was glad she talked that way, since it let him off the hook, he was just one more of her bad French novels.

He liked talking to her about almost anything else. He even liked hearing her talk about sex when she got off the topic of her sex life in general and just talked about the two of them. "I noticed the way you looked at me at the clambake," she said. "Admit it. That was just plain lust. I understand—it was early in the summer, you hadn't seen anyone in a bathing suit for a long time."

"No," he said.

"Be honest, now. When I was helping you with the clams, wearing my bathing suit and your old rubber boots, and my thighs were turning pink from all the steam. Come on. Just for an instant you had evil thoughts. Say it. 'I had evil thoughts. . . .' "

He said, "Hell, Elsie, I thought you were being a good scout." It drove her nuts.

"You jerk!" She regrouped to get the better of him. "Too bad for you, then. There were at least five guys at that clambake who thought I was cute as hell." She started to count on her fingers.

"Okay, okay." He would have liked to think that when she pulled on the boots and waded in to help him she'd looked good by accident. He wished it all to be an accident. But he could give up that little clambake accident. What he really didn't want to hear was that she'd drawn the look Charlie gave her, that she'd enjoyed Charlie's look. "You're right," he said. "I burned my fingers twice on account of looking at your legs." But that was just a cloud of ink he squirted so he could slip away.

This was one of the many times he felt her urge to draw everything in him up to the surface. The farther down it was, the more she wanted to get at it. Sometimes he felt the pleasure of it, he liked the feeling that she put all her skimming and diving into getting at him. But, once in a while, he felt a third, completely different way: that all the skimming and diving, all her sexual eagerness (which could get as edgy and probing as her conversation) were just the small broken-off pieces of her that swam to the surface—that really she had a quieter, larger nature in her. He still liked all that top-water busyness, he was still charmed by her tern-self—and so was she, it probably felt good, as good as flying and wheeling and swooping. But he also got a sense of that part of her that wasn't so sparkling with seizures and escapes. Far below all the different things that she thought she was, that she wanted to be, that she feared to be, there was a part of her that was more gently defined, more easily receiving and more easily flowing out, defined less as a shell or carapace or hard shore against the waves and more as a bay as it becomes deeper and vaguer, undefining itself into the broader sea.

That sense of her, but also his connection to her childhood (sharpened by their talking, and splintered into their sexual thrill), and his tender admiration and liking for her were all troubling thoughts. So then he would think of the thoughtless fainting of their first falling into her bed. If the whole thing had stopped after that time he wouldn't have felt so guilty. It had washed over him, a freak wave.

He still didn't know what he was doing, but he did know he was coming to Elsie on evenings he told May he was going to the Neptune, and on afternoons when he said he was going to get something for the boat.

Now the sex was sex. Variable but recognizable. In that sense, he knew what he was doing. It was talking with Elsie that kept changing. He still told her she was nosy, he still kept his mouth shut about some things—Parker, for one—but he told her a lot about himself he'd never told anyone, not even May. He told himself that he'd never told May because May hadn't ever asked. But in truth he knew that May would like to know everything Elsie pulled out of him. He told himself that that was just the way it was, that Elsie was good at asking questions. And he could tell Elsie stuff he'd done, stuff he'd thought, and Elsie wouldn't get upset. Even when Elsie found fault with stuff he'd done, she didn't come down all that hard, perhaps because of what she'd told him about herself, but perhaps because she imagined herself doing it, good or bad. May would have held it at arm's length, would have sounded warnings.

It was when he drove away from Elsie's house that he felt full guilt. He'd stomp down on the gas and drive fast out her driveway, bottoming out on the crown, whipping the sides of his truck with laurel branches that cocked on the wide wing mirrors.

His work habits gave way. He barely touched the boat for days, just did the wiring with Eddie and told Charlie how to put in the wheelhouse windows.

He talked to the boatyard owner about using the owner's new trailer to haul the boat to the yard, about using the old marine railway to launch it. The owner said, "You got her finished?" Dick said, "No. I'm just planning ahead."

"Well, don't show up the week after Labor Day," the owner said. "That's when all them yachts come out. In the spring it's all spread out. Anywhere from Memorial Day to July. Fall, they all want it the same time."

Dick dropped by to see Joxer Goode at the crab plant. Still not buying crabs. But Joxer had financed the new freezer system, got a new investor, though he didn't have a dime to spare. Joxer said, "Will you come by when you get your boat finished?" Dick said sure. Joxer's tone was one Dick hadn't heard. They were equals, but it was based on Joxer's bad luck, not on any gains Dick had made.

Dick stopped by Schuyler's new cottage, found Marie sunning herself in a lawn chair on the wharf that stuck out into the creek. Dick could smell the coconut oil ten feet away. Marie said that the phone company hadn't put the phone in, so she hadn't heard from Schuyler. "And I can't call anyone to come do anything about the house. There isn't a single thing I can do. It's sort of delicious."

Charlie and Tom went by in Dick's skiff. Charlie slowed down, waved, headed toward the cut. Marie raised her head, Tom waved. The wake, which had rolled up the bank under the wharf, slid back out.

Marie said, "Your friend Parker isn't back, is he?"

Dick said, "No. Not that I know."

Everything he saw was part of his familiar life, except where he stood. And the part of himself that was heading for Elsie's. Every time he talked to someone he felt odder and odder. The yard owner, Joxer, Marie. How odd it must look to Charlie and Tom to see him there. He should have been in the skiff. How odd to see his skiff, when for years he'd been in it, turning his head to look at the point.

Marie slid her sunglasses up her nose with one finger and began to read again. Dick said goodbye. She turned her face toward him, her lips moved silently, "Bye-bye."

Dick decided he'd better take *Mamzelle* out on his own. He'd take Keith college-boy and Charlie. Parker would still get the boat's share. No sense in letting everything stay idle. The weather was good, would hold for a few days.

Dick went home. May was in the garden. He went past her to look at his boat. As he pulled back the plastic sheet from the doorway May said, "The Buttrick girl was here. She said you wouldn't mind her taking pictures of your boat."

Dick didn't say anything. May said, "I let her, I didn't know. Is that all right?"

Dick said, "Doesn't matter."

"Have you thought of asking her to lend you some money?" May said. "I hear Joxer Goode's still shut down, so you can't look to him. I know you won't ask Miss Perry, but you could ask the Buttrick girl. The Buttricks just sold their whole lot to the development. And God knows they bought it cheap enough."

"That was a long time ago."

"Still . . . It ought to be on their mind, now they've made such a profit."

Dick said, "If Parker shows up, tell him I've taken his boat out. I can't wait around."

"You going to ask the Buttrick girl?"

"If I decide to."

May looked at him so long he felt alarmed. She said, "You've worked so hard, I hate to see you give up now."

"I'm not giving up. Jesus, woman! I'm going out."

"I never thought I'd have to tell you to do something about the boat. It's been—"

"Then don't tell me. Don't tell me what to do with the boat. I told you already, if I don't get her in the water by September, I'll sell her as is and get a regular job. You'll be satisfied one way or the other."

May sighed. "It's true I couldn't stand another winter like last one. And the one before, and before that. It's not just the lack of money, it's the way you are on account of it. On account of the lack of your boat. The boys and me get to feel every bit of what you feel about banks, the price of lumber, anything that goes wrong. So if you don't raise the money, if you sell the boat, the rest of us won't be any better off. You say *I'll* be satisfied one way or the other. I'm saying *you'll* be sour one way or other. The only way you won't be sour is if you finally get your boat in the water. You won't get the money quick enough putting out to sea. It may suit you better to get knocked around some by salt water, but the plain truth is you've got to do it the way everyone else does it—get your nerve up and go ask."

Dick said, "I'm not going to talk about it with you. What do you think Joxer Goode was here for? I went and *cooked* for him, I went and waited on his friends to get him over here to look at my boat. I asked him, I damn near pleaded with him. Were you blind that day? Deaf? Have you been blind all summer? This whole summer I've been making money. I poached those clams, and you complained. I did that clambake, and you said I worked the boys too hard. I've gone out with Parker and stuck swordfish and brought back more than four thousand dollars, and you complain about Parker. You don't know what you're talking about."

"I know you've done all that," May said, "and I know it's not enough. And I know you haven't asked Miss Perry, I know you haven't asked the Buttricks. So don't tell me you'll sell the boat, don't tell me you'll cut off your arm. Just don't you come in all next winter and make the house stink with your moods. Not unless you've gone round and—"

"And begged—" Dick said.

"No," May said, "you just tell them how you figure to make money, how they'll get their money back. But if it does come to begging, I'd rather you begged and hurt from begging than have you sit around oozing poison for another year. I won't live like that. It may be the only way you can drive yourself as hard as you do, but I can't let you put me and the boys through it. So you go ask."

Dick knew enough not to get mad. What May said wasn't just her nagging. It was a well-seasoned bitter complaint. In the end what May said was hard but true. It wasn't worth arguing over the details. About the boat, she had him pretty well pegged.

May sat down on an upside-down washtub. She put her arms across her knees, her head on her arms. She didn't cry. After a bit she got up and went back to hoeing the weeds out.

Dick had no exhaustion to match hers, not this week. No salt of work. He felt rotten with his secret sweet.

May stopped hoeing and looked at him. He said flatly, "I'm thinking about it."

"I didn't say anything."

May looked like winter. Not bright-blue winter but drizzling, tired winter. On this summer day, the sun still above the trees, May in the middle of her bell peppers and summer squash, in front of the square of tasseling sweet corn, she was the only thing that hadn't absorbed the summer, that hadn't flourished.

Dick felt the justice of the claim she made. He felt it the more since she spoke from the middle of bleakness. But he doubted he could bring himself to ask Miss Perry. He could hope Parker would get back. But even if Parker paid up, he'd be short.

He felt the embarrassment and danger of his next thought

before he fully knew what it was—May *wanted* him to go see Elsie. Dick saw himself coming back late, May stirring in bed, himself saying, "I did what you asked, I went over to see the Buttrick girl."

Perfect. Just perfect. Go all the way, Dickey-boy. Be a player.

Dick wondered if it was in any way possible that he could have been pushed into asking Elsie if he and Elsie hadn't started up.... It didn't matter, there was no way, not after what he'd been up to.

Dick now couldn't wait to get out to sea. "This next run'll be a short one," he said. "I'll be careful with Charlie, you needn't worry. The weather's good. There's nothing can hurt us in summer."

"The Buttrick girl told me you saved her life," May said. "That was summer."

"Oh, that," Dick said. "That wasn't—"

"She told me what happened. So don't put Charlie out in the skiff. You keep him on board," May said. She added, "The Buttrick family ought to have that in mind too. They..." May cut herself off. She knew you didn't mention help of that kind. You salvaged ships, not people. If your life was saved, you were grateful; if you saved a life, you claimed nothing.

Dick was glad May bit her own tongue. He was too stung with shame by his other thoughts to correct her.

He pulled the plastic curtains shut across the front end of the shed. He didn't want to look at the boat. He shouldn't touch her, he shouldn't even go near her in his condition. He should go out to sea in Parker's tub.

*B*ut still Dick didn't put out to sea. His temptations continued, though their tone and nature changed. He resisted these no more successfully than the first.

Their sexual encounters had changed rapidly from the initial weightless cloud-tumbling-into-cloud. The second time he'd come to her house, the day had been clear, the light harsh. He'd come back on purpose. But she kept the lead. In the cab of his pickup on the way to pick up her Volvo she'd been chatty and cozy, leaning against him until he had to say, "Look, Elsie, I know about half the guys driving pickups up and down this road." She moved way over to her side but still punctuated what she was saying by sliding her bare foot up under the cuff of his pants.

On the way back she passed him in her car just before the turnoff to her little arc of access road. She practically forced him onto it, but he charged after her and took the turn up her driveway so close he could hear fine gravel pinging his bumper, then green branches hitting her car and his bumper in one sweep. He could see all this from far off—there he was, a crazy teen-ager. She seemed to know it—she jumped out of her car and ran around toward the pond, laughing, and, come to think of it, pretty nimble for someone with sore muscles. He rushed after her clumsily, as if he was running through a thicket, batting away briars and vines, the last threads of his good sense. She ran herself into a corner of the tiny lawn between the bull briars and the pond. Run, run, as fast as you can, you can't catch me, I'm the Gingerbread Man. Her underpants and sneakers became teen-age litter on the grass.

The day after, he'd left Eddie doing the wiring in the wheelhouse, Charlie and Tom painting. He reminded himself to tell the same lie to May and to Eddie. In up to his chin now, planning his craziness.

Once again, Elsie stayed a step ahead. She had a little lunch tray set for them, little napkins folded under the forks. "Would you like me to fix you a drink?" And she seemed to have a touch with the way time moved, as though she could pull time out of the air and wind it round him. He felt immobilized, but not at a loss, since nothing else could move either. When she loosened him, let a little time writhe down his wrists and ankles, he moved, but only inch by inch. When they finally stretched out on her bed, he was naked but subdued, balanced between pleasurable impatience and pleasurable patience, happy to let her control him, tilt his urges against each other. She knew what she was doing, he said out loud she knew what she was doing. With her fingertips and then with practically nothing but her breath she kept him up in the air as if he were a plume of down. She'd send him up and then let him sink, eddying and side-slipping back down. Then back up higher, a little higher each time.

She reached up to his mouth once with her hand—turned her head to say, "You're grinding your teeth, don't grind your teeth" —and slid her fingers into his mouth, just touching his side teeth and gums in a way that made his jaw go slack. He heard his breath, felt his breath as though she'd made him part of his own breathing.

But afterward, while he was still astonished by her physical delicacy, she roughed him up before he was quite ready for it. She said, "You know what I like about having you come in my mouth? I feel like a blind person—you know how they say blind people feel with their faces so they can practically see a building? Same thing...Now I've felt it this way, the next time you come in my cunt I'll practically see it. ..."

He was just getting over the effect her words had had and understanding what she meant when she laughed. "You should see your face now. You're really shocked. I should think you'd like the idea. ... Or is it another hippie girl with hairy legs?"

"No..."

"You'd just prefer a prettier piece of poetry."

"No. It was just sudden. I'd just as soon have stayed a little lazy."

"Well, yes." She took his head between her hands, but then sat back on her heels, her eyes turning beady as a bird's. "You know, I once asked a doctor if a shot of sperm had any nutritional value. He said, 'Certainly, it has about the same number of calories as a slice of white bread.' "

"Now you're doing it on purpose."

"I am. I can't help it, you make it so worthwhile. When I shock you, I feel as if I've shocked a whole layer of granite."

He tried not to think about her when he wasn't with her, but of course he did. One of the most unsettling thoughts that came to him was that the things he liked about Elsie were at odds with each other. That wasn't how it was with May, May was a single settled person. He stopped there—he didn't want May and Elsie getting together in his mind.

After the first delirium—a word Parker used to describe his shore leaves, along with lotus-eating and postcoital amnesia—phrases Dick found leaking into his thoughts no matter how often he bailed them out—Dick and Elsie fell into an odd mental intimacy, which, like the other stuff he liked about Elsie, had its opposed charges. It was cozy but high-strung, idle but energetic, aimless but part of a design. She could be absolutely sympathetic ("Good God, Dick, I don't see how you could stand it!") but absolutely remorseless about drilling into him for the facts and the tone of his life. The rhythm of her inquisition was vaguely familiar to him, but he couldn't place it for a while. They spent a couple of afternoons just lazing around. Dick was secretly relieved that the sexual schedule was less urgent, though there was still an erotic shimmer to just coming up to her house. It occurred to him at last what the rhythm was: A blue heron wading in the marsh on her stilts, apparently out for a stroll—suddenly freezing. An imperceptible tilt of her head—her long neck cocking without moving. No, nothing this time. Wade, pose. Abruptly, a new picture—a fish bisected by her bisected beak. Widening ripples, but the heron, the pool, the marsh, the sky serene. The clouds slid across the light, the fish into the dark.

He told her about this picture. She said, "I liked it when you thought I was like a tern."

"You're like a tern. You can be all the birds you want. You . . ." He bit his tongue. He'd been about to talk about her croaking like a shypoke.

"I was certainly an ugly duckling."

"Come on, Elsie. You were kind of a tomboy, is all. You weren't ugly. I remember seeing you and Mr. Bigelow go out in the blue canoe, come surfing in over the sandbar. It looked nifty. You were a cute kid. Brown as a berry. Your hair coming out from that Red Sox hat you used to wear all the time. It seems to me you wore that hat everywhere. Except when you went in the general store, then you'd clutch it in front of you."

"I was covering my chest. I was embarrassed when I first got bosoms. No bosom was okay. And real bosoms would have been okay . . . weird but okay. My sister and mother and Mrs. Bigelow all walked around as though they were normal. That was the summer I was thirteen."

"I guess. You still called me Mr. Pierce. I went into the Coast

Guard right after, I don't think I saw you again until you were sixteen. That summer with you and your baseball hat was the last time we farmed Sawtooth Point. We picked a hundred and thirty bushels of sweet corn an acre. Your father came out one evening when I was in the field, offered me a ten-dollar bill to pull the poison ivy out of the raspberry bushes. I said sure, I'd get around to it. But then it turned out Mrs. Bigelow, who was the one put him up to it, she had in mind I was to do it *right then.* Because you were all going to have raspberries for dessert that night. She was nearby, just hanging back on the lane by your tennis court. So when she heard me say I'd get around to it, she came up to coax me. I didn't mind being a part-time farmer for my old man on top of working at the boatyard, but I wasn't keen on becoming Mrs. Bigelow's gardener. I didn't say anything for a bit. I wanted to be obliging, but I didn't want her to get in the habit. . . . I still hadn't said anything when she reached into your father's pants pocket, pulled out a five-dollar bill and slipped it into my shirt pocket. She said, 'To insure promptness'—and she made that little sound, you know, sort of a little two-note laugh she used to put on the end of everything—"

"Yes—actually it had three notes, it was a little rising trill. We used to call it Aggie's hemi-demi-semiquavers."

Dick laughed at that.

Elsie said, "Could you tell she was fucking my father?"

Dick didn't know where he was.

Elsie went on, "I didn't know she was, not then. I didn't find out until I was sixteen. The year you came back. We'd all been on Sawtooth Point together ever since your father sold us the two house lots. Our two families built the tennis court together—that is, we got Eddie to, but Dad and Timmy Bigelow were out there, Mom too. Aggie didn't do outside work, but she made lemonade. And the blue canoe. The blue canoe belonged to all of us. My sister found out first, then the Bigelows' son, then me. Then my mother. She says that wasn't the only reason they got divorced. Timmy—Mr. Bigelow—didn't find out for years and years. Just last spring. Some burglars thought their house was an empty summer house and broke in, discovered Timmy and Aggie. They tied them up. They broke open a box they thought was Aggie's jewelry box. It was old love notes from my father. The notes were lying there at Timmy and Aggie's feet after the burglars left. They, I mean Timmy and Aggie, had to lie there together for hours. Nobody came until morning. They lay in front of all those strewn *billets doux*. . . . The burglars opened them. I guess they were looking for bonds or something. Timmy could read them—well, of course he knew the handwriting, but he could read some of the lines . . . fond and apparently graphic letters." Elsie laughed. A little venom in it. She said "Oh, Aggie . . . 'Lay not your treasures up on earth where thieves break in. . . .' You know, if Timmy wasn't so sweet the whole thing would make me laugh. If he'd been the kind of man who could have laughed at her, just laughed in her face . . . Because it's so pathetic. Now she's an old hag. She's got something wrong with her, I mean, she's sick with something and completely dependent on Timmy. But I'm afraid he was just hurt, lying there facing this secret that was ripped open in front of them."

Although Elsie was being kind enough about old Mr. Bigelow, there was a bitter triumph in her voice when she talked about Mrs. Bigelow that Dick found repellent but fascinating. When Elsie broke in on *his* story, he'd been irritated, then stunned by *her* story. He still felt irritated, maybe because Elsie was putting his story in its place, just a complaint from the handyman, pretty much of a nothing story really, nothing like the inside story. And yet he was thrilled, in fact a little turned on by her malice.

Elsie said, "You know, I *remember* Aggie's jewelry boxes. They were covered with some kind of silk quilting. When Sally and I were little, she used to take us up to her room and fix our hair. I had long hair then. She'd take out her bracelets and let us try them on. And sometimes she'd put makeup on our faces—it felt wonderful—she had cool, light hands. I used to close my eyes and wish it would go on forever. . . . I used to wonder—I mean afterward—where she and Dad did it. Now I wonder where she kept that box of secrets. And did she take them out and read them late at night? Maybe it didn't matter about not having Dad, maybe all she needed was a secret. And at last it's been ripped open."

Dick said, "Does that happen a lot in the big-house set—some guy running off with someone else's wife?"

"Oh, they didn't run off. After it came out—except to Timmy—Dad just split. It wasn't 'Women and children first.' It was 'Every man for himself.' Maybe that got to Aggie, that she was more hung up on him than he was on her. She got her hooks into him because he was weak and she lost him because he was weak. So she got what she deserved. Except for Timmy. She doesn't deserve Timmy. I really adored Timmy when I was little. He's too nice, though. I never wanted a boyfriend like him."

"I wish you could have just heard yourself. There wasn't anyone in that story you didn't scalp. And Aggie—"

"I can say anything I want about Aggie. You know why I started working for Natural Resources? I mean, I believe in saving nature . . . but part of why I started is that I get to be in the same sphere as Aggie—her favorite place in the world is this part of South County. She's one of the four grown-ups who discovered it. Anyway, I get to be here too, but in the job I do, I'm her opposite. She's an idle, feminine, scientifically ignorant, snobbish, physical coward. I'm a hard-working, tomboyish, scientifically educated, socially declassed jock with enough nerve to go out in rough weather in a small boat." Elsie paused. Dick was about to take her down a notch by bringing up how pale around the gills she'd been on account of the sharks, when Elsie looked up at him and said, "Otherwise I'm exactly the same kind of bitch Aggie is."

Dick knew she meant it, but he didn't know which way she meant to go with it. Away from him? Toward him? Maybe it was just one of her solo aerial maneuvers, one of her swoops to see how fast she could go.

He said, "Well, neither one of us is about to get a good-conduct ribbon."

"I wasn't thinking of good conduct. I was thinking of my bad character. My secret, outlaw nature. *You'll* end up with good conduct again. *Won't* you?"

Dick didn't say anything for a moment. Then he nodded and said, "Yup. I'm not running off anywheres."

"You'll go home. That's right. You should go home. I wouldn't want you anywhere else. Safe and sound. And I'll be here, locking up the big bad secret."

Dick wasn't sure if she was stinging him or stinging herself. He said, "Well. You want me to go now?"

"Oh, for God's sakes!" She made an exasperated humming noise. "You know, sometimes you're ... For God's sakes, where's your sense of ..."

"Of what?" Dick said. "Direction?"

She was revving too fast to think he was funny. "Where's your sense of ... play, your sense of timing, your ..." Elsie took a breath and said, "Your sense of me!"

She hovered for a second and then Dick saw she was going to laugh. He watched her laugh get the better of her, and he felt a current of pleasure he'd never thought of looking for.

By now some of the lobster in the pots he'd set would begin to eat each other.

Or a big eel would get in, go after a lobster, get hold of its claw, lash it back and forth, and tear hell out of the inner netting.

Pots would work themselves so far into mud or onto the wrong side of a rock, the gangions would break when he pulled the trawl.

Or a dragger would have steamed through with her net set, torn up a whole trawl.

Dick called Keith college-boy again. Someone else answered, said he didn't know where Keith'd got to. Dick left another message. High time to pull the damn pots.

Dick started for the Neptune—have a beer, maybe see if he could pick up a hand for one trip.

He couldn't get past Elsie's driveway.

He thought if one day Charlie was driving the pickup, Charlie would suddenly find himself in front of Elsie's house. The horse knows the way.

He told Elsie that. She was delighted. He was getting so he told her everything.

Elsie said, "That must have actually happened when people drove horses. What a way to be found out! I think there's a Maupassant story about that. No—no horses. Just the son taking over his father's mistress."

She got him a beer. She drank wine. She kept beer in the icebox for him.

The house seemed very bright, sending out a whole roomful of light through the picture window. She said, "Dick . . ." and stopped. She said his name intimately and familiarly, but in a way that made him feel unfamiliar.

"Yuh."

"Never mind, I'll get back to it. After you've settled down. Is it my imagination or are you awfully restless?"

"No. Just worried about all those pots."

She didn't ask about the pots. She settled back in her chair, stretched her legs. "Have you seen Mary Scanlon?" she said. "I'm worried. I think her father's awfully sick."

She was slouched so low she used her stomach to set her wineglass on, kept it upright with one finger. "I saw Miss Perry's light on last night. Very late. I'm afraid she may be in her manic wind-up before her depression. Have you seen her lately?"

"No."

"Jack came over to look at the cottages. . . . They've sold more than half already. He came by here this afternoon. I thought it might be you."

Dick still felt unfamiliar. He knew all the people, was interested in the news, but disliked the skimming, didn't like Elsie skimming. . . . He couldn't tell; what the hell did they do over at the Neptune but trade "Did-you-hear-about?"'s?

"You know," Elsie said, "I'll bet I could get Jack to invest in your boat. He's still feeling abashed—at least toward me—about developing Sawtooth Point. And he loves to think he's connected to life at sea."

Elsie got up and turned off the overhead kitchen light. He was grateful for that. But on the way back she put her hand on the top of his head and said, "Jack would do anything for me."

Dick pulled his head away.

"*Be* touchy about it," Elsie said. "It's a good idea." She settled back in her chair. "I'm feeling oddly psychic these days. I can *feel* things. . . ." Then at last she turned full toward him. "Well, *you* must have psychic feelings. I've read that Icelandic fishing-boat captains find herring by having dreams. Do you have dreams about lobsters? Is that how you find them?"

"No." He gave it a try. "No, their life is way down there. I can figure it out. . . . Look. Let's skip lobster, I spent all day worrying about lobster."

"What about swordfish? Do you dream—"

"I had two knacks. When I was a kid, I had two knacks that impressed my father. One was I could get in our skiff to go after stripers and I'd get a feeling. I'd get out to the sandbar and I'd get a kind of nervousness along the inside of my forearm. It would be one forearm or the other. That was the side fish were on."

"Really? Like dowsing for fish?"

Dick wished he hadn't brought it up; Elsie often wanted a lot of back and forth about stuff that wasn't going to get any more settled than it was. He said, "I don't know about dowsing. Wasn't anything mystical. What it probably was, was there was so many little clues I couldn't figure them one by one, so I just got one general feeling."

"You want to try it? I've got a spinning rod."

"That was when I was a kid. Besides, stripers aren't running now."

"Well." Elsie said this flatly. Dick thought she was trying to draw him.

"You don't have to believe me, I wonder about it myself. I can't say for sure. I'll tell you, though, I've been out with skippers used to taste the bottom. Captain Texeira used to use a lead line, even though he had a depth finder. The lead had a place to put a plug of wax, a little piece of the bottom would stick to it, and he'd take a lick. Maybe to double-check where we were, maybe he could tell

something else. One thing's sure—just about anybody can taste
the difference in sea water when a little curl of the Gulf Stream's
broke off and drifted in."

"I'm not interested in reducing it all to common sense," Elsie
said. "I'm more curious about the inspired flashes. But what was
your other knack?"

"I could feel the tide. I still can, just not as well. I'd be in school
and I'd start thinking about doing something in the pond and I'd
know—"

"That's not so amazing, you'd've seen it before you left for school."

"Yeah. Maybe that was all it was."

"No, go on. Don't—"

"Maybe you're right. But I didn't calculate. I didn't remember
what I'd seen in the morning and then count the hours. I just felt
it. Especially if the tide was coming in. I'd feel it rising in me. Up
my arms and chest. Of course you could be right—it mattered to
me, so I kept track without knowing I was keeping track."

"No. I've read about that feeling."

"Yeah, well, then I guess it's okay to have it."

"Jesus, Dick, chill out." But then she went on as though she'd
been talking along without his saying anything. "Actually, this
was in a story, so maybe the author just made it up. It was a very
sexy story. We were actually assigned it in French class. Incredibly
sexy. I mean, I'd read Catullus but this was amazing. . . . I wish I
could remember—"

"Are all these French stories the same thing as your bad French
novels?"

Elsie took him in again. "Well, fuck it, then. You *are* on edge. You
want to go to the Neptune?"

"I don't seem to be able to get there." Dick laughed.

"I mean you and me."

Dick shook his head.

"All right, we'll go in separately."

"Elsie, it's a fishermen's bar."

"I've heard women go there."

"Yeah. Either they're with some guy or they're not."

"Yes, those are the two alternatives."

"Don't be dumb. If they're not, then they're expecting—"

"I'll go in and expect, then. You may have to be quicker than you think."

"Elsie, we can't go to the Neptune. I know all those guys."

"Well, *what,* then? Now you've made *me* restless." Elsie got up. "Come on. We'll go out in the blue canoe. I know where it is. We'll go up one of the creeks. What's the tide now?"

"Almost full. I looked."

When Elsie was unlocking the boathouse by the Wedding Cake, Dick thought maybe this was what she'd had in mind all along— her asking to go to the Neptune was just to use up his saying no. He was thinking of digging his heels in; he couldn't think of a reason, except he didn't like to be managed.

He saw a shooting star. Elsie said, "Look!" but she was looking at the water, which was shot with phosphorescence where she'd dumped the canoe in.

When they got in front of the breachway they could see flashes of white where the larger waves broke on the bar. The wind was fresh, the tide still running so hard it almost swept them up Pierce Creek. Dick, in the bow, paddled hard to nose them over into Sawtooth Creek. Elsie laughed. "Now, there's *another* story . . . 'Look what the tide washed in.'"

They glided up Sawtooth Creek. They only had to paddle enough to steer. They reached the pond with the flounder hole, and the current grew vague. They drifted. The wind in the grasses shut out the sounds from Route 1. It was the dark of the moon; the tide was going to brim up well into the marsh. It was bright with starlight. Another shooting star, and another—the August meteor shower.

He felt the canoe wobbling. He turned toward Elsie, who was taking her jeans off. She had to stand up to work them over her hips. She sat down again to pull her sweatshirt over her head. Before he could say anything, she put a hand on each gunwale and flipped herself over the side. The phosphorescence bubbled around her. She came up, brushed her hands over her face, and then dove down. He could see her go deep through the water, outlined by the glow of plankton she set off, her legs elongated by the trail of light she left in her wake.

She came up. She said, "Come on in, it's great."

"I don't want to get wet."

"You're no fun."

"How you plan to get back in?"

She reached up across the canoe, put some weight on her far hand, and rolled in. She flicked water at him.

He said, "I don't want to get wet."

"Come here. I remember that story now. Come here, in the middle."

Dick turned around on his seat. She took his hand and pulled him closer. She sat on her heels on one side of the center thwart. He knelt on the other.

"I can't remember what it's called . . . '*La Marée*.' Maybe. Two cousins, a boy and a girl, in Brittany. They're wading in the sea, the tide is about to come in. The boy is like you, he can feel the tide. Maybe they *are* in the water, that'd make it . . . No, they're in a *marsh*, I seem to remember having to look it up . . . *roseaux*, reeds. The boy makes her take his prick in her mouth. But he makes her stay completely still. Nothing can move except the tide. He can feel the tide coming in. He feels himself as the tide, her as the—what? —the land about to be flooded? Anyway, he holds her still. She's scared, but she adores him. No—we don't know what she thinks, maybe that's what I liked, I had to imagine her.... The tide comes up to her waist—which is to say his shins—then up to her breasts— I may be making this part up—then up to her shoulders. It's Brittany, the tide comes in faster than you can run. He can feel the tide in his body, his blood expanding. He feels her terror, but then he feels her change, she feels the tide too. I did make that up. *He* can feel the water on the fingers of the hand that's holding her hair. His body is taut. It's unbearable." Elsie stopped. "What do you think?"

"You're just full of your bad French novels tonight."

"This is a short story. I remember reading it, I was in college, I'd never been good at French, I had to look up a lot of words. *Frantically*." Elsie laughed.

Dick said, "I'll tell you what I think. I think the next part is they both drown." He was in a rage. With everything. With his clothes, with his leather work shoes he didn't want to ruin with salt water, with his body, with her stories, with how beautiful she'd looked underwater, with her *playing* with everything—she was like a kid in a workshop, picking up everything she didn't know what it was for.

The canoe drifted up the pond, got caught sideways in the creek to Mary Scanlon's restaurant. He looked up at the thick stars.

Elsie said, "Fine. Good. I see that you're..." She turned and pulled her sweatshirt on. When she stood up with her blue jeans in her hand, he stepped out into the mud and wrenched the canoe. Elsie tilted out.

The creek was chest-deep. She had trouble getting to the far bank; once she started to wade, her feet got stuck. She swam free and got a hand on the bank. She said, "Shit! Where are my pants? The key to the boathouse ... You asshole!"

He swam across. She started to pull herself up the bank by tugging on the solid spartina roots above her. He got his knees on a shelf of mud and grabbed her. She shoved him hard with her heel, but her shove made her slide back too. She dug her hands into the bank. She still slid belly-down into the mud, now awash with salt water. Dick pulled her sweatshirt up around her head and arms, held it with one hand like the neck of a gunny sack. He scooped mud onto her back, onto her butt, onto her legs. It spread like very thick paint, thick as toothpaste but black, even by starlight you could see it was black.

Elsie wriggled back out of the sweatshirt. She spun around and threw a handful of mud. She dug into the bank for another handful. He picked up her feet and twisted her over onto her front, holding her legs up like the handles of quahog tongs. Her arms sank into the mud halfway up to her elbows. He let her legs down and straddled her, slowly poured ooze onto her shoulders, the back of her neck. He reached over her shoulders and pulled a wave of mud under her breasts, under her stomach, up into her armpits. He unstraddled her and sifted mud onto the bare spots on the back of her legs, smoothed it out.

"Okay," Elsie said. "Pull me up."

He slithered his arms around her and raised her to her knees. She caught her breath, then stood up and slowly smeared his cheek. She unbuttoned his shirt and painted his chest. She pulled at the waist of his pants and ladled in a handful of mud. She said, "On second thought," and undid his pants and tugged them down. She smeared his legs.

"I see," she said. "You've been painting me black to make me disappear."

His pants were around his calves, his work shoes stuck in the mud. She yanked him over. He caught himself on his forearms so his hands didn't sink in but a couple of inches. She put her hands on his back, climbed over his shoulders on her knees to bog him down. She started to pack him with mud. He wriggled forward and raised himself on his forearms. She slid down his back. He raised his legs, trying to catch her between them, to snare her in the triangle of legs and furled pants. She squirmed sideways, slid off his legs. He curled around on his side and grabbed her leg. His hand slid down her calf as if her leg was an eel, but he got a good grip on her ankle. He pulled it back past his waist. He could hardly see her. She was disappearing like an eel in mud. They were both disappearing. His hands were blurred with fine mud. He put his free hand on the back of her other leg, trying to get his fingers around it so he could slide down to her other ankle. His hand slid on past the inside of her thigh, the last bit of paleness in the dark. His hand slid on into the cool mud, but on the top of his forearm he felt heat, which startled him as though it was light.

They lay still.

His feet were in shallow water. He felt the creek stirring against his feet, tugging his pants as it flowed by, pushing up into the marsh. He felt Elsie move. The outside of her thigh brushed his face. She slid toward him a little, onto the thicker part of his forearm. He lay his forehead on her as she rocked slightly, like a boat on a rippled pond.

He was giving in to her imagination now.

He hadn't known what he was doing before. (What had it felt like, all that tussling around? Just their outer shells . . . Like handling some guy you knew who kept popping off at you, but who was too drunk to fight? Like punishing a child?)

He turned his head so his cheek was flat against her. He could feel her muscles moving softly—her coming was more in her mind still; when she got closer she would become a single band of muscle, like a fish—all of her would move at once, flickering and curving, unified from jaw to tail.

His mind was half in hers. He felt her still loose-jointed drift—only an occasional little coil in the current tugging at her harder, moving her toward the flood.

The tide came all the way up.

He felt all of her pass into him through his forehead: the effort of her body as if she was swimming upward, then the uncurling as she stretched out to catch the break, body-surfing a wave bigger than she'd thought, caught in the rush.

He felt it—she had an instant of fear—he didn't hear it but he felt a bleat from her as though her lips were pressed against his opened forehead. Then she breathed—he felt her body move as if her mouth opened on all of him—she took a breath and let herself go tumbling.

After a while they moved up the bank as though they had to escape the flood. They clambered onto the table of higher ground, onto the spartina. He sat to untie his shoes, and Elsie clambered on his back as if she couldn't get enough of clambering. He got his feet out of his pants and made a bed of them for her on the long flattened stalks.

Everything was brighter than in the creek—all around them the even tops of the spartina caught flat shadowless starlight.

He reached under her back to smooth out broken stems. For an instant he felt her feel his body, felt her register him, his inner sounds, the outer wave of them pressing toward her. And then they both fell into their own urgencies, overlapping disturbances, like waves from separate storms, at first damping, then amplifying each other.

They lay still in their pit of gray light. Her cheek moved against his. He had no idea what her expression was now—maybe smiling, maybe recovering herself the way she laughed at herself after she cried.

She moved her head and kissed his mouth. It didn't make her clear to him. Pretty soon she'd start talking.

She stayed quiet, though. She wasn't coming back so easily. He caught one more feeling from the heavy stillness of their bodies. Both of them this time—no matter what silly game she'd started—

they'd both been caught and tumbled hard and carried this far. They were both stunned by sadness.

And then they had to get up and find their clothes, foolish people again. The blue canoe was still caught sideways across the creek. Elsie's sweatshirt was on the bank. Dick's paddle was in the canoe, but Elsie's had floated away, along with her jeans and the key to the boathouse. And the key to her car.

They left the canoe on the grass above the boathouse and walked back to Elsie's house. Elsie pulled the hem of her sweatshirt down to miniskirt length when a car drove by them on the point. And again when they scampered across the four lanes of Route 1.

Dick got into the shower with his clothes, got the mud cleaned off inside and out. The solar-heated water began to run out. Elsie didn't have a dryer, so she put his clothes in the oven. Dick picked up his unfinished glass of beer from the arm of the sofa. He felt dull about everything now. Dull but unfamiliar again. He felt a sliver of hope that everything here was so askew, so unfamiliar, that it wouldn't show noticeably in his general life.

*A*t last Dick got hold of Keith college-boy. Dick spoke to him agreeably and reasonably. Keith hadn't heard from Parker either, and agreed they shouldn't just hang around doing nothing, the boat doing nothing. They'd leave that night.

Charlie was pleased about going. Tom wanted to go too. May said no. Dick said to May that he'd gone out on a lobster boat when he was Tom's age. May said, "Not on one of Parker's boats. And not all three of you on one boat. No."

Dick told Tom, "When I get my boat in, we'll get you some sea duty."

Dick took the pickup to go get some more replacement pots. He was only half surprised to find himself jouncing up the dirt road to Elsie's, running in low so as not to jar loose the lashed stacks of pots.

Elsie was getting ready to go out to a garden party at her sister's. He told her he'd be at sea for a few days, going out this evening.

"Oh no," Elsie said. "I wish you'd told me."

Dick said, "I didn't know for sure until just now."

Elsie looked at her watch. She went to her curtained cubicle and got a red wool sash which she wound around the waist of her white skirt. She put on a pair of sandals, took them off, and put on a pair of high-heeled shoes. She looked at them, looked up, and asked Dick what he thought. Dick said, "Fine." Elsie took them off and said, "I wish you'd told me. I'm still on leave—I could have gone with you."

Jesus, Dick thought. But why did that surprise him?

Elsie put the sandals back on. She said, "I found out about a preventive for seasickness, but you have to start it the day before you go out. I'd love to go out again."

"That's up to Parker."

Elsie looked at the sandals. She said, "I know—I'll wear the sandals and borrow some decent shoes from Sally. You know, what I can't wait for is when you get *your* boat in. Maybe I'll quit Natural Resources and crew for you. I hope your bunk room's going to be nicer than Parker's."

Dick didn't know whether Elsie was serious. He said, "Parker's boat is the worst you're likely to see. Around here at least."

Elsie said, "Who *are* you going to get for crew? I mean for *your* boat."

"One thing at a time. It's not certain I'll get her in the water."

"I wish I'd known you were going," Elsie said. She tied a silk bandana over her head, pirate fashion. "What about this? Does it make my face look funny?"

"No," Dick said.

Elsie put on dangling earrings. She said, "And these? Don't just say fine."

"You look like a gypsy fortune-teller."

Elsie changed them for little pearl studs, straightened the collar of her blouse. "You're right, this is better. Do you wish you didn't have to leave? Why don't you tell Parker to wait a day?"

"The sooner I go, the sooner I get back. And you've got your party to go to." He held back from Elsie that Parker was up in New York. There was a crazy lurch to his life, there were people running loose all up and down the coast with secrets that could undo him.

Elsie said, "What time are you going out tonight? I could get back...."

"I'm taking Charlie this trip," Dick said. "I got to get him squared away. It's his first time offshore."

"Well, then, I might as well spend the weekend at Sally and Jack's."

Elsie packed a tote bag, crammed in her tennis gear. She slipped a wristband over the handle of her tennis racket and zipped the racket head into its pouch. She looked at herself in the mirror. She said, "This is dull." She took off the bandana, ran her hand through her hair. She got a lavender chiffon dress from behind the curtain and held it up in front of her. "What about this?" Before Dick said anything, she ducked back behind the curtain. She came out wearing the dress, holding the front up by its strings. "The only problem is it's backless and I'll stick to the carseat. I can always hang a towel over.... What do you think? Here, could you tie these things, they go behind the neck.... Not so tight." She stepped away from him. "Any strap marks? Or is it all tan?" Elsie turned her back to the mirror and craned her head around. "I guess that's okay. You're not much help, are you?"

She slipped on a bracelet, held up the long earrings to her ears. "What do you think? The dangling ones, right?"

"Yes."

The phone rang. Elsie picked it up.

"Oh, hi. No, I haven't left yet. . . . Well, sure, I could, but how will she get back? I mean, I thought I'd spend the night, if that's okay with you. If the problem is she can't find your house, she can follow me. . . . Oh. Well, then, she can drive my car back and I'll get home somehow. Doesn't Jack have to come look at the construction site or something? Or maybe she can stay over too. . . . Look. We'll just play it by ear. Do I have to call her, or . . . ? Tell me the number. . . . Okay. We'll be there. Bye." Elsie put the phone down and said, "Damn. Now I have to pick up that ditz who lives in Miss Perry's cottage. Do you know her? Phoebe Fitzgerald." Elsie laughed. "Her one claim to fame is that she got lost in the woods last year."

Dick said, "I know who she is. It was Eddie Wormsley found her."

Elsie laughed again. "Is that right? Is *that* right? Did Eddie say anything about her?"

"He liked her. He said she was kind of shaky at the time. I think he asked her out but she said no."

"Aha," Elsie said, "I can't wait to get her talking. Maybe I can put a good word in for Eddie." Elsie dialed the number. "Phoebe Fitzgerald? This is Elsie Buttrick, Sally's sister. Yes, that's right. I wasn't sure you'd remember. Sally tells me you need a ride. . . . Sure, no trouble at all . . . I know the house. Are you all set? Well, I'm not dressed yet, but I'll be along in, oh, just a little while."

Elsie hung up.

Dick said, "What do you mean, you're not dressed? You going to change all over again?"

"Maybe I will. Maybe this dress is too gauzy, just too helpless."

Elsie struck a pose, her body leaning to the right, her arms flung back to the left, palms up. Dick laughed. Elsie said, "A little too much fleeing nymph, know what I mean?"

Dick said, "You could strap your gun belt on, that might even things up."

Elsie laughed. Then she said, "I don't know, I guess it's okay." She took Dick's hands. "I was feeling a little bit wanton a minute ago. Now I just feel tender. And that makes me feel sad and weak. Know what I mean? I was getting ready to be ravished on the floor. Now I just want to be sure you'll come see me when you get back. Monday night? It doesn't matter how late. Or even Tuesday morning, just come wake me up."

Elsie leaned on his chest, her arms around his waist. Dick felt awkward and uneasy, his hands miles away from him, the thick pads of his fingers still farther away on the soft sliding of her back. Little Elsie Buttrick, fresh as paint. Great big Elsie Buttrick, on top of it all. But now there was a tinge of pain to her.

There wasn't a bit of satisfaction in seeing how all her dresses, her big black tennis racket, her Volvo, her solar house didn't weigh in for much. She was a little bit spoiled was all. The two of them were exactly the same kind of damn fool. But for some reason she was going to get more of the pain. He felt terrible about that.

She was going to get more of the pain, but he was going to sustain more damage. He wasn't going to stop just yet.

It was on his way out along the dirt road that he knew he'd got a fresh jolt from Elsie. All that about the clothes was silly. Maybe she'd done it to annoy him, but she'd done it just to be silly too. She wasn't careful with him. She wasn't careful with herself. He admired that—it wasn't as easy as it looked. Whoever she was at the moment, she came right ahead, swarmed right into him. Good for her.

He'd been about to blame her for his not working this last week. Wrong. And he'd been trying to work up a notion that he deserved this fooling around as recompense for all his bad luck. Wrong.

He didn't understand it all, but it was pretty clear that he'd been stuck for several years. He'd blasted himself loose. That's what he'd been doing all summer. Even that half-assed clam poaching. Going out with Parker, going along with Parker.

He'd been thinking all his thoughts as though he was still stuck—lodged in tight among the impossible banks, Sawtooth Point, everyone else floating free and easy, just him stuck. Wrong again. He was on his own. He used to think that bitterly, that he was on his own in the worst way, imprisoned up Pierce Creek by his father's failure, by the way everyone turned away.

He'd blown himself out of all that, without knowing what he was doing. Or maybe he'd known. But he'd damn well done it, and he'd better look out where he was going now. Adrift or under way, he was afloat on his own.

For years, the way he'd been good, the way he'd been an ill-tempered son of a bitch—both had been bound by habits or inheritances. He'd gone along set ways. He wasn't done with them yet, he wasn't sure he wanted to be done with them. Even wanting his own boat, wanting to be skipper of his own boat, was a set way. What was odd as odd could be was that now he'd put parts of his life into other people's hands—Parker's and Elsie's—outside of rules in either case, nothing but their fluid wills, he was on his own.

On the way out through the swordfish grounds Dick noticed that the water temperature was too high in some places, about right in others. He started checking the thermometer frequently. They didn't see any swordfish. They pulled and reset the pots and headed back in toward the swordfish grounds. The conventional wisdom has it that you don't see swordfish finning when the tide's running hard. No one's completely sure why, but it was handed down that way, like the optimum water temperature for finning, sixty-four degrees to sixty-eight degrees, though you hear some people swear by the lower and others by the upper end.

What Dick found was that there were narrow tongues of water the right temperature, strung along drift lines. These could have been upwellings of cooler water, and maybe some mixing as the set of the tide stretched them out. He figured if the swordfish hadn't left the grounds they had to come up to get rid of their worms, so they'd concentrate in the right-temperature water, the tide running or not. Worth a try.

Charlie spotted the first one. They'd scarcely hauled that one in when Charlie sang out again. The second one felt like three hundred pounds.

Charlie sang out a third time toward evening, but whatever it was disappeared before they got to it.

Charlie said, "I'm pretty sure. Looked too high to be a shark. I'm—"

"Okay, okay," Dick said, "I believe you. You go back up tomorrow. We'll stay out another day."

Charlie said, "You'd better tell Mom."

Keith laughed. Dick looked at him enough to shut him up and then showed Charlie how to use the VHF radio to raise someone at the Fishermen's Co-op. "Okay," Dick said. "Now, what are you going to say?"

"I say, please telephone May Pierce and tell her we'll be late 'cause we're into a whole mess of swordfish."

"Jesus!" Dick said. "This radio isn't a goddamn telephone. Everyone listens."

Keith laughed. Charlie was laughing too. "I know *that*," Charlie said. "I was *joking*, Dad."

Dick grunted. He said, "Well, what *are* you going to say?"

"I say please tell May Pierce our estimated time of arrival is Wednesday."

"Good. That's fine."

"I'm sorry, Dad, I thought you'd know I was—"

"I don't know what you know and what you don't know. So when I ask you something, you just tell me plain."

"Okay. Sorry."

"It's okay." Dick felt foolish, and still irritated. But there was an echo—it was partly hearing Charlie say "May Pierce," the funny way that hung in the air. It was also that Charlie was feeling good enough to get sassy. In an uncomfortable way, all this pleased Dick.

At dawn the tide was running more or less the same pattern as twelve hours before. A few patches of fog, but clear enough. Charlie spotted a fin right after breakfast. Dick couldn't see it. He headed the boat where Charlie pointed, and after a minute Dick made out the fin.

When they hauled it on board it felt like another two-hundred-pounder. That was it for the morning. But three in sixteen hours—sailing up these tongues of cool water was like wading up a stocked trout stream. Dick had Keith come down to take the wheel. Dick brought a cup of soup up to Charlie in the crow's nest. "You aren't tired, are you?"

"No."

"Well, watch yourself. You know what they say—one hand for the boat, one hand for you."

"I know, Dad."

"Okay. We're making money now. So I just don't want..."

"Dad, you're getting worse than Mom." Charlie put his sunglasses on. "What is it, anyway? I'm doing okay so far."

"Yup," Dick said. Charlie looked strange to him here, his eyes narrowed behind the glass, his face dark and hard under the visor, behind him the blank sky and sea. Dick said, "You're doing good. You got good eyes."

Charlie turned away. The praise made him look young and soft again. "Remember what I told you," Dick said. "Don't look hard all the time, let your eyes unfocus, then—"

"I remember," Charlie said.

"Okay. Finish your soup so I can take the mug down."

Charlie laughed. He said, "It's weird, I never realized how alike you and Mom are."

They got another fish before supper, smaller, under 150 pounds. Dick was tempted to radio the Co-op to check the price, but he didn't want to tip off any other boats. They could lock on to *Mamzelle* with their RDFs in the minute or two it took to talk to the Co-op.

Nothing more that day. Dick wanted another day.

After supper he took Charlie with him to check the lobster in the live wells and to see that the swordfish were iced right.

Charlie asked him what was the most swordfish a boat had ever brought in.

"When I was with Captain Texeira, we got twenty fish in eleven days. That's the most I've ever heard of. Next trip out we got nine in two weeks. The trip after that, nothing. And nothing for the rest of the season. That was the summer you got your bicycle."

Charlie touched the hole in the swordfish.

"But I'll tell you," Dick said, "I'm making more money off of these four than I did off of those twenty, even though I was the one that stuck all twenty. And if I were on my own boat, I'd make more off of two than I will off of these four or those twenty. That's how it works. I knew that all along, but I never paid enough attention to the arithmetic."

Charlie said, "Did you ever miss? I mean, when you were on Captain Texeira's boat."

"Yeah," Dick said. "Five men and the skipper watching their shares go down-a-down-down. Pulling that slack line back in . . . But I made a worse mistake than missing—I didn't keep my mouth shut. I blamed the man at the wheel."

"Was it his fault?"

"That's not the point. It's the captain's place to say. Or not to say. You can *look* at the guy who screwed up, you might even have a little talk in private. You don't sound off in front of everyone."

Charlie nodded. Dick added, "That's not so likely to be a problem for you. You've got more good sense than me. I mean me when I was as green as you."

"But *was* it his fault?"

"He came in too fast, but I should have stuck that fish anyhow. You sure you understand what I just told you?"

"Sure," Charlie said, a little carelessly for Dick's taste. Dick worried that he'd praised Charlie too much for one day.

Charlie said, "When are you going to show me how to use a harpoon? If we see a skilley can I try?"

"I'll show you this winter. You got to practice before you try on something live."

Charlie said, "I have practiced *some*."

"No," Dick said. "You got enough other stuff to learn this trip. Anyhow, your mother said to keep you out of the skiff, and she wouldn't like you leaning out of that bow pulpit any better."

Charlie didn't say anything. Dick saw his face close over, not in a sullen way, just go blank. He was a good-looking kid. Dick was surprised how much Charlie looked like May. Charlie turned and went topside. Dick stayed below, caught by something in the dim light. May's face more than seventeen years back, in the same kind of bad light. He remembered where—the hospital corridor, taking her to see his father. May's face plain and broad. A solid woman at twenty-two, not a girl. Willing to take on his trouble. Without any nonsense, willing to go back to the dark, cold house in Snug Harbor. Her hands were warm from her wool mittens, which she left with her wool hat and scarf in the front hall. She still had her coat on when she turned down his tufted bedspread. The two of them pale and dry and hot against the salt damp in the house. He'd felt she was a lot like him, a lot like the slow serious parts of himself that he thought were okay. She didn't have his temper, thank God for that. She was patient and stubborn, she could wait out his temper. Now he thought for the first time of what she'd do if she found out about him and Elsie. She wouldn't leave him. She might go off for a bit, but she wouldn't leave. She'd stay, but she wouldn't forgive him. She wouldn't turn the boys against him, but she'd make him take it out of himself week by week, day by day, until he was as clean as her kitchen floorboards, mopped every day, scalded and steel-wooled every Saturday. He'd told her it was no way to treat wood. She paid no attention where she had the upper hand. She'd hold a hard mortgage on him, one that might outlast the two on the house.

But that wasn't the worst. There was a good part of her that settled for the way their life went, and there was another part, maybe smaller, but still part of her, that couldn't help looking for the weakness in him. Even faced with his infidelity, she wouldn't say it right out, but she'd think, I always knew there must be a reason why you don't rise. He'd be able to read her mind. It would be in her, stuck in her, a lump of contempt. She would still go to bed with him, the food wouldn't be any worse, she wouldn't even keep him from going to the Neptune.

No outburst, no keeping him on a leash. She'd do it worse, she'd accept it.

Before he went topside to take the wheel, Dick looked around the dim hold. He might as well not keep Charlie at sea any longer. Give May that at least. Even if they got extra lucky with more swordfish, May was right. He'd never get his boat in the water working Parker's boat for him.

Dick sent Charlie up to the office to collect for the swordfish and lobster, while he and Keith hosed down *Mamzelle*. Dick wanted the kid to see the deductions for bait, fuel, and dock fees, to see what a crew member's share of all that swordfish and lobster looked like after deductions. How the boat's share got the owner just about half of everything without his even being there.

Dick said to Charlie, "If Parker'd been along, he would have a right to another share for being skipper. You see how it usually goes?"

Charlie was too pleased. Dick sent him back up to the office to get some small bills. Dick made up an envelope for the household, both monthly mortgage payments and a little extra for groceries. "You understand that in summer we get off easy because of your mother's garden. And summer we get free clams and flounder."

Charlie was still pleased. Dick let it go. He said, "Well—it was a good trip. You earned your way."

Charlie asked Dick to hold on to his share, put it toward Dick's boat. Dick said, "It's your money, Charlie."

Charlie said that he'd just as soon get it back when Dick's boat was in the water making money. Before Dick could say anything, Charlie added, "And I don't want to make Tom feel worse for having to stay home. If he sees me with all that money . . ." Dick let that go too. Charlie was high from a good trip, nothing to worry about with that. And that Charlie transformed his own excitement into eager good will . . . Dick didn't want to knock that down either.

They tossed their sea bags into the bed of the truck, Charlie with a little flourish that made Dick laugh. Charlie hitched his trousers and strode around the back of the pickup. The kid had a little roll and swagger to his walk. Dick stopped himself from saying, "Don't bump your head getting in."

Charlie gave May the household envelope. She made a fuss, got into a better mood than Dick had seen her in for months. She started fixing a big breakfast, and Charlie started talking to her about the trip, day by day.

Dick went off to take a hot shower. He could hear May oohing and ahing.

He turned the water on. He understood his pleasure at Charlie's pleasure, he understood his uneasiness and his urge to bring Charlie down some. What Dick didn't understand was the feeling of bleak despair that hit him now. Here he was flush with two thousand bucks, more than half of it unquestionably his. Flush with a good haul of lobster and swordfish on account of good luck and his knack. It was his marked charts, not Parker's, that they'd set the pots by. His measurements and reckoning that got them into those swordfish.

And there was still a chance Parker would show up from New York and pay him.

He was closer than he'd ever been to fitting out his boat. Time was short, and the list of things he needed was long—there was the loran, five thousand bucks. And then a depth finder, a bilge pump, another payment on the engine. The pieces of equipment and what they cost tumbled through his head as clear as ever. But it *wasn't* that. It was something else he couldn't bear. It wasn't worry or too much work or even facing pain. It was as though he was suddenly weakened by a causeless ease. Something already in him was shifting loosely and lightly. It wasn't a temptation to give up, but a sensation that he already had.

It wasn't until he'd eaten his breakfast—May and Charlie were still having a pretty good time at their end of the table—that he squeezed down on himself.

He got up and said, "I'm going to see Miss Perry. Talk about money."

May looked up. She looked alarmed.

May said, "What . . . ," cleared her throat, and started over. "Have you thought about how to put it?"

"I'm going to do something you want me to do," Dick said. "Don't get fussy about how I do it."

Dick pulled into Miss Perry's main driveway and then the side drive to her house and into the white-pebble circle around the enormous weeping willow. Dick got halfway around the little circle before he saw Elsie's Volvo, parked with its nose sticking onto the flagstone path to the back of the house, its tail out so far in the circle he couldn't get around without tearing off pieces of weeping willow.

Jesus, he thought, Elsie too.

He marched up the steps to the front door and rang the bell before he could start thinking about it. It was Elsie who opened the door.

"Good God," she said. "Dick. Where have you been?" He took a breath in. Elsie said, "And what are you doing *here*?" Dick let his breath out. Elsie said, "Look, this isn't a good time. I mean, it was very clever of you to figure out I was here, but this just isn't a good time. I'm going back to my house in a little while. Say a half-hour."

Dick said, "I came to talk to Miss Perry."

Elsie said, "Oh."

"Is Miss Perry in?"

"Well, yes. But this isn't a good time. She just got back from a doctor's appointment. It's a little bit complicated."

Dick said, "Is she sick?"

"It's her . . . you know, her annual spell."

"I thought that was more toward the end of the summer."

Elsie said, "Well, yes. It usually is. But I've been—or, I should say, her doctor and I have been—trying to talk her into taking a drug, and all our talk seems to have upset her. Look, can you come to my house in a half-hour? Or maybe you can just go over there now. Just go on in. I'll be back, and I'll explain it all then. She'll be glad you called on her. I'll tell her."

"I came to ask her to lend me money."

"Oh." Elsie stepped back. "Oh dear. I don't know. Look, I've got to arrange some things. Captain Texeira's coming over, and then the doctor's going to call, so why don't you go on to my house. I'll see you there."

Elsie closed the door. Dick stood there. He felt too reckless and lightheaded to feel he had shamed himself, but he could tell he was going to feel shamed. He got back in his pickup. When he got to the crossroads of Miss Perry's lane and the dirt road, he stopped. What was the point in going to Elsie's house? But, then, what was the point in going home?

When he got to Elsie's house, he sat in his truck and smoked a cigarette. He lit another but put it out. He went into the house.

He felt odd being there alone. He was glad to feel odd, it kept his thoughts from settling. The scarlet curtain was drawn back from around the bed, the bed unmade but not messy, just the near corner of the covers flapped down, two pillows on top of each other.

The sun was bright on the little pond and on the slant of the greenhouse roof.

On the table by the window there was a plate with a wet peach pit and a coffee mug. A letter addressed to Elsie, several pages covered with handwriting on both sides. Next to it a tablet of paper and a pen. At the top of the page only "Dear Lucy" in Elsie's writing.

These pieces of interrupted activity made the house even more charged with stillness.

Elsie didn't come in a half-hour. Dick waited. He was made uneasy by the peach pit and the unmade bed. He threw the peach pit in the trash and tucked in the bedcovers. He sat back down at the table by the window. He let his mind go lax. Nothing here in this bright room. The sun moved across the pond, across the slant of glass. Now his thoughts began to settle. What had he done? His face felt cold, but busy with sensation. He'd blurted out how he needed money. Why did that feel so bad? He'd made himself more naked in front of bank officers, in front of Joxer Goode. The difference was that with those people he had an argument. They stood to gain if they used him shrewdly. Neither Miss Perry nor Elsie really knew the argument. They weren't fighting for advantage.

They didn't set themselves out as being in business. Going to them was begging. There it was.

Dick thought he'd leave. Maybe write a note to Elsie saying he'd changed his mind. He felt weightless again, as though he'd been cut loose and might end up anywhere. Was this what Parker felt like all the time? Was this what it felt like to be a player? Or did you find yourself feeling like this and that's when you had to decide whether you were a player? Parker wasn't tied to anyplace or anyone. That part was how Dick felt now, but the difference was Parker wasn't scared so much as dizzy about it. Once Parker started moving dangerously, he thought it all out. And Parker grinned. That was a difference too.

Dick thought of Parker's grin. He saw it clearly. For the first time in all the years he'd known Parker, Dick noticed there wasn't quite enough flesh between Parker's nose and Parker's upper lip. No wonder Parker had paid to get his teeth fixed, even before he paid to fix his boat. Parker couldn't help that grin. Was that how it worked? Parker was just born with that short upper lip and couldn't help living up to it? Or had that lip shortened up a hair's breadth with every quick trick Parker pulled? With every sly dollar he conned from tourists, insurance companies, his crews of green college kids? Captain Parker's Pep Pills for Sleepy Sailors.

Dick stopped. What was he up to? Blame it all on Parker? Dick had always known how Parker lived. If he'd gone along with Parker, it was because there was a piece of him that wanted to be just as sly. Dick couldn't claim he caught that disease from Parker. He'd gone poaching clams all on his own, no matter that was small potatoes. And the way he felt about banks, if he could have robbed one without inconvenience, he just might have.

And it had been Dick's idea to get Schuyler on board and stick him with the bill for the spotter plane. That was pure Parker, and Dick had done it.

As for Parker's drug run, Dick had balked at that, but he'd gone ahead. And to be honest about that, he had more worry that Parker was going to stiff him than he had remorse. Goddamn right. He couldn't get any more mortgages on what he owned, so he'd taken one on his being a free citizen. No interest, but lots of penalty.

But mainly here he was fooling around with Elsie. Parker didn't have a thing to do with this.

With every minute of waiting, Dick saw more and more clearly how Elsie was linked to every piece of his life. To his father's land, and even to his father's death by that odd condolence. To the bright rich people who now inhabited his father's land by the salt pond—Joxer, Schuyler, the whole clambake. To Natural Resources, for God's sakes. To Miss Perry. To his own sons. Dick remembered Charlie's startled look of longing at Elsie's legs when she'd whipped off her skirt to go swimming.

Charlie's dreams might be full of Elsie—Miss Buttrick to him. Charlie's puppy love merging with Charlie's first spasms of billygoat anguish. Banging his head on a tree for sweet Miss Buttrick, for her complete sweetness as she bent over him at her ecology class, her sleeve touching his hand as her finger touched the powder on a butterfly wing. Gritting his teeth at night, thinking of the terrible things he wanted to do to Miss Buttrick's body, imagining with equal and simultaneous shame and pleasure Miss Buttrick saying "No, Charlie," Miss Buttrick saying "Yes, Charlie."

Dick cringed. He didn't want to get that close to that part of Charlie.

But the thought of Charlie clung to Dick's mind; Dick's actual pleasure—accomplished not ten feet from where he now sat—seemed pale by comparison with Charlie's dreams.

Dick was finally getting rid of Charlie's daydreams when Elsie came in the door, down the two steps. He stood up. She put her pocketbook on the table. One hand on his shoulder, she kissed him shortly. She said, "I thought you told me you'd be back day before yesterday."

Dick thought of what to say—"We got into some fish" was answer enough for anyone—but the sight of Elsie in a blue seersucker woman's suit, dressed up as soberly as if she worked in a bank, and Elsie's face cocked to one side in such a perfect imitation of a wife waiting for an answer, not May, not May now, not May ever—this was an affronted wife out of someone else's life, someone wearing a suit and a tie to match her suit, someone who would say, "I'm terribly sorry, darling—I got tied up at the office" —all this was so far from Dick, so far outside what he'd just imagined, that Dick was popped right out of a straight answer.

He felt himself slide back into himself, reinhabit his body, from his vacant face down to his wide feet in his tight good shoes. He looked up to Elsie's face, still cocked, her chin stuck out, her forehead furrowed up. When she folded her arms across her chest, he started to laugh.

He tried to stop. Elsie said, "What's so funny?"

Dick shook his head. Elsie said, "It's the whole thing, is it?"

Dick said, "That's right," and sat down.

Elsie said, "You son of a bitch."

"It's not the whole thing with *you*," Dick said. "It's everything right now."

"You liar," Elsie said. "You think you can get away with anything because you still think I'm just a spoiled brat."

"You're wrong there," Dick said. "That's just one thing I think you are."

"You asshole!" Elsie wasn't out-and-out screeching but there was some screech to her voice. It struck Dick as odd that Elsie was losing it. In all his set-tos with yachtsmen, bankers, and such, Dick had been the one to lose it. The other guy may have been mad too, but it was Dick who lost it. Just now he'd been a little riled, but he didn't want Elsie to lose it.

"Aw, come on, Elsie. I couldn't use the radio, for God's sakes. The operator at the Co-op is nosy as hell. And Charlie was on board, remember how close by everyone the radio is? I know I said I'd be back, but if you get into fish, you—"

"I don't give a damn about your calling in. Though I'll bet you could have thought of something if you'd tried just a little. You could have sent some innocent message, you could have asked if I still wanted a basket of lobsters even if you were going to be late."

Dick said, "I'm not too good at thinking up things like that."

"But what is rude, what is unspeakably rude, is your sitting here going har-har-har like a big oaf! I come in, you've been gone nearly a week, and you laugh in my face."

Dick said, "I wasn't—"

"And in fact the first person you go see is Miss Perry."

Dick said, "It's hard to explain. I was—"

"I'm sure it is," Elsie said. "In that case you could at least have had the grace to lie and say you were looking for me."

Dick didn't try to say anything.

Elsie said, "Do you know what Captain Texeira does when he gets back to port? He phones Miss Perry. If he comes in late at night and can't call, he leaves flowers. She finds a little flowerpot on her front step and she knows he's back safe. And he named his second boat after her."

Dick was afraid he was going to laugh again. Flowers. Him and Elsie Buttrick arguing about flowers. He got up and walked to the window, looked down at the pond.

"I don't have one boat, let alone two. I'm not sure I'll ever be the kindly soul Captain Texeira is, even if I do." The pond was glaring, exposed as muddy by the midday light. Dick said, "I told you why I was going to see Miss Perry. I can tell you too that I don't want to. I'm going 'cause it's rock bottom. It came to me this morning when I got in. This trip I did as good as I could hope for, I had as good luck as I could ask for, and it ain't enough. If it was just me,

I'd give up, I'd salvage what I could from the goddamn boat and beg for a job. That's what May would have wanted a year ago. *Now* she wants the boat in the water because she says I'll be poison to her and the boys if I give up. And she's right. I could bring myself to sell off the boat, but I couldn't do it cheerfully. Even if I got fifty or sixty thousand for her, that money would evaporate. If I back off now, I won't ever get a boat. So I'm willing—just barely willing—to go begging to Miss Perry. I knew this morning, if I didn't do it that very minute, I wouldn't ever do it."

Dick heard Elsie moving around behind him. After a while she said, "Let me get this straight. You want a loan."

"That's right."

"You're not begging. A loan isn't begging. I know you went to Joxer Goode—"

"Joxer Goode is a businessman. He stood to gain. But even talking to *him* I felt I was stripping myself naked. I'll tell you something I don't like to remember. Joxer asked me about collateral, and after I'd listed the house and truck I said, 'There's my eighteen-foot skiff and there's the boys' little skiff.' "

Elsie said, "I don't get it. What's so bad about that?"

"Jesus, Elsie. It was like I was going into the next room and coming back with the boys' piggy bank. It's the boys' boat. And it was so . . . puny. Joxer's a decent enough guy, so he didn't laugh. Not to my face at least. But there I was in front of him, turning my pockets inside out. I might as well have been taking off my damn pants, I might as well have said, Go on and take the boys, take May. They'll pick crabs for you, they'll clean your house. . . ."

Elsie said, "I don't think he saw it that way. I understand how you feel—"

"Do you?"

"Yes, I do," Elsie said. "Goddamn it, I do. And it's wrong of you to think I don't."

Dick turned around.

"It makes me mad," Elsie said. "The way you think of me. You should have made this clearer to me before now. Much clearer. Either you think I'm a moron, or you don't trust me. I know things, for God's sakes. I built this house, I live on a salary. And I'm trustworthy." Elsie pursed her lips. "I'm not perfect, but I'm trustworthy." Elsie suddenly deflated. She said, "I know it's complicated. I mean, we *are* having an affair and that's always more than anyone imagines. . . . And I'm tied up in odd ways with all sorts of people you might not trust—there's my brother-in-law for one, building his dream resort for the right people on Sawtooth Point. He's not a bad person but . . . One thing I've always felt is how unfair it is that my family just swooped down on Sawtooth Point. And now my sister and brother-in-law are doing it again. I've always felt my family owed you something. And I understand how hard you've worked. I feel guilty. I can even imagine that it might make you angry to come here and see this house."

"No. Jesus, Elsie, I don't hold your house against you. And if your father bought land from my father, that's their business. My old man needed the money. And it was later when he sold the rest of the point. Once he knew he had cancer, he was scared they wouldn't treat him right if they thought he couldn't pay his bills."

"It's funny—these last couple of weeks I've softened up a lot. I've never laid around so much in my life. I've never spent so much time in bed."

Elsie cocked her head. "Is that so? Sloth and lust drive out anger and envy. So what does that make me? Some siren luring you to a doom of pleasure in her enchanted cave?"

"No."

"Do you want me to start nagging you about working on your boat?"

"No."

"Do you think we should stop? I mean, do you think there's some correlation between our affair and your not working on your boat?"

"No."

Elsie said, "You always get so gloomy when I ask you questions. Submerged swamp Yankee. But it does you good, you know. On a scale of one to ten, how guilty do you feel about sleeping with me?"

Dick said, "Jesus, Elsie."

Elsie laughed. "Isn't our little spat cheering you up? It does me."

"Come on, Elsie. Don't just fool around. I've screwed everything up. I've blown it all into the air. Every goddamn thing."

Elsie sighed. "I suppose I should be a comfort to you. The problem is, every time we get all cozy and tender, we don't have sex. But go ahead. This is my last good deed of the day, though. I've spent all morning driving Miss Perry to her doctor and back." Elsie took off her jacket, sat down on the sofa, and said, "Come on over here." She took his hand and held it between hers on top of her knees. "Tell me one thing that makes you think you've fucked up."

Dick shook his head, but went ahead and said, "You know most of it. I just told you about why I don't want to go to Miss Perry."

Elsie said, "I'll tell you about that in a minute, that's not out of the question at all." Elsie reached up, stroked his head and said, "Something else."

Dick leaned back and said, "I think Charlie's got a crush on you. While I was waiting here I couldn't get it out of my head that he spends time dreaming about you."

"Oh. Yes. I see." Elsie cocked her head. "Don't worry. He may have a little sneaker for me but it's tiny. And I think he has a girlfriend in school. But no one will find out about us. You don't have to worry, it really is all right."

Dick let go. He thought he might regret it, it might be games to her. But the effect of her saying "I know, it's all right" was too much relief to resist. He told her he was the one who'd dug the clams from the bird-sanctuary beach. "I know. Don't worry." He told her he'd once smuggled coke in his boot. He told her he'd done it again. Recently. "I know," she said. "That's probably why Parker and Schuyler went to New York."

"I didn't get paid."

"Don't do it again. You'll be all right if you don't do it again. It's good you didn't get paid. That's all right."

He told her about the detective on the dock, the dog, the whelks. "Jesus," she said, drawing in her breath, "don't try *that* again." She laughed. "Whelks!" She said, "It'll be okay. Parker's got enough sense to let Schuyler do it his way. Schuyler probably sells it where he plays squash."

As she said "squash" soothingly, Elsie took Dick's head between her hands. "You really are miserable," she said. "You really do feel just terrible."

Dick had never imagined such indulgence, such soothing, indulgent pleasure.

Elsie pulled him toward her so he lay with his head in her lap. She smoothed his forehead with her palms, closed his eyelids.

Dick said, "I sometimes feel like I'm caught already. Like there's a whole other force nosing around, nothing clear or smart about it, just a bunch of dumb sharks, they can't see anything, but they're nosing around."

"I know, I know," Elsie said. "But they're not after you. Believe me, you're not what they're after." She smoothed the furrows in his forehead with her fingertips. She said, "And Parker won't sell you out. He might use you and cheat you, but I'm sure he wouldn't ever turn you in."

"It's not just that," Dick said. "I'm all spread out, everything can go wrong."

"It won't," Elsie said. She kissed his temple. "It's going to be all right. Really. May doesn't have a clue, I can tell. You're going to get your boat and be busy. You and I will be friends. You'll see. Miss Perry is going to lend you the money. It's all set."

Dick said, "What?"

"Maybe I shouldn't have stuck my nose in, but there wasn't a lot of time—she's going into her depression. You don't have to go see her."

Dick started to get up.

"Not yet," Elsie said, putting a hand on his chest.

"No," Dick said, "Jesus, Elsie . . ."

"It's all right," Elsie said. "I know I should have checked with you, but it's set now, and I want you to let me help. Miss Perry wants to do it. We talked with Captain Texeira, who came by, and he said you're good, that your boat's a good investment. She's going to lend you ten thousand. You pay back a thousand a year plus ten percent interest. And I'm going to lend you a thousand that I borrowed from my brother-in-law."

Dick was silent. It was tumbling on him. He wasn't surprised, it was part of the way things were going, more invisible force disorienting him, dislocating him.

"The reason she's doing this," Elsie said, "I mean apart from her deciding it's a perfectly good kind of investment—and of course her liking you—is that she wants things to be in good order around here. And her idea, somewhat feudal though it may be, is that you ought to be able to maintain your family's place in the community. So."

Dick shook his head. Elsie put her hand on his forehead. "I know it's not exactly the way you'd like it. But that's the deal."

Dick had been feeling a drugged pleasure at Elsie's reassurances. That was gone now. But his attention didn't come right to the present, not entirely. He had a moment of fear as complete as he'd had on the hummock in the salt marsh lying flat beside the skiff. It wasn't that he thought of himself as a criminal, but that there were people in uniform who thought he was. They knew someone was hiding in the salt marsh. They wanted to know his name. Once they had his name, that would be it. He imagined an office, a desk, a sheet of paper with his name on it. There was a force there—in the office, in the desktop, in the paper. The force wasn't in the truth or not of what it said under his name. It was the power of duplication that terrified him—office after office, desk after desk, paper after paper. The power of his name on those papers to draw him to office after office . . . It wasn't a fear of a trial or prison, it was of the tedium of plastic chairs, each chrome foot on a square of pale linoleum, square after square, pale brown, pale green, gray.

He stared at Elsie. Her sharp, tan face, the white collar of her blouse, the single-pearl earrings. Lipstick for her morning with Miss Perry and the doctor. A navy-blue velvet ribbon pulled her dark hair back from her high forehead and made her look like a nice young girl.

Elsie's forest-green uniforms were all on clothes hangers for the moment, her .38 revolver shut up in the chest of drawers next to her jewel box. Her red bathing suit was hanging by one strap on a hook by the shower, the backless party dress on the same rack as her uniforms. What did Elsie think of the undertow in those linoleum-tiled offices? It wouldn't scare her, it was another game she knew how to play.

Elsie said, "I promise you this is all for the best." She put her hands on his shoulders. She smiled and said, "Say something."

Dick brushed her hands away and sat up.

Elsie said, "You sometimes make things harder than they have to be."

"You're right," Dick said. "That's one thing different between you and me. I make it hard. You make it easy. For you it's almost nothing at all."

She said, "Oh, for God's sakes."

"I'm being dumb," Dick said, "I can see that. I'm being a pisshead. It's just going to take me a minute."

"No, you're right in a way. I see it's not as simple as . . . I see I've been very forward about it, and you're right to resist. I mean, especially if I gave you the idea that I did it because I felt guilty about my father's buying your father's land or because you saved my life. Or, God knows, if you think the main effort of your life is suddenly in the hands of a couple of women—I'm trying to see this from your point of view, you understand—a couple of women who don't really know anything about boats." Elsie sat up square on the sofa. "But one thing Miss Perry and I both know is that Joxer Goode would have loaned you the money if his freezer hadn't broken. So why can't we step in? Especially since Miss Perry got some advice from Captain Texeira."

Dick nodded but didn't say anything. He was having a hard time concentrating on how reasonable she was being.

"And Miss Perry and I both know this is just the last little bit. Just the last tenth. Less than a tenth, if you count all your labor. Do you understand that Miss Perry and I aren't just . . . jumping in blind?"

"Yeah," Dick said. "I can understand that part."

"And this is a *loan.* No one's giving you anything. You'll have to pay it back." Elsie laughed and poked his knee with her forefinger. "Miss one payment and Miss Perry and I may just repossess your ass."

Dick moved away from her touch. He jerked to his feet. He stopped at the plate-glass window. He would have left the house, but he couldn't turn around to face her.

She said, "Oh, Dick—"

"Don't talk."

He was trying to disconnect what was driving him away from her. Her last little jolly joke. Her flock of reasons. He could see her telling it all to Miss Perry—and Captain Texeira. That too. He couldn't hear her voice, but he saw her hands moving, the lapels on her jacket moving like gills. Her face shining with her good deed. Maybe when she asked her brother-in-law for a thousand she'd been dolled up and half naked in her backless dress.

He knew that was terrible. He knew he was being disgusting.

It was the two of them who had mixed everything together. She was caught too. Maybe she was trying to get clear and this was the way she knew how.

He shook himself, breathed through his nose. Now he was angry because he couldn't think straight. His anger eased off. He felt depression come in and flatten his anger.

"Well," Elsie said, "I can see you think I've done something wrong."

Dick said, "You wouldn't tell your brother-in-law's business to someone else. You wouldn't try to do his business for him without his say-so. You wouldn't tell people what kind of trouble he's in. But someone who was last seen earning a few bucks fixing a clambake for the gentry, why, anything at all you can do for him, he ought to be pleased."

"That is just so wrong!"

Dick turned to face her. He said, "No. Maybe it's not so simple as that for you. Maybe the complications make it hard for you to see it as plain as that. I shouldn't boil up about it either. There's so much else mixed in."

"So much else to get mad about?"

"No. You know what I mean. I see how you've made some efforts so your life doesn't just stick close to shore. Some of that's just for your own fun. But you aim to do good. I see that."

Elsie looked down and straightened her skirt across her knees. "I'm . . . I really don't dare say anything." She folded her hands in her lap, her eyes still down.

Dick couldn't believe he'd ever slept with her, so trimly rigged out in blue and white.

At the same time he had a sharp sense memory of her—his face over hers, her clenching her jaw, breathing fast and shallow, then going rigid with a hiss that frothed through her teeth.

Elsie looked up at him, looked him over. He felt the knot of his tie on his throat, his shirt collar riding as high as the lowest razor scrape. His scrubbed hands stuck through the ironed shirt cuffs.

Elsie stood up. "Look, Dick, I may not have arranged it perfectly. . . ."

Dick said, "The thing is, I pretty much have to go along. On account of May and the boys."

"Well, there you are," Elsie said. "It does come down to that."

A t Miss Perry's door for the second time that day, Dick was impressed with the stonework. The doorway was round-arched, made of gray stones rough-hewn to the size of bricks, except the keystone, a handsome wedge the size of a loaf of bread.

Dick said out loud, "Christ Almighty," and rang the bell. A nurse in a navy-blue jumper opened the door. Dick told her his name. She said, "Just a sec," and left him in the front hall.

Dick had been in the house before, but the clearest memory now came from when he was seven. Because he'd been scared that time too? He recognized the walking sticks with carved heads hanging in a rack on the wall. He looked down at them. They had been at eye level then. They had terrified him. The Indian head, the bulldog with red garnet eyes, the eagle's beak. The relief of the plain ivory handle. The blackthorn topped with a two-humped gnarl, yellowish in the fissure. It had been most terrifying because it was trying to be something, caught half alive under the layers of shellac.

The nurse came back and led him into the house. Miss Perry was in the library lying on a sofa, a thin wool blanket across her legs. Her glasses lay on her chest. Her white hair was pinned up, as usual, but was untidy. Even in the dim light Dick could see her eyes were red.

"Please sit down."

Dick looked around, found a straight-backed chair. The curtains were drawn across the tall windows on either side of the fireplace. At one narrow end of the room there was a bull's-eye window high above the bookshelves. The outside shutter was closed.

"I'm afraid you see me at my worst."

Miss Perry's voice was so low Dick could scarcely hear her. He started to move his chair closer, but she raised her hand. He sat down again.

"I don't like to see people when I'm this way."

Outside it had been a hot day. Here the air was cooler, but motionless. Dick began to sweat.

Miss Perry said, "Elsie and the doctor want me to take a drug. '... let me my senses in Lethe steep.' That is a line from Webster. Neither Elsie nor the doctor understands why Lethe is terrible. I quote Webster. Webster is morbid, melodramatic, inferior to Shakespeare. But Webster is apt for the way I am. Webster is glittering and unwholesome. I should get him out of my head, but I can't. The trouble with Webster is that he didn't meet life head-on the way Shakespeare did. His plots are full of drugs and potions. 'Sweetmeats which rot men's nostrils.'"

The nurse came in with a tray. Miss Perry said, "Would you like some tea?"

Dick said, "No thank you."

"No tea, nurse, thank you all the same."

"It's all made. I'll just put it down."

Miss Perry closed her eyes. "This is like Elsie. Elsie has become insistent too." Dick winced.

The nurse said, "Let's just give it a try. If you don't like it, I'll take it back out, but I bet you end up liking it." She left.

Dick felt terrible for Miss Perry. He'd been momentarily baffled by her talk about Webster—he'd thought it was the Webster who wrote the dictionary. When he got clear of that idea, he saw what she meant. It also came to him that he'd never heard her be rude, he'd never heard her complain. For that matter, he'd never heard her talk about herself at such uninterrupted length. She'd always seemed to have a built-in conversational timer—it was as though a bell rang in her head every so often and she'd cock her head and switch over to asking about May and the boys or how the lobster season was. But now . . .

And there was that remark about Elsie—it sounded like Elsie had pushed the old lady hard about taking pills. And maybe about the money.

Miss Perry looked at the tea service. She said, "I suppose it *is* teatime." She pushed herself up to a sitting position and poured two cups. She eyed a plate of little sandwiches. "And what are those? I have no idea. Do you know what those are? What's *in* them?"

Dick ate one. "It's crab." He held the plate out to her. "It's fresh. Maybe Joxer Goode's back in business."

Miss Perry shook her head, took a sip of tea, and leaned back. "I feel like such a child. I simply can't do anything. I'm absurdly exhausted without having done anything."

Dick cleared his throat and said, "I'm sorry you feel so bad."

"Each year I say to myself it won't happen, and then I simply let down. I don't go to pieces. I simply let down."

Dick could see that. He felt some sympathy, which he knew was useless. He had no business being here. His being here was just making Miss Perry struggle. She as much as said she wished he hadn't seen her like this. He wished he hadn't seen her like this too. Her naked eyes were bleary, unfocused, unguarded ... worse than unguarded—feebly guarded. The way she looked was like the way she talked: signs of distress but no signal he could respond to. She wasn't crazy, she could see what she was like and she would remember it.

Another painful thing was how *almost* herself she was. It was like standing onshore and watching a boat just getting into trouble. Her bow still rose to the waves, you could see signs of life, someone at the wheel, someone moving on deck, but she wasn't right. You could imagine she'd fouled her prop or her rudder or lost power. You could imagine, but you couldn't tell. And you couldn't help. You could hope she'd get help, or better yet recover herself, but all you were was one of the gawkers. You'd seen her graceless, even if you kept your mouth shut.

Miss Perry said, "Elsie was to drive me to church this morning, but she sent for the doctor instead. I must let her have her way sometimes, I suppose." Miss Perry's face was turned toward the back of the sofa. Dick saw that she was really talking to herself, or that she would rather be talking to herself.

Dick was angry with Elsie. And then angrier with himself. What had got him in here was his own distress. Elsie's part was only that she'd told Miss Perry about his trouble, told him about Miss Perry's. Elsie, with all her young and easy sympathy, thought that trouble was just trouble; she had no idea how heavy the sense of fault was, and how heavy the shame of being seen.

Miss Perry rang for the nurse. Dick got up and said, at last, "Thank you. That's what I came to say."

Miss Perry didn't speak for a moment. Then she said with some difficulty, "I am afraid that I have already reached the point at which conversation is too perplexing. I'm sorry...."

Miss Perry was distracted by the nurse, who came in and began to put their teacups on the tray.

Miss Perry said, "Please don't do that until I ask you." She turned to Dick. "Please go away. You must come again." She was out of breath. She said hoarsely and fiercely, "But not now. Now you all must go." She tucked her head down to one side and pushed her hands at them.

When Dick and the nurse got to the walking sticks, the nurse said, "Don't take it personally." The bulldog head, the bulbous gnarl of the blackthorn. He felt a fear of Miss Perry's illness. And a simultaneous revulsion from her body and his, as if he'd bludgeoned her.

*D*ick stopped at the end of Miss Perry's driveway. This time he turned away from Elsie's house. He drove home and walked into the kitchen. May looked up. Dick said, "Miss Perry will do it. She's lending me the money." There it is, Dick thought, I've closed the circuit. No way to turn it off now.

He sat down and covered his eyes with his hand. He felt dizzy and undone. May looked up. She came over and touched his shoulder. "You'll pay it back. She's a nice woman, but you've earned your way. You'll make it good."

Dick felt May's power. He wished he could receive it.

He said, "There's another thousand too. Elsie Buttrick wants to lend it."

May tilted her head. "It's not a whole lot, is it? But it's something."

"It was Elsie Buttrick went to Miss Perry and set up the ten thousand. Miss Perry is just into her spell. Elsie's the one in charge of looking after her this year."

"That's good," May said. "When do you think you can put your boat in?"

"Depends. If I can get the loran without too much wait. If I can get Eddie to help with the wiring. If I can use the boatyard to launch her. Another week or ten days."

May nodded. "And when can you start work with her?"

"Depends. If Parker agrees that half the pots out there now are mine, on account of what he owes me. And if I can buy out some more from him—then I'll have pretty near a thousand pots out there to start with."

Dick got up and looked out the back window at the shed. What he'd just said to May sounded strange to him. It was all reasonable, but he didn't feel connected to it. The boat, the engine, now seemed less physically true than when he used to see them in his dreams. His resolve then had been bright and sharp. The boat's lines had cried out to be made whole. And the spurts of anger every time he went out in his skiff past Sawtooth Point—they'd helped.

Could it be that he'd gone to bed with Elsie Buttrick because she was part of Sawtooth Point? Because she was one of the Buttricks, the Perryville School, the life of tennis courts and sailboats that had overgrown the point, squeezed him up Pierce Creek to an acre of scrub? Of course, it had squeezed him into a concentrated purpose too.

When the boat was half done, he'd been the boat's other half. Now the boat was almost whole, he'd hoped he'd feel whole. He didn't. He'd got himself into all this mess.

May said, "Call the boys in, would you? They're down at the wharf. Supper's ready." When he didn't move right away, she touched his shoulder again. "Dick. Maybe you don't know how hard it was. Maybe you thought it was just giving in, and so you thought it'd be easy. Going to those people and getting money is work. You have a good supper and a good sleep, you'll be all right."

Dick said, "I'll get the boys."

A North Star loran. Five thousand bucks. Eddie Wormsley looked over Dick's shoulder as he wrote the check on his account at the Wakefield bank. Elsie had called once to get his account number, and again to tell him the ten thousand was deposited. The dealer went into his back office to call the bank. He came out all smiles. It was Eddie who thought to ask for help with the hookup. The dealer agreed, he had a man free.

Eddie also came with Dick to buy the radio. Eddie was having so much fun it carried Dick along.

By the end of the week they'd spent the ten thousand on the loran, VHF, RDF. The sonar took the swordfish money. They got the stuff hooked up. The antennas, along with the topmast and crow's nest, had to wait till they pulled the boat out of the shed.

Eddie was with Dick when the boatyard manager came to talk about launching. All three of them walked out to the shed. Dick held the plastic sheet aside. The manager stepped inside and said,

"Jesus H. Christ!" Eddie laughed and stamped his feet and said, "You're goddamn right." Dick said to the manager, "You think you can move her?"

"Goddamn," the manager said. "That's just fucking amazing." He bobbed his head down. "I didn't do you a bad turn, then, laying you off."

Dick said, "I never held it against *you.*"

The manager walked around her, checked the cradle and poppets. "We can do it. So long as you don't mind what happens to the shed."

Dick said, "No. The shed don't matter."

"Okay. We can do it. This'll be the last piece of business for the marine railway. You'll have to arrange something over by the state pier in Galilee if you want her hauled after this. I got a new boatmover but it can't haul you, big as you are. Just yachts from now on. I'm tearing out the old rails."

Eddie said, "So you'll put Dick's boat in for old times' sake?"

The manager looked sideways at Eddie, then back at Dick.

"I'll do right by you. I got to make it a job, but I'll do right by you. We'll do it Monday. I got yachts coming out every day from now till mid-September, but I'll fit you in Monday, for old times' sake. It'll still be four men and the use of all that equipment."

Eddie said, "We could keep the cost down if Dick and I—"

"No," the manager said, "my insurance is only good if I use guys on my payroll."

"How about if you could use some piles," Eddie said. "I got some I cut this past winter—big straight ones, size of phone poles."

Dick said, "I'll take care of it, Eddie. I got some more money in the hole."

The manager left. Eddie said to Dick, "I know he's going to need those piles. If he runs the bill up on you, we'll stick him for the piles come October."

"Yuh."

"Look, Dick. You're all set with this, right? You don't strike me as feeling as pleased as you might."

"Yuh. Maybe I'm tired. Maybe I don't think it's all there yet. Maybe when I see her in the water." Dick made a little effort. "Look, Eddie. You've done a lot of work for me."

"Not that much," Eddie said. "I'm glad to see things work out. These last couple years, I've been doing okay. I wouldn't want my luck to turn."

Dick knew what he meant—if you don't help out, it shows up sooner or later. Dick thought that might be why he himself was feeling so skittish. He'd been pretty much living for his own boat. He couldn't count helping out Parker, he'd been in that for the money—whether he got the money or not. He couldn't count hauling Elsie out of the drink—he'd turned that into something he sure as hell couldn't call helping out.

Eddie said, "Well, then. See you Monday."

"See you Monday, Eddie."

Dick called Elsie again Sunday evening. He'd talked to her the two times on the phone, but he hadn't been back to her house all week. Now she made it easy for him.

She said, "I ran into Eddie Wormsley yesterday. He told me the two of you were up to your eyeballs putting in all that stuff you bought. Look, I've got your other check here. Do you want me to drop it off or will you come by? Why don't you come by?"

"Yes," Dick said. "I'm at home now."

Elsie said, "Ah."

Dick said, "When's a good time to pick it up?"

"Right away would be a good time."

Dick looked around the kitchen. The boys were setting the table, May was at the stove. "After supper," he said, "if that's convenient. How's Miss Perry?"

"Fine," Elsie said. "No. She's not fine. I'll tell you about that later. It's no worse than usual, at least that's what the doctor says. How are you?"

"Fine," Dick said.

Elsie laughed and said, "Fine. We're all fine. Come over."

Dick cleared his throat. "It turns out I will need the money after all, so I'm—"

"Dick, hey, Dick," Elsie said, "just come over."

"All right," Dick said and hung up.

When Dick said he had to go out to pick up some more money, Charlie asked if he could come along. Dick said no, because after he picked up the money he was going to look in at the Neptune to see if Parker was back.

May said, "Parker? I thought we'd be shed of Parker now."

"I told you I got to see him about the pots. What you boys can do is make sure the way is clear for when they show up with their rig. They'll be here first thing tomorrow morning."

Charlie said, "What do you mean, Dad?"

"What the hell do you think I mean? All that junk in the yard—the bait barrels, the sawhorse." He couldn't think of anything else. "I want all that junk out of the way," he said.

Charlie said, "We can do that tomorrow."

"You do what your father says," May said. "And I don't want you going to the Neptune anyways."

Tom said, "Charlie's too young to go to the Neptune."

"You'd better pick what's left of the corn and tomatoes," Dick said to May. "When they make the turn to back that rig in, they may have to run over the south end of the garden. You boys help your mother with the garden."

Might as well go all the way, Dick thought. He pulled out onto Route 1 in front of a station wagon and got honked at when the pickup misfired. The station wagon swung round him and passed. Dick worked the gas pedal twice, sped up, and passed the station wagon on the right. He cut into the left lane in front of it, then slowed down to get into the left-turn lane. The station wagon honked again, a fading blare as it went away toward Wakefield.

Make it perfect, Dick thought. Be dumb-ass sullen with Eddie, a son of a bitch to May and the boys, leave them working, go off and topple Elsie one more time and take her money too. Along with the old lady's when she's out of her mind. Perfect.

As he went up the narrow lane to Elsie's house, he knew that in some cracked way he meant it straight. Tie it all up. Make it as bad as could be and leave it all onshore when he took the goddamn boat out.

*E*lsie seemed to know what he felt like. She'd made a dent in a bottle of wine before he got there, and she poured some more for the two of them with a sloppy flourish. She drank off half of hers, put her glass down, and stuffed an envelope into Dick's pants pocket.

"Before I forget," she said, "my rich brother-in-law has some advice that goes along with that. It's his money after all. He says you shouldn't sign your boat up with Joxer Goode. He thinks Joxer's not going to make it."

Dick said, "The halfway-decent ones don't do too good with money, do they?"

"It seems that way. But you'll do fine. You'll be all right on your own now."

"Yuh."

"Don't be hard now. We'll have a bottle of wine tonight. Tomorrow I'm going on the wagon. I'm going to devote myself to Miss Perry for one more week, and then I go back into uniform. And you're off to sea in your brand-new boat." Elsie patted his arm. "I have some advice for you too. Be cheerful, be blithe." Elsie laughed.

The sun was lowering and turning red. It shone under the crowns of the tall trees and under the eaves of the side porch. The long sideways light picked out the half-empty bottle, the glasses, the polished wood. It flickered on Elsie's face and hands as she picked up her glass of wine and brought it to her mouth through a bar of sunlight.

The room was as bright as a county fair.

The pond was in shadow, black and distinct down below the glitter of the greenhouse roof. The near shore and the big rock were vague in shadow.

They both looked down at the pond for a while. They kissed in a tired, restful way. Elsie laughed, shook her head, and tugged him by the hand to go for a swim.

They didn't stay in the water long, but it was almost dark when they got out. They stopped to look at the moon, almost full. Elsie dropped her clothes in the middle of the room and picked up her glass. He could just see it move, a piece of light in the near dark. Her body was as darkly distinct as the pond.

She seemed fuller and softer than ever before.

It was hard to tell distances in the dimness, so it was a surprise when he reached her with his outstretched hands. Her skin was cool, a little dispiriting. Her lips and tongue were warmer, spongy and acid with lukewarm wine. She put her arms around his neck and began to dance slowly, tugging herself up on her tiptoes. She said, "You don't mind if I'm a little sloshed, do you?" She began to hum along to her dancing.

She turned her head sharply. He heard a car an instant later. The headlight beams popped through the side porch. Elsie said, "Oh shit," and rummaged for her clothes in the dark. Dick got his pants on just as there was a knock on the door. Elsie said, "Just a minute, who is it?"

"It's Mary. Mary Scanlon."

Elsie said, "Coming," and turned on a light. "Just a second, Mary." She looked at Dick, who was stuffing his shirttail into his pants. She turned again when she got to the door and waited while he buckled his belt. She gestured to him to sit down and opened the door.

Mary Scanlon, all in black, stood at the top of the three steps, looking taller than Dick had ever seen her. She towered over Elsie. Mary's face looked pale and bony under her black hat. Her face was set in a way Dick had never seen. He stood up, half-expecting Mary to denounce Elsie and him.

Mary said, "Oh Jees, I'm sorry. I didn't mean to barge in." Her face slowly became puzzled.

Elsie took her by the hand and said, "Oh, Mary, I'm sorry. I called last week, but . . ."

"I've been up at the hospital the whole week. The funeral was yesterday."

"Oh, Mary, I am sorry. How's your mother?"

"She's okay. My brothers are staying on a few days. I thought I wanted to be alone, but when I got this far I couldn't face it, so I thought I'd drop by."

Elsie took Mary's hands, guided her down the last step, and hugged her. Dick put his hands in his pockets, and ran into the envelope. Elsie led Mary to the sofa and sat down beside her.

Mary looked up and took Dick in. "My father died."

Elsie said, "Are you tired? Would you like a drink?"

Dick said, "I'm sorry, Mary."

"He was good about it," Mary said. "He was really good about it. Part of it was that the cancer spread to his liver and they say that's painless. They say it even makes you euphoric. And he hated being old, so..." She turned to Dick. "But you've been through all this. And it must have been harder for you, you being an only child, and your mother already dead when you were just a kid."

Dick felt pinned by the turn of her sympathy toward him.

They sat in silence, Mary the most composed. Elsie asked again if Mary wanted a drink. Mary turned down the wine but asked for a short whiskey. She said, "Am I the only one?", so Dick took one too, with a beer chaser.

They sat in silence again. Dick felt the power of Mary Scanlon's gray gaze changing the air of the room, like the first cold day of fall, a fair warning. He felt the justice of her coming to put an end to his desire for Elsie. Dick said, "That was how Elsie and I got to be friends, when she came to the boatyard to say she was sorry to hear about my father."

"No, that wasn't it," Elsie said. "I had my schoolgirl crush long before that."

Mary looked at Elsie. "Even then."

Elsie said, "Even then what?"

"Even then you were taking up with us micks and swamp Yankees."

"I don't see why you go on seeing me like that."

Mary smiled. "Okay, okay—you're just one of the guys. I guess it's seeing your sister and that husband of hers come over here in their coach and four to survey their domain. It reminds me you didn't start out just folks."

Dick thought, This is more like Mary. More like having a beer with her while she took the paint off someone at the bar.

But this was Elsie's house. Elsie looked unhappy and fragile curled in her corner of the sofa, her hair wet, her eyes squinting into the light from the standing lamp behind Mary. Dick got up and turned the shade away. His attention went back to Mary. He felt he should do something more for Elsie, but he couldn't.

Mary took off her hat, and said, "I haven't been to mass for years. Except for funerals. Maybe it's my middle age, but I'm beginning to like it again. We all went to mass again this morning."

She laughed. "One thing the old man said . . . I guess it was a couple of days before he died. My mother got this priest to come see him, a young priest, just a kid. But my father disapproved of deathbed confessions. Too easy. So the old man says he's not going to confess. But the priest hangs around, tells a few stories, and gets the old man talking. The old man tells a few stories himself. The priest says, 'Well, Mr. Scanlon, you've had a pretty good life.' The old man says, 'I have.' And the priest says, 'But there're probably a couple of things you feel sorry for.' The old man says, 'There are.' So the priest tries to finish it off, he slips in, 'Because they offended God?' The old man lifts his head up and says, 'No. Because they offended *me!*' " Mary laughed and looked at Elsie, who looked terrified. "Oh Christ," Mary said, "maybe you had to be there."

Dick laughed. Mary looked at Dick, her gray eyes growing wider and brighter. He could see why she'd scared Elsie.

Mary said, "Or maybe you have to be Catholic." She laughed again. "One time my father was working in an office, when he was a salesman for the lace company. There used to be a lace mill here in South County, made lace as fine as any in the world, won a gold medal at the Brussels fair. Anyway, my father used to do this Gallagher and Sheen routine with another salesman standing around the water cooler.

" 'Say, Mr. Gallagher?'

" 'Yes, Mr. Sheen?'

" 'I hear the new Pope's got all the cardinals on their toes.'

" 'Now, how'd he do that, Mr. Sheen?'

" 'He raised all the urinals in the Vatican.' Ba-da-da-dom. No, wait. So they all laughed, all except this one young secretary. My father turns to her and says, 'I'm sorry, dear. Didn't you think that was funny?' And she says, 'Oh, I'm sorry, Mr. Scanlon, I don't know what a urinal is—you see, I'm not Catholic.' "

This time both Elsie and Dick laughed. Mary sighed. She said, "It got to be a family joke. If someone was being dumb, the old man would say, 'I'm sorry, I'm not Catholic,' and we'd all break up."

"How old was your father?" Dick said.

"Eighty-four. My grandfather got to be ninety-eight. My grandfather came over in time to fight in the Civil War. My father was drafted in World War I and got shipped all the way back across the Atlantic to France. So I suppose I'm lucky I got here at all, what with a famine and two wars. I had a cousin who got killed in World War II, but by then I was safe on first.

"My father was the tail end of his family, and I'm the tail end of mine. My brothers all have white hair, for God's sakes. The oldest one just retired from the Navy. And I remember my grandfather from when I was little, and he was in the Civil War. My father remembered twenty-dollar gold pieces, when that was a whole payday." Mary laughed. "At mass one day—just over here in Wakefield—they passed the collection plate and my grandfather reached into his pocket and tossed his penny in, you gave a *penny* in those days. Just as the plate reached the end of the row, he realized he'd put in his twenty-dollar gold piece. He started to reach for it, but my grandmother pulled his arm back. He whispered to her what he'd done, and then she started pushing him to get up and get it back, but by then the collection plate was going up the aisle like a bride to the altar. My grandfather said out loud, 'No, Mary. I gave it to God—and to hell with it!' "

Mary laughed and looked at Elsie. Elsie laughed. Mary poured Dick and herself another shot. Mary said, "One thing that was nice about this last year was the way the old man's childhood came back to him. He'd always talked about his life as a young man— being in the Army, working for the lace company, the mills closing, having to start all over, having to move to Pawtucket. Hard-times stuff. But this last year it was all the stuff when he was a little boy. He remembered these hills here when they were pastures, filled with sheep.

"When he was a little boy he had a crush on the prettiest girl at the mill. Mabel O'Brien worked a treadle—pumping away all day, her skirt hiked up to her knees, her calf muscles swelling under her white stockings. She had three bastards by three different men. We think of that time as repressed and intolerant, as though sex got invented in 1960, but there's Mabel O'Brien, and she went to mass every Sunday with her three boys. The old man remembered her at the Saturday-night parties. It was lovely how clear the old man saw Mabel O'Brien's legs. Working the treadle or prancing around the O'Briens' big kitchen on Saturday night. I'd go to the hospital and sit while he and his roommate would watch the Red Sox game. The old man would take a little nap and then wake up from a dream—almost all his dreams were of his childhood here. He saw Mabel O'Brien's legs, of course, but everything else clear as day too. When he was eight he used to collect the men's hot lunches from all the wives—the Irish workers lived at the top of the hill in company houses—and he'd load all the lunch pails in a barrel he'd nailed to his sled, and just as the noon whistle blew he'd shoot down the hill, his legs wrapped around the barrel, his face freezing in the wind where he peeped around. He'd coast up to the door of the mill, and the men picked out their lunch pails and let him come inside to get warm, and they'd all talk a blue streak. There was no talking allowed during work, so they were all busting. He heard their voices in his dreams—most of them still had brogues in those days. And he remembers them not being able to stand still after being stuck at the machines. They'd arm-wrestle and dance and challenge each other to walk on their hands. My father's father was famous for being able to jump over a dye vat from a standing start. My father saw him do it. He'd crouch down and disappear behind the vat and suddenly there he was flying through the air. I'd always thought the mills must have been hell, but when my father was dying it all seemed paradise to him. The way he talked, it was as though he'd never known anything since. He'd wake up from his nap and tell me about his sled shooting down the hill. Near the end he only felt hot or cold in his dream memory. And even taste. He dreamed of the first time he tasted maple syrup. None of them had ever tasted it. Someone gave them a bottle. They'd never seen it. His mother gave it to him as cough medicine until someone showed her how to make pancakes.

"And Mabel O'Brien, he adored her. They used to have parties in the O'Briens' kitchen, just up the hill from the house he lived in. After the dancing and singing they'd tell stories. It was mostly ghost stories, you know, a man out alone at night and he hears a banshee. Terrified the old man, he was only six or seven at the time. One night he stayed later than anyone in his family, and he was scared to go home alone. Mabel opened the back door for him and the light from the oil lamps shot out along the snow right down to his own back door. So he started running down the beam of light from the open door and he could hear Mabel's father shouting, 'For God's sakes, shut the door, Mabel!' But she kept it open. 'Shut the door, Mabel, we're perishing!' But Mabel held on till he got safe inside his own house." Mary leaned back and put her hands over her eyes. "You know, it's not so hard that the old man died at eighty-four, though I'm sad enough for that. But it's him as a little boy I see. It's Tommy Scanlon, running down the path alone, little Tommy Scanlon, scared of the dark."

Mary began to cry. Elsie put her arm around Mary. Mary pulled out her handkerchief and blew her nose, then she got up and poured herself another shot. Dick got up, and she poured him one too. She slipped off her shoes so she wouldn't be taller than him, put her glass down, and held on to him hard.

Elsie said, "Are you a little jealous of Mabel O'Brien? I would be."

Mary laughed. "Sure I am. But she never knew how he adored her. And look what she did for him at the end."

Mary sat back down on the sofa. She made room for Dick between Elsie and her and patted the cushion. "She must be dead now. She was ten years older than the old man."

Dick squeezed in. "What happened to her?" Dick said. "Her and her three boys?"

"I don't know. Her father died, and she and her mother raised the three kids. She kept on till the mill closed, but what happened after that, I don't know. Oh. Her mother worked as a maid for one of the few lace-curtain Irish families in town. So one time Mrs. O'Brien—Mabel's mother—came into the parlor to clean up, and the daughter of the family and two girlfriends of hers were smoking cigarettes. Mrs. O'Brien said, 'Shame on you girls. Nice girls don't smoke cigarettes!' And the daughter said, 'How can you dare to say that to me, Mrs. O'Brien, when your own daughter has three children out of wedlock!' And Mrs. O'Brien says, 'That's a different thing altogether! Mabel loves children!' "

Mary laughed, and it brought some color back to her cheeks, but at the same time she began to sag with fatigue. She finally leaned over toward Elsie, who put an arm around her.

Elsie said, "Spend the night, Mary. There's a bed on the porch. We'll have a good sleep and a good breakfast, and then we'll go down to see them launch Dick's boat."

Elsie took Mary's glass from her hand, and walked her to the sleeping porch. She sent Dick out to get Mary's suitcase. Elsie took it in to Mary. Dick sat and listened to the two women talking softly. Then Mary passed through in her nightgown, her red hair straight down her back, her toothbrush in her hand. When she came back out, she gave him a kiss that smelled of toothpaste and whiskey.

Mary went to bed. Elsie came out. She sat beside Dick on the sofa, one leg curled under her. She finished Mary's whiskey and blew out a long breath. She said, "I can't tell if she's okay or not. I don't know what it's like."

"He was eighty-four," Dick said. "She seems pretty clear about that. And she's here with you."

Elsie nodded. "Is the way she was the way people are at wakes? All those jokes? Was that a wake?"

Dick laughed. He said, "I'm sorry—I'm not Catholic."

"Don't tease me," Elsie said. "I feel very odd."

Dick was touched by Elsie. He took her hand. "Maybe you're being too good again, feeling like you're becoming Miss Perry."

"Not as good as all that," Elsie said. "I was about to screw your brains out when Mary came in."

Dick shook his head. He still wasn't used to her talking like that.

"It wasn't just jokes," Dick said. "You can tell she liked her old man."

"That was nice, the story about Mabel O'Brien," Elsie said. "I think I'd rather be as nice as Mabel O'Brien than as good as Miss Perry."

Dick laughed at Elsie's getting herself in the story somehow. Then he felt bad for her again. He said, "Maybe you are."

"Why'd you laugh?"

"Here you are all grown up and you're like a kid worrying about whether people think you're nice."

Elsie looked suspicious.

Dick said, "You're nice—you don't have to worry."

"What I'd like is for you to like me even if I'm not nice," Elsie said. "That's one of the things I like about Mary. She just likes me whether I'm nice or not."

"Well, sure," Dick said. "That's not so hard."

Now Elsie laughed at him.

"I made you a little boat-warming present." She got up and gave him a package. He opened it. It was a thermos bottle done up to look like a White Rock soda-water bottle.

"Thank you. I can use a thermos."

"Look at the White Rock girl."

Dick held the thermos out under the lamplight: the White Rock girl—kneeling on her rock, bare except for a little wisp of a skirt, and little dragonfly wings on her back.

"You don't see?" Elsie said. "Look. That's the pond. That's the rock. And that's me."

"Jesus, Elsie."

Elsie laughed. "I made this myself. Used an old label, put in my picture and used photo offset. It looks like the real thing, doesn't it?"

"I guess it does. Where in hell am I going to keep this?"

"On your boat."

"Jesus, Elsie—I don't know."

"Look—if *you* didn't recognize me, who will?"

"Who took the picture?"

"Oh, for God's sakes, Dick. Just tell me I look gorgeous."

"You do. I don't know though. I'm going to have Charlie and Tom on board sometimes."

"They won't be able to tell."

Dick looked again. "I guess that's right."

"But *you'll* know it's me," Elsie said. "Oh. Do you mind if I shoot some film tomorrow? I've still got Schuyler's camera here."

Dick was struck by how agile she'd suddenly become again. It was as though she was making herself the way she was with him before. It had crossed his mind that she might want to go outside with him, find a nice spot in the grass, damn the mosquitoes, full speed ahead. The idea had struck him, but he was relieved it somehow didn't seem likely now.

He didn't know whether he should speak plainly. He wasn't sure she understood their sleeping together was over with. He didn't dare ask what she thought. He was still bothered by the thermos— he looked at it again, a nice thermos, glossy with thin, even coats of varnish, the picture label set in nicely. The whole thing had taken some work.

"I really like this," he said, "even though I don't see where I'm going to fit it in. Do you see what I mean?" He put the thermos down and took her hand. "Jesus, Elsie, I don't know what to do about all this. I could give up the going-to-bed part, but then what? There's something I'm going to miss. I don't want this to be like the one time I went to the West Indies. But my life is going to be on pretty regular courses. If I come up here to see you, there's a chance I'd just float right up to you again. That day I picked you up in the rain I wasn't planning on anything. I don't say I hadn't taken notice of you. But suddenly there I was."

Elsie laughed. "Yes," she said. "You're a sweet man sometimes."

Dick shook his head. "There's two things I swore I'd never do. One is be caretaker for a summer house, the other is mess up my family."

"You haven't done either one. You went along with what May wanted when you borrowed money from Miss Perry and me. You know, even if May found out about you and me, I'll bet her chief complaint about you would still be that you've been bitter, jumpy, pigheaded, and generally impossible. As marriages go, that's about par for the course. And as men go, you're not so bad. If you get a little nicer and more cheerful now that things are picking up for you, May'll be okay."

"You're pretty damn free and easy."

"I know," Elsie said. "And that's not even the worst thing about me."

Dick laughed.

"Don't worry," Elsie said. "No one's going to know. I'm going to be the soul of discretion."

"But what are we—"

"We'll see," Elsie said. "Whatever it is, it won't be bad." She got up and walked him to the door. She came out to his truck. He put the thermos in the glove compartment and sat, hanging on the steering wheel. Elsie leaned in the open window.

She said, "Maybe we'll be like Miss Perry and Captain Texeira." She stuck her head in and kissed him briefly. She said, "We'll see. We'll both be around for a while. You go on home and dream about launching your boat. I'll come and take pictures. Around noon, right? It'll be okay, I'll bring Mary."

As he drove down the narrow driveway he saw she'd whirled him around another way. He'd as much as said it was over. He especially felt the weight of his remark about Elsie and him having wired into each other when his father died, a remark that had slipped out but that he'd considered so light as to be secret to himself. He now heard it as so heavy and doltish that he jammed the brake on with disgust. No way Elsie hadn't finished the thought for herself: And here's Mary fresh from *her* father's funeral to snip us apart. Elsie at first had protested, she'd said no, her schoolgirl crush started before that, before he knew anything about it. And yet she'd gone on to agree with him in some way, had gone on to send him home. And now he could feel himself turning, felt a pull that whirled him as neat as a wrestler's trick.

He switched the engine off. It didn't matter whether he was

making it up. When he said she was good, she'd said no, she was about to screw his brains out.

If he'd been paying attention when he drove off, he might have seen her stop at the front door, her hand slow on the knob, just touching it. If he'd turned the motor off then, she would have turned.

Now she'd be brushing her teeth. Or finishing off her glass of wine. Maybe pacing the room. Maybe stepping outside once more, going down to the pond in her bare feet.

Dick walked back up the driveway, staying on the grassy crown so he wouldn't make the gravel crunch. When he got to Mary's little pickup he carefully skirted it, stepping along the edge of lawn, moving slowly so as not to rattle the forsythia tendrils that just touched the side of Mary's truck. When he turned to face the house, he saw the lamp on the sleeping porch was on. Just turned on? He couldn't see very clearly. The waist-high planking cut the lamp from direct view. The overhead moon shone down bright enough to dazzle the screen mesh. He moved beyond the forsythia, stopped behind a new-planted hemlock, still shorter than him. Mary was awake, he heard her voice. He saw Elsie leave the sleeping porch. He could wait until Mary went back to sleep. No. Elsie came back. She sat down beside Mary's bed. He heard a scrape of chair legs. He could make out Elsie's head through the screen. He started to leave, decided to wait until Elsie left. At this point all she had to do was turn her head to see him scuttling away.

His ear became accustomed to the insect drone, and he could make out Mary and Elsie talking about some friend of Elsie's, a woman who'd been married to Jack Aldrich before Jack married Elsie's sister.

The mosquitoes began to find Dick. Served him right.

Elsie's voice. "... Lucy had an IUD all along. Jack's an asshole in some ways, but he didn't deserve that. The poor man was probably worried about his sperm count."

Mary's voice. He couldn't hear what she said.

Elsie said, "Oh no. He wouldn't do that. They make the man beat off in a Dixie cup. Anyway Lucy told *me,* after their divorce. But she still wouldn't tell Jack. Lucy and I had a big fight. I told her she was a really hideous liar. She said it wasn't a lie, she just hadn't told him *anything,* and apparently he never asked, at least not directly. I haven't ever had a fight like that with anyone else. I've quarreled with my sister, but that's nothing. I have fights with Jack, I've told you about some of those, fun really. But I still feel terrible about Lucy Potter. So of course *now*, irony of ironies, *now* I get a letter from her. She's getting married again. Wants me to be a bridesmaid."

Mary's voice.

Elsie said, "Well, sure. But the irony is that it's the mirror image. If it's true."

Mary's voice.

Elsie said, "I'll tell him sooner or later, sure. That's not the issue. Or, rather, it is the issue. Sooner still leaves a choice."

Mary's voice, loud enough for Dick to hear the words—"Oh, Elsie! Absolutely not! Don't even think—"

Elsie said, "Don't get mad at *me.* I'm not the one to convince. If . . . I mean, it's all if. If I am. If I tell him right away."

Dick understood that Elsie was pregnant. No if.

Her talk of adopting, her plan with Mary Scanlon. Her brightening up at the Mabel O'Brien story. And what was this about Elsie's friend Lucy Potter? He didn't figure that, but he didn't need to.

From his crouch behind the hemlock he sank to his knees. Jesus H. Christ. He wasn't as angry as he thought he might be. Elsie hadn't lied to him yet—maybe that was it. He hoped it was a girl. There was that thought, quick as a shooting star.

But right away he felt the punishment of that: they wouldn't be father and daughter.

He sank back on his heels and felt the envelope crinkle against his thigh. So what was that? A fee, a goddamn stud fee. Sly Elsie Buttrick. So the Buttricks could buy that too.

For a moment he was on the edge of tearing up the check. Or walking up to the porch.

He heard Mary Scanlon laugh.

He crushed a mosquito with his forefinger under his earlobe.

Trust Mary Scanlon to see the joke.

Mary was sitting up in bed now.

Elsie said, "I could apply for maternity leave, but then they might be able to fire me for moral turpitude. I'll talk to a lawyer. But I think that the best thing is to pretend it's adopted. That takes care of my career, and it would make things easier for Dick. I could go stay with my mother in Boston for the last five months. I'll apply for educational leave, enroll in some courses. You could have this place to yourself for a bit. And you could look after building the wing for yourself."

"Sounds nice—a few months in Boston," Mary said. "Suppose you meet someone in Boston and suddenly decide to get married."

Elsie laughed. "I don't think so."

Mary said, "Have you ever thought of getting married just to give the kid a name? Then you could be a divorcee."

"I don't see any likely candidates. Besides, I want the baby to have my name."

"What if Dick wanted to marry you? I mean get divorced and—"

"Oh no," Elsie said. "He wouldn't do it, I wouldn't want him to. I don't want that, I don't want this child to start out by ruining someone else's life. As it is now, I don't think anyone's going to get hurt."

"Maybe not," Mary said. "The kid will be a bastard. Maybe that's not being hurt. If Dick doesn't find out, that seems hard, but I guess you could argue he's not hurt. You could tell him it's adopted, but he's not a dummy, you know. . . . Or suppose you tell him. What then? Suppose he says get an abortion?"

"No," Elsie said. "I'm pretty sure he wouldn't. But I'll have to see. I can't imagine what he'll *feel* like. What do men feel like? Suppose I tell him I picked him—won't he be flattered? Isn't it a good deal for a man? No diapers, no grocery bills. His genes getting a free ride."

"Elsie. I don't think it's that easy, Elsie."

Elsie's head sank below the screen, then came up again slowly.

Elsie said, "But you're still game? You'll still be the godmother? Move in here with us?"

"Sure," Mary said. "We'll give the kid a nice home." She laughed. "You know what some guys are going to think, just the two of us living out here in the woods? A couple of middle-aged dykes."

"Let 'em. It'll keep the riffraff out."

Mary said, "My social life isn't so good I can afford to keep the riffraff out."

"Oh, Mary," Elsie said. "Don't be absurd. You're gorgeous, you're smart, you're funny, you're a great cook. And when you're managing Jack's restaurant, you'll be meeting all sorts of people. And you'll have this nice house to bring them home to."

"Yeah, sure. Life begins at forty. Look, I'm not complaining. We'll have a good time. But before you go adding a wing to your house, maybe you should make sure the rabbit died."

"I've got a doctor's appointment next week. But I'd like you to move in anyway."

"We'll figure all that out," Mary said. "Right now I'm really bushed."

"But you'll come with me to the launching?"

"Oh yeah. Dick's boat. Sure, if it's not too early."

"Noon." Elsie's tone still hovered and soared, as if it was all a breeze. "It's a beautiful boat. Dick's his usual grumpy self about it, but it really is amazing. I know it's presumptuous, but I'm terribly proud of it. Of him."

Mary's voice was muffled again, but it sounded like she'd had enough, didn't want Elsie to get wound up again. The light went out.

Dick got up on one knee. For a second he was confused, lost in the dark, thought he was still hiding in the salt marsh. He could barely feel his body except as dull weight.

He hadn't figured there were so many ways to get in trouble. He made his way back to his pickup and let it roll down the driveway, almost to Miss Perry's, before he started the engine.

When he slipped into bed he thought he'd have a hard time getting to sleep.

May woke him up once to stop him snoring. May had to shake him awake again in the morning when the boat-moving rig pulled off Route 1 into his yard.

*I*t took longer to load up than he'd figured, but it went okay. Backing in, the tractor's front wheels swung round and tore up half of May's garden. The trailer moved back into the shed a yard at a time, taking the weight of the boat frame by frame, as Eddie and he dismantled the cradle.

The wheels of the trailer sank in a half-foot, leaving a double trench from inside the shed, out across the garden, through the backyard, and around the side, slowly coming back to grade as the wheels ran up onto the packed grit and shells of the driveway. The boys ran out onto Route 1 waving red handkerchiefs tied to sticks to warn off traffic. Dick's truck didn't have flashers, so Eddie tailed the boat in his pickup. Dick pulled out and swept past, leaving May to bring the boys along in her car.

By the time they got the two miles to the boatyard and rolled the boat onto the marine railway, it was close to noon.

The manager let his men off for a half-hour lunch. Dick raised his eyebrows. He took a deep breath and took the manager aside to ask, as calmly as he could manage, if the half-hour for lunch was going on the bill. The manager pinched the bridge of his nose, closed his eyes, and said, "No." He opened his eyes and said, "Look, Dick. It's all going fine. The boat's in the yard. She's on the railway. It's time for my boys to have their lunch. It's when you hurry that things slip. *You* know that." He nodded toward the harbor. "The tide's still coming in, another half-hour there'll be even more water. You don't want her to bounce when she slides in." The manager added, "All you boat owners are alike—expect everything to fall into place just 'cause you show up." Dick was stung. The manager shook his head. "Hey, Dick. I'm kidding you. That's what *you* used to say when you worked here."

Dick sent Charlie and Tom off in May's car to get their skiff off *Mamzelle,* Tom to bring the skiff back up the harbor from Galilee, Charlie to drive the car back. Dick wanted the skiff to tend his boat once she was at a mooring. May offered to go back and get him a sandwich. He was in too much of a fuss to eat. He got an oar from the yard's store, got in a dinghy, and floated over the rails, poking down with the oar around where his boat's stern would splash in. His hands were so fluttery, he almost dropped the oar.

Plenty of water down there. What was he fussing about? He splashed a handful of water on his face.

A man in red pants and a white tennis hat hailed him from the dock. Dick cupped his hand to his ear. The man said he wanted his dinghy back. Eddie was on the guy like a shot. Dick watched

Eddie's hands open like flowers in front of his chest, his head cock to one side. The man's eyes followed Eddie's to the boat. The man lifted his hand to catch Dick's attention. "Okay, take your time." Dick paddled back in anyway.

Dick said he was sorry, he'd thought the dinghy was a yard boat.

The man wanted to chat. He said, "That's some boat. I didn't think they still built commercial boats out of wood." He looked at Dick again. "Didn't you use to work in the yard here?"

Dick recognized the man's face, couldn't place him. The man pointed to a large catboat at a mooring. "You worked on my boat a couple of times."

Dick looked. "Yeah. I remember your boat. An old Crosby."

The man seemed pleased.

Dick said, "You used to let the Perryville School kids take her out."

The man said, "That's right, that's right!" He was quite excited by this recognition.

Dick looked down the channel to see if the boys' skiff was in view.

"Your boat wasn't built in this yard," the man said. "Was she built in a Rhode Island yard?"

Eddie said, "You could say that—he built her himself in his backyard."

Dick looked up toward the parking lot. He saw Elsie's Volvo. Then Elsie and Mary coming round the yard office.

"Good for you," the man said to Dick. "That's something I've always wanted to do myself."

Dick said, "Something I've always wanted to do myself is be a brain surgeon."

The man lifted his face in surprise. Then hurt spread across it slowly, like the stain of a dye-marker at sea.

Eddie said, "Dick. Jees. Take it easy."

Dick breathed in and out through his nose and shook his head at himself. He said, "Yeah. I don't know why I said that. Sorry."

The man said, "I take your point. I only meant . . . congratulations on succeeding where so many merely wish."

Elsie and Mary came down the gangplank to the dock. Elsie said, "Good. We're not too late. Mary brought a bottle of champagne for May to christen her with." She turned to the old man. She said, "Hello, Mr. Potter," and kissed him on the cheek. She introduced Mary Scanlon to Mr. Potter. Then Dick and Eddie. Mr. Potter shook their hands.

Dick felt stupid and mean all over again.

Elsie looked around brightly. "Are your boys here? I don't see them. I stopped in to see Miss Perry on the off chance she might be able to . . . She sends her congratulations. Captain Texeira was there, so he came along."

Mr. Potter asked after Miss Perry.

"Much better," Elsie said. "Would this be a good place to take pictures, Dick? Or should I get up someplace high and shoot down? There's sort of a splash, isn't there?"

"Not supposed to be. She's on a marine railway, she's not going to skid in."

"Oh. Well, maybe Schuyler will get here. He's back, so maybe he'll show up and we can use two cameras."

Dick felt a terrible new intimacy, as though he and Elsie were stuck to each other, floating through the air out of control in front of a crowd, which Elsie didn't notice or didn't care about, because she kept pressing her face in to him. No, she did notice, because she was also waving to the crowd.

Dick shook his head.

"Dick," Elsie said, "maybe the roof of that shed." She really did put her hand on his forearm. "I want to be sure to get May in."

"Fine," Dick said. "Anywhere out of the way."

He saw the skiff at last, coming up the channel. He looked up to the parking lot and saw Charlie drive in. Parker was with him.

Dick said to Eddie, "Have Tom stand by with the skiff right here."

He walked up to the parking lot. The manager was rounding up his crew.

Parker slapped Dick on the shoulder.

"How you doing, old buddy? Goddamn, look at that! There she is, your own genuine, self-financed, offshore boat, fully guaranteed for five years or fifty thousand miles, whichever comes first. Who-ee!"

Charlie laughed.

"Now, that is a boat, son." Parker shook Charlie's shoulder. "And your old man's the one that built it. What do you think of that?"

Charlie was embarrassed.

Dick said, "He knows the boat. He did some work on her too."

"Well, there you go," Parker said, releasing Charlie's shoulder. "Say, Dick, I hear you took *Mamzelle* out while I was gone."

"That's right," Dick said. "Somebody had to check those pots."

"That's what I'm saying," Parker said. "I'm obliged to you. Maybe we can have a little talk later on in the day, catch up on each other. After you get squared away."

Parker strolled off to look at the boat. Charlie's gaze followed his wake. Dick felt the air was filled with secrets.

Charlie said, "He was on board when we got there, so we explained, and he just got in the car with me." Charlie sounded dubious.

"That's fine," Dick said. "Your mother just sees the one side to him. I wouldn't want you boys to ship out with him, but he's . . . got his good side."

Charlie said, "I guess he's got a sense of humor."

Dick looked sideways at Charlie to make sure it was his son who made this remark. Nothing to it really, but it came out so flat, saying just so much.

Elsie came fluttering around the corner of the office. "Dick, come on! And here's Charlie! Good. You go stand by your mother when she breaks the bottle. Tom's already there."

Dick said, "Jesus, Elsie. I just want to put the boat in. See if she leaks. I don't want a side show."

"The trouble with your father," Elsie said, "is that he takes gloom pills."

Charlie laughed.

"It's a Yankee superstition," Elsie said. "You think if you're grumpy enough you'll have good luck. But just this once, Dick, don't be a wet blanket. Everybody else wants a little celebration."

Elsie went back toward the boat. When Dick and Charlie came round the office they saw there was a crowd. Elsie strapped on her camera and climbed a ladder to the roof of the shed.

Mary Scanlon had rigged a bottle of champagne on a yard of ribbon and was holding it out to May. May said to Dick, "It won't hurt the paint, will it?"

Mary Scanlon said, "No, I've practically sawed the bottle in half with a glass-cutter."

May said, "What do I say?"

Mary said, "You say, 'I christen you *Spartina*.'" Mary turned to Dick. "Is that right, Dick? It's what Elsie told me." Mary turned back to May. "And then you let loose with the bottle. You can't miss."

Mary waved to the manager, who was at the controls of the marine railway. He gunned the engine and then cut back to idle.

Dick said, "*Spartina-May* is what she's called."

May said, "I can't say my own name."

"Come on, May. Say her full name."

"You do it, Charlie."

Mary Scanlon said, "It's got to be a woman."

Mary held her arms up over her head.

Now that everyone was quiet, the crowd seemed even bigger. Captain Texeira with his hat in his hand. Joxer Goode. Elsie's sister and her husband. Eddie Wormsley down on the dock holding one of the lines. Parker grinning at Schuyler and Schuyler's wife.

Dick looked away from the people, down the harbor. The south-west onshore breeze was just picking up, a cat's paw flickered toward him, relieving the dull surface of the channel.

May held on to his arm, took a breath, and said in a high voice, "I christen you *Spartina-May*."

The boat was already moving when May finally let go of the bottle, which broke neatly in two on the bow, gushed, and then dribbled foam from the dangling neck.

Charlie said, "Way to go, Ma."

For the time it took the boat to run in and float up from the carriage, Dick felt squeezed tighter and tighter, and then released as he came loose with her. Now it was just the two of them. He felt her press up from the water, felt her colors bob into order: her gray hull, her royal-blue waterline, and a slice of her rust-red bottom as she rode light in her first taste of the sea.

*D*ick didn't remember speaking to anyone, or even having lunch. It was only when May reminded him to thank Mary and Elsie for the champagne bottle and the picnic basket that he figured he'd eaten. Dick let Charlie and Eddie Wormsley show people around for a while. Then he moved *Spartina* to her mooring. Dick kept the boys' skiff and stayed on board for the afternoon. He didn't do any work. He just looked at everything, touched everything, listened to the soft creak of the hull in the wake of passing boats. He went home for supper, but went back on board with a mattress for one of the bunks and spent the night. In the morning he turned on the bilge pump. She'd taken on a little water, about right for the first day. By the third day she was bone dry in the morning, completely made up. In his time on board Dick had rigged the antennas and the crow's nest.

He took Charlie, stopped off to pick up Parker, and went out for a quick shakedown cruise.

Even with full fuel tanks she rode high. Dick could feel her dance as soon as they slipped through the breakwater. He hadn't filled the water tank or taken on any ice for the fish hold. He pumped some sea water into the lobster well, and that settled her a bit.

Dick let Charlie take the wheel and went below to listen to the engine. Parker came along.

"Plenty of power," Parker said, "and, my God—look at your lobster tank—you're pretty optimistic."

"Seven thousand pounds," Dick said. "It's about half of what Texeira's boats'll take. But, then, they stay out twice as long. I figure I'll be staying out ten days when the weather's right."

"And you figure what for crew?"

"I'd like two, and a boy during summer."

"And how many pots?"

"Well, now," Dick said, "let's talk about pots. You and I started out with just about fifteen hundred, maybe a thousand of them yours. But every time we lost or busted one, I replaced it. So by now we're even."

"Hold on, Dick, just a second there. When we lost a pot, who says it was mine and not yours?"

Dick said, "It was me put out a new one."

Parker said, "But if it was one of yours got busted, you don't gain a pot. Don't you see that?"

Dick said, "Let me put it this way. You owe me money."

Parker said, "That's right. You got a little money coming to you."

"Not so little."

"Well, Dick, here's how that works—once I had to bring Schuyler in to help out when your first run didn't work out, that kind of rearranged things. You can see that, can't you?"

"You're heading south," Dick said. "You don't want pots. You don't want to hire a tender to bring in all them pots. It'd take you a month to bring them in on *Mamzelle*. And, selling them dockside, you wouldn't get much even if you were willing to sit around waiting for the different skippers to come in. Now, I'm willing to take over your pots and call it even."

Parker laughed and went back up on deck.

Dick knew his own position was unreasonable. But he also knew Parker was impatient. Parker had never stayed north past the first week in October. Parker might go out with *Mamzelle* another two times. Maybe he could bring some pots back on her, maybe use a tender and bring in a bunch, and maybe he could peddle them. Parker was sharp enough, but he didn't have patience. Dick could wait.

Dick spent the rest of the afternoon checking out the loran, the RDF, and boxing the compass, lining *Spartina* up on Block Island, on Brenton Reef, on Point Judith Light.

Parker started up again when Charlie was out of the wheelhouse. Parker said, "You're being an overreaching Yankee son of a bitch, but I'll tell you what—I'm not going to spoil a beautiful friendship—"

"Okay," Dick said. "You're right. Let's not have any hard feelings. We'll just divvy up the pots and not even try to make a deal. I'll take all the pots east of Lydonia Canyon. That's about half."

"Hold on, Dick, just listen to me a minute. I'll call it fifty-fifty on the pots. Now, that's something right there. You buy my pots. I'll give you the twenty-five hundred dollars I owe you toward the purchase price. . . ."

"How much per pot?"

"Ten dollars."

"Parker, me and the boys can make them cheaper than that. You keep your half of the pots and pay me the money you owe me. And that ain't any twenty-five hundred."

"I cut Schuyler in."

"Bullshit, Parker. You may have given Schuyler a slice of the pie, but the pie got bigger." Parker kept his face still, but his eyes registered. Dick said, "Schuyler went to his club, saw some friends, and made out like a bandit. And I figure the reason you're back here so late and I had to run your boat for you is 'cause you went to Virginia and made a down payment on your new charter boat."

Dick thought that scored a hit too. Before Parker could say anything, Dick called Charlie into the wheelhouse and asked him to fix him some tea.

Dick said to Parker, "You want some tea?"

Parker nodded, waited till Charlie went below. He said, "Schuyler had me over a barrel. You're going to have to be a little less mistrustful, Dickey-boy."

Dick said, "Don't give me that shit. If Schuyler had screwed you, you wouldn't be smiling at him. I saw you and him, you both looked pretty happy. But I'm not happy. You want to hear why I'm not happy? It's on account of when I got you out of that salt marsh and found your boat for you in the middle of nowhere, and on account of once you were safe on board you said, 'Sorry, it didn't work. No money!' Well, now it worked. And I'm not even asking you for money. Just some pots you got no more use for."

Parker, who'd been looking a little numbed by Dick's outburst, suddenly brightened. "You don't want money. I can see that. You certainly don't want a check. But maybe you're afraid of cash too."

Parker lifted an eyebrow. "Now, I wonder where you got the money to put this here boat in. Joxer Goode? Maybe one of the conditions was you dump your old buddy Parker. No more fooling around with the notorious Captain Parker, not if you're going to be an associate of a fine old New England family."

Dick smiled. His guesses had scored better than Parker's.

Dick said, "I'm my own old New England family."

Parker laughed. "I was afraid of this, son. Having your own boat is going to your head. You know, you ought not to get shed of me. What I've done for you, that's more than the money I've made you, is I've kept you disreputable. You're not so bad when you're messing around with me. But if you get all reputable ... I don't know, Dickey-bird, I just don't know."

Dick said, "I guess you've got me. I'm scared of your money— you give me five thousand dollars and watch me fall to pieces."

Parker didn't say anything. Dick took another compass bearing and checked it against the loran reading. Good enough. He rolled up the chart and pigeonholed it.

Just as he did that, he felt a lurch. It was so nearly physical that he looked around in alarm. The sea was calm. It was Elsie. He thought of Elsie. As he was riding high, sticking it to Parker by being single-minded and hard-ass, all his single-mindedness and hard-assedness dove into a trough.

What had Parker said?—that Parker kept him disreputable. If only that was all there was to it.

Dick looked at Parker. Parker hadn't noticed anything, was standing there trying to come up with an answer.

Dick thought of their trip south. On their way they'd gone up Long Island Sound and toured New York City. They'd steamed around Manhattan in that yacht, Parker naming skyscrapers and bridges. When they'd left the bay to go outside, just as they got to Sandy Hook, they'd run into a built-up sea. They'd plowed up it, up and up and over. And then plummeted—the whole bow end just fell down into the trough. She buried her bow. Water boiled past the wheelhouse. Dick's feet flew apart so he had to hang on to the wheel. Parker fell on his ass. Even before she broke free, while he was still trying to get up, Parker was talking. "Goddamn! Last time I was here I told them about that. I told them about that damn hole in the water. Goddamn New Yorkers never fix anything."

Now Dick thought, What the hell. Why spoil old times? He said, "Look. I don't want to argue. You do what you think's fair."

Parker came up beside the wheel. He said, "Well, screw you too. Take the damn pots. I don't want to hang around here, don't want to go out there again. I'm going south. . . ."

Dick realized Parker thought Dick had spun him around. Dick said, "Don't get all huffy about it. I don't want you to go away thinking I've gouged you. Look. I still owe you the boat's share for the last trip. I'll bring it by your apartment."

Parker said, "I gave that up. I'm staying on *Mamzelle.*"

Dick laughed. "You son of a bitch. You *are* about to head south."

"Look. I'm giving you the pots."

"You aren't leaving 'cause you're in trouble, are you?"

"Naw. If I was, I sure wouldn't leave in *Mamzelle.* I got a man in Florida says if *Mamzelle* can make the trip down there, he'll buy her."

Dick said, "She'll be better off down south, with her hull."

Parker said, "And if she can't make it, I got her insured for all she's worth."

"Not exactly in love with her, are you? I suppose you got your charter boat picked out?"

"Forty-five feet of space-age paradise. Fastest boat of her size. Four chairs. Flying bridge. I can get to the fishing grounds in one hour, or on out to the Gulf Stream in a day. The going rate is seventy-five dollars a head for a day's charter. That's six hundred dollars a day for a party of eight. The mate works for tips. So the six hundred is all mine. Spend two hundred on fuel, I'm still doing as good as a doctor or a lawyer. And, like them, even if I don't produce I get paid. Winter in Florida, spring in Virginia Beach, come up here for the tuna derby in August. But I don't have to be anywhere if I don't want. I make my nut for the year in Virginia Beach. The rest is fun. The only thing I got to worry about is herpes."

Dick said, "That's why God made it, Parker." Charlie came up with two mugs of tea. Dick let Charlie take the wheel, told him the bearing.

"And what did he do to keep you in your place? He didn't need to do nothing. You already got winter with thirty-degree water—waves as big as a barn—ice in your rigging. Dickey-boy, I admire that you built yourself a boat, but I don't envy you."

Dick thought that there were days in these waters he wouldn't trade for anything. Even December, fair days after a gale, the sea still shaggy with white crests, the sky a blue as pale and hard as a Portuguese glass float. He'd still be going out no matter what kind of mess his life was onshore.

They came in through the breakwater, dropped Parker off at his boat. One of the smaller fishing boats was being hauled. When he got to the top end of the salt pond, he saw that one of the larger sailboats was being hauled too. It was after six in the evening.

When he passed the office the yard manager called out to him, asked him when he was going to move *Spartina* down the harbor.

"Another day or two. What's the rush?"

"There may be some bad weather. I don't want your boat swinging around here in a storm."

"I'll be out of here tomorrow. I'm going out. When I get back, I'll tie up down in Galilee."

"You may not be going out. There's a hurricane coming out of the Caribbean."

"They usually pass out to sea," Dick said. "Is that why you're hauling boats so late at night? Every year everyone gets all edgy about hurricanes. We haven't had one hit hard since '54."

"Maybe we're due."

"No such thing as due. Of all the hundreds of hurricanes that have started up in my life, only four have hit shore: '38, '54, and then those two little ones in 1955. Nothing since, and that's more than twenty years. I'm not saying we won't get one. I'm just saying there's no such thing as *due.*"

Dick realized in mid-speech that he himself was working on an even dumber theory than *due.* He was figuring on *not due.*

He drove down to Joxer's plant. He'd noticed on his way in that Captain Teixeira's *Lydia P.* was tied up at Joxer's pier. The *Lydia P.* received satellite weather-pictures, flashed them on her computer screen.

Dick ran into Joxer at the foot of the pier. Joxer was supervising his plant crew as they nailed up shutters over the windows and piled up sandbags along the cinderblock walls.

Dick said, "You're taking this pretty serious."

"I talked to Captain Teixeira," Joxer said. "He's pretty serious."

Dick asked the *Lydia P.*'s first mate if he could come aboard to talk to the captain. The mate sent him up to the wheelhouse.

Captain Teixeira laid it out for him.

There were two storms. The second one, Elvira, was moving faster than the first, Donald. If Elvira caught up with Donald, the combined storm might pick up speed. Usually hurricanes moving up the coast followed the Gulf Stream and moved out to sea before they hit New England. But if a hurricane was moving fast, over thirty-five miles an hour, it could override this tendency to move toward warmer water. There was also a weak Arctic trough over central New England, and that tended to invite a storm in. The winds at twenty thousand feet over the storms, which, according to one theory, steered a hurricane, were out of the south. Captain Texeira had ordered his bigger boat, *Bom Sonho,* to head southeast from Georges Bank. She was fast enough to get to mid-Atlantic.

Captain Texeira said, "Even if the hurricane does curve out to sea, in two days she'll be safe to the southeast."

"What about the *Lydia P.?*"

"I don't know. I don't know. I won't stay in this harbor. The breakwater may prevent a hurricane wave from coming up the harbor full-force. You remember '54—boats thrown up across Route One, right up the hill, forty feet above the water.

"If the hurricane tide goes up twenty feet, all those yachts back there will yank their moorings right up. The harbor of refuge just out here will be for Coast Guard and Navy ships. Perhaps other ships. That'll be up to the Coast Guard. They may let the *Lydia P.* lie to, there. There may be room, it's almost a square mile inside the breakwater. But even there you have to depend on the other ships' not breaking loose, or dragging their anchors. I don't like to depend on people I don't know."

Dick was sobered by Captain Texeira.

Captain Texeira said, "My wife wants me to stay at home. My nephew is competent to take the *Lydia P.* out to sea, he's been the acting skipper half the time for the last five years. But what if something happens? How do I face his mother—my sister? The *Lydia P.* is insured. She's my second boat. But if she stays here and she goes down, my nephew and all the crew are out of work for a year while I have a new boat built. I think I can take her east of the storm. But the storm may move east. And then she'll be in the worst quadrant."

Dick said, "Why not go out and if the storm moves east then you move back to the west, into the easier half. You have plenty of speed."

Captain Texeira shook his head. "A storm this size, the swells go far ahead of her, several hundred miles. They can be so big you can only go half-speed, maybe less. And they may be spread out two hundred miles across."

"So you think we may get hit this time."

"I don't know. NOAA doesn't know. Nobody knows. If the storms link up, if the big storm is moving forty miles an hour when she passes Cape Hatteras . . . if, if, if. I'll know more tomorrow, but tomorrow may be too late to take the *Lydia* out to sea."

Dick thanked him. He drove back to the yard. There was a crowd now around the office. Dick peered over the shoulders of the people in front of the door. He saw that the phone on the manager's desk was off the hook, the manager was trying to get out the door. When he finally popped through he went by Dick but turned after a few steps. "You going to move *Spartina*?"

Dick said, "Look. I feel like a damn fool—after we just put her in. I'll get Eddie's flatbed, rig my old cradle on it, and if you haul her, we'll take her out of here."

The manager shook his head.

"I got twenty-five, maybe thirty boats ahead of you. They've been customers for years. They've all heard the news. I can't haul *Spartina*. No way."

The manager turned toward a man who began to speak to him. The man got in one word, the manager said, "I'm sorry—I'm talking to Captain Pierce."

The man said, "I've been waiting—"

"I'm talking to Captain Pierce."

The man made a show of keeping the lid on. He said, "Very well. I'll phone you at home."

"I'm not going home. I'm not answering the phone here. You want your boat hauled, write her name on a piece of paper, sign it, put the time which is now eighteen forty hours and have it on my desk. No promises."

The man left.

Dick said, "I owe you near to a thousand bucks. For that I get to see a yacht owner go away pissed off, and I get to be called Captain Pierce. Life is full of satisfactions."

The manager said, "Look, Dick. I'm sorry. That guy's an asshole. If it was him or you I'd haul you. But I got to go by rules, I got to have a system for the whole crowd. I'll put you on the list, that's all I can do. I got to be fair."

"Can I use your phone?"

"Sure. Just leave it off the hook when you're done."

Dick called his insurance agent at home. Busy. Called his office. Busy. He got in his truck and drove to the guy's house in Wakefield. The guy's car was there so Dick kept knocking till the door opened.

Dick told him he'd like to up the coverage on *Spartina*. "Sure," the guy said, "I'll see what I can do. But you remember how I explained it to you. There's a little lead time. It'll be easier once your interim policy is in effect."

Dick said, "You told me *Spartina*'s covered with an interim policy. I wouldn't have gone out today without that. So just up the interim policy."

"That's what I'm talking about. The interim policy. I'm pretty certain I explained to you it would be a few days. That'll be the ninth. Today is the sixth."

Dick turned aside. If he looked at the guy's face, he'd get mad. He took a breath and said, "So any damage before September ninth, I'm out of luck. After that I'm fine."

"Yes."

"So if *Spartina* is a total wreck, let's say as of one minute past midnight September ninth, I get a hundred and fifty thousand dollars. One minute before and I get nothing."

The guy said, "It does seem—"

"Yes or no," Dick said. "Just tell me have I got it right?"

"Yes."

"And where is this written down? I mean, where do *I* have this written down? Is it on that piece of paper you gave me?"

"Yes."

"The ninth it is, then. That's two days and five hours from now. If there is any doubt in your mind as to when any damage was sustained by my vessel, you be sure to check with Captain Ruy Texeira. You know Captain Texeira?"

"Yes, I do—"

"Good. I will be in radio contact with him or with one of his vessels, and you be sure you check with him, you *verify* with him that *Spartina* is well as of the first minute of the ninth of September. Now, if by some chance I'm not around to collect, you still owe that money to my family. Is that right?"

"Yes. You remember when I wrote the policy we discussed the eventuality that—"

"Good."

Dick drove back to Galilee. Joxer's plant was now fully bulwarked with sandbags on the south and east sides. Captain Texeira was still on board the *Lydia P.*

Dick asked him if he was taking her out.

Captain Texeira said he was. Dick said, "Good. I'm taking *Spartina* out. What channel will you be on?"

"Fifty-six."

"Okay, good. I don't receive the satellite picture, so if I can get the word from you I'll be much obliged."

Captain Texeira sat down. He was silent for a long time. At last he said, "You were in the Coast Guard in '59."

"Yes, sir."

"Were you out in that little hurricane?"

"Yes, sir."

"This will be bigger." Captain Texeira's head tilted forward, and the flesh of his face sagged.

Dick said, "Captain Texeira, there's lots of reasons. My insurance starts in two days. I may seem to be running around like a chicken with its head cut off, but there's one big reason. If I lose my boat, I'll be a slave."

Captain Texeira shook his head.

Dick said, "I'm not doing this because you're doing it, you're not talking me into it. I have my own reason, and I have my own boat. You can't take me on your conscience."

Captain Texeira nodded. Dick started to leave. Captain Texeira took him by the arm. "If you do get caught, don't fight. You understand? More power isn't the answer. The shape of your boat is the answer. If you punch hard against a big wave, it's harder for her.

"If you let her yield, she'll move right. The wave is a wall if you run at it. If you move with it, it's a wave. But you used to have a temper—you used to like to get tough."

Dick said, "Look. There's one last thing. My insurance policy starts on the ninth. One tick after midnight. I plan to call you then so it'll be on your log that *Spartina*'s okay."

Captain Texeira nodded.

Dick considered asking him to log in the message no matter what. At the last minute he kept quiet.

Dick shook hands with the old man and left the *Lydia P.*

*D*ick stopped at home just long enough to leave a list of chores with Charlie. He was in and out so fast May didn't have time to ask questions. He filled his new thermos with coffee, took a six-pack of the boys' Cokes.

He got Charlie to drive him to the yard and ferry him on board. He told Charlie to load the little skiff in the back of the pickup. The whole family was to go up to Eddie's in case there was a flood. Charlie and Tom were to pull the plug on the big skiff and sink her in the creek filled with stones. Take as much stuff as they could in the car and the truck, but especially the books. If there was time Charlie and Tom could board up windows, but the main thing was to be up at Eddie's before the storm hit.

It wasn't until Dick climbed on board *Spartina* that Charlie seemed to realize what Dick planned to do.

Dick told him to get going. He wouldn't let go, he just stood in the skiff and hung on to *Spartina* with a frown on his face.

"I haven't got time to fool around," Dick said. "If I leave now, I can keep up with Captain Texeira. I'm just doing what he's doing."

Charlie said, "I'll come with you."

"No," Dick said. "Look—you get your mother and your brother up to Eddie's. That's your job. I'll take care of the boat. That's it, Charlie. I'll see you in three days."

The yard was in so much chaos it would have taken too long to top off *Spartina's* fuel tanks. Dick stopped at Joxer Goode's. The *Lydia P.* was gone. Joxer hailed him and lugged out a sack. "Captain Texeira left this for you. It's a survival raft. Strobe light, water supply, automatic distress transmitter."

Dick said, "I see he expects the worst for me."

"It's for the regulations," Joxer said. "If the insurance company asks if you were properly equipped..."

Dick signed for the fuel and stowed the survival raft in a locker in the wheelhouse. He backed *Spartina's* stern away from the pier and made a turn toward the breakwater. He felt her squat down with the push, then come up. He'd keep her light for a bit. When the sea kicked up some, he'd take on sea water in the lobster wells.

Beyond the breakwater the sea was calm. There was a slight swell, the troughs so wide it was almost imperceptible.

He suddenly felt exuberant. *Spartina* was only a few knots slower than the *Lydia,* and maybe two hours behind. It was true that in a day they'd be a hundred miles apart, but Captain Texeira would have figured on at least that as a margin of safety.

In another hour Dick had left Block Island off *Spartina's* starboard quarter. He could see *Spartina's* bow shadow racing across the water. Behind him the sunlight was shot with red. The long mare's tails overhead were soft pink ribbons. He'd be okay, they'd do fine—so long as the engine kept at it. Sounded fine.

So he'd burn a full tank. An expense with no return. Small dues, especially if he'd be one of the few boats still able afterward.

He fastened the wheel, made a mug of soup, put two Hershey bars in his pocket, and came back to the wheel. He decided to save his thermos of coffee for the long night. It was darkening in the wheelhouse, though the surface of the sea still shone. He could just make out Elsie's picture on the thermos. His mood was still up. So he'd laid up for a week or two in Elsie's bed. What man would have said no? For the first time in quite a while he thought of her with pure, dumb pleasure. The light through the trees falling across the room. Her compact body magnified by her energy. Who landed who? She'd wanted him, and he now felt the flattery of her wish. Why not?

She wasn't helpless, she knew what she wanted. She *liked* him, for God's sakes. He let that in too, not just flattery, some comfort. She was a tough cookie, abrupt and full of quick turns. And curious as a seal. But she'd been good to him, nice to him, coaxed him right into the middle of her life. Why stand off from her? She wasn't going to cling, that was clear, she was one to take care of herself.

Dick switched on the chart light and got a loran reading. Good enough, rolling right along.

By midnight he was getting a little tired. The swells, still farther apart than any he'd ever run into, were bigger now. He couldn't see them very well, but he felt them as *Spartina* took them on her starboard bow, chugged up them slowly and then slid over the top with a little pitch and roll.

After an hour he checked his position again. The swell had slowed *Spartina* considerably.

He called the *Lydia P.,* got Captain Texeira's nephew. Their position was well east of *Spartina*'s. The hurricane had grown. *Lydia*'s satellite picture showed that the two systems had linked up and had picked up some speed. The storm center was more than two hundred miles off Cape Hatteras and moving due north at about thirty-five knots, maybe more. If she didn't curve, she would plow into New England somewhere between Old Lyme and the middle of Cape Cod. The Rhode Island shore was the bull's eye between those two points.

It looked as though Captain Texeira had made a good guess and a good move. Dick saw that *Spartina* wasn't in quite as good a position. The diameter of the hurricane was now almost four hundred miles. If she hit dead on the mouth of Narragansett Bay,

Spartina would have to be at least two hundred miles to the east. Since midnight *Spartina*'s progress eastward was down to six knots. There was no wind to speak of but cutting across the swell was like mountain climbing. If the forward edge of the hurricane was now pushing past Hatteras at thirty-five to forty knots, it would reach *Spartina* in ten or eleven hours. *Spartina* would be, at best, 120 miles east of the eye. She'd get caught. Not in the fiercest winds—those were tucked in tight swirls around the center. But even halfway out to the edge, according to the reports that the *Lydia P.* had, the winds were full hurricane force, and since *Spartina* was going to be in the eastern sector of the storm, where the counterclockwise swirl was blowing in the same general direction as the overall movement of the hurricane, he could add those forty knots to the force of the wind.

If the two storm centers hadn't linked up, he'd have been in dandy shape. Neither storm by herself had been bigger than 150 miles in diameter, and *Spartina* would have been forty to fifty miles east of the eastern edge. Sure—rough seas, some gale-force wind, but nothing to worry about. But now that the hurricane had doubled up, the eastern edge was reaching out for *Spartina* like a big paw.

Another problem Dick foresaw was that, if he was pushed too far north by the southeast wind, he'd end up over Georges Bank. It was almost as bad as a lee shore. The waves, as they felt the tug of the rising bottom of Georges Bank, would bunch up, grow steeper, break.

Dick had been at the wheel of a Coast Guard vessel in '59, winds at just hurricane force. At half-power, bow into the wind, she'd still been moving backward. If everything the *Lydia P.* reported was correct, *Spartina* was in for winds some forty knots harder. Dick couldn't calculate the force exactly. He'd read that the *force* of the wind increased not just with the velocity of the wind, but with the *square* of the velocity. So a sixty-knot wind pushed at about fifteen pounds a square foot, but a 120-knot wind pushed not at thirty pounds but at almost eighty pounds a square foot.

If *Spartina* caught a wind like that broadside, it would be like being pushed by a tugboat the same size as her.

Dick looked at the chart. It was easy, on paper, just looking at numbers and lines. *Spartina* laboring eastward at six knots. The hurricane boiling northward at forty knots—right along 71°30′, as though it was a rail. He could hope the storm would slow down. If she slowed to thirty knots, he'd get out almost to her eastern edge. If she slowed to twenty knots, he'd be able to slip beyond her reach. Right out there with Captain Texeira's lucky ships, even now the *Bom Sonho* headed toward the Azores, the stars shining on her.

Dick checked with the *Lydia P.* every couple of hours. The hurricane was still coming at full speed, straight as an express train. The distance between the *Lydia P.* and *Spartina* was now greater than could be accounted for by their different hull speeds. It was the size of the swells that was cutting *Spartina*'s way.

At what should have been sunrise, light began to ooze through the cloud cover, an amber glow with tinges of green. The swell, now visible, was enormous. Every time *Spartina* reached a rounded crest, Dick could see three or four crests to the south. The swell seemed almost stationary, foothills of a mountain range.

At ten o'clock he checked the barometer. Twenty-eight. He was about to call the *Lydia P.* once more when he looked to the south. He didn't need to call. He could see the abrupt line where the amber glow of the cloud cover and round swell gave way to darkness. And yet in the darkness there was a flickering. At first he thought it might be lightning, then he thought it might be whitecaps catching the last light. Before he got close enough to decide, his visibility dropped.

He was scared, but his fear seemed remote from his body. He

drank a Coke and ate a Hershey bar. He took out another Hershey bar but left it in its white inner wrapper in his jacket pocket. He turned on the pump and put some more sea water in the lobster wells. He hooked the door to the wheelhouse open and ran a twist of wire around the hook and eye. One thing he didn't need was to pop the windows out when the pressure dropped.

When the first wind hit, he watched the needle on the dial of the anemometer. It spurted up to seventy and then fell off as *Spartina* slid into a trough. He eased back on the throttle. The seas were steeper than the swell had been, but not as high. The peaks were blown flat by the wind. He caught the anemometer dial out of the corner of his eye. The needle flung itself all the way to the right. *Spartina* moved nicely into the next trough, and Dick eased up even more on the throttle. He couldn't see anything beyond the bow except water. He had no sense of its movement, whether it was coming at him or whether it was rising or falling. He felt *Spartina* rise. He watched the needle spurt to the right and then fall back. He was puzzled for an instant, but then felt *Spartina* nosing down into the dark of the next trough.

From the noise of the wind and the quick scribblings of spray across the glass in front of him it seemed he was engulfed in speed, but the one true sense he had—hearing and sight conveying no meaning—was of slow motion.

He caught a glimpse of the anemometer needle slack at zero. He realized the cups had blown off.

He checked her depth. Plenty of water under her.

He broke off a bit of chocolate every half-hour. Then he realized he was making time drag on him by checking his watch. He saved the last bit of chocolate for a lull.

It struck him as odd that his legs got tired before his arms did. And as his calves and thighs began to bother him with twinges, his confidence weakened. He felt tired and stupid and unlucky.

There came a lull. For a terrible moment he feared it was the eye. The eye would be a disaster. It would mean the storm had curved out to sea toward him. It would mean that the winds yet to come would be violently opposed to how the sea was running, *Spartina* would be caught in confused seas, freak waves. But it was just a lull. The wind still southeast as far as he could tell, *Spartina* tucked into the lee of the mountainous seas. In his momentary panic he'd forgotten to eat the rest of his Hershey bar. In the next trough he mashed it into his mouth and got both hands back on the wheel. When *Spartina* was deep in the trough, the windshield wasn't lashed with spray. He could make out just enough of the hole he was in to see *Spartina* as a bug in a toilet bowl.

He tried to calculate how long before the storm would blow by. If *Spartina* didn't get pushed north, and the storm kept moving at forty knots, it would be less than ten hours. He'd have to wait for another lull to check the loran against the chart, to see if *Spartina* was making any headway.

Eventually the wind would move from southeast to south, and then around to southwest. By the time he'd be leaving the storm at the bottom of the cyclonic movement, the wind would be all the way around to the northwest, maybe down from hurricane force to gale force. The thought of coming out the bottom cheered him up. So far *Spartina* was taking it. Still tight as a tick, still coming up nicely.

The weak point was him. He began to swear at himself. He swore out loud, calling himself a stupid son of a bitch, a dumb asshole. He was trying to numb some sharper thought of what he really was. Stupid was just making a mistake. There was something in him that had done worse than that, that had prepared him for deliberate harm to himself. *Spartina* was fine. Captain Texeira was right about her lines, she gave no flat argument to the force of the seas. He'd done that part fine. But he'd left some bad part of his effort inside himself. Perhaps it was the part he'd thought was tough bitterness, but now, washed once with a terror that he might give in, it turned out flawed. Worse than flawed—rotten. Worse than rotten—rotting, spreading rot.

He ran out of cursing. He shook his head. He was afraid he was getting a little dingo, as though he'd got dizzy from too much sun.

He held on. He felt thick and dull but okay. Maybe he should have taken a nap while *Spartina* was steaming east, before the swell got too big. He spent a long time deciding whether to drink another Coke or to crack the thermos of coffee. He leaned over to pick a can of Coke out of the cooler in the locker. As he stood back up, *Spartina* suddenly slid forward as though she was greased. She stuck her nose into a wave. He felt her held down, caught, then lifted by the bow and spun sideways. He leaned against the spokes of the wheel. No effect. She fell back on her beam. He clung to the wheel post with one hand to keep from falling over. For a long moment he had no idea where she was or which way was up. Then she came back on her own. He felt her stern wag, but he couldn't tell whether it was her answering the helm—still hard over—or a lucky push of the sea. And then she was nestled in the next trough as though nothing had happened. The inner rasp of adrenaline smoothed out. The taste of zinc left his mouth.

He felt a slow roiling of his sense of *Spartina*. He'd made her. He'd made her, but now she was the good one. She was better than him. It wasn't alarming to hear this news, it was deeply, thickly soothing. She was lightened of a dangerous disabling weight. She wasn't him. She'd become separate from him, and yet she was staying with him.

He feared he was getting dingo again. But at least his nerves had pricked him awake. No need for the can of Coke. He glanced around his feet but couldn't find it. The thermos was still stuck in its bracket over the locker.

He willed himself to keep attentive to *Spartina*'s motion, but some of his thoughts began to wander. He found himself thinking of the books Miss Perry gave the boys. He couldn't get the one he disliked most out of his head. A Christmas book, not a birthday book. He could see the pretty fluffy drawings of curly-headed boys and girls, the boys in sailor suits, the girls in billowed dresses under pretty fluffy summer clouds. Everything puffed—the children's hair and cheeks and clothes, the pretty cloud above the pretty children. *A Child's Garden of Verses.*

He said out loud, " 'O Leerie, I'll go round at night and light the lamps with you!' " He couldn't remember any other part of the poem. Except the title—"The Lamplighter." The line played itself again in his ear, "O Leerie, I'll go round at night and light the lamps with you!" And again. He felt the little poem tug at some other thought, as though it was the current in a salt creek tugging at a stick half on the mud bank, half bobbing in the water.

He'd read all those damn little poems to the boys. He wouldn't have guessed they'd have stuck. It came loose: "Now Tom would be a driver and Maria go to sea, And my Papa's a banker . . ."

The boys had said, "Miss Perry says 'pa*pa.*' 'And my pa*pa's* a banker.' It goes 'pa*pa.*' And Miss Perry says 'Mar-*eye*-ah.' Not 'Mar-ee-ah.' "

It came again, trickling into his ear. "—and Maria go to sea, and my pa*pa's* a banker and as rich as he can be, But I, when I am stronger and can choose what I'm to do," he shouted out loud, " 'O LEERIE, I'LL GO ROUND AT NIGHT AND LIGHT THE LAMPS WITH YOU!' "

He found the line turning to Charlie. When Charlie was six and seven, he'd admired everything Dick did. Every dumb ordinary thing. If he split wood, dug clams, or opened a beer, Charlie would be there with his face swiveled on him like a searchlight.

Tom hadn't been like that. Of course Tom'd had the problem of keeping up with Charlie, that'd kept him more closed in, he'd had to pretend to be indifferent to anything he couldn't do or understand—until he got it and could spring it on Charlie whole. But Charlie had followed Dick around like a duckling—Charlie's wide-open face had looked at Dick like Dick invented everything they found in water or mud—lobster, fish, clams. That knives could cut, that boats could float. O Leerie, I'll go round at night and light the lamps with you.

Dick now thought it amazing that Charlie hadn't turned sour when Dick did. Charlie hadn't followed him into bitterness, he just wandered off his own sweet way. Maybe he'd found another Leerie to go round with.

What faint light there was began to darken. Dick could still see the dark of the sea against the lighter blur of sky, but now he lost his short glimpses across the trough to the defined planes of the wave face, facets of chipped flint. He still had a sense of the enormous distance between waves. Each trough a small valley. And he had an even more puzzled sense of whether it was *Spartina* who moved toward the wave or the wave which came toward her, until she lifted up and went blind in the blown spray across her windshield.

It was full dark when he sensed that the seas were growing confused. From the direction of the spattering across the windshield he figured the wind had pulled around to the southwest. Maybe west. The main roll of the sea was still from the south, but he could feel *Spartina* responding to bulges and shoves of wind on her starboard bow.

This was good news and bad news. The good news was that the wind shift meant *Spartina* was getting to the bottom of the hurricane. The bad news was that she might take some funny bounces. He couldn't see how high the seas were running, but the time *Spartina* spent climbing seemed shorter. It took him a while to figure out what else was different—it was the pitch of the wind.

The higher register was intermittent and more variable, rising and falling, instead of solid noise. And he could hear *Spartina* now. He couldn't hear the engine, but at less than half-power that wouldn't be very loud. What he could hear was her timbers working, groaning and creaking.

As she rolled to port in a little cross sea, he felt his right foot nudged by the Coke can.

He scooped it up, popped the top, and sucked it in. He hadn't realized how dry he was. Almost immediately he began to sweat. He felt it popping out on his forehead and running down his sides. He reached for the thermos of coffee but put both hands on the wheel as *Spartina* slid sideways and rolled sharply to starboard. He turned his head at the first noise. It sounded as though he was grinding his teeth but it was the port section of window. In the glow of instrument lights, he saw the black window turn crackling white. He ducked away, his left hand still on the wheel, his right hand skidding on the floor. His left hand came loose. He was flattened against something, he couldn't tell what. He was being pulled sideways. His left hand found an edge. It came to him slowly that what was pulling him was water.

He felt it pull past his waist, past his knees. He was lying against the door of a locker. It occurred to him with careful instructional slowness that the reason he was lying on what was normally an upright door was that *Spartina* was over on her starboard beam.

He was too dazed to move his body, though he felt his hand move under his face, brush his cheek. After an instant he felt his feet touch the floor. His senses cleared enough for him to feel *Spartina* coming back. He turned and grabbed the edge of the instrument shelf and then the wheel.

Spartina was more or less on her feet. There were no lights on the instruments. Only the binnacle light was still on.

He wasn't sure, but he thought he remembered seeing bluish

light when he was lying down. The wiring shorting out from the water? Where had all the water gone? He began to shake now. The weight of the wheelhouse full of water could have pushed her over—with all that weight so high she could have turned turtle.

He leaned over and opened the locker door with his right hand and groped for the flashlight. He shone it first on the broken window. There were a few pieces of glass in the frame. He knocked them out with the flashlight so they wouldn't blow loose. He shone the flashlight around the wheelhouse. There was an inch or two of water left sloshing around. The instruments were still in their mountings. The loose charts were gone. There was a soggy piece of one plastered to the jamb of the doorway.

He put both hands on the wheel, breathed through his nose. The open door was a piece of good luck. The water had poured out the door before its weight rolled *Spartina*. Once out on deck, it'd just slid away.

Of course the other piece of luck was that he hadn't gone out the door too. And surfed on over the rail.

He could feel his hands shaking, even though they were tight on the spokes of the wheel.

In the lull of the next long valley he tried to turn his mind to sealing the broken window.

It was on the lee side now, so the wind wasn't blowing the spray in, but another freak wave and he'd be up to his knees again. And if *Spartina* buried her bow again . . .

He could feel the edge of adrenaline ebb away. He looked for something to seal the hole. He thought of the mattress on the bunk. The wheelhouse door. The locker door.

The problem kept him in an alert state of indecision. He could hear the noise of the wind humming across the open hole. He lost track of time.

What brought him to was that he had to take a leak. He shook his head. He realized he'd been close to nodding off on his feet. He unsnapped his bib, shoved it down, and pissed into the inch of water still sliding around his feet.

He examined the window with the flashlight. Maybe not as bad as he thought. Only three feet by two feet. He took the thermos out of its bracket and put the flashlight in its place. It shone bleakly on the dead instruments, on the film of water at his feet. He drank the coffee and tossed the thermos into the locker.

Spartina took a wave over her bow that danced around the wheelhouse. By the flashlight Dick saw a bucketful of wave spill in the window. It was the locker door banging loose that nudged him. He filled his jacket pocket with nails. He took a cat's paw from his tool box and tore the locker-door hinges loose.

In the next long trough he held the door up to the window. It didn't fit, but better too big than too small. In the relative lull of each trough he banged in a couple of nails, through the plywood door, into the frame.

Back at the wheel he looked sideways at it. It looked like hell. One good smack of another cross-wave and it'd come flying in and he'd be lying on it like a damn Indian yogi on a bed of nails. He got his screw gun out of his tool chest. He couldn't remember if the batteries had got wet. No. The locker door had been closed then. He was clumsy with the screw gun, he wasn't used to using it left-handed. He zapped the first screw in askew, but the next six spun in straight. He was sweating again. The piece of plywood still seemed ominous. He got a short piece of wire and used his left hand to take some turns around the knob of the locker door. He made the other end fast to a bracket on the wall. At least this way, if the whole thing got knocked in, it would pull up short before it took his head off.

His jumping around and banging had revved him up some. Or maybe the coffee was kicking in. He checked his watch and turned out the flashlight. Getting on to midnight. Unless *Spartina* had drifted back a whole lot, she should be coming out.

He could feel the seas diminishing. The crests were steeper—he could hear them sizzle over the bow—but the size of everything was settling down. The time in each trough was shorter, and the time climbing the next wave. He felt a small upward pressure of hope through his chest and shoulders. And a pain in his rib cage, a twinge in his right side when he breathed. He couldn't remember hurting himself.

He began checking his watch too often. He'd wait and wait and then sneak a look, only to find that what he'd hoped would be an elapsed hour had only been fifteen minutes.

At three in the morning he began to talk to himself. "No more looking. Forget the goddamn watch. The watch is nothing to do with it." He pushed the watch up under his sleeve so it wouldn't be so easy to get a look at it.

He wasn't surprised to hear a brass band playing. It came from somewhere off the port bow, somewhere beyond the boarded-up window. It was playing a march. At first he couldn't hear it well enough to tell what march it was. Then it came closer and he heard piccolos tweeting above the melody, and he recognized "The Stars and Stripes Forever." He began to march in place, picking his knees up until they hit the wheel. He heard the trombones and sousaphones take it, and then the whole band crashed into the big wide-open part. He sang along. "Be-ee kind to your web-footed friends, for a duck may be somebody's mother. . . ."

The band stopped. Those weren't the real words, but what the hell . . . he'd got the goddamn poem right.

He took a deep breath and let it out through his teeth. Jesus. He was going nuts. Completely nuts. Into the wide blue yonder.

No, not completely nuts. He wasn't *doing* anything crazy. He just better watch himself. It didn't matter what he heard or what he thought so long as he kept *Spartina* headed up. She'd do fine, if he could just watch himself.

Then he began to suspect that something had gone wrong. That the waves that had whomped down on her had spread her, had pulled her deck planking apart. That each time a wave spilled on her, she was taking on water through the gaps.

Or something was up with the engine. Something was working loose. One little spot of metal fatigue was working. If anything was wrong below, there wasn't a damn thing he could do.

He looked at the compass. He was a little surprised to find that, although he was still taking the seas more or less bow on, *Spartina* was headed southwest. There was less spray, and what there was was rolling rather than driving across the windshield. He couldn't tell for sure which way the wind was blowing. It would still be pretty stiff even if he was past the southern edge of the storm.

He said out loud, "One thing at a time. Wait'll it gets light. Once it gets light, you'll see what's going on. Once it gets light, you'll wake up some."

But when it began to turn light, he felt more and more exhausted. Each shade of lighter gray in the sky seemed to sap him. He began to blink off and on, sleeping for a few seconds like a porpoise. It wasn't doing him much good.

By six the gray light was brighter than anything he'd seen since he hit the storm. It wasn't clear, but it was clearing. The seas weren't huge, but were steep and sharp-crested now that the wind wasn't tearing off the tops. But it wasn't the condition of the sea that was his problem. It was his own condition. He hadn't done anything dumb yet, but he was getting to a state where he wasn't sure he could watch himself.

He held on for another hour. He tried jigging and jogging in place to get his blood moving. It pepped him up some but at the same time made him feel more lightheaded. He began to fear he was just going to give way. The fear sent a ripple of energy through him, but it wasn't enough.

At last he recognized that he was done, that he'd have to put all his trust in her. He slipped the loops of inner tube over the spokes, cut back on the throttle to idle, and broke out the sea anchor from the one intact starboard locker. He put her in neutral. He tucked the bulky canvas and the stiff hemp bridle and line under one arm and went out the door. Just aft of the wheelhouse he clipped onto the lifeline and made his way onto the foredeck. When he glanced at the wheelhouse he saw that the paint looked like it had been sandblasted. In places it was down to bare wood.

He got the sea anchor over the side, made the end of the line fast, and paid off the coil.

When he turned the corner to go back into the wheelhouse he was pulled up short by the line to his waist.

He said, "Wake up, dumbo." His voice surprised him. It sounded like somebody else.

He got back to the wheel and watched the line to the sea anchor. As the bow rose he saw a length of the taut line slice up out of the water and shake off droplets. Setting out a sea anchor had always struck Dick as something like flying a kite, except, once you got the big canvas cone out there, it was supposed to fly you.

He didn't know exactly where *Spartina* was. He knew roughly— east of the gap between Monomoy and Nantucket. With the wind out of the northwest and the seas southwest, he wasn't going to drift onto anything but plenty of water. All he needed was to rest his legs for a half-hour. He pulled a life vest out of the locker. It was thick enough so he wasn't sitting in the puddle of water that was sliding around. He set his back against the one remaining locker door. He felt his shoulders and neck sag with relief. He tightened up again as he thought to clip his line to the locker handle. He sagged back again. The pale sun was near the top of the open door.

He stretched his legs out straight and felt them ease. He thought, Okay, just a few minutes of this. Just till the sun gets a little higher. As his eyes closed he thought, This may be the dumb thing I've been trying not to do.

*H*e woke up from the tugging on his lifeline. He was on his side, looking out the wheelhouse door. The sky had darkened some. The far-off clouds were as puffed as those in *A Child's Garden of Verses*.

He lay for a moment longer, half dazed, half alert to his own motion as he rolled fore and aft, snubbed on his roll toward the doorway by the line. His hands were wet, his left cheek was sticky with salt water. The motion would have been comforting except for the tug at his waist.

It was when he touched his puckered hand to his face that he woke up fully. In a sudden panic he tugged himself upright by the lifeline. Through the windshield he saw the huge glowing western sky, shooting off reds through the clouds. *Spartina*'s gray foredeck gave off a pretty violet as it dipped and caught the early-evening fall of light. He saw the line to the sea anchor stir in the chock.

He said, "You're a lucky son of a bitch, you dumb son of a bitch."

He let *Spartina* lie to a while longer. He found a Hershey bar and a last swallow of cold coffee in the thermos. He felt slow and strangely heavy when he moved. He was dully stiff all over except for his side, which hurt sharply. All in all, not so bad.

As long as she was lying to with some comfort, he got his sextant and stepped outside the door. The wind was fresh, and the seas still running fairly high, but regular. It took him a long while to get a reading, even with his back braced against the door. His legs were still wobbly, and his hand-eye coordination was slow.

After he'd worked out the bearings, he swore at himself. The chart had washed away. He pawed through the shelf of the intact locker and got a larger-scale chart. His notion of *Spartina*'s position was worse than approximate, but even a mile of error wouldn't kill him.

Spartina had been pushed north some. She was about forty-five miles east of Stone Horse Lightship off Monomoy Point. That suited him. He'd take her home along Cape Cod—some seas might be running, but the wind would keep him offshore. He checked the tide table. If he got a move on, he could catch the tide turning his way from Woods Hole to Cuttyhunk, pick up a few knots for that leg. With luck, he'd be home for breakfast.

He took another ten minutes to go below and fill the thermos with tea and condensed milk. His appetite grew sharp, but he kept himself from shoving in too much at once. He settled for a cup of instant chicken-noodle soup, hot enough so he had to drink it slow. He wrapped two cheese sandwiches for later.

The sun was down. He swore at himself, and by last light he ran the bilge pumps. They spat, then ran heavy enough so he came to attention. They eased. He went below for a look, the lights down here worked, just a quick glance at everything. Nothing wrong he could see. That amount of water could come from a lot of things. Maybe one of the wells wasn't tight, or had sloshed some when she'd been knocked on her beam end.

Just before going back on deck, he stood still. He'd spent quite some time right here, a few hours pretty nearly every day for the better part of four years. But holding on now, listening to her move, her wooden creaks and sighs clear in the silence of the engine, he felt she was all new to him. He knew where everything was, it wasn't that. But this view of her took him by surprise, like when he'd walked in to see May after Charlie was born.

He went back up, cranked the engine, took in the sea anchor, and got her under way. She wasn't home yet.

He saw the first light, counted the interval . . . one thousand nine, one thousand ten, blink. He knew where he was. He'd be able to pick up the light at Monomoy, some more lights along Cape Cod, and through Vineyard Sound he'd even be able to see the islands.

At first light he was in Vineyard Sound. The Vineyard was a dark rise against the eastern sky, but Naushon, Nashaweena, Pasque, and Cuttyhunk turned from granite gray to purple, from purple to rose as the early light touched them. *Spartina* picked up some speed as the tide began to run hard with her. When he pushed past Cuttyhunk he saw Two-Mile Light flash around, a dart of unnatural strobe-silver about to be subdued by day.

And then Sakonnet Point. Then Brenton Reef Light, off the bow, and then abeam. And dead ahead Point Judith. He said, "Now you smell the barn." And for the first time it occurred to him to wonder what kind of shape the barn would be in.

As he came up to the harbor of refuge he could see the tide still dumping, pushing out a steady pulse of muddy water through the gap in the breakwater. When he nosed *Spartina* inside and headed for the breachway into the salt pond, he was hailed by a Coast Guard tug. He cut the throttle back and let her come alongside. A Coast Guard lieutenant addressed him through a bullhorn. "If you're going into Point Judith Pond . . . watch out for floating wreckage. It might be better . . . to wait for the tide to turn . . . before you go in."

That speech was polite enough, so he put her in neutral and came out on deck to acknowledge it. He saw there was a seventy-foot fishing boat on the Galilee Road.

The hands on the tug threw him a line, and then another, and he pulled *Spartina* against the huge bumpers of the tug and made her fast.

He pointed at the boat on the road.

A chief said, "It's worse inside the harbor."

"How long till low water?"

"It should've been slack now," the chief said, "but that's a lot of water in there."

The tug was bigger than *Spartina* but her afterdeck lower, so when the chief ordered coffee for Dick, the seaman he sent to fetch the pot had to reach up to *Spartina*'s rail to fill Dick's mug.

The lieutenant and the chief told Dick that this was worse than '54, but not so bad as '38. So far as they knew, no one was killed, at least around here. They'd been in Wickford when it hit and just got to the harbor of refuge this morning. For the moment they were standing by for any distress signals, and after a bit they were going to help clear the channel.

Dick was grateful for the coffee and the news. But when they looked *Spartina* over and asked him where he'd been, he felt uncomfortable.

The chief noticed the bare patches on the wheelhouse, and some more along the hull. The lieutenant asked if his crew was below.

Dick said, "I took her out alone," and was embarrassed. He saw himself standing there naked, stripped down to his folly. His affection for *Spartina,* his pride in her, his satisfaction that he'd done okay handling her, and his relief at being home were gone for the moment. He knew what he'd think of some damn fool who took a boat alone across the path of a hurricane. He'd admire his luck, but he wouldn't admire him.

Without raising his eyes, he said, "I got sideswiped some by the other side. I'd hoped to get clear to the east."

The lieutenant said, "How long have you been out?"

The chief said, "Looks like more than sideswiped."

"Three days."

"You must be tired," the lieutenant said.

"You been on your radio?" the chief asked. "Let someone know you're back?"

"The radio's out."

The chief said to the lieutenant, "Maybe we should contact the station, sir. They may have this vessel missing." He turned to Dick. "At least we didn't have to go look for you."

The lieutenant ordered a seaman to get on the radio. He turned to Dick. "What's the name of your vessel?"

"Spartina-May."

"Is there anyone you'd like the station to call? Of course the phone lines may be down."

"Eddie Wormsley. In Perryville. That's where my wife and kids are."

Dick started to ask what the damage was like at the top of the pond, but these men hadn't been there, and Dick didn't want to hear what they'd only heard.

He said, "I'm going to go take a look at something. I'll be back when the tide turns."

He cast off from the tug and headed out the west gap in the breakwater. It was less than two miles to the opening into Sawtooth Pond. It took him a minute to take in what was different about the beach. There wasn't a single beach house. There had been two dozen, not to mention the trailer camp on the high ground of Matunuck Point. The old undermined seawall, a ruin for twenty-five years, was unmoved.

When he got just outside the cut to Sawtooth Pond he saw that the storm had torn it wide open. It had been fifteen yards across, now it was fifty.

Looking up the cut, he saw the Wedding Cake was still standing. He got out his binoculars. The fretwork on the front porch was smashed, some of the shutters were torn off, and the windows were broken. The paint was scoured even more than *Spartina*'s. The wind would have picked up sand from the top of the dunes and blown it at the house like birdshot.

There wasn't a tree or a bush upright on Sawtooth Island. Just a few pieces of wood wedged among the close-set rocks.

The tide was still running out of the cut in slow brown coils that were laced with grass and leaves and the occasional whiteness of a split branch bobbing just under the surface. A whole willow swam by looking like a giant jellyfish. Darker, heavier matter was moving too. Dick put *Spartina* in neutral and let the wind back her off the junk spewing and spreading in the slow coastwise current. Looking at the flow, Dick realized the sandbar had been cut by the storm—there seemed to be a sea-dredged channel through it.

The cottages which were set back up Sawtooth Point looked okay, but the ones right along the creek had taken a beating. Schuyler and Marie's had a line of water stain and flecks of grass, seaweed, and silt up to the second story. The picture window was smashed and the waterfront porch was half torn away and sagging into the creek.

Dick wondered how far up the creek the surge had gone. Could be his house was flooded.

He looked beyond the flat shore up to the tangled growth covering the Matunuck Hills, then back along the dunes, where the low grasses had held on, and then to the confluence of Saw-tooth Creek and Pierce Creek and the low table of spartina that spread out between them. His calculations of damage gave way, not to another thought, but to a rush of green. He lowered the binoculars. The air was scrubbed so clean, the wind had winnowed the dead brown away so completely, the green was so bright in the morning light that particular blades jumped across the water to his eyes. Green against the black muck of the marsh, green against the crystals of new-sifted sand, and green on the hills against the quick blue sky.

Just this place, the shore from Green Hill to Galilee, the upland from the beach to the Great Swamp, the Matunuck Hills, and Wakefield, just five miles wide and five miles deep, was just about all the land he knew. He hadn't thought it could come on him like this. It was as if he'd been blown clean as the marsh grass, been scoured even more than *Spartina*'s wheelhouse or the Wedding Cake. Each time he looked along the stretch of land, the green came into him like a stroke of paint on parched clean wood.

He saw a jeep coming along the bird-sanctuary beach. He let *Spartina* blow a little farther offshore, then put her in gear and made his way cautiously back through the breakwater.

*H*e followed the Coast Guard tug in through the breachway, keeping an eye on the tug's wake and the water slipping by her hull for anything likely to foul his propeller or even just give it a good whack. He didn't have time to take more than a quick look to port toward Joxer's crab-processing plant. The roof was still on, the sandbags still piled against the walls and windows. The *Lydia P.*

wasn't home yet. There seemed to be some damage to the tightly clustered houses in Jerusalem. The bridge across the slough from Point Judith Pond to Potter Pond was out.

On the other side of the channel, the piers by Galilee were a shambles. The Co-op and George's Restaurant were still standing, but all the smaller buildings and sheds were scattered in pieces all the way to the Escape Road. There were some trucks and bulldozers at work clearing the road and parking lot. The boats that had been hauled far back and tied down looked to have scraped through okay. One near the pier had a utility pole across her deck, her bulwarks smashed, but her hull intact. The boats left in the slips were better off the closer they were to the dock. The outermost boats must have provided some shelter, even after they sank. The innermost boats had been smashed around on top, but their hulls seemed to be tight. *Mamzelle* was on the bottom. Even at low tide Dick could only see a bit of her wheelhouse. The rest of her superstructure was gone.

The tug stopped at the state pier. Dick went on up the salt pond slowly. All the little islands had been engulfed. It was hard to tell the ones that had had cottages on them from the ones that hadn't— every islet was evenly littered with broken lumber.

Dick had to feel his way. The channel had been redredged to eight feet the year before, but he wasn't sure what the storm might have done. Some of the channel markers had survived, but they were so few and far between he had to piece out a lot of the zigs and zags from memory.

The moorings in front of the boatyard were swept clean. The boats that hadn't been hauled had either broken loose or gone to the bottom. He saw a couple of submerged boats tugging heavily on their half-submerged mooring buoys. Dick could also see from far off that the water had surged at least twenty feet. Some of the boats that had torn loose were splattered against the abutments of the Route 1 bridge over the north finger of the pond.

He wouldn't have to argue with the manager about finding a vacant mooring. What he might have trouble with was finding a loose dinghy to get himself in from the mooring. The docks and the sheds were in pieces. The office was caved in on the near side. He wondered if the phone worked. He went into neutral and looked for a safe mooring, well clear of any hulk.

He saw his pickup moving slowly across the bridge, followed by a Natural Resources jeep. They stopped way up in the parking lot, unable to find a way through the scatter of boats, some still in their cradles, some toppled but whole, some stove in, and some snapped in half.

Dick pulled up to a fragment of dock. He thought he might hose off some of the salt from *Spartina,* but he was relieved when he found the dockside spigot didn't work. He leaned against a pile, a little dizzy from fatigue and the phantom motion of *Spartina* in his legs. May and Charlie and Tom stood on the bulkhead, unable to get down to him because the gangplank was gone. Charlie finally jumped down. The piece of floating dock lurched. Charlie got to his feet and hugged him.

Dick said, "Yeah, I'm back," and Charlie made way for Tom.

Dick said, "You boys see if you can get your mother down."

Eddie swung May down by her hands and the boys caught her. May found her footing and stood for a second. Dick folded her in. For a moment he was giddy with the feel of her back under her dress, her hair against his face, the real gladness with which she held on to him.

She raised her head. He could see her go back to being of two minds. He said, "She did fine. It was the only thing to do. I got her out past the worst."

May studied his face but didn't say anything. Eddie jumped and grabbed his hand. "By God, you did it, Dick."

"She did fine. She's a good boat."

"Well, by God. You must be tired."

"Tired enough." Dick turned to Charlie. "You boys see if you can find some kind of dinghy so I can put her on her mooring."

Elsie was standing on the edge of the bulkhead. She was in her uniform, and had her movie camera on her shoulder. She said, "Welcome home, Captain Pierce."

Dick nodded. "Well, I kept your investment afloat. Yours and Miss Perry's."

Elsie shook her head. "Good God."

Charlie and Tom shinnied back up a pile next to the bulkhead. Eddie made a stirrup of his hands and hoisted May so she could reach the top of the wall. The boys pulled her up. Eddie came back and cast off *Spartina*'s lines, and Dick backed her off the float, picked up the mooring, and shut her down. The boys pulled an aluminum johnboat down the ramp and paddled it with pieces of plank out to *Spartina*'s stern, laughing and splashing.

"God," Dick said, "what kind of a Chinese fire drill you boys running here?"

Dick looked down at them. They were glad to see him, no two minds about it.

"Come on, Dad, get in."

"Well, hold her steady, Tom. I didn't go through a goddamn hurricane to come home and capsize."

"Come on, Dad. We're holding on."

Dick lowered himself in and thudded onto the seat. His ribs hurt. His legs felt like barrels. "Now, don't you boys do anything rash. I'm too old to get wet."

Tom said, "You *could* use a bath, Dad. I thought you put a shower on *Spartina*."

"You just tend to your paddling."

The boys churned away, and the johnboat wobbled her way toward shore. Dick turned sideways and touched them both, Tom on his knees as he sat in the stern, Charlie's back as he knelt in the bow.

"You boys get Miss Perry's books out?"

"Yes."

"You sink the big skiff like I said?"

"Yes."

"You took your little skiff to Eddie's?"

"Yes."

"But you didn't think to bring it down here to get me off."

Charlie said, "Oh."

Tom said, "Jees, Dad. Elsie came by and told us you were coming in. We just came."

"Never mind about the skiff, then. You did fine." Dick felt he should say more, but he also felt blocked. What was wrong with him? He made an effort. "And you got you and your mother safe to Eddie's."

Charlie said, "Yeah. There's no phone and no electricity, but we were okay."

"You ought to see the road," Tom said. "There's stuff all over it."

"But you were okay at Eddie's, were you?"

"Yeah," Tom said, "it was neat. The eye went right over us. We were down in the cellar and you could hear trees cracking and the wind blowing and then it got all quiet."

"But you were all okay."

"Mom was worried," Charlie said. "She was worried about you. I explained it to her, how you were out beyond it. Even down in the cellar you could feel the whole house shake, and it was hard to think there was someplace where it wasn't stormy."

Dick nodded. May had a right to be mad at him. The thought tired him.

They hauled the johnboat up the ramp and walked up to the pickup. Elsie pulled up alongside in her jeep. "They got you back on the job," Dick said. "I guess that was your jeep I saw on the beach."

"Yes, I recognized *Spartina*. I almost drove into the sea. I—"

"Thank you for bringing May and the boys."

Elsie said, "It's good to see you back. I'll go tell Miss Perry. She asked after you." Elsie laughed. "It's odd. The hurricane seems to have snapped her out of her spell. You didn't hear anything about Captain Texeira, did you?"

"Not for a while. My radio went out. But the *Lydia* was well east of *Spartina*. She should be okay. You could ask the Coast Guard."

"Okay." She paused. "See you later. I'll be driving around all day, but you can get me on my CB."

The boys climbed into the bed of the pickup. Dick let Eddie drive. They had to run a slalom course along Route 1. There were trees down, bits of fence, roofs, brush. There were tongues of silt in a couple of low places where the water had licked across.

"You seen the house?" Dick asked May.

"No."

Eddie said, "I'll go take a look with you after you get some rest. I got to help clear some roads this morning."

Eddie drove right on by when they passed Dick's driveway on the other side of Route 1. Dick craned his head to see, but the grove of bushes in the median strip cut him off.

"I'll take you down later," Eddie said. "Let's go get some breakfast."

Dick figured Eddie had taken a look and it was pretty bad. For some reason this didn't dismay Dick. Maybe he was too tired to worry anymore. He felt odd. He recognized he'd been his old crusty self with the boys, but he felt different. It just didn't show yet. This was fine with him, he didn't believe in sudden change. What he did like was the idea that feelings already in him had been laid bare to himself by the storm, some bare rock of what he really cared about.

Eddie said, "I guess your boat's proved her worth. You could probably sell her for two hundred thousand. She's passed the hardest test there's likely to be."

Dick shook his head. "I've never held with that idea. You see a big fancy sailboat for sale in Newport, the ad says 'Two trans-atlantic crossings.' You're supposed to think that's good. What it really means is she most likely needs some work. I probably took four or five years off *Spartina*'s life." Dick laughed. "I took her from maidenhood to middle age without much joy of youth."

May said, "I guess you didn't get as far out as you thought you could."

Dick took May's hand. She let it lie in his. "May, I figured it the best I could. And it worked out okay. Not perfect, but okay. I recognize it was hard on you, and I'm sorry for that."

May didn't say anything, but she didn't take her hand away.

Eddie said, "You won't have any trouble getting a crew. The boys'll figure you can get through anything."

Dick said, "Not if the whole story gets out. I'm not sure I'd sign on myself with a skipper who'll do any damn thing to save his boat. I'd rather be with someone who'll let a boat go. Gets every-body back, or, better yet, keeps them at home. Now, if the word is that I was just following right behind Captain Texeira and didn't have much trouble, then I'll get someone to sign on, someone who's been around a while."

May said, "At least it didn't cross your mind to take Charlie."

"You're right," Dick said, "it didn't cross my mind."

Eddie swung the pickup up the Ministerial Road and, after a slow half-mile through twigs and small branches, into his driveway. "Here you are," he said, "your home away from home." He came round and opened the door for May. He said to Dick, "You want me to fix you some breakfast?"

"I'll get it," May said. "If you don't mind, Eddie. The boys can help you in the yard. I'll fix something for all of us."

May took Dick inside and began to cry. She rolled her forehead on his shoulder while she cried, and then began to thump her head against his chest. Dick stopped her and held her still and said, "It won't happen like this again, May. It just won't."

She said, "Maybe not," and went to the stove. She said, "There's no running water but I'll heat up a bucket so you can wash up."

"I'm sorry, May."

"I brought your razor and your toothbrush. They're in the bathroom. You left without them."

Dick laughed. "I knew there was something I forgot."

May didn't laugh, but when he held her hips from behind and pressed against her back he felt her ease up. Not give in, but ease up.

Eddie had given May and Dick his own room. Dick scrubbed off, shaved, and brushed his teeth. He went in and lay down for a minute. He heard the boys come in, May and the boys setting the table. When he woke up he heard the same thing—May calling the boys in and the clink of plates. But when he got up he found it was suppertime.

*D*ick had wanted to spend the day raising the big skiff. He'd wanted to make a list of repairs to *Spartina*'s wheelhouse and check the hull and go see his insurance agent. Everyone else had been working. Eddie had been out on the roads all day, the boys had been busy in Eddie's yard, and May had done a load of wash by hand and hung it out.

At supper Eddie said, "If the power don't come back on soon, I'll lose what's in my freezer." But that was his only complaint. He was making good money. He'd run into half a dozen house owners who wanted him to clear their drives and yards and do repairs. Eddie said, "I could turn the corner, I could turn out to be a general contractor. I already built some sheds and garages cheaper than those prefabs they sell at the Wakefield Branch, and people like 'em better, they like that log-cabin look. And now I'm out on the road and people see me, they make a deal. The phones are still out, so they can't call anybody else. And Elsie's been putting out the word. She got me on her CB this afternoon, told me to go by and see some folks and put in some estimates on boathouses. I should get some signs: 'This boathouse being repaired by Edward Wormsley ST3-7801.' No, a P.O. box. And a sign for right here: 'Hurricane repair. Inquire within.' I'll tell you what you could do, Dick, is line up some boat-repair contracts for this winter. I'll help you haul 'em, we got my flatbed with the hoist. I'll build cradles here in my yard. I got plenty of wood. Six or seven of those'll get you though the bad part of the winter. There'll be weeks you won't be going out at all."

Dick nodded. "First I got to go out and see if the storm left me any pots. I may have to make quite a few."

"First you may have to make a new house," May said. "We can't camp out on Eddie all fall."

"I don't see why not," Eddie said. "I'm all alone except when my boy comes on weekends. We can fix up the back room for your boys. I'll bunk in my boy's room. We could have a pretty good time of it."

"Oh, Eddie," May said. "We can't . . ."

"And, come November, Dick and I can shoot a few geese. Take Charlie and Tom. Maybe a deer or two. Turn your boys into woodsmen."

Dick nodded, but didn't say anything. He already was too obliged to Eddie.

"We could make pots in the basement," Eddie said. "You, me, the boys. Get my boy off his motorcycle, make him pitch in. Regular assembly line. Make enough pots each weekend for you to add a trawl every week."

Dick said, "What about your firewood business?"

"I'm way ahead. Way ahead. When I cut up the trees I'm hauling now, I'll be two years ahead. There's only so much firewood to be sold around here. I'm branching out."

"Well, May's right. I got to look at the house before anything else." Dick got up, pulled out his truck key.

Charlie and Tom asked to go. Dick said, "I want to get a look by myself first." He feared he was being a little hard again. "We'll all go tomorrow. I'll be right back after I get a look. I remember building it. I'd like to just get a look by myself."

But when he came to his driveway, he lost his nerve. He decided to look at the cottages on Sawtooth Point, a benchmark, so he could say about his own house, "It's not so bad, could be worse."

The cottages just off the road inside the entrance were all right. Someone had covered the windows, left openings to equalize the air pressure so nothing popped. Some water had got to them but not really in them. Dick circled around to the Bigelow and Buttrick houses. The Bigelows' was banged up but okay. It was a bit higher than the Buttrick house. The Buttrick house was in trouble. A corner had been undercut and lurched a foot toward the pond. The house was still up, but half the window frames had popped out. A lot of planking had sprung loose. The corner post itself was standing but skewed.

It could be worse. Maybe they could jack up the corner, replace the post and ... Probably not.

Dick went on to the Wedding Cake, walked around it. He realized how smart his great-uncle had been about one thing. The Wedding Cake was near the end of the point but was up on a knob. The water had reached it, but hadn't even got up on the high seaward porch. Just left debris and seaweed on the steps and the huge granite blocks of the above-ground foundation. The wind had done what it could, but the fretwork and windows and shutters were all it harmed. Dick felt a rise in his mood—good for Uncle Arthur. Good for the Pierces.

By the seaward corner of the house there was a tanker truck with the Salviatti Company emblem on it. Dick was puzzled for a minute, then saw the hose. They'd been spraying a truckful of fresh water down the lawn to get the salt off. They could have used that water on the potato field behind the Matunuck beach, maybe saved a crop instead of a lawn. It was their money, they could do what they pleased. It was their house now. But they should still be grateful to Uncle Arthur.

Dick started back up the point. In front of the Van der Hoevels' cottage he saw Parker's VW station wagon. Dick parked alongside and started down the path. From *Spartina* he'd seen that the porch had been knocked into the creek, but the main part of the cottage was standing, although the doors and windows had popped. Dick was about to shout to Parker when he heard voices. The low sun was in his eyes. He took a step forward into the shadow of the house. His foot crunched on a piece of glass. He looked down at it, and then up when he heard a woman moaning. He saw Marie's head appear in profile in the side of the bay window. There was no glass in it, though the network of lozenge mullions was half intact, sagging outward.

Dick thought she was crying over her house. Her head moved backward and disappeared. Her arms and hands reappeared. She picked up the long cushion of the window seat, shook it, flipped it over, and ran one hand over it. Her head reappeared, her cheek drowned in her loose hair. Her hands slid along the cushion and braced against the windowsill. Her shoulders were moving as though she was sobbing. She lowered her forehead onto the cushion.

Dick began to back away. He hadn't thought she'd have cared so much about the cottage. But maybe they were wiped out. Uninsured . . .

Her head and shoulders were suddenly covered. It was so abrupt Dick jumped sideways. She made another noise. It took him a moment to realize she was laughing. What was covering her head was her long skirt, flipped up.

Dick's right ribs hurt from having jerked so suddenly. He tucked his elbow over them and kept crabbing away, off the path now, in between the ornamental bushes.

Well, that's another way to take it, he thought, when your house is coming down around your ears. Now he was into the raspberry bushes. He ripped his pants leg free from a tendril. He looked back, ashamed but prickled and heated up in spite of himself.

Schuyler's head came forward, his chin on her back. It wasn't Schuyler. It was Parker.

Jesus, Parker. Of course. It was Parker's car. You son of a bitch, Parker. You'll do anything.

Dick turned away, tucked his chin down. He clambered over a skinny uprooted pine. He got his hand gummy pushing away a branch. He was surprised at how churned he felt, how nasty he felt himself. He was angry that he was stuck with seeing it. Angry at the sharp sticky impression he carried away. Angry that he looked back once more.

They were just rearranging themselves. Dick backed away. They got up lengthwise on the window seat, face to face, their feet toward him. He almost laughed when he saw they both had their sneakers on. Two pairs of sneakers. All four sneakers allemande left, and do-si-do. Bow to your partner.

Dick got back to the road and climbed into his truck. He hesitated to start it. He heard Marie's voice, a faint high note. He turned the key.

He said out loud, "Goddamn," but he carried away the sight of her hair on her cheek, her hands sliding on the window seat. She'd turned the goddamn cushion while it was going on! Against the sound of the motor running and the wheels crunching, he imagined noises from her thin-lipped mouth, blown open like the fancy windows of the cottage.

"You son of a bitch, Parker," he said, but he couldn't shake it, he was talking to himself. "Go back to sea, get out of this."

He was about to go by the turn to his house. He thought, They'll ask what I saw.

He parked the truck at the head of the driveway. So far so good. The boys had done a good job with the front windows, boarded them up good but left some room to breathe. The chimney was toppled. The silt line was above the windowsills. It could be worse.

When he got to the back he took one look and sagged. He looked again and sat down on the end of the driveway. He picked up a handful of gravel and let it trickle out.

It was his own goddamn fault. It wasn't the boys' fault, he hadn't told them. *He* hadn't thought of it, no reason for them to have thought of it.

There was a piece of *Spartina*'s old cradle sticking through the wall, half inside the house. Through the hole around it, he saw a flap of black paper, broken studs. The broken clapboard had been plucked away. Must have happened early—a lot of wind had worked it over.

Another piece of cradle had cracked into the southeast corner post. It wasn't as obvious as the hole in the wall, but the post was probably broke. He didn't get up to go look.

He couldn't have put the shed and cradle in a worse place if he'd meant to. Due southeast. Might as well have aimed a cannon at the house.

He made a right angle of his thumb and forefinger and held it up toward the corner of the house. No question about it, the roof was off line, the corner was sagging.

He sat there. The longer he sat, the better it got. The house was insured, the bank holding the mortgage had seen to that. The boat hadn't been, so if something had to get hurt, this was the place.

The boat was okay, May and the boys were okay, he was okay. He owed something to the storm. He might as well pay here.

The kitchen door was gone, the screen door too. There was a last bit of light coming from the sky shining on the wet slime on the kitchen floor.

His butt was getting cold. He was tired. He'd only been up a couple of hours and he was ready to climb back in bed.

May would take it hard. First thing she would take in—well, maybe second thing after the hole in the wall—would be what was all over her nice kitchen floor.

He got up to go look at his wharf. He'd better go look now, May wouldn't take it right if he wandered off to see it tomorrow.

The wharf was fine. He couldn't believe it. It had mud, weeds, and sticks all over it, but all four posts were solid. Why shouldn't it be, dummy? It let the water through, nothing to push against. The flat part was flat, nothing sticking up, the water just flowed flat across the top.

Of course that was what got *Spartina* through too. There wasn't anything solid sticking up on her but the wheelhouse. And what there was of her to push against was curved—her hull was as curved as a pumpkin seed. He thought, We did okay, Uncle Arthur and me.

He stood on the wharf and looked across Pierce Creek. A few big trees were down, and the smaller stuff was stripped. He could see clear across his bit of land, across Sawtooth Creek, and onto the salt marsh, rustling and silver in the last light.

He began to cry in gratitude. He stopped and washed his face in the creek. He laughed at himself. He said, "I could have had lots more swept away. I could have been swept away along with them fornicating ants in tennis shoes."

He started for the truck. He'd tell May it wasn't so bad, could be worse. Get her to have a drink with him. Get her tipsy on a drink or two. Get in his lawful bed.

Dick heard an engine. It was just dark enough to see headlight beams swing through the trees. He went back up the path and recognized the close-set squint of jeep lights.

Elsie got out the passenger side and asked Dick if he could give her a ride home. He said yes and Elsie sent her partner away with the jeep.

By the time Elsie walked to him, the jeep was in third gear on Route 1. She took his hand and said she was sorry his house was so hard hit.

Dick said, "It could be worse. How'd your house do?"

"The greenhouse roof has a hole in it. Mary and I got the big window covered. It's okay." Elsie let his hand go and said, "I'm bushed. I've been chasing folks out of their wrecked houses all afternoon. Some people wanted to spend the night in houses that would cave in if someone sneezed."

It took Dick by surprise that she leaned in to him just then, pulled herself in with her arms around him. He'd forgotten how short she was, how compact and strong. She put a hand on his chest and tilted her head back. "I'm glad to see you. I'm glad I saw your truck just now." She touched his cheek. "Come on, Dick. You can be a little glad to see me. A little gladness isn't going to kill you."

She kissed him on the cheek. "Okay," she said, "I don't mind a more chaste tone, just so long as you're glad to see me."

Dick said, "Yeah, I'm glad to see you."

Elsie said, "In spite of yourself," and shook his upper arm. He'd forgotten she had tomboy gestures like that, especially when she was in uniform. They were as surprisingly off center as when she got dolled up in lipstick and her backless dress.

"Oh," she said, "Captain Texeira's back. He stopped by to see Miss Perry."

"Did he leave flowers?"

Elsie laughed. "Yes. I don't know where he found any, but he did." Elsie added, "Oh, hey, could you do me a favor? While it's still light enough?"

What Elsie wanted was to go into the salt marsh with his truck. She said, "I know you know where the old causeway is." She laughed. "I want to get something I saw from the beach."

They drove into the bird sanctuary and then out onto the marsh, slithering a little in the debris that had caught on the slight rise made by the submerged slabs and boulders of the old causeway. They got to the little plateau of marsh where the *Spartina patens* gave way to *Spartina alterniflora,* a little salt meadow between the salt marsh and the back of the dunes.

Dick turned the truck so the beams shone where Elsie pointed.

"Do you see it?" Elsie said. "There it is. The blue canoe."

Dick shut off the light and they walked out to it, their feet squeezing up water through the matted stalks. Dick called to Elsie, who was ahead of him, to slow down. "There may be some funny holes in here." She waited for him and took his hand. They walked another fifty yards, steadying each other hand in hand, but when they got close, Elsie hurried ahead.

She walked around the canoe bent over, her hands on the gunwales.

"I don't believe it! It's whole!" Elsie's voice sounded girlish. "It must have just surfed up here on the surge. Or sailed along in the wind. And caught here in the grass. When you think of everything else that's smashed . . ."

Dick peered toward Sawtooth Pond. In the evening light he could just make out the silhouette of the rocks on Sawtooth Island. He said, "It must be a mile from the point."

Elsie came round to his side of the canoe and began to cry, holding on to him like a crying child.

After a bit Dick said, "What is it? What is it, Elsie?" He thought she might be about to tell him she was pregnant. He felt his worry about her turn, just a little shift that changed it from being hard-pressed and taut to being tender.

Elsie said, "Jesus. I don't know why. . . . I've only cried two times in ages, and both times it's been with you."

Dick shifted his foot that was getting wet in the hole it had made.

Elsie said, "Maybe you're the only person I know who's as tough as I am, maybe that's why."

"I don't think so."

Elsie wiped her eyes. "This was just old, old stuff. Sally and me. And poor old Mr. Bigelow. And everything."

Dick said, "I thought you were going to tell me you're pregnant." He was instantly sorry. She went stiff and turned away.

After a bit he said, "Here, you sit in the canoe. I'll slide you along."

Elsie sat in the canoe facing him. When Dick pushed it, his feet sank in six inches. The canoe lurched forward a yard, but Dick couldn't get his feet free, and he fell on his knees. Elsie laughed. Then she said, "Come sit with me for a minute."

They sat in the seats, facing each other, their hands on the gunwales. Elsie said, "I'm glad we're here. I like the marsh."

"Wait till the mosquitoes come out."

"I think the storm cleared them out," Elsie said. "How'd you guess I'm pregnant?"

Dick lowered his head.

Elsie said, "I'm glad you guessed."

Dick had been about to lie a little, tell the truth a little—say that his truck had stalled and he'd heard her talking to Mary Scanlon. He let it go by.

"I'm going to have the baby," Elsie said. "I want to. I'm glad you're the father."

Dick looked up at the sky and got dizzy. Elsie said, "No one will know. Well, Mary will know. And I'll tell my sister. I don't have to tell Jack."

"If you tell your sister, she'll tell Jack. You can't be married and not tell."

Elsie looked surprised. She said, "Does that mean you'll tell May?"

"I didn't mean that," Dick said. "But it seems like I ought to. It might end us."

"You mean you and May," Elsie said.

It took Dick a second. He said, "Yes."

"I don't want to have an abortion," Elsie said. "I've thought about that, and I won't do it. I have friends who've done it." She hesitated and said, "I did it once, and I won't do it again. And I won't give the baby away. There's not anything I'm sure of, but I'm surer about this than about anything else." She leaned forward and put her hands on the thwart between them. "But what I *can* do is say to the people I have to say something to that I adopted the baby. I've talked about that enough so it'll fly. And I'll raise the child. I've got enough money. And if it's not enough, one of Jack's virtues is that he's generous. If Sally asks him to help, he will. And eventually I'll have some money from my mother's side. My father may have some too. And of course Mary will be around. I won't ask her to pay for the child, but she'll help with the house. But mainly I can do it myself. No matter what."

"No matter what," Dick said. "That's what it comes to. No matter what."

"Oh, Dick, I know. I know it must seem to you I'm being high-handed."

"I didn't mean it that way," Dick said, "I didn't mean you're getting your way no matter what. I meant there's a life no matter what. No matter what you or I think. I got to admit I've worried some. I'm still worried about how it's going to work out if I tell May. If I tell the boys. If they forgive me or don't forgive me. And I worry how I'll feel having a kid who's not in my life. You got pregnant. I got you pregnant. No matter how we say it, you're pregnant. No matter whether you should have said what you were up to. You were up to something, weren't you?"

Elsie said, "Yes. I wasn't as cold-blooded as ... I mean, in some ways it was an accident. I could make a case that in the heat of the moment I forgot I was off the pill. And that the next time it should have been okay. But in some way, yes. I knew it might happen. But I'm going to take care of it. That's what I meant by 'no matter what.' I mean to handle it. I'm in a position to take care of—"

"Yeah," Dick said. "You said that. You've got the money."

"I don't just mean money. Though I've thought a lot about my being a rich kid. Not so rich, but I know what you mean when you think 'rich kid.' I've made fun of myself too, I mean, I've asked myself how brave I'd be, how full of mystical life force I'd be, if I were completely broke. Is the life force another middle-class privilege? Suppose the answer is *yes*. Then I say, so what? But now, you tell me something. You don't want me to get an abortion, do you?"

"No."

Elsie sat up straight. "I'm glad about that. I . . . By the way, are you mad at me?"

"No. I have been. I'll tell you what's hard for me. The way I feel about the boys. I've been hard on them, I haven't done everything just right, but I know what it's been like being a father."

"Yes, you're a good father."

"There's the way I feel about the boys . . . and then there's this. You can talk about your life force and your money, but all this . . . I don't know what to call it. It doesn't fit with anything I know."

"I know. I know what you mean." Elsie's voice was soft. "I've done at least one thing I didn't want to—I've disturbed the pattern of your good habits."

"How do you mean that?"

Elsie said, "I mean the balance of your force field, your network. The way you care for your family, the way you get along with someone like Eddie, the way you are with Miss Perry. And, I suppose, the way you were angry about Sawtooth Point and the toy-boat people." Elsie hunched her shoulders and crossed her arms as though she felt a chill. "I suppose what I mean is I haven't been a good ecologist."

Dick snorted. "What the hell does that mean? You're the ecologist and I'm some endangered species? You're the game warden of my, what-do-you-call-it, my *habitat*?"

"Don't get mad," Elsie said sharply. "You're just as high and mighty as I am. And you're meaner. You practically spit when you say 'summer people,' or 'toy boat.' At least I'm sympathetic to your getting on *your* high horse." Elsie stopped herself, took a breath. "I admire what's good about your life, for God's sakes. I don't look down, I admire just about everything I mentioned—you and your boys, you and how you work and your boat and going to sea. The time you took Miss Perry and the boys fishing, that whole afternoon was one of the reasons I . . ." Elsie stuck her hands up in the air and then held her head. She said, "That and the way you talked to me about being scared of sharks when I got stuck in that little boat. . . . I didn't pick you out of a catalogue, for God's sakes. I know you. I mean, in my own fucked-up, neurotic way, I fell for you."

Dick was alarmed but satisfied to hear her say this. He still had Parker and Marie on his mind.

Elsie said, "What got more complicated—I mean I could have let that go by—maybe just gone back to having a little crush on you. But then I wanted to be friends too, and that kept me bumping into you. So here I am going to be a mother. It takes my breath away too, you know. So naturally I see it's not easy for you. I can see how this last part isn't your idea. I can see that my child and I—or at least this child—is going to make a claim on your thoughts. I'm to blame for that, for what it does to you, no matter how completely I take care of the child." Elsie said this carefully, and even submissively, and then stopped. Dick didn't see what she was submitting to.

She said, "I could go away. I mean I'm going away anyway, before it shows. But I could stay away. If you decide not to tell May, it might make it easier if I'm not around."

Dick said, "If I *do* tell May, it'll be hard on her if she has to keep running into my bastard." Elsie winced. "If I *don't* tell her, she'll believe what everyone else believes. You went down to Boston and adopted a baby."

Elsie looked surprised. Dick didn't see why until she said, "What makes you think I'm going to Boston?"

She was too quick for him. He didn't flinch. No sense in weaseling anyhow. And for some reason he didn't mind letting her stick him on this one. It crossed his mind that they must be friends if he didn't mind letting her take a swipe at him, if he trusted that, after she tore into him for a bit, she'd settle down, go on with him.

He told her she'd talked about Boston when she was talking to Mary Scanlon.

"Mary?" Elsie said.

"Mary didn't tell me. I heard you talking to her. The night she came from her father's funeral. I came back up—"

"Where were you?"

"I was walking back up your drive."

"And you heard us."

"That's right."

"So you just stood there listening in."

"I did."

"You sneaky son of a bitch!"

"What I heard sounded sneaky enough."

That stopped her. Dick wished he hadn't said it like that, but it stopped her.

When she spoke next, she was careful again. "I don't know what you heard me tell Mary, but what I just told you is true. Do you want me to say it all over again? When we made love that first time, whatever I was thinking, it wasn't cold-blooded."

"No," Dick said.

"Good." Elsie cocked her head. "Of course maybe it would be easier for you to think it was all my plan. I just siphoned it out of you, you know, like someone stealing gas out of your gas tank. A sly little succubus stealing your seed. Maybe I'm an alien and I came down on a flying saucer and flew away with a specimen for our earthling exhibit. You like it better that way?"

Dick said, "Okay. I got the point."

Elsie said, "Listen, earthling. You have been selected as a suitable type to release your earthling essence." Elsie switched into a squeaky robot voice. "For this experiment I have assumed a receptacle-type earthling body. Beep. You are injector-type earthling? Beep. You will now begin process. Beep."

"I got the picture, Elsie."

Elsie laughed and laughed. When she stopped, she said *beep* once more and knocked herself out all over again. Dick waited.

The sun was long down, and the sky was losing its glow. He could just see her face when it tipped up, her single pearl earrings little moons in the dusk of her dark hair, her teeth as white as the moon.

He got out of the canoe. He said, "I got to get home." He took her hand to help her out. When she got to her feet on the soft earth of the marsh he put his arms around her. He felt awkward. "I don't know, Elsie." She felt small and cold. As he pulled back, his hand caught on the handle of her revolver. "Damn, Elsie. What're you wearing your gun for?"

"We're on special duty. They even called up the National Guard. In case of looting."

Dick said, "Pistol-packing mama," and began to laugh.

"You think *that's* funny?" Elsie said. "Mine was much funnier."

The canoe slithered along easily on top of the marsh. He could pull it by the painter with one hand. Elsie took his other hand. She said, "One of my problems is that I like hanging around with you. What do you say we keep it a secret, keep on hanging out together?"

"I know what you mean," Dick said, but he couldn't say any more.

"At least for a couple of months," Elsie said. "Just hang out some. I won't use my ray gun on you. I'll be off to Boston by Christmas."

They got to the truck before Dick answered. Dick slid the bow of the canoe up on the roof of the cab, and he and Elsie lashed it on.

"We'll see each other," Dick said. "I don't know how much hanging around I'll be doing. You've seen my house. And I got to check my pots."

"I could go out with you to check the pots," Elsie said.

"You remember how sick you got last time?"

"I'll take seasick pills."

"I'll have Charlie along, and another hand too."

"I could help."

"What's Charlie going to think? And, more to the point, if May gets to know about you and me, it would get to her a lot more if she knew you'd been out on *Spartina* with Charlie and me."

"Maybe not," Elsie said. "Maybe she'll take it that I have some decent good will toward her children. She'll be reassured I'm not out to break up a family. Maybe—"

"Maybe," Dick said. "You're a great one for saying *maybe*. But there's some things there's no maybe about." He felt he'd been a little short and hard. He added, "You can see that, Elsie. There's some things there's just no point in being fanciful about." Elsie cocked her head in a way that irritated him. He said, "Maybe May'll be overjoyed about the whole thing, want the kid to come stay with us. Maybe she'd like having a little baby girl to fuss over now she's through having kids of her own. Maybe she'll want us all to move in together at Eddie's, maybe you and her'll sit around together shelling peas while I'm out on *Spartina*."

Elsie said, "You want me to ask her?"

Dick felt the unpleasant glitter of Elsie's nerve. It exasperated him—just when he was feeling sorry for her, she'd get pissy. But that was the way it was with her. She'd be going one way and then dart off another. Whether this was a skittish fashion she'd picked up from the kind of people she grew up with, or whether this was her own nature, he couldn't tell. Maybe she couldn't tell either. Whichever it was, it made him skittish along with her. He sometimes liked the feeling—he had to admit that—but it made him doubt her. Not her liking for him or even her intentions of loyalty, but her place in a life like his.

It saddened him. They got in the truck and drove slowly back on the causeway. She put her hand on his arm and said, "I'm sorry." He was still sad. Elsie said, "The Eskimos live like that.

I read a book about the Greenland Eskimos, it's no big deal for them who gets into whose igloo."

"There you go," Dick said. He laughed. Sooner or later she did get him laughing. "We'll just leave that book around for May to pick up and our troubles are over."

The other thing he'd miss was telling her stuff. He couldn't tell May about Parker and Marie. If he did, he knew how May would take it—get those slugs out of my garden. He understood that, he had that feeling too. But Elsie would crack up when he told her about Marie's skirt suddenly flopping up, about the two pairs of sneakers. And what else would she say? He couldn't tell. There was something to be said for that, for not being able to tell which way she'd fly.

It didn't change the fact that he was in trouble.

But when they got to her house Dick said, "There's this to be said for having kids." And he told her about the middle of the hurricane, about how he'd started thinking of Charlie, how he'd kept repeating to himself, " 'O Leerie, I'll go round at night and light the lamps with you!' "

She was puzzled for a bit. He explained some more, told her about reading to the boys when they were in bed, about how when Charlie was six and seven Charlie had followed him around, admiring everything he did, wanting to do what he did. "O Leerie, I'll go round at night and light the lamps with you!"

And Elsie did surprise him. She said, "Oh shit." Dick looked at her. She said, "Why did you tell me that? What am I going to do if it's a little boy—is that why you told me that? Because I'll never be Leerie to a boy?"

Dick felt whirled away a hundred miles. "No," he said. "I just wanted to tell you."

"Why did you tell me *that*?" She was still irritated and puzzled. "The only point to it I can see is that little boys need fathers." She opened her door, but turned back to say, "That is just narrow-minded. Even if you're right, you're wrong."

She was out. "Elsie." She started for the house. He shouted, "Elsie! You forgot your canoe!"

She said, "Put it in the garage." But she came back.

He said, "Look, Elsie. All I meant was—"

"Yes," she said. "All you meant was . . ."

"All I meant was to cheer you up, for Christ's sake. Just that it's nice having a kid around."

Elsie said, "I see," but helped him stow the canoe in the garage alongside her Volvo.

Mary Scanlon came into the garage from the house. She gave him a hug and patted him on the shoulder. "Elsie told me you got back okay. Can you stay for supper? I made a stew, plenty for everyone."

"I ate, thanks. I got to get home."

Elsie hadn't moved. He said, "I'll be by. Maybe we can go see Miss Perry. Talk her into hiring Eddie back to clean up her driveway."

He drove along the narrow lane down the hill, branches switching the sides of the truck. He saw his mistake. The stuff about remembering Charlie as a little boy was for May. The other story was for Elsie. He said out loud, "Watch yourself."

He drove to the boatyard to take a look at *Spartina*. He took his big flashlight, found the buoy with the beam, ran it up the mooring pennant to the chock. Okay.

The only electric light visible was from the South County Hospital high on a hill above the salt pond. Emergency generator. No traffic to speak of. Halfway home Dick cut off his headlights, drove slowly by the light of the moon. He got his story straight. Sawtooth Point. House. Blue canoe? Yes, blue canoe. *Spartina,* had to check on her.

What surprised him was how he was still looking forward to

getting under the covers with May. How soft her lanky bones could get in a big soft double bed. How she got to like it if he took the time to mess with her hair, comb it out with his fingers.

He switched the headlights back on to go up Ministerial Road. In some ways he was a vile son of a bitch, maybe May and Elsie could get together on that.

Eddie was out. May said he'd gone to check on some woman who lived alone up by Miss Perry's. May was at the kitchen table drinking coffee in her nightgown and wrapper. The boys were watching TV on a battery-operated portable. "Hey, Dad," Tom said, "we saw you on TV. You and *Spartina* were on the news. And that man who's a friend of Miss Buttrick, you know, the one that makes movies? It's his pictures."

Dick had misgivings.

He put them out of his mind. Most people had plug-in TVs and the power was still off. The boys at the Neptune, for instance, wouldn't have seen it. Charlie said, "What's the house like?"

"Could be worse," Dick said. "We'll go by in the morning. You boys don't stay up too late." He was pleased to see May put her cup and saucer in the sink and glide down the hall carrying the kerosene lamp. When he came into the bedroom she turned the wick way down. She didn't even ask why he'd been gone so long.

When she was unpinning her hair he said, "It's nice in here. You look nice.... I'll do your hair." He took out the hairpins slowly.

She said, "Isn't it odd, living in a strange room like this?"

"Well. Yeah. We're okay here—it's Eddie's house. It's not like it's a stranger."

"I don't mean that. I mean I kind of like it, being in a strange house. It's like we're going to a motel." May blushed.

God Almighty, Dick thought. It's the whole county carrying on.

*T*hey all went to the house first thing in the morning. Eddie said right off, "It looks worse than it is, May. When I get off work, I'll help Dick jack up that corner—make all the difference in the world."

But he cautioned the boys not to go inside.

Dick opened the storm-cellar door. Down inside, the water stood pretty near up to the tops of the bait barrels. But they were still tight, still standing in rows.

He ran the outlet hose of Eddie's pump as near the creek as he could. It was mostly salt water in the cellar and he didn't want any more salt on his yard.

He figured he'd better get the insurance agent to take a look while things were still at their worst.

When he got to the insurance office in Wakefield there was a line coming out the door. They were giving out numbers like at the supermarket meat counter. He got 102, the head of the line was 37.

He picked up some sandpaper and paint and drove to *Spartina* to dab up the worn spots in her coat.

The manager had his crew cleaning up the yard. Dick took the johnboat out to *Spartina* and set to work. The sun was hot, a late-summer day in September. Even working slowly on account of his sore ribs he worked up a sweat. At midday a little onshore breeze blew across the salt pond, dried him up nicely. He thought of getting the boys, but didn't want to break this thread of pleasure. His ribs felt better in the sun. Maybe it was just bruises and pulled muscles.

He finished sanding and touching up the front of the wheelhouse. He found a can of lukewarm Coke in the corner of the locker. Good enough. Everything he did, everything he touched or smelled gave him pleasure. He couldn't figure it, he hadn't felt so good for years.

He stripped the wood off the broken window. He was still working slowly and pleasantly. He felt as good as a bee inside a flower. He wondered if May ever felt so good tidying up the house when he and the boys were out. He opened up the wiring, tried to see where it'd shorted out. He'd get Eddie to check it. Even messing with the wiring didn't irritate him. The breeze came in the window and out the door, cleaning out the damp. He pulled the mattress on deck to air it out, and he couldn't pass up lying down on it in the sun.

He woke up from a simple dream—bright-blue sky and flat-bottomed clouds piled in billows against the westering sun. An easy waking—in front of his eyes was blue sky and flat-bottomed clouds.

Elsie was sitting on the hatch cover next to his head.

She said, "I like you having a boat in port. I can always find you." He sat up. "When I was a little girl I used to go visit old Mr. Hazard in his bookshop, it was like having a little tea party whenever you felt like it. A floating balloon on a string, give it a tug and down it comes to you. Have you had lunch?"

Dick rubbed his eyes, sniffed the air. He wasn't sure where he was with Elsie, but she seemed cheery enough. He said, "I had a Coke."

Elsie opened up her lunch box and began to lay out food on the hatch cover. Dick said, "I ought to get back to work." She peeled a boiled egg and gave it to him. She said, "Get a cup, I'll give you some iced tea. It won't take a second, I want to tell you something funny."

He got his White Rock–girl thermos and unscrewed the cup.

"Now, that's funny too," Elsie said. "You have to admit."

"You're in a pretty cheery mood."

"I am, I am indeed. Here's the funny thing. I was moaning around about how I might have to resign if the department won't give me leave. I even went and talked to the new headmaster at the Perryville School—Jim Bigelow, you remember him? The Bigelows' son . . . Anyway I was thinking I could teach science there when I get back. But here's what was going on. My rich Republican brother-in-law is in with some guy who wants to run for governor in a couple of years. But the Republicans don't have enough women. There's a not-bad Republican woman in Congress, and their thinking is that competent women can update their image. So this guy asked Jack for a list of women who were likely candidates for appointments to this and that, and Jack told him about me—degree in forestry, pioneer woman in Natural Resources, years of good and faithful service. All of this leaks out. Everything leaks out around here. So when I went in to ask about extended leave, before I open my mouth, my boss tells me he's heard I'm on the emergency hurricane task force. Two months' TDY. And my promotion is coming through. His whole tone was 'You're on the way up and don't forget your friends, Elsie.' And here I was going to beg. . . . After the emergency-panel reports—Jack is on it too—though how he's going to square that with being a partner in Sawtooth Point . . .

"Anyway, after the panel writes the report and fusses around another month or so explaining it, then I get to go back to school for a management course for a term. I can do that in Boston, drive to school from my mother's house. And the department pays for it *and* they pay me my salary *and* a per diem. That takes me up to June. Then I'll have enough accrued leave and sick leave to stay at my mother's for three more months. The whole thing makes me laugh. I mean there I was about to throw in the towel and it turns out like this. From knocked-up and driving a jeep to being some kind of executive trainee with rumors that I'm a hot item. Ms. Buttrick as part of the new gender-ticket. Anyway that's why I'm dressed like this." Elsie flipped the hem of her green uniform skirt and touched the little black tie on her white shirt. Her badge was on her starched breast-pocket.

Elsie said, "Of course there may be hell to pay later. I mean if Jack finds out he was touting me as Miss Responsibility and all the time I was carrying a baby . . . But the timing works. . . . And I feel lucky. No, not just lucky, I feel really good. I mean I *have* worked hard, I *am* a perfectly good person for this. I know what I'm talking about, and why shouldn't I go on working and have a baby if I want?"

Dick was dizzied by Elsie. Glad for her. Also charmed and touched by her in a way he'd mislaid recently.

He said, "That a girl, Elsie. Go ahead and get what's coming to you."

Elsie laughed. "When someone says, 'You'll get what's coming to you,' it makes me look over my shoulder."

"I don't mean it like that."

"Oh, I know." She touched his forearm briefly in her summer-party style. Intimate, easy, one-way. She laughed again. "Here's another funny thing, speaking of getting what's coming to you. I saw Schuyler for a second. He's absolutely cleaning up. He's into his Mr. Zip-zip-zip mode. He's been to Boston and New York and he's got a deal for his documentary. He's sold the whole film, with all that stuff we shot on *Mamzelle* and some other footage—and what he shot during the hurricane too. You know what he did? He stayed in Galilee after it was evacuated. He was in a kind of pillbox with his camera, and he got shots of roofs flying through the air, the surge coming right over the breakwater and over the docks. He was up the slope a bit or he would have drowned. As it was, he was waist-deep in water in his pillbox. He got that footage processed and sold clips to the TV stations in Boston and Providence. He wasn't in Galilee when you got back but he had someone else working for him, so he's got shots of *Spartina* coming back up the channel."

Dick said, "The boys saw that on TV."

"And he's going to use what I shot that morning you came in. I must say he's sort of insufferable in his ruthless show-biz mood. I gave him the film of *Spartina*'s homecoming and he asked me why I hadn't gone out with you."

"You wouldn't have seen much out there. Just a lot of water close to."

"Anyway he's on a roll. I'm not sure he deserves it, but he's going to be a golden boy again. He does have nerve. In a funny way the nerve that it took to stay in Galilee during the hurricane is the same nerve that he uses to make deals. What pleases him even more than the money is getting back on top. He went to some TV executive in New York who wouldn't return his calls last year. Schuyler had found out the executive's boss wanted the film clips, and Schuyler kept getting up to leave. 'I made him grovel' is what he says. He's so full of himself he's about to pop. His wife can't stand it. She put up with a lot during the hard times. She really admires him for his jauntiness when he's down. She forgave him for all sorts of stuff. . . . It's odd. They're very like each other in lots of ways. They think alike, they talk alike, they even look alike. But he's neurotic in an active way, and she's so passively neurotic she could spend the rest of her life in a deck chair. She seems to soak up Schuyler's thrashing around in his desperate funny way. He *is* very funny—when everything is about to cave in and he's dodging bullets. But when he's doing well and is plugged in right, there's no buzz for her. In fact, she's *repelled* by him when he's in good order. She really is a kind of vampire who sucks up his desperate energy."

Elsie stopped, her hands in mid-air. "I'm being a bitch, aren't I? What I don't like is I'm harder on women than on men. Is that right? Have you noticed that? Or in this case is it that the two of them are both spoiled, but Schuyler is at least redeemed by his work? So I'm just... Of course he is being monumentally self-centered these days. .... But, then, he's still funny. Of course maybe she's just as funny but doesn't say it. But, then, that's her fault for not speaking up."

" 'But, then,' " Dick said. " 'But, then.' But, then, maybe he talks so fast she can't get a word in."

"Ah." Elsie straightened her legs. "Okay." She pulled her uniform skirt up above her knees to sun her legs. "You know the way I talk to you has changed. The only other people I talk to like this are my sister and Mary Scanlon. I used to talk to you more the way I talk to Jack, sort of put-up-your-dukes.

"I realize I'm just pouring out now, but it's because I may not get to see you so much. .... Still. I'll try. It's funny because at the same time I'd like to just sit here and not say a thing." Elsie reached in her lunch box and unwrapped a sandwich. "Here, have half. It's huge. Mary made it. She baked the bread too."

Dick took half. Cheese and bean sprouts and fancy mustard. The bread was cut so thick, he had to stretch his mouth open. He watched Elsie smooth her skirt between the back of her thighs and the hatch cover. The problem hadn't gone away, but here he was eating Mary Scanlon's bread, being warmed by the sun, cooled by the sea breeze, and feeling the blue sky press closer and bluer and yet open up out to sea, channels of light into the distance.

Everything might be okay. Days like this day might be ordinary. May might say, "Well, all right, Dick, but don't you do it again." She might say, "Well, she's a nice girl and you can go on being friends so long as you behave yourselves." She might say, "I always wanted a little girl and Elsie'll just have to bring her around as often as she can."

Spartina swung a little on her mooring. If he was going to tell May, it would make sense to wait until he'd been out a couple of times and some money was coming in. Get the house back in shape. Maybe get her a dishwasher.

Dick burst out laughing at himself.

Elsie looked over at him, pleasantly curious.

He said, "I was thinking along, and I got to where I go out and buy May a dishwasher."

Elsie looked puzzled, then laughed.

"If you tell her," Elsie said, "you don't think she'll leave you, do you?"

"No. Now I've thought about it, I don't think so."

Elsie said, "I hardly know her."

"If I've got a halfway-decent number of pots left out there, I can make seven, eight thousand dollars by Christmas. Net. That's more loose money than we've seen . . ."

"There isn't anything I can do," Elsie said. "I can't think of anything that wouldn't just make it worse. There isn't anything, is there? I can't even imagine her mind."

"I'll be doing more than imagine one of these days."

"You've made up your mind, have you? Maybe you could wait till Christmas, when I'll be gone. Wouldn't that be easier?"

Dick nodded. He said, "I guess I ruined your picnic."

He was about to say something else, when he surprised himself by taking hold of her stocky slack calf, running his hand up behind her knee. He pulled his hand back.

Elsie cocked her head. "That's something else I've wondered about. I mean, you could say to yourself, 'In for a penny, in for a pound.' Or 'Might as well be hanged for a sheep as a lamb.' Or you could say . . . what?"

Dick shook his head.

Elsie said, "I'm sorry, I'm being flip, but I can't stay this earnest for very long."

Dick shook his head again.

Elsie said, "I see. I've lost my looks, my girlish figure is gone."

"Come on, Elsie. Quit fooling around."

"I'm just kidding, for God's sakes. I mean you're the fellow who started playing with my leg—not that it wasn't nice, absent-minded though it may have been. No, look, don't mind me. Okay? I'll start over, I'll be serious."

Dick said, "You go ahead and be whatever way you want. You can say anything you want about this pickle, and it'd be true." Dick paused. "Maybe not. I wouldn't want to say we're like Parker and Marie."

"What?" Elsie said. "What do you mean? What are you talking about?"

Dick thought he'd told her. It worried him he wasn't keeping straight what he'd told who and what he hadn't. He said, "Parker and Marie."

"What *about* Parker and Marie? Do you mean Parker told you he'd . . . Parker might *say* he had, Parker might say *anything*. Or do you mean their characters in general? Of course in some horrible way it makes sense. She's furious at Schuyler. . . . You do mean something in particular?"

"Yes."

"Well, how do you know?"

Dick was sorry he'd brought it up. He felt the mattress, it was pretty well dried by the sun. He got to his feet, picked it up, and headed for the cabin.

"Where are you going?" Elsie said. "You can't leave now."

He went below, tossed the mattress onto a bunk, and came back on deck.

"Tell me," Elsie said. She made room on the hatch cover. "Sit down and tell me."

He wondered how on earth he'd ever thought he'd like telling Elsie this story. He must have thought that she'd see what was funny, that she'd make it lighter. Now he was irritated at her eagerness. He was embarrassed. And he was fearful that one way or another the story would stick to them.

"Dick, for God's sakes," Elsie said.

He told her, not looking at her. He started with his walking around the Wedding Cake and his reflections on his great-uncle Arthur. That made her impatient. When he got to Parker's car she shut up. He told it step by step, trying to make it far away and funny, right down to the two pairs of sneakers doing their barn dance—"Duck for an oyster, dig for a clam."

Elsie said, "Good God." He looked up. She put her feet together and pulled her skirt down over her knees. "There's a grisly little tale." She puffed her cheeks and blew out her breath. "Poor Marie. I'm sorry I was so mean about her just now." She shook her head. "I mean, *Parker.* Poor Marie. And that sort of thing gets worse as you get older.... And Parker is such a tick.... He looks like a possum snout. I wish you hadn't told me about it."

"You told me to tell you."

"Well, once you brought it up ..." She paused and looked baffled. She said, "You did bring it up."

Dick saw it coming now. He couldn't think fast enough how to fend it off.

"In fact," Elsie said. "Well, shit. That's just mean. We aren't ... I don't see how you could think of ..."

Dick said, "I said we *weren't* like Parker and Marie."

"You said you *hoped* we weren't like Parker and Marie."

"What I said was—I wouldn't want to say we're like Parker and Marie."

"That's worse," Elsie said.

Dick said, "What I meant was ..." He shook his head.

"What *do* you mean?" Elsie said. "What could you possibly mean?"

"All I meant was, it got to me."

She said, " 'It got to me, it got to me'—what does that mean? It means you think we're just one more possum-snout fuck."

He shook his head, but she didn't see him. She hugged her knees to her and lay her forehead on them.

"No," Dick said. He stood watching her for a few seconds. In the silence he heard noises from the yard, the tractor throttle going up a notch, the ringing of an end of chain. As if he was falling into her mind, he sensed a close darkness, and then, fresh and bare as a pulled-up root, her wish. It was so close to his senses it was as if he plunged his face into it. He felt the sting of her feelings like the smell of a root drilling up his nostrils. She wanted her child—and what she was going to do about having her child—to come out of what was good in her, and she wasn't sure what that was. Everything in her could go either way. For all her quick nerve, she still wasn't sure she'd absorbed enough good from doing a job, from living here, from wanting to be rooted in this heap of hills, rockbound ponds, scrub woods creased with streams running down to the salt marsh. All this tag end of a glacier: half tumbledown and useless disorder, half a fertile accident for ingenious, stubborn little forms of life accommodating to the old wreck and spill of rock, on and on to the way it was now, still half a disaster, half a wonder. Here it was again tumbled down and flooded, and here they all were, plants and animals, at it again in the old accident.

It seemed to him he caught this picture from her, and along with it her wish to be formed by it, her wish to be complete by aligning herself with invisible forces, even though she only half-believed in their coherence, and only half-believed they could apply to her.

But her wish was so strong he felt it, and felt her buried half-belief too, like his own in its distrust of people and in its hope for the rightness of the natural world. He kept on sliding into her sense of things until it seemed for an instant they were swimming together, coming up for air in the flat-rock pond by her house, coming up together by the overhanging rhododendron, their coming up setting floating green leaves bobbing around them—instead of facing each other askew on board *Spartina* in sight of the boatyard, within hearing of the tractor, the squeak of a long nail being pulled out of hard wood, the tractor chain ringing again as it went slack and fell.

*B*ut there they were, two bodies in the sun, what they'd left of the food sitting on warm waxed paper.

Elsie sat up straight.

Dick said, "Elsie . . ."

"Yes." She came up snappish.

Dick said, "Forget all that about Parker and Marie. It didn't get to me on account of us. At least what we have is an honest mistake."

Elsie laughed. She said, "So that's what it is. Great, that's great." She laughed again, hard enough to annoy him.

Dick set his mouth shut. She'd had her feelings hurt and now she was going to stab at him a couple of times, until she cheered herself up. He didn't mean to put up much of a fight. He was still considering his discovery that the better part of energy and power in Elsie's life didn't come from being a rich kid. It came from ordinary life. When he put it like that it sounded so simple it sounded dumb. She wouldn't be pleased to hear it, at least not in the mood she was in now.

Elsie said, "You can't just say forget it."

"I'm sorry you took it wrong."

"I'm not so sure I did. Maybe you're thinking about my sneaky ulterior motive. But maybe you're worried that *you* had some creepy little thrill. Maybe what you saw in Parker was something you hadn't admitted to yourself, some little element of class rage. Don't lose your nerve—go ahead and admit it."

"You're on the wrong track, Elsie."

"No, I'm not. I'll tell you one thing you couldn't have built this boat without."

"I know. Without that money you got for me."

"No, something more important than that. You wouldn't have got this boat built unless you were furious. Hours and hours—no, *years* of class rage. You shouldn't have named her *Spartina,* you should have named her *Class Rage.*"

Dick felt himself twist with that. He got up, turned away from her, and held on to the wire of the lifeline. It was too thin to grab hold of hard enough. He said, "You don't know what you're talking about. You don't know about this boat." He felt the thin piece of truth in what she said, the sharp little wrongness of it. He'd been a son of a bitch, he'd been bitter and hollow and stupid, but not about *Spartina. Spartina* had come through him untouched.

He said, "What's this class-rage shit? When I think of the dead-beat rich around here, these assholes with their toy boats, I think of them one by one." He saw that wasn't a very good answer, so he said, "And what I think of them—or you—is nothing to do with my boat. Nothing! You want to call something class rage, call your kid class rage."

Before he felt the harm of what he'd said, even before he felt astonishment, he felt the air go dead between Elsie and him, as though she'd stopped transmitting or receiving.

He turned around but didn't look at her. He said, "Aw shit, Elsie, I don't mean that. You pissed me off."

"I know," Elsie said. He looked at her. She wasn't mad. She looked at him calmly. She said, "I meant to get you mad. I shouldn't have. . . . It's a dumb thing to do. Of course I got back a little more than I bargained for." She waved what he'd said away with the back of her hand. She sat comfortably, her weight and energy all within her again, balanced. She said, "Sometimes when I'm impatient for what's next, I either make jokes or start a fight. I used to think it was pretty neat of me, it showed I was a live wire. I guess what it is is a way of being intimate and heartless at the same time. Where were we? I mean before . . ."

Dick said, "Slow down."

"That's true too," Elsie said. "I sometimes think if I slow down or stop I'll get caught, I'll be seen, I'll be visible some way I don't want to be. What's odd is I'm perfectly willing to be seen being bad . . . well, bad in some clever little way. But I'm secretive about being good. I mean, there is a part of me that's just a plain dull good girl."

"Is that right?" Dick said. "Just a dull good girl—no more to it than that?"

"Of course there's more to it than that," she said agreeably.

"Then don't exaggerate," Dick said. "Don't swing back and forth so hard."

"Okay, chief. Whatever you say."

She was now as tucked in as a tern on the water, rising and falling with the waves that pillowed her.

"Just a good Girl Scout," he said, trying to keep his distance. He couldn't resist her when she settled down.

"Uh huh."

He said, "You aren't sick or anything, are you? Mornings?"

"No, I've been fine. I guess I'm lucky."

She held her hand out for him to help her up. After she got to her feet she shifted her weight and sagged a little. She held on to his arm and bent over at the waist, let her head hang down. After a moment she stood up straight. "Just a dizzy spell," she said.

"You want to sit down again?"

"No, I'm fine." She kept her hand on his arm.

"You want a drink of water?"

"No. I'm fine, really."

He looked over at the yard. He saw some of the visors of the workers' caps point toward Elsie and him.

"I know you from years ago," he said. "Coming through this very yard here. I know what you're like now. I think you're as good as Mary Scanlon or Miss Perry. Of course you're your own wild bird too."

He felt her draw back. Was she on guard against him, against his saying his feelings? Or maybe she was, you know, *pained* he wasn't saying it just right. . . . To hell with that. Then he thought she might be afraid he was setting her up for a final word. But at last he couldn't see any way to go but dead ahead. He said, "The thing is, there's a lot that feels . . . incomplete. I don't mean the physical side. . . ."

"It'd be hard to call that incomplete," Elsie said. "I mean, taking the point of view of the egg."

"Stop fooling around for one goddamn minute." He looked at the yard. The crew had got back to work. "But in a way that kind of answers something I was wondering about. Which is, I used to wonder if we could've just got to know each other. Like Mary Scanlon and me."

"Just a couple of good scouts?" Elsie said. "Or is class prickliness the problem? Or do you wish I'd have let you go on being the wholesome boy you were?"

"No." He was going to tell her to shut up, but she became still. He said again, "No. I'm talking about something else. I like Mary a lot, but if I don't see her for a while it's okay. Forget Mary. What's hard to see is how to keep seeing you, that part of you I got to know *besides*. The part that's like getting echoes."

She didn't say anything. He wanted to say more, but he couldn't. He turned to see if she was going to say something, but she'd turned away. He had no idea. He'd just as much as said he could read her mind, and now he couldn't tell a thing she was thinking.

At last he said, "Okay. I guess all that doesn't cut one way or the other. It doesn't let us out of trouble."

She turned back to him, her face drawn down. She shook her head. "No. Still in trouble. I'd better take the dinghy back."

Maybe he'd been wrong when he'd been grandly picturing the way she felt for the natural order of things. Maybe she was way ahead of him, thought he was a fool when he talked about echoes, thought he was whining when he talked about trouble. She was the one used to not living in her everyday bones, used to flying above the rules. He wouldn't wish them on her—Get some rules, Elsie. Get back in your everyday bones.

He said, "Yeah. I got to get back to work too."

He took her hand to help her into the dinghy. She cast off but floated nearby for a bit, just holding the oars in the water. She said, "I meant to make it easier. Just tell you I was all set. About my job." She slid the blades out of the water. "Will you be able to come see me?" She took one little stroke. "Mary and me. Maybe you could come see Mary and me."

He had the rest of the afternoon to let it sink in. No matter what he said or how he said it, no matter if she misunderstood him or understood him, he wasn't going to make anything better for her.

*D*ick went out on *Spartina* two days later. Even with Eddie and Charlie helping, it took longer to get her ready than he'd planned for. Dick took Charlie along. He also got Keith college-boy, since Parker wasn't taking him south just yet.

It was clear breezy weather, not too choppy to spot the buoys, though a little tricky to haul the trawls. As he feared, he'd lost a lot of complete trawls to the hurricane. No buoys to be seen anywhere near where he'd left them. The pots were down there somewhere, probably with lobster in them, and trash fish. Little aquariums of starving creatures at the bottom of the sea.

He brought as many of his extra pots as *Spartina* could carry below and on deck, but it wasn't near enough to fill in the blanks. Even when he found a buoy and hauled the trawl, there were a few pots stove in, or missing where they'd snapped the gangion.

But all in all it wasn't the worst he'd feared. The good news came when he got back to port and sold his lobster. The price was way up, higher than it had ever been. Lobster were scarce—everybody was missing pots, and half the offshore lobstermen were fixing their boats, if they still had boats to fix.

Dick wanted a quick turnaround. He had to let Charlie off to go back to school, which had finally opened two weeks late. Dick sent word with Keith to ask Parker if he'd care to come along while he was waiting for his insurance money. *Mamzelle* was a total loss. Dick took over her berth near the Co-op. Parker said yes, but a few hours before *Spartina* was to leave, Parker showed up on the dockside with a very small Vietnamese man.

"I got some business to tend to," Parker said, "but this fellow's willing to work for a half-share. Save you some money."

Dick said, "Just how green is he?"

The Vietnamese man spoke up. Dick didn't understand him, thought he was speaking Vietnamese. The man repeated himself. Dick understood that the man was trying to introduce himself. Dick looked him in the face. The man said his name a third time. Something something Tran. Tran something something. Dick liked that the man said it just as slow and patiently the third time. Dick said, "I'm Dick Pierce." Tran's hand moved at his side and Dick stuck out his hand. Tran's hand was as small as Elsie's. "Well, look, Tran. You understand English?"

Tran said, "Yes, sir."

"You been on boats?"

"Yes, sir."

"You know what a winch is?"

Tran pointed to the winch.

"You know what a self-tailing winch is?"

Tran shook his head, said, "No, sir."

Parker said, "He knows all kinds of stuff, he just don't know the names."

Tran said, "Yes, sir."

Dick said, "So how am I going to tell him what to do?"

"I can learn the names, sir."

Dick said, "Parker, what's the deal here? You got something going?"

Parker took Dick to the wheelhouse.

It turned out Parker had set up a lobster-pot factory near Westerly. He employed all of Tran's family. Parker had rented a truck, and was selling pots from Wickford to Westerly as fast as his Vietnamese assembly line could turn them out. The family wanted one member to get work on a lobster boat. Maybe just to see how the pots actually worked.

Dick said, "What are you paying these guys?"

Parker smiled. "It's piecework. They're still paying me off for the tools and material, so I ain't paid them nothing yet. I gave them a loan to get through the month. And I'm getting a job for their boy here. Look. Give him a try. The boy don't work out, send him back. I done you plenty of favors, think of all them pots you're hauling."

"Half of them busted loose."

"And you figure that half must be mine."

Dick didn't want to have any more deals with Parker. He could go to the Neptune that very evening, pick up a good hand from a broken boat.

But there was something about the little guy he liked. Dick said, "I could use some pots."

Parker said, "I'll sell you a hundred at two bucks over my cost. You can't get them cheaper."

"That's just a couple, three trawls. I got to take that many each time I go out."

"Okay, I'll sell you a hundred and fifty. When you come in, we'll see what else I got on hand for you. I got this family going six days a week. We'll make some for you this Sunday. I figure for the next month we won't be able to keep up with demand. All these skippers are fixing their boats, no time to make pots. They're itching to get out while lobster are sky-high. You ought to be glad you know me well enough so I'll sell to you on credit. Everybody else is paying cash, and everybody else is happy."

Dick said, "You put them hundred and fifty pots on board by tonight, I'll take your boy half-share."

Tran turned out to be quick with his neat little hands. First haul he emptied and rebaited pots almost as fast as Keith. Next haul he was just as quick. He had good eyes, could spot a buoy between swells at a fair distance. Dick let him take the wheel some. The kid had a feel for it.

He picked up the names for things, a lot of them on the way out. Keith was a better teacher than Dick, and could understand what Tran was saying. And Tran understood what Keith said. Dick had to say everything twice. Dick gave Keith credit, though he still didn't like him. Dick did like Tran.

Some cold weather moved in, and the little bugger nearly froze. He hadn't brought but one change of clothes, and the warmest thing he had was his denim jacket. Dick suited him up in old foul-weather gear, rolled up at the cuffs three times. If he kept Tran on into the really cold weather, he'd have to buy him a survival suit. He wondered if the Co-op had one small enough.

Dick had enough pots set to stay out seven days. He sent word through the Co-op to May and Parker that *Spartina* was coming in. Parker met them at the dock in his huge rented truck. Parker would only sell him another fifty pots. Dick looked at the stacks of pots still on the truck. Parker said, "Those are already bought at a price you wouldn't want to pay."

Parker came into the wheelhouse while Keith and Tran unloaded the lobster and stacked the fifty new pots on board.

"How'd my boy work out?"

"Another couple times out, he'll do."

"His brother's a good boy too. Hard worker."

"Not on my boat."

"I'm taking Keith south pretty soon."

"Fine with me—I need someone with a little more time in. What is this, anyway? Your conscience bothering you about your Vietnamese? Another two months it'll be winter, a lot of folks'll have time to make their own pots—you explain that to them?"

"I'll tell you, Dick, they're real bright people, real bright—but they can only take in so much at a time. I'm not their employer, you understand. I just set them up. I rented an old barn, sublet it to them. They sleep in the loft, work down below. Their house is gone, they were living at a Catholic church, crammed in with a lot of other folks. Bunch of old Army cots where they used to run the bingo game. They looked a little aimless there. I'm giving a little focus to their energy, is all I'm doing."

Parker poured himself a mug of coffee. He glanced at the picture on the thermos. "They changed the White Rock girl again. I remember when the White Rock girl and *National Geographic* and Venus de Milo colored-pencil sets was the only place you could see bare tit. Nowadays . . ."

Dick found he was furious. Repelled by Parker. At the same time he kept on liking him, kept on knowing that Parker liked him. Parker had told him all along—Parker was a player. What that meant was that Parker could cheerfully cut Dick out of five thousand dollars and keep on liking him. It was a game, nothing more than playing cards. Parker obeyed his own golden rule. He did unto others as he figured they'd do unto him. And he kept on feeling friendly. Feeling just as friendly as when he was doing a favor—taking Dick to see an alligator, swinging the fancy yacht in toward shore so Dick could see pelicans. Parker had no idea that turning on the intercom while he was fooling around with his English girl was anything but a joke. And screwing Schuyler's wife.

Dick shook his head. "You'll do anything, you get the chance."

Parker looked up. "You still want to argue about those Vietnamese? You feel so bad, you pay Tran a full share. As far as I'm concerned, I'm doing the same by them as any businessman would. The only difference between me and a bank—and you know what banks're like—is I don't hide behind rules and middlemen. It's just me. I'm doing it right out front, and in this particular case I'm doing more than a bank would do. And a hell of a lot faster. But maybe it's not the Vietnamese. Maybe you're still smarting over your five thousand, now you lost some pots. You think I went out and busted the pots I gave you?"

"No," Dick said, "I'm not griping about the pots. I'm not griping at all. I hope you get all your insurance money for your sunk boat, and I hope you get your fancy new boat. I'm just seeing what runs you. You could no more keep from working a deal than you could keep from eating. And I got to say, you do keep busy. A nibble here, a nibble there."

Parker said, "You got something on your mind?"

"Yeah. I was wondering if you screwed Marie on account of Schuyler was greedy about selling your coke."

Parker looked at him. Parker smiled, and then laughed out loud. Parker shook his head. "I'll tell you why I'm enjoying that. It's sort of peculiar." Parker rubbed his chin with one hand. "How'd you find out? I didn't figure she'd talk much about it. But maybe she got together with Elsie. That's okay. So long as she don't talk about drugs."

"I saw your car at her cottage."

"You saw my car."

"I saw your car and I heard her."

Parker laughed. "Hearing things again, Dickey-bird? You can't say I tuned you in on this one."

Dick didn't say anything.

Parker said, "What was peculiar was—I'm getting back to your question now—was this: She'd sort of been a bitch all along, you know the way she was with us that morning, all depressed but snotty to everybody. When I ran into her after the hurricane—she and Schuyler moved up to the inn in Wakefield—she was all revved up. She was still being snotty about Schuyler"—Parker mimicked Marie—" 'How'd you like the big city with Schuyler? Did he take you out on the town?' But she was laughing about it. Then she said, 'Did he treat you fair on your deal?' I said, 'He got a little more than his share, but I'm not complaining.' She looked at me and I just knew. Even if it might take a while, we were on. She was one of them who like to pretend nothing's going on till it's too late. So we drove down to look at their cottage. She kept talking the whole time. I was getting interested enough. We'd get going some, and then she'd spin away and go look at something else. It was okay, sort of a tease to keep me on my toes. But when it came right down to it, she shut up. It needed a little something, so I whispered in her ear, 'I'm only doing this 'cause Schuyler cheated me.' She loved it. So I said, 'He didn't cheat me much. About a thousand.' She got into it some more. So I said, 'Maybe less.' How'd I know that was the stuff? It was just a lucky guess. I mean, the idea had come up. But, to get back to your question, Schuyler gouging me a little or my doing a little rag-doll dance with Mrs. Schuyler Van der Hoevel, neither one has been what you'd call preying on my mind. I'll tell you what it is—I've got lots of energy, I can't wait around like this without getting up to something, it's the kind of boy I am."

"You don't worry about it, do you?"

"I told you, it don't prey on my mind."

"What if Marie tells Schuyler?"

"What if. But I don't figure she will."

"Why's that?"

"For one, she couldn't be bothered. That's the way she is, kind of inert. That's part of her charm, if you choose to take it that way. For another, one thing women have is a sex imagination. The whole thing is more in their heads. And what that means is it *does* prey on *their* minds—they dress it up, they replay it in their heads. So they naturally figure a man is going to do it the same way. And it wouldn't do to give someone you're married to a script like that, something they're going to keep on imagining about. I've never had a married woman to tell on me. It's not just an act for them, it's a whole soap opera. You understand what I'm saying?"

With bleak distaste, Dick had to admit Parker seemed to know what he was talking about. As Dick applied Parker's theory to his own coming problem with May, his good mood from several clear days at sea covered over with gloom. It angered him that Parker could get things figured in that slick way of his. It angered him that he was tempted to ask Parker what he should do. It angered him that there was so much confusion, so much thrashing around, in his own efforts to think. Buy her a dishwasher. Good, Dick, take care of everything. He was unfit for this kind of duty. He pictured himself talking to Eddie about it. Eddie wasn't any fitter than he was.

"I'm off," Parker said. "I got to make a delivery. I'll be in touch."

Dick got *Spartina* squared away, put her in her berth, paid Keith and Tran. He sat by himself for a bit in the wheelhouse. When he got on the road, he overtook Tran, who was on a bicycle. He told Tran to put his bike in the back of the truck and climb in.

Dick thought again how Parker was on to something about women's imagination, even a plain-thinking woman like May. The boys away all day. No surprises in her work, no little puzzles. No boat, no sea. Nothing to take her mind off it.

Captain Texeira fired him. As the loan officer at the bank pursing his mouth. As Joxer Goode asking about collateral.

Captain Goddamn Pierce. His saying "Goddamn" wasn't the worst thing—it wasn't necessarily the hard-ass sons of bitches that humiliated you.

Dick wasn't all that worried about the old man, but he was sorry about Tran. The way things had gone, Tran would have rather pedaled home on his bicycle.

Dick still couldn't figure what he liked so much about Tran. Part of it was Tran reminded him of when he'd been the kid on board. Let the kid do it, that way he'll learn. And Tran reminded him of a different way to take it—he wasn't as sour as Dick had been. Tran was quiet and serious and earnest about it all, reminded Dick of Charlie. And for all his being a bronze-colored fellow, what with his small hands, his small bones dwarfed in the foul-weather jacket, he reminded Dick of Elsie. He'd even picked him up bicycling on Route 1, took him home, and caused trouble.

Dick said "Goddamn" again and laughed. He was still in that other trouble.

Dick had another surprise when he got back to Eddie's. He'd figured May would get on the subject of when he was going to get their house fixed. He and May went to the bedroom. May sat on the bed. She had something on her mind, but it wasn't the house.

He gave her the money for the month and told her about the

One of the pleasures of being at sea was you didn't think about sex much. Hardly at all. It just disappeared. That's why it had been so disconcerting to have Elsie on board *Mamzelle*. In a way that had started that whole line of trouble. These last two trips had been good; making money was just part of it, another part was the gentle oblivion.

He asked Tran where to turn off. Tran was embarrassed, finally said, "Another ten miles."

"Jesus, Tran. You can't bicycle all this way. The weather's going to turn cold. You understand? I'll pick you up day after tomorrow. You be all ready to go, I'll come get you."

Dick went into the barn with Tran. Parker was right, the whole family was in assembly-line stations: banging together the frames, bending the wire mesh on a jig, tying in the entrance cone and wall of the parlor with needle-nose pliers. Even with all that wire, the pots had to be weighted. At one of the stations the smallest kids were lining the bottom with newspapers soaked in cement. They sloshed some more on to bond the little slab of newspaper-concrete.

When Tran came in, the family quit one by one to come up to him. Then each one stepped back on line.

In the time Dick stood there, a pot came out the end of the line. The old man came up to Dick. Tran spoke to him, then introduced him in English to Dick. "Father. Captain Pierce."

Dick said, "I never seen a pot built so fast. Looks pretty good."

The old man nodded. "Good, thank you."

"Tran did okay on the boat. I'll take him out again."

"Good, thank you. Tran is able-bodied."

"Yeah, he's okay. Look. What does Parker pay you for your pots?"

"Captain Parker pays us. Then he drives the truck, and the men wanting pots pay him." The old man smiled. "Tran is okay on your boat?"

Dick figured he could get the price out of Tran next trip out. Get rid of Keith, get an older hand, keep Tran. Then work on a better deal on the pots through Tran.

Dick said, "Who's going to sell the pots when Parker goes south?" The old man looked puzzled.

Dick said, "Who's going to drive the truck after Parker has gone away?"

"Driving a truck will not be a problem." The old man spoke carefully. Dick was now sure the old man was just being careful, not dumb.

Dick said, "When I come back to pick up Tran day after tomorrow, I'd like to put another thirty pots on my pickup. You get Parker to call me tonight or tomorrow." Dick wrote Eddie's number down.

"Captain Parker is a old friend of yours?"

"Oh yeah, Parker and I go way back. You don't mind if I take a look at what you got stacked up there?" Dick nodded at the rows of pots near the double doors of the barn, six pots high, six pots deep, and at least ten pots long. A lot of good cheap pots.

Dick relaxed some. He'd had a couple of jarring nervous impulses. One was a worry about Parker gouging these guys and leaving them in the lurch. The other was a hot spurt of greed seeing the stacked-up pots—not just to replace his missing trawls, but to get a hold of all these pots before the other boats did. He opened and closed a couple of the pots on top. He imagined the barn door opening, Eddie's flatbed backing up to the pots. . . .

Spartina could just carry all these, if they stacked them high and lashed them down. But he couldn't afford this many, not cash money. He *could* manage a hundred each time he turned around. Of course, in November he'd have to start moving all his trawls in closer so he could duck back into someplace safe if the weather turned.

The old guy and Tran hovered by him. Dick said, "I'll try to get Parker to agree to a hundred of these. And, Tran, you get yourself some wool clothes, you understand? Summer's over. I'll get you a survival suit at the Co-op, but when I come get you, you better have a sea bag full of long johns and sweaters. I can't teach you much when your teeth are chattering."

The old guy said, "When do you pay Tran a full share?"

"The more he learns, the more he earns."

"Christmastime?" The old guy said.

Dick hoped the old guy was as pushy when he was dealing with Parker. Dick said, "He's still the boy. That's just one week he's put in."

"Twenty years old. You call him boy?"

"He's the boy till he can do all the stuff needs to be done. I'll teach him. He pays attention, he'll be full-share in a year."

The old guy spoke softly, but he kept coming. "Tran spent time on fishing boats, more than a year, three years." The old guy held up three fingers. "How long you have your boat? Captain Parker says your boat is brand-new."

Dick said, "Goddamn." Tran spoke to his father in Vietnamese. Dick said, "Goddamn!" more angrily, but he kept his temper. He looked at Tran and shook his head. "You tell your old man not to screw up a good thing. I'll see you day after tomorrow. You get them wool clothes, and you stand by to load my truck with pots."

Dick left. He gunned his truck some so they'd hear it. He saw in his rearview mirror he was burning oil. He said out loud, "Goddamn! Next thing, I'll need a new truck."

He thought of what Elsie would make of all this. It made him laugh.

It wasn't surprising the old man came on the way he did. He'd been dealing with Parker, didn't know any better. Dick recollected he himself had some greed in his mind, maybe it'd showed in his eyes. The old man was foreign, probably didn't know there was some things you push back and forth, some things you don't.

With a little jolt Dick saw himself as Captain Texeira when

Vietnamese family. He said he'd like to put some of the money into buying a bunch of pots cheap. May nodded, said at least the food bills were low, what with Eddie having cooked up pots of stew with the meat that had thawed at the edges when the power was out. Then she asked him for a hundred dollars for herself. When he asked her what for, she was embarrassed. She wouldn't say right off.

Dick said, "Look, I'll give you the money, May. What the hell, it's not even a quarter-trawl of cheap pots."

May twisted her mouth at that, not angry but peevish.

Dick tried to brighten things up. "I'll give you the money. It's coming in regular for a change." He opened his wallet and held out five twenties. She took it and put it away in her purse. He saw she was peeved with herself. With her back to him, she said, "I'm going to spend it on a makeover."

"Good," he said. "Whatever it is, good."

"I'll tell you what it is," she said.

"Don't have to," he said cheerily.

May said, "It's a beauty treatment. You learn what makeup and what kind of hairstyle and what color clothes you ought to wear." She was furious now.

"You look pretty good to me." No help.

May said, as if Dick was dragging it out of her, "Eddie invited over that woman he's been helping out. The one he met when she was lost in the woods. He cuts wood for her, fixes her storm windows. He was over to her house cutting up a tree across her driveway, and he asked her to come back for supper." May paused and said, "She's the same age as me. The boys have seen her, she works at the library and she substitute-teaches. She has a daughter the same age as Charlie. When she told us about her daughter and her thinking of where to go to college, Charlie and Tom couldn't believe it, she looked so young. They said so. Eddie laughed and said, 'It is hard to believe, isn't it.' All three of them stared at her till she was embarrassed and talked about something else."

Dick cleared his throat. "I know who you mean. I don't think I've seen her, but Eddie's mentioned her."

He heard his own voice come out far off like an echo. For a second he feared he'd said, "Elsie's mentioned her."

May said, "She looked at me when they were all looking at her. She just took a quick look sideways."

May didn't say anything for a while. Dick didn't see what he could say.

May said, "She didn't get dressed up to come here. She was wearing a checked shirt and slacks. Her hair was nice, all clean and fluffed up. She had on a little bit of eye makeup. And a little bit of lipstick. Her hands were pretty. Her slacks were kind of baggy with pleats, but she had this wide belt so her waist was pinched in. You could see her toes in her sandals. She didn't paint her toenails but they were nice too. She had little tiny pearls in her ears—"

Dick said, "Well, hell, May, she did get dressed up."

"No, she didn't. It's not just getting dressed up. It's every day. She takes care of herself. She gets her hair cut right. Her shirt was just a regular checked shirt. It had brown and pink and white and real little blue lines, but it was just right for her. Of course her skin was good anyway. She just knows how to take care of herself."

Dick said, "Well, she's a divorcee."

May looked at him until he felt dumb. She said, "That makes a woman better-looking, does it?"

"All I meant was—"

"You spread that secret around, everyone's going to try divorce."

"All I meant is, she don't have much else to do all day."

"If you mean she's not cleaning up after a bunch of oafs tracking low tide through her house, you're right about that."

Dick said, "The boys not doing their share around here?"

May sighed. "The boys're doing their share all right. And Eddie does a lot. Cooks some too. I have more free time around here than I ever had."

"Well, good, May, you deserve it." Dick thought of the goddamn dishwasher again. And then of the free time May would have to think about things.

May said, "You got your boat now, and when you're ashore you got the boys and Eddie to do your will. And you go to the Neptune, and you've got Parker to get into trouble with. When I picked crabs at Joxer Goode's, I at least had all of the other pickers to talk to. He didn't mind us talking so long as we filled our boxes. You told me to quit, so I quit. Here comes this divorcee of Eddie's, she says she likes living alone. Alone! She sees Miss Perry every Sunday, she's friends with both Buttrick girls, she goes to their parties. She's friends with the librarians and the teachers, and she goes to see friends in Boston. That's on top of Eddie running up there as soon as there's something she can't fix herself. Alone!"

Dick didn't say anything.

"The boys're getting grown up and on their own," May said. "Tom's fifteen. When school's out, he and Charlie spend more time with Eddie than with me. They work with him all day, every Saturday."

"Pretty soon we'll all go work on our house together," Dick said. "The insurance money'll come through...."

"Did you ever ask what I thought about your spending three weeks out of every month at sea?"

Dick was stung. He was about to say, "What the hell you think I was building a boat for?" He swallowed it. May got up from the bed and looked at her watch. She said, "The boys'll be back from school in an hour. You want to take your shower?"

"Eddie still out?"

"He comes back late these days. Around six."

Dick didn't want to go to bed with May in her state, but he was afraid he'd cause more trouble if he didn't want to. He said, "Maybe you'll feel better back in your own house."

May didn't say anything for a while. Then she said, "It's funny. I didn't think I'd like living at someone else's place. But it's nice here."

"It is," Dick said. "Eddie's handy at making things homey. Steady Eddie. You ever think you'd have been better off married to someone like Eddie? Nice and homey. Good disposition."

May surprised him by laughing.

"Poor old Eddie," she said. "He's never going to get anywhere with that woman. It's not just on account of her being up there with the big-house people. I don't know about that. But if she *was* interested, he's too nice. It's okay the way he helps you out, the way he is with the boys. But with her he's too bent-forward and agreeable."

Dick couldn't believe her mood had changed so suddenly—she sounded almost cheerful about Eddie's problem.

"He gives up his own mind," May said. "He just turns into a feather pillow for her. I think she had more fun out of Tom than out of Eddie. Tom got a little sassy, and you could see her perk up. I don't know what she would've done if you'd come in the door in one of your slam-bang moods. Probably gone down on her knees to help pull your boots off." May laughed again. She'd brightened up entirely.

Dick said, "I thought your complaint was I was too disagreeable."

May said, "I'm saying that to show what she's like, not to encourage you." She added, "Nobody wants things all one way or the other. Go take your shower."

*T*hat fall Dick and May spent in Eddie's house was companionable. *Spartina* brought in pretty good hauls. Even with time out for some November gales, Dick got out more pots, found a window of bright, cold, calm weather in December. He'd hired an old Portuguese who suited Tran and him fine. The food on board was excellent—both Tran and the Portuguese, Tony Pereira, took an intelligent interest in meals on board. The food at Eddie's was good too. Eddie took out his crossbow and shot another swan for Christmas dinner. Dick had never figured on how cheering good meals could be.

But Dick still hadn't told May about Elsie. That worry would swoop in on him so that he was stabbed with panic. But then it would leave quickly. Later he realized the sharpness was dangerous: it made him think he was actually paying a price for things' going well; when the stab of panic was over he was lulled back to regular life.

He told May in January. There'd been a foggy thaw and all of them had gone down to their house with Eddie. The insurance money had come in and was enough so that Eddie and what was now Eddie's regular little building crew could do quite a bit more than just shore up and patch the old house. They were going to add a little greenhouse on the south side, and a screened-in porch off the kitchen. May was very pleased. Eddie went back with the boys to start supper. Dick went down to check the wharf. When he came back, May was poking in the garden with a spade fork. There were beads of foggy dew on the nap of her new wool coat and on her cut-short hair. Her cheeks were pink from the little bit of digging she'd done. Dick told her she looked pretty good. She stopped digging. "It's not just those beauty treatments," he said. "Maybe it's things looking up. That was a bad patch last summer. I see now it weighed you down too. Maybe even more than it did me. I was almost crazy with getting that boat in. It's sometimes easier to get through something like that when you're a little crazy. But that made you the one had to be normal, had to keep things going. I can see that must have been hard."

May was happy to hear this. She took his arm, brushed the water drops off the cuff of his slicker.

Dick said, "That stuff with Parker. God, I got up to crazy stuff. You were right to get me to go to Miss Perry after all. I damn near missed that on account of her going into her spell. But you were right to get me to do it."

"You won't have any trouble making that payment, will you?"

"It's not till the end of next August. Even with a bad swordfish season, it's no trouble."

"And you don't have to deal with Parker."

"Parker taking me on his boat is how I made some money. I didn't actually get money for his little smuggling deal."

May said, "Well, you're clear of him. And you won't have to do a clambake for Sawtooth Point. And you won't have to fool with that fellow that was making the movie, that friend of Elsie Buttrick. I heard things about him. . . ."

"We did get him to pay for the spotter plane. Some of that turned out lucky. Even poaching clams out of the bird sanctuary made some money. But that was another piece of craziness."

"Wasn't it the movie fellow that caused the accident where Elsie Buttrick fell overboard?"

"No, that was her getting the outboard foul of the line."

May said, "Well, even that turned out to the good, then. She ended up lending you another thousand. And your boat came through the hurricane."

Dick said, "Elsie's going to have a baby."

May seemed to know everything just from that.

She walked off a short way, then came back to face him. She looked at her watch. "We have to get back soon. It is your baby?"

"Yes."

"So all that about how near crazy you were, you told me that by way of an excuse."

Dick hadn't thought of that, but now he saw it might be true. He didn't say anything.

May said deliberately, "You better tell me some more. One thing you better tell me is how come an up-to-date woman, gone to college, gone to two colleges, how come she gets pregnant? Or was it out on Parker's boat? And she didn't . . ."

Dick said, "I guess she made a mistake." Dick could see anger move up May's face. But May didn't explode.

May said, "This was last summer? Before you put the boat in? How long did all this go on?"

Dick looked away. "Once or twice. No, two or three times."

May laughed at him.

Dick felt that. He said, "I'll tell you exactly. It was right after Parker's smuggling run. Elsie was on duty for two nights. She was riding her bicycle home and I gave her a ride. It was raining."

May shook her head. Dick heard her teeth grind.

Dick said, "Then Parker was in New York, so when he wasn't back after a week or so, I took his boat out. And it was all over with."

"Then she loaned you the money."

"That's right. She loaned me the money. She was taking care of

Miss Perry, and she talked to Miss Perry and set that up, and she talked to her brother-in-law and got another thousand."

"She's a real friend of the family," May said and went to her car. She opened the door, paused, and added, "When she came to Eddie's to tell us she'd seen *Spartina,* I guess she knew she was pregnant then, she knew she was carrying your child."

May started the car. Dick barely had time to get in and shut his door before she pulled off.

During supper May scarcely showed signs of trouble at all. She talked to the boys and to Eddie perfectly naturally. She went straight to the bedroom right after the washing up. Dick listened to the NOAA weather forecast. Not good. He watched the first half of a Celtics game with the boys and Eddie.

May was lying in the middle of the bed. Dick went back out and got some extra blankets to use as a mattress.

When he came back in and dumped the blankets, May said, "And what about the baby?"

Dick was surprised at her tone. She didn't sound mad. She sounded worn out.

She said again, "What are you going to do about the baby?"

"What do you mean? You want her to get an abortion? It's too late."

May shook her head slowly. "I don't mean an abortion. I mean you taking care of your baby. How do you plan to do that? No matter what—even if you got a divorce you'd still have three kids and two mothers. That's what you got, no matter what."

Before he got alarmed, Dick had the funny feeling that he was playing checkers with May, and May was making two moves each time it was her turn.

It was the mention of divorce that alarmed him. He said, "This is my family. What we got here. You and me and Charlie and Tom. I never said divorce. I never thought it."

"What are you going to do about your baby?"

"Look. Elsie was planning on having a baby all along. She's getting Mary Scanlon to move in with her, in that new house with her, and the two of them were going to adopt a baby. They found out it was too complicated. So when this came up, they figured they'd take this one. They're going to say it's adopted. When Elsie comes back from Massachusetts, that's what they're going to say."

May was silent. For an instant Dick thought this time he'd been the one that got in two moves. Then he saw he was worse off.

May said, "So Elsie didn't make a mistake."

Dick fumbled a minute before he said, "It was a mistake, and then they figured they'd go ahead and take advantage of it."

"*They,*'" May said. "I'm too tired to go on listening to you. I've never heard you so shifty. You sound like Parker. I can't pay attention to it. You go back out on your boat and think about this—what are you going to do about your baby?"

Dick woke up when he heard Eddie's truck leave. He heard May in the kitchen. He got up and stood behind the bedroom door listening. The boys weren't there, must have left for school. He was sore from lying on the floor, so he got sidetracked by the thick quilt covering the bed. He wrapped himself in one of his blankets and curled up on top of the quilt. He hadn't been in bed so late in months. He hadn't been so tired in months. Not since after the hurricane blew itself out and he slept away a day on *Spartina*. He'd never taken a nap ashore in his life. Except the time he drowsed off in Elsie's bed one of those afternoons. That recollection snapped him awake. What struck him as odd was that the sensations were so alike—waking up in Elsie's bed, with that same feeling of two pressures—alarm and satisfaction. It took him a minute to identify that, although he was in trouble, he was satisfied by what May had said, by how she was taking it.

May woke him up to tell him Tran and Tony had both called to ask when they were going out. She made him breakfast while he tuned in the weather. No better. He called Tran and Tony.

He spent the morning fixing some pots in Eddie's cellar. May called him for lunch but otherwise didn't talk to him. She didn't seem mad. Just slow and far away.

The wind backed into the northeast and blew hard for three days. It turned cold.

May said he could get back in the bed to sleep.

For three days they were alone, in and around the house all day, from breakfast to when the boys got home from school. May talked to him some about other matters. She also felt free to make comments about Elsie's having a baby. Dick understood he wasn't to answer back, just pay attention and give whatever facts May might ask for.

He didn't dare say out loud he admired the way May was acting. She was taking her own time. She was hard, but she wasn't asking anything for herself. He could see it weighed on her steadily and she was carrying it. He went about his business.

Eddie had brought back a wood sailboat from one of the wrecked boathouses he was rebuilding. It was on a cradle in one of the sheds. Dick set to work on it during the day. At night he went down to the cellar for an hour or so to mend a few more pots.

May came down and said he could go to the Neptune if he wanted. He knew what she meant—his working extra hours didn't count that much one way or the other.

*D*ick went down to the harbor to check *Spartina*. As he walked past the Co-op the radio operator called out to him. She had a message for him from Woods Hole. He couldn't think of anyone he knew there. Even when he read the message he wasn't sure it was for him. From Neptune Documentary Film Co. Woods Hole, Massachusetts To: Capt. R. Pierce, master of *Spartina,* Galilee, RI . . . Tune in Channel Two Boston, 2000 hrs, 18 Jan.

He got off on the wrong track for a second . . . thought of channel 2 on the CB. Then he figured a TV channel. Schuyler's movie? Why didn't he put his name? Then he figured it was Elsie. That was why there was no name, why it was phoned to the Co-op, why she'd put that it was from Woods Hole. Dick couldn't recall the real name of Schuyler's film company—Elsie'd told him each of Schuyler's films had its own company—but maybe she put Neptune because she meant him to watch it at the Neptune. . . .

It was still blowing a little on the 18th. He went to the Neptune. Neither the Celtics nor the Bruins were playing. He bought a beer and asked the bartender to tune in Channel 2. A couple of guys Dick knew said they wanted to watch a cop show. He bought them each a beer and said if it turned out this wasn't a movie about around here, they could switch back.

The teaser was an aerial shot of the harbor of refuge and Galilee. The guys called to a couple of their buddies.

At first Dick didn't recognize Schuyler's voice narrating. It was a slow, serious baritone, none of Schuyler's usual prance. What he was *saying* was more like Schuyler, little jabs and twists:

"Rhode Island—poor cousin to Massachusetts" . . . "Most densely populated state after New Jersey" . . . "Lowest educational level of any state outside the Deep South" . . . "Highest percentage of people whose first language is not English" . . .

Dick thought of what Mary Scanlon used to say—"Rhode Island is not a high-expectation state."

There was an aerial shot of palaces in Newport—". . . glittering remnant of the robber barons, but the greater part of Rhode Island is as desperately poor as West Virginia.

"According to a Ph.D. thesis on state governments, Rhode Island came in second only to Louisiana for the title of most corrupt state legislature.

"If Rhode Island were a country, it would be part of the Third World. The largest employer is the military. Tourism is the major moneymaker, although most Rhode Islanders benefit from it only in service positions. The bulk of choice real estate is in the form of second homes or resorts run by absentee corporations.

"There is a seafaring tradition, and there is—still—a fishing fleet. By comparison to the high-tech factory ships of Russia, East or West Germany, Japan, or the tuna clippers of our own West Coast, the boats and methods are quaint. But it is still possible—barely possible—to wrest a living from the sea."

One of the guys said, "Who the fuck this fag think he is?"

During the introductory narration, the shots kept alternating between luxury and what was meant to be seen as squalor. A fancy restaurant. Then, at the phrase "lowest educational level of any state outside the Deep South," there was a shot of the crab pickers at Joxer Goode's plant. Dick knew that some of those guys were hired out to Joxer from the state school for the retarded. Dick had always thought Joxer was doing the crazies a favor while he got some real cheap labor. In the pictures Schuyler shot, the camera lingered on the retarded men and women in a half-light that made them look like driven slaves. The soundtrack left out the Muzak Joxer piped in that the poor guys sort of bobbed to, so their movements all looked like some necessary part of a hellish assembly line. Then there was a shot of a mansion from the ocean walk at Newport, with a pack of guard dogs snarling behind the ironwork fence. Then a shot which Dick recognized as his own backyard, and the outside of his patchwork boat shed. Then the Wedding Cake. At the phrase "wrest a living from the sea," a long shot of Dick tonging quahogs.

A guy said, "Hey—that's Sawtooth Pond."

Dick thought of leaving before the boys at the bar recognized him. He couldn't move without making a big effort—the boys were now two deep behind the bar stools.

Schuyler had rearranged things so that the launching of *Spartina* came before the shots of lobstering or harpooning swordfish from *Mamzelle*'s bow pulpit. Schuyler'd made it look like *Spartina* was the only boat in the movie.

Schuyler's voice-over—"According to OSHA, fishing and coal mining are the two most dangerous occupations in America. On board this fishing boat sometimes there is camaraderie, sometimes a good deal of tension." And there was a close-up of Dick's face for the first time. He turned to the camera and said, "If you go over, we pick the fish up first."

The boys laughed. One said in a mock singsong, "Ooh, Dickey, he thinks you're cute. Wants a little of that camaraderie." The boys quieted down at the shots of pulling pots, emptying them, and rebaiting them. No faces, but Dick recognized his old gloves with duct tape around the middle finger. One guy yelled, "Short! That lobster's a short!" but no one laughed.

Then there was a sequence that puzzled Dick—underwater shots of a pot settling on the bottom. In the corner of the picture there was an inset rectangle with elapsed time—oo:oo.

One of the guys said, "That's that old URI movie. It's infrared or something."

At first Dick thought that was just like Schuyler—fake a little, bullshit a little, steal a little, stitch it together. But then Dick got to like the contrast of the seabed to how things looked on the boat—cluttered, noisy, and bouncing around.

Elapsed time 02:38, the first lobster. Jump to a little later, three more. First one still can't figure out how to get in.

Back upstairs. Long shot of Elsie in the dory. The guys couldn't tell who she was, but they figured out what was wrong quick enough. "Look there—that asshole's fouled his line."

Good shot of shark fins. One of the guys hummed the theme from *Jaws*. They laughed. A shark jostled the bow of the dory. Dick hadn't seen that at the time. The boys settled down for a bit, then cheered half-derisively and laughed when Dick hauled Elsie up, her feet running in mid-air. "Look at the little bugger go!" "Ain't that the Vietnamese kid that's the boy on *Spartina*?" They laughed again at the shot of Elsie from the rear, crawling to grab hold of the hatch cover.

Dick felt as if his head was in an oven. It was a relief when the movie went back to the lobsters. Elapsed time 09:43. A whole workday for one lobster to get in. He's reaching for the bait with one claw, can't get it. He's using the other claw to keep the others out, jabbing and thumbing with it. But it somehow seems slow and quiet down there. For all the lobster scuttling, scuffling, and claw waving, it's peaceful. They take their time between moves. Their feelers sweep out in slow arcs like unhurried casting with a fly rod. Even the quick tuck of the tail when a lobster drives himself backward seems calm. He darts once, then settles, his tail spreading out like a Spanish lady's fan, the rows of walking legs touching down as light as a spider's on her web.

The last rectangle gets crowded with big numbers. A lobster is in the parlor. A second one is just inside the entrance, keeping the crowd out. The line is around the block; it's like *Star Wars* at the Wakefield theatre. Dick shook his head. You could get on edge about it, pretty discouraged at how slow they go about getting themselves caught. But he found himself soothed by the way everything wafted, by the watery gentleness of time down there. He'd never seen this. He'd thought about it of course, knew about it mechanically, but never seen it this way. But then it occurred to him he'd seen something like it: newsreels of astronauts on the moon—heavy-shelled, weightless creatures finding their own slow way, not in rhythm with the click of earth-surface readouts, their large motion as liquid as the silt they stirred up.

Send these brave lobsters to the moon.

Dick didn't mind now about all the lobsters that didn't get in the pot. He was pleased to see what he'd never imagined—that he'd spent a lot of his life dropping pots onto the moon.

The movie jolted back to the surface. Dick's gloved hands moving fast, grabbing lobster out of the netting. Side view of his face, but you could still read his lips—"Fuck you, Schuyler."

The guy next to him back-handed his shoulder. "Jesus, Dick. You're on fucking educational TV." Laughter. Dick tipped his head. Let him have his joke. They weren't so bad, a little rowdy was all. Dick wished the movie would get back down to the seabed. But it was in his backyard. A shot of May in her garden. Looking pretty good. One of the guys at the bar leaned forward to say something. Another guy knocked his forearm.

May said, "When do you want your supper?"

Dick's voice—"When I get back."

They all whooped it up. "Keep her right in line, do you, Dick."

Okay, Dick thought, I'm an asshole.

A while later there was Dick back in the bow pulpit, leaning forward with his harpoon. Dick heard the tail end of Schuyler's voice—". . . requires strength and timing."

"Hey. He does think you're cute."

Dick shoved the harpoon.

"Give it to me, Dick. Put it in all the way."

Dick said, "Blow it out your ass."

Then there was *Spartina* sliding out the channel past the sandbagged crab-processing plant. Shots of boats being hauled.

"That's *Swiss Miss*."

"Where's *Bom Sonho?*"

"She was out with *Lydia P.*"

"Yeah. That was just before the hurricane."

Then they all shut up when they saw the sea come up over the breakwater.

They sat still and watched boats crack like nuts. One broke loose and lifted up onto land and rolled—they could scarcely believe their eyes—she goddamn rolled across the parking lot in the white surge.

Then you couldn't tell. There was stuff moving, but you couldn't tell. Blackout, but the soundtrack kept going for a bit. Then quiet.

The next day. The guys stared at the harbor. They spoke up again to say the names of boats they saw, boats they couldn't see.

There was *Spartina* riding off the beach. Dick remembered Elsie had been in her jeep. He remembered looking at the hills, the scrubbed beach, the green shoots in the salt marsh. All he could see now was how beat-to-shit *Spartina* looked. The movie could erase what he thought. But it didn't erase completely. It left little bits of his life all lit up.

There was another shot of the wrecked boats at the state pier.

The men on either side of Dick pulled away from him.

There was the scene Elsie shot of the boys and May at the boatyard. Schuyler—but maybe it was Elsie—had put in music. Dick was glad Elsie hadn't recorded what they'd all said to each other. But the music was bad. It did just the wrong thing. It was happy-end-of-the-movie music. It stank, and Dick saw how some of the stink was going to stick to him.

Some of the guys still weren't working. It didn't surprise him when one of them said, "And here he is with us today. Luke Skywalker."

At last someone else said, "Hell, there were a couple of lucky ones. Texeira's boats were out. You got to choose lucky or good, choose lucky."

"Hey, Dick. They pay you? For being in their movie?"

Dick said, "No. Nobody paid me."

"I heard they loaned you money. The money for your boat."

He left the bar. Stood by his pickup. Didn't feel like driving home. Sooner or later May would hear about the movie. She'd smell a stink too. Different, but just as bad. For a moment he thought, What the hell have you done to me, Elsie? You thought *Spartina* was a work of art, put her in a movie, put me in a movie, made a fool of me.

"Wrong." He said it out loud. He put his hand on the door handle. Might as well blame his truck. What kind of a sorry son of a bitch was he? He had his boat. That's what he'd wished for.

The weather was colder. The stars were steady, the moon clear.

And what had Elsie got? She'd got a wish too, more of a bend in her life than she'd thought of.

*T*he weather did clear. It was a little breezy, but Dick called up Tran and Tony.

They got *Spartina* out to the near edge of the banks, where they still had a few sets of pots. They'd moved most of the others in close enough to get out and back pretty quick, not as far out as this. When they were hauling one of the trawls, the line snapped. Dick heard the crack and the whistle. When he came out of the wheelhouse he saw the line had whipped forward over the wheelhouse and sheared off the VHF antenna and cracked the radar casing. Neither Tran nor Tony was hurt. They'd hit the deck when they'd heard the line hum just before it broke.

The damage was easy enough to fix, but he couldn't tinker with anything delicate while *Spartina* was bouncing around in the chop. He took her into Woods Hole. As they came in at the end of the afternoon, he saw someone waving from the beach just north of the harbor mouth. The waving kept up. He put the glasses on it and saw the figure dragging a foot in the slope of hard sand. It made a big E.

After they docked, Dick let Tran and Tony go ashore for a meal. Elsie showed up, bundled up in foul-weather gear.

She'd come down from her mother's to stay at a friend's house . . . give her mother a break, they were getting along fine but . . . And she craved some sea air, so . . .

She was grinning down at him from the dockside while she said all this. He climbed up. Elsie held on to both his hands. She said, "I'm glad to see you! Come on, I'll buy you a meal."

Dick said sure, but he had to wait for either Tran or Tony to get back. He didn't want some wharf rat pinching something off *Spartina*.

He helped Elsie down on deck, she weighed a ton. He took her to the wheelhouse, which was warm.

Elsie said, "Turn around a second."

She shed her foul-weather gear. When he turned back to face her, she stood sideways, pulling her wool jumper tight to show off the jut of her basketball stomach.

Dick was taken aback. He hadn't thought of getting to see this part.

"Amazing, isn't it?" Elsie said. "The only part I don't like is that I can't go out much in case I run into someone I know. Even people I don't know but who know me—it turns out my mother's house is right down the street from Phoebe Fitzgerald's ex-husband. I sneak out at night in a big overcoat and go to the movies, but that's it." Elsie climbed back into her foul-weather gear. "Anyway, I recognized *Spartina* from the beach. *You're* someone I can run into. . . . Look, let's go eat. Leave a note for your crew. We can ask the harbormaster to keep an eye on *Spartina* till they get back."

Dick didn't like to ask favors, but he didn't want to say no to Elsie. He felt a terrible weight suddenly, not of trouble or sorrow, but of Elsie's good cheer.

At the restaurant he started to tell Elsie about telling May, but she cut him off. "Later," she said. "Let's just eat. This is my first social life since Thanksgiving."

She drove him to the cottage where she was staying. It was dark. "It's a friend's summer house," she said. "She's in Boston."

She asked him to start a fire in the fireplace while she made coffee. She brought a bottle of Irish whiskey out with the coffee. "I'm not drinking, but you go ahead."

She was in a wonderful mood. She'd eaten a huge meal, right down to pie à la mode and a glass of milk. She talked about how cozy Woods Hole was in winter. "I like walking around the harbor at night; it's like a little cup of tea with the mist coming up like steam. My sister's coming up here tomorrow, just for the day." She took his hand again. "And Mary Scanlon's come to see me a couple of times. She's going to come for the birth. In fact everybody's going to be there then. My mother, my sister, and Mary." Elsie laughed. "You want to come?"

Dick said, "Look. I got to say something. We haven't really talked about this. I got to know about doctor's bills and the like. I'd like to put some money aside for that. And for other things."

"Dick, we did talk about that. I told you about that already. I'm doing fine. I mean, right this minute I'm getting paid a salary."

Dick said, "I've got to do it. It's not just because it's May's idea. I thought about it and she's right. I see she's right."

"Ah." Elsie folded her hands in her lap. After a minute she said, "Was it terrible telling her? Are things okay? That's a dumb question. I guess I hope she blamed it on me. Did she? You know, call me a tramp and a slut? It's funny, I've been feeling very close to her. I mean, this baby is related to her babies."

"No," Dick said. "She didn't blame it all on you. She didn't even get that mad. Not that way. It's hard to explain. I've got to say I admire the way she feels about it—so far as I understand the way she feels." Dick was suddenly glad to be seeing Elsie, to feel the relief of talking to someone who was in the same trouble.

"It'll be a while before things settle down," he said. "If I had to guess, I'd say things'll be okay eventually. Not the same, but okay, if I make amends."

"You buy her a dishwasher yet?"

Dick looked at Elsie.

"Oh, come on," Elsie said. "No. I guess I shouldn't tease you. I'm sorry, I can't help it—part of this *is* funny. Me transporting myself across state lines. Elsie, the unindicted co-conspirator disguised in a man's overcoat. I feel like an anarchist carrying a bomb." She put her hands on her belly, said, "Boom!" and lifted her fingers.

"There is this side to it," she said. "I'm not killing anybody with my crime. I mean, it's not bad *that* way. I get to have my deep outlaw wish, and it's a baby."

Elsie sank down after that little spate of bright talk. She said, "So May didn't blame me, she didn't call me a cheap slut?"

"I said she didn't blame it all on you. She might not even think you were bad to her personally. You just ignored her. If she was going to call you anything, I guess it'd be *spoiled*. But I'm not sure I get everything May's thinking. I've never had to forgive anybody. At least not anybody in my family. For anything so definite . . ." Dick thought of how he finally forgave his father so many years after his father's death. But it wasn't for any one thing the old man had *done*. He shook his head and said, "I'm no one to go by about that."

Elsie said, "Don't go gloomy on me." She started to get up, said, "Don't just sit there, give me a hand." He pulled her up. She shook the skirt of her jumper loose from where it clung to her tights. "I used to laugh at Sally when she was pregnant, struggling up out of chairs. Thank God, I won't be pregnant in summer—I even feel too hot now." She took her boots off by stepping on the heels. She held out a foot for him to pull her wool sock off, then the other foot. She went around to the back of the sofa and took her tights off, leaning on it with both hands as she trampled them off her ankles and feet.

"I'm not spoiled," she said. "If anybody was spoiled, Sally was spoiled. When Sally was pregnant, Jack hovered around her like a hummingbird. And he kept telling her how beautiful she was. I used to laugh at him. I don't now. Everyone should get to be a little spoiled when she's pregnant."

Dick said, "I was just guessing when I said May might have thought you were spoiled. And anyway that was about the way you were last summer. I told you May wants me to put up my share of what it'll cost."

"What exactly does she mean by that?" Elsie said. "I think I see, but I'm not sure."

"She doesn't want me owing anything," Dick said. "I understand that part. That's one way of making things come out quits."

Elsie said, "Well, as a practical matter, I'm on Blue Cross. And as for the kid's clothes, Sally's got trunks full of hand-me-downs. *Trunks.* Girl's and boy's, so we're covered both ways. But if May wants you to do something—"

Dick said, "*I* want to do something."

"Okay. I won't argue about it. But I don't want to feel I'm making things hard for Charlie and Tom. I mean, there's still Charlie and Tom, even with Miss Perry's books. God, it does get complicated. We'll all be taking care of someone else's kid before we're through."

"Miss Perry's books?" Dick said.

"Oh," Elsie said. "Oh dear. I thought . . . Of course it was a surprise to me too. Oh shit, you're going to get mad at me again."

Dick said, "What're you talking about?"

"When I was talking to Miss Perry about the loan for your boat, I asked her about selling some of Charlie's and Tom's books. Not the readers' copies they've got but the good ones in Miss Perry's library. She said no, they were for Charlie's and Tom's college. I didn't ask what she thought they were worth, but it sounded a little grandiose. I mean, *college.* I thought she might be a little addled. But I looked the books over one day—she's got them all together in her library—and I made a list. I could tell that some of them are first editions, but some I wasn't sure of, so I took down the date and city, all that stuff. When I was in Providence one day, I went to a rare-book dealer and showed him the list. He said a lot depends on the condition of the book. They looked pretty good to me, and I told him that, and he gave me a rough estimate. . . . Look, I know I stuck my nose in again. . . ."

"What'd he say?"

"Tom's are worth more than Charlie's, though Charlie has one that—"

"What's it all come to? All totaled . . . more than a thousand?"

"Twenty thousand."

Dick laughed. "You must've got something wrong."

Elsie said, "Nope. You know what amazed me? *The Wizard of Oz.* A nice edition is worth more than five thousand dollars. That's what put Tom's books up so high. That was on Tom's Christmas shelf. Louisa May Alcott, Hawthorne, John Greenleaf Whittier... I can't remember them all. I've got them written down, but the list is back at my house. There's one the dealer couldn't price exactly— *The American Practical Navigator* by Nathaniel Bowditch. That one stuck in my mind. It's a little beat up, but it belonged to Oliver Hazard Perry, it's got his name on the fly leaf. If it's his signature— and I'd guess it must be—it may put Charlie's share up to Tom's. Of course, Commodore Perry may have owned several. It's sort of a manual, right? It came out in the early 1800's, but it kept getting updated, so he may have kept getting new ones. The Navy probably issued them. . . . You could sell it back to the Navy!"

Elsie was cheery by now.

Dick felt a weight pressing at an odd angle. He said, "I didn't know she was up to anything like that. I surely didn't know."

Elsie came round the sofa and knelt in front of him so she could see his face. "I was afraid you'd take it this way," she said. "But it's good news."

Dick shook his head. "It's too much money."

Elsie said, "It's a lot of money, but it's not *that* much."

Dick snorted. Elsie sat back on her heels. She said, "What I mean is that it won't pay for four years of college, not with room and board. Even if they just go to URI."

"Just," Dick said. "Everyone can't go to Brown and Yale."

Elsie moved a few steps on her knees and hoisted herself up, her hands on the arms of a chair. She said, "Don't take it out on me. And don't start that class-rage shit."

Dick didn't say anything.

Elsie said, "You know, it's just as spoiled to be as touchy as you are about everything as it is to think you can get away with anything you feel like."

"No," Dick said. "You can't say I'm just being touchy. There's something strange about not knowing how much your own kids have. There's something strange about all that money growing in the dark."

"Well," Elsie said, "she didn't give anything to you, she gave it to Charlie and Tom." Elsie laughed. "You aren't jealous, are you? You're not worried she loves them more than she loves you? She did lend you some, but you have to pay yours back."

Dick looked at Elsie. She'd turned impish again, grinning and poking. She said, "Maybe you're annoyed she's setting your boys free from you. You are sort of a tyrant, aren't you? But there isn't anything you can do about this. As soon as the boys turn eighteen, it's just between Miss Perry and them." Elsie laughed again. "There is an irony here—last summer you were scrabbling hard for every penny. You conned Schuyler into paying for the spotter plane, poached clams out of the bird sanctuary, ran drugs. . . . There was no stopping you. But now—now you want to give it all away. Pay for my baby. Make poor old Miss Perry take back her presents to your children."

Elsie was nettling him, but she was also jostling him out of his sense of oppression.

"You know," Elsie said, "Miss Perry sold me my five acres at way below market value. Why can't you be as cheerful and grateful as I was?"

Dick said, "Passing money from rich to rich isn't the same."

Elsie laughed at him. "I wish I was as rich as you keep thinking I am. Get it straight, will you? I'm not rich, I'm privileged." Elsie cracked herself up over that.

Dick didn't laugh. He still hadn't made his good reasons clear to her. "Look. I'm as fond of Miss Perry as anyone, but there's a mockery in it. Whether she meant to or not, it mocks me. For four years I tried to borrow money from the bank. We didn't eat red meat but once a week and that was hamburger. An awful lot of fish, which none of us like all that much. I was hauling pots, building boats for other people when I couldn't afford to work on my own...and that whole time, all those years, one of my kids has some...*storybook*...worth five thousand dollars! Goddamn. I built a whole catboat and didn't get five thousand gross."

"I understand," Elsie said. "I agree that what some people get paid is crazy, how people get money is crazy. Miss Perry thinks the whole thing is crazy too. She sold an old painting she'd never liked much—she was horrified at what it brought in."

Dick said, "Horrified. Yup."

"She knows that people get rich by chance. At least she's a rich person who admits it. And at least she's generous. I admire what she's done, and I think you should too. If she'd said straight out to you, 'I'm going to help send your kids to college,' you might have given her a flat no. She's given your kids some things she owned. It didn't cost her anything. She let them catch a ride on this crazy inflation. If you weren't such a prickly bastard, you'd be generous about it. You could be a perfectly nice man, you know. You *are* a perfectly nice man when you're not being a tightwad."

Dick said, "I'm no tightwad."

"Yes, you are. It's just as stingy and graceless to tighten up when someone's being generous to you as it is to be a miser. It's just as unsympathetic, just as defensive. It's all the same old Yankee vice."

Dick let what she said lie on him. It wasn't just one of her nettles.

She got up from the armchair, hoisting herself on the arms. She stood in front of him. "I've gone too far," she said. "I don't know why I do. I'm sure you and Miss Perry are nicer with each other than you and I are." She took his head in her hands, ran her thumbs across his forehead until they met. She laughed a little and said, "At least in some ways." She parted her thumbs slowly. "Models of comportment."

He scarcely felt her fingers and thumbs, but he felt her presence. It concentrated around them, began to tug him up from a depth as though he and Elsie were being hauled together, thrashing in the same net, not touching the weave yet, still darting this way and that but feeling everything lift—what was there, what was around them—feeling the water bulge upward, the turbulence push on their lateral stripes.

He thought maybe Elsie wouldn't notice, would just go on talking. He closed his eyes, opened them, saw her puffy bare feet. As she swayed a little, her feet spread at the edges.

He was still sitting on the sofa. Maybe she was still talking, maybe she still had her hands on his head. Elsie and he were all alone now, submerged together. No old light falling from a single star, not this time. It was all undersea, briny and blind. He felt her as though he were a fish, no hearing, just flutters of her disturbing the water. He felt them on the stripes along his flanks. Flutters on one side, then the other. Then flutters pressing equally on both flanks, running from gills to tail—that's how he felt her dead ahead.

He was baffled by feeling. He was deep and dumb as a fish. He felt the pressure this way and that as she moved. Maybe she wouldn't notice his hulking attention, hovering and swiveling in the stream of presence she sent out.

"Are you tired?" she said. "You must be tired."

He looked up at her face. Maybe he would just sink. Maybe he could just give up and sink.

"I suppose you've been up since dawn." She put her palm on his forehead. He felt her palm and leaned into it. He pushed himself up from the sofa. When his face came up to hers and up a little higher, she let her hands fall along his shoulders and arms. She said, "Oh my."

He kissed her. He held the sides of her belly. "Oh my," she said, "I ought to talk you out of this." He kissed her again, moved his hands to her shoulders to steady himself.

"Well, yes," she said. "But listen."

He looked at her face until he saw it clearly. His sense of sight helped him veer off. Part of his imagination told him this would be a disaster, would shackle him to trouble for the rest of his days. But most of him was for going on, for finding her. He was touching her, his hands on her belly.

She put her hands over his, held his hands tightly while they rested on her belly. If she raised him too quickly, he might burst.

"I'm glad, I really am glad," she said. "But listen. . . ."

Years ago he'd dived down to wire the bolt of a shackle on a mushroom anchor. One of the workers at the boatyard had screwed it shut but forgotten to wire it before he chucked it in. Not far down, maybe fifteen feet. He'd gone in in his skivvies, over the side of the yard skiff. He'd hauled himself down on the chain. Just five feet down in the silty water it was dark. Fifteen feet, not even a memory of light. He'd reached the shackle, got the wire in the eye, and twisted it round, his legs hooked around the stem of the toppled anchor. When he was done, he panicked. He'd forgotten which way was up. Dumb, dumb as could be, all he had to do was let go and he'd go up. Plenty of air in his lungs. But he'd gone dumb for a bit—it seemed long but it was probably just a few seconds. He'd clutched the stem of the anchor, couldn't get himself to turn it loose. Didn't even know he was holding on. He was all blank mind. Lost his body. In his blankness he couldn't imagine anything, let alone what was holding him down there. Then he was loose. He saw dim brightness where he was headed, and that seemed to take a long time too, the brightness getting brighter.

The relief hadn't been air or light. Or, after a jumbled second, being able to hear the two guys in the skiff talking to each other; nothing was going on for them, they were just passing the time, no time at all. The relief had been finding his fingers and toes, he'd been as dumb as that.

Now he popped up in front of Elsie, saw the corners of the room, the lamp, the fire. Amazed. Amazed at what he'd wanted, amazed at how completely.

Elsie was talking still. He pieced it together now—she'd been explaining in her seesaw way why they weren't going to, but how glad she was, how nice he was, how funny it was. . . . He'd caught some of it. She'd been interrupting herself, but her voice had been steady and soft.

She held on to his hands while they sat down on the sofa. They slumped back. She was amazed too. She unbuttoned his shirt cuff and peeled it back, shoved back the loose sleeve of his union suit. She kissed his forearm, then put her hand on it. His arm lay between them. A plank lodged between two rocks after a big tide. He was relieved after all to be inert, glad she was soothing him.

Elsie lifted her head to speak. Dick said, "Don't say any more, not just yet."

Elsie said, "You'll be glad."

"Yeah, you're right."

"You don't want to go, do you?" The way she said it she didn't mean anything, it was just a light breath.

"No, let's just stay a bit."

They sat up till past midnight. Elsie talked, took naps, got up to go to the bathroom or get a bite to eat. She started, broke off, and resumed various conversations, in between various silences.

Elsie apologized several times for not making love. "I hope you don't think I'm just being good. Or that I'm suddenly scared of being bad."

Dick was amused, now he was calm.

Later on she said, "This isn't any kind of self-pity—some attempt to get more."

Dick was briefly impatient. "I wish you'd quit being so suspicious of yourself. Or of someone. It sure isn't me checking up on you."

He was interested when she gave a real reason. "There are going to be lies about all this—about having a baby," she said. "I didn't see that as clearly as I do now. There are some lies I can't do without, so I don't want any extra ones. Extra lies or extra truths—you'd either have to lie to May or tell her. If we..." Elsie twirled her hand.

Dick nodded. Was it being pregnant that had cleaned up the way she talked?

Elsie said, "I don't care what May thinks—no, I do care—I mean, I don't care if . . . What I mean is I feel a bond to May, whatever she thinks. Her children and mine are related."

"You said that," Dick said. "It sounds simple and cozy when you put it like that. But I know it's not."

"If you were an Arab sea captain it would be that simple. Me in Abu Dhabi, May in Kuwait. You sailing back and forth between us in your dhow, praising Allah."

"Yeah. That'd take care of everything all right."

Elsie laughed. Then she said, "Look. As long as we're getting rid of unnecessary lies . . . But, then, this may make you feel better about Charlie and Tom's book. . . ."

"Skip the backing and filling, will you?"

"You remember I told you Jack would do anything I asked? Well, when I started to talk to Miss Perry about your loan, she didn't seem . . . I mean, she was just too far along. . . . It *is* true that Captain Texeira said it would be okay to lend you the money, but he said it to me. I didn't think it would be good to try to explain to Miss Perry. So I just called Jack."

"What are you saying? He's the one? But the note I signed was to you. Because you said you had Miss Perry's power of attorney."

"Well, that's what I thought I should clear up. Jack loaned me the money, and I loaned it to you."

"Jesus, Elsie." But he wasn't really angry. It seemed farther away than he'd thought. He felt some dismay as he reasoned it through, but not anger. He said, "So your brother-in-law figures I wheedled ten—no, eleven thousand dollars out of you on top of knocking you up."

"I was afraid you might think that—I mean, that you'd think *he'd* think that. So I didn't tell him what it was for."

"He didn't ask?"

"No. It's hard to explain. . . . It's not just that he'll do anything for me.... Every so often he likes to do something that makes him feel madly extravagant. But when Schuyler paid me what he owed me, I paid Jack some of what I owe him. So really we're almost down to the simplest situation of all, which is your owing me eleven thousand dollars, and nobody needs to know about that except you and me. And after all—considering all the serious things everyone's been doing—the money part is just comic."

"Jesus, Elsie." But he didn't care to set her right. He couldn't figure why. Maybe it was because Elsie had saved him just now in a way that absolved her of all her meddling. Maybe it was that the better part of five months at sea on *Spartina* came to him now to let him worry less about how he stood onshore. Or maybe it was because Elsie had been the one who kept them from sinking into worse trouble, so that he wasn't the captain of this enterprise, the only one in charge making everything right....

And still later Elsie said, "Is this how you and May got married? I mean, two people have this flare-up, it's all perfectly natural at first. The woman fills up with a baby. Then it's a social problem— in comes her father, the preacher. The man makes an honest woman of her. They get stuck with a life together. I can't imagine putting up with that." Elsie looked thoughtful. She added, "As it is, I don't resent you at all."

"Is that so?" Dick said. "That's good. In case you worry about the way you may have led me by the nose, I better say I don't resent you either."

"Well, all right," she said. "Have you noticed that we're passing up some chances to have a fight? Maybe because we're passing up our chance to ..." She waved her hand again. "Maybe it's because right now all I can think about is food."

But she curled up again between him and the corner of the sofa and dozed off.

He felt peacefully attached, but snipped free from wanting anything. He was clear enough for the first time to see how wanting had tugged him hard through the last few years—the long wish for his own offshore boat; the sudden pull of an old surprise that had sucked him in close to Elsie.

Now none of that was wishes anymore. In the little hollow of that shock he wondered what he would want next. He didn't know, but for a long second he got a sense of what it might be. Whatever it was was invisible but real—maybe a wish to be part of something bigger, as though the shell of his boat, of his family, or even of Miss Perry's arrangements was getting tight enough for him to molt.

For a moment he felt whatever it was was as huge as the horizon, always there but you never get there. Then he thought it was a little thing, the spark in a herring's tiny brain that made it splatter upstream with a shoal of other herrings, a little dot that drove its body in a long line.

The size of it flicked from big to little and then vanished. Maybe he had it all wrong, it wasn't a straight-line wish he needed, no new course ruled in on a chart.

What he thought next was how quick it would all go. No matter what he set out after, his life wasn't more than a puff, a cat's paw just shivering the water. You only saw it whole if you were a ways off; you only felt it if you were inside it.

That was one way to look at it all—from outside it was quick. But, sitting here, breathing slow, and, for all the rush of these pictures, barely thinking, he felt completely still in time.

Time slowed up. Then, without moving, time slipped both ways at once. Part of it came from Elsie sleeping: there she was a sixteen-year-old girl, her quick-bird hands curled up, a little girl still younger, his father was still alive, he himself was young, he could feel how little he knew, his mother was alive, she was sleeping, everyone was there.

The future was nearby—for a moment he thought he was there too, or maybe he'd been there and back. He felt that future the way he felt the past still. All at once.

He snorted at himself. This was what old folks thought when their eyesight went and they sat at home remembering, thinking they remembered.

Then, from years ago, he remembered standing watch on a Coast Guard vessel. Near the end of light on a short, cold day in the North Atlantic. Checking out icebergs north of the shipping lanes. Dick saw one, sang out, and looked down to find the officer of the deck. Okay, one mistake—keep your eye on the ball. When the officer looked it was gone. Dick looked and it was gone. The officer asked the radar man, who said there was nothing on the screen. An hour or so later, they picked up a blip on the radar, turned out to be one huge iceberg. The officer and Dick were baffled. The skipper said it could happen like that—you sometimes could see things beyond the horizon. The Eskimos knew about it. Arctic and Antarctic explorers. Called "superior mirage" or "looming." The old man couldn't explain it, just that it had to do with layers of air of different temperatures. He said to Dick, "Tell me, Pierce, did you notice if your iceberg looked like it was upside down?"

"No, sir." When he tried to remember, he couldn't picture it.

Now, here in the cottage in Woods Hole, he saw it. Piled up like a thunderhead, an anvil of opal. It had been upside down.

Dick's watch officer said, "Something you didn't know about, huh, Pierce?"

"You and me both, sir."

The old man said, "That'll do, Pierce."

He liked the old man. The old man had tried to get him to stop being a wise-ass. He'd been a wise-ass. Now at last he let go of being a wise-ass. Of layers and layers. Wise-ass was just one. He let go of being himself.

He was still again, without thought, on watch, just seeing the way things would work out: him staying at home, putting out to sea, the familiar waters from Galilee to Georges Bank, from Georges Bank to Galilee. The house was there on Pierce Creek, there was the salt creek, the salt marsh, the salt pond. He wasn't going anywhere. So how would things happen? He'd stay in his life no matter how often or how far he put out to sea. The future was that a lot of things would move on away from him—was that it? Charlie and Tom would move on away; it didn't mean they'd leave, it was that what they wanted and what they'd get done would move on away, link up with things he'd have less and less to do with.

He guessed he'd always known neither Charlie nor Tom would work on his boat. It didn't bother him, it had been a good part of his wish while he was building *Spartina*. It'd helped. You don't get everything. He'd tell them it was all right, so long as they understood he'd have liked to have them along.

He wondered if he'd get a second boat. There seemed to be another boat. . . . He'd always wondered how Captain Texeira could own two boats, could stand the strain of worrying about the boat under his feet and the second one over the horizon. Maybe Captain Texeira wasn't a worrier. Or had enough trust in his nephew to set him free as skipper of the *Lydia P.*

Dick looked at Elsie under the lamp. It hadn't dawned on him till now that he'd have to trust her. No matter whether they managed to stay in touch, she'd be pretty much on her own with the child. Not easy for her, she was sometimes oddly young for thirty-three; no, thirty-four now. He got a sense of her as older, everything older and all right. But it wasn't going to be easy for him either. He'd got that right in the first place, when he'd stooped in the bushes and heard, felt alarm and anger and then a terrible forlornness. Feeling forlorn would keep on, but it wasn't so terrible, eased somehow.

He'd guessed back then in the bushes the kid would be a girl, and he seemed to know now that was right. His second boat, his daughter, were there in the future, not visible to him but bumped into by some blind sense, like coming up Pierce Creek on May's baking day—if the air was still, or he was to windward, he didn't have to get there and taste it to know.

His sense of the future, of other time, left him on a little shift of wind.

What was with him now was just himself, scoured. And time once again ticking.

Elsie shifted and worked her bare feet under the ham of his leg. He got up and fixed the fire, looked for something to put over her.

There wasn't much to the house, he didn't need to turn on a light to find the bedroom. One bed, a folded afghan at the foot. His fingers felt the holes, the lay of the yarn, the tighter twist along the scalloped edges. He came back into the light—only the color of it was a surprise.

Elsie opened her eyes when he covered her. She said, "Oh, good ... What time do you have to be at your boat?"

It seemed a very hard question. Before he got around to it, Elsie nodded off.

After a bit he thought, I don't *have* to get there any special time. I'm the captain.

He felt the return of figuring logically as if he was putting on clothes after being naked.

He didn't want Tran and Tony to start worrying. But he could use a little sleep. He went back to the bedroom and got hold of another blanket. There was enough room for him to stretch out on the sofa, his head at the other end from Elsie's. He took his boots off, thought he'd better wash his feet.

While he was sitting on the edge of the tub, Elsie came into the bathroom, hiked up her jumper, and sat down on the toilet. The noise woke her up completely. "God, I sound like a cow pissing."

When she was done, she pulled herself up on his shoulder. "One thing I won't miss is peeing five times a night."

She stayed while he dried his feet. They arranged themselves on the sofa, their feet and shins overlapping.

"There are things I miss," Elsie said. "Being in my own house. The salt marsh, the sea. And I miss Miss Perry. I even miss work."

"They're all right there," Dick said.

Elsie turned out the light.

Dick didn't go to sleep. Sometime in the last months, sometime in there between the time his boat had been in doubt and now, he'd changed, been breached as wide as the cut from the sea to the salt pond, and been washed of the worst of his bitterness. Curled up now in his own skin again, he had no way of seeing whether it was the storm or one of his own crazinesses that had breached him, or whether it was a goodness of his or of someone else that had kept him rooted soundly while his bitterness went out on the ebb.

It was odd—no question but that the worst bitterness was gone, though he couldn't say when or how. He fiddled with answers: maybe it was just plain getting his head above water, just being able to relax about putting bread on the table. It seemed more than that, though—he could have just had a job, and May and him could've put bread on the table.

Maybe it was May having a right to bitterness and choosing another kind of feeling. Not that she didn't get angry, but her anger was solvable, approachable; he could find his way back to her. She had put up with a lot, with no more vengeance than speaking her mind, telling him things he could do to make it right. She'd let him back in bed without too much fuss. It had been a good winter since then, he'd been fond of May lately in a way he hadn't felt for a long time. Another thing he hadn't put into a thought till now: when it came to regular homecoming, regular get-your-ticket-at-the-station, all-aboard, down-the-line, Kingston-next, next-stop, Kingston, on-time, and home-for-a-hot-supper, May had Elsie beat hollow. Even with her hair cut short and dyed. Now her hair was short, taking out her hairpins was what he missed—picking them one by one, letting his hand full of pins brush by her mouth so he could feel her breath getting short and quick, taking out the last couple of pins real slow, letting the ends scratch along her scalp a little the way she liked, fluffing out her hair, then combing it out straight with his spread fingers, starting at her forehead and going back to her neck, his little fingers getting in behind the tops of her ears, she liked that part a lot too, so well that it was often about then that she'd get her embarrassed half-smile on her face and switch the light off.

It was a funny damn thing to think of. He saw the funny side of how he'd just been carried away, grabbing a hold of Elsie when she was so pregnant she was tipping over.

He was like a green kid when he was around Elsie. This time it was her good sense that had kept things in order. And that was a funny thing too, Elsie having good sense, at least when it came to sex. She'd changed some too. Still quick and tart, but sweeter. Easier and sweeter and more connected . . .

And so he came onto his own change again, not just that his worst bitterness had drained, but his feeling of his distinctness. He'd spent a lot of time trying to make himself distinct by doing distinct things. His life on land was boats he'd built, bigger and bigger, until he built a boat that was big enough. That's how he would have put it. Or he might have put it that his life was distinct things: father's death, marriage, house, Charlie, Tom.

Even the skill that got him onto boats when he was young was his seeing what was distinct before most people could—he could make out the edge of a swordfish fin while the fish was still submerged way off, indistinct in the roll and glimmer of the sea.

He saw himself black against the sun, going out to the bow pulpit. Ease on up, on up over that fishy shape. He could see his shadow out in front of the shadow of the bow, a stiff cutout dancing on the bronze water. He saw himself held cocked just before his arm moved down, became one shadow with his body. The fish was away, stuck deep and fast, took the line out, took the silver keg—a bright eye that saw that fish clear down a taut line into its toggled wound.

Dick's arm twitched. Elsie stirred, rolled her belly sideways against his clean feet. Dick lay still.

And there was fixing a position on the surface of the sea. There was sounding out the bottom of the sea—the shelf, the canyons, right down to the ledges and cracks where hard little lobster scuttled around. The pots settled and gave off their rot day and night. Lobster crawled their way in, dreaming that fishy perfume, not dreaming how hard and fast they'd be. The water came in and out, but the distinct lobster was stuck in the distinct pot.

This time it was a blotched red buoy that kept an eye on these comings and goings, down the warp into the dark. More lines—a wand atop the buoy, a radar reflector atop the wand, a six-pointed, twelve-faced crystal that made a nice blip on the screen; no matter what course you came in on, it blinked right back at you, brought you straight in. He'd been measuring everything in hard lines. He'd measured himself in hard lines. Where would he be, what would he be, without hard lines?

He tried to sit up, almost called out to Elsie.

What would he be without the hard things he was right about? If his bitterness had drained, what would he be, how disabled? He didn't want to be like Eddie. It was hard to say about a friend as good as Eddie, but he didn't want to be that soft-shelled. In a way Elsie was right to say class rage—he'd been made by enemies. It was natural. How else did nature work? He'd used some of his tricks to show up the piss-to-windward sailors, wasn't much maybe, but it marked his territory. And *Spartina*. What had he ever got by letting up?

An answer came from a funny direction. He thought of Mary Scanlon talking about her father. Fresh from his funeral, she told his jokes, even told his dumb jokes. He was a man Dick might have put down as just another gabby mick. And here he himself was remembering her remembering her father's remembering. Little Tommy Scanlon whizzing down the hill at the noonday whistle, poking his cold face around the barrel on his sled, carrying the lunch pails to the mill, where his father was foreman of the dye works, where little Tommy Scanlon saw him jump over the dye vat . . .

Mary Scanlon sifted her old man like flour through her fingers.

Dick thought he'd be lucky to get as fine a sifting from his own kids. Include the one still in Elsie, now pressed against his feet. No building a boat, no hard craft of his would keep him from their judgments.

But that wasn't the only reason he thought of Mary and her father, to worry about how he'd be remembered. Not just for that. It seemed to be to get him to relax about something he'd always known—that they all flowed into each other. All of them set about the salt marsh in the little towns and the houses on the hills—they all got mixed in, they stayed themselves. Permeable, yielding to each other, how could they stay themselves? The notion was as dizzying as the notion that time moved through them, that they moved through time. They changed and changed and stayed the same.

They were here, they were gone, they were somewhere in time.

But if there was no time that mattered but the time that was inside them, then they'd be nowhere.

He'd been scared by that thought before, shuddered it away before. Now it stuck him, as if it was angered by what he'd thought before, angered by his airy-fairy kindly-light notions of time as wave, in motion through a sea that was always there. Of all of them as waves in a life that was always there. But what if you go into the dark—you go in, you don't come out?

Old geezers sitting around the Neptune near to closing time on a quiet night—he'd heard them say, "Best thing I ever did was have kids." It had always sounded feeble to him. Now it seemed completely empty.

They were all down there trying to wire the shackle. Each one of them alone, clinging to the stem of a mushroom anchor with one breath inside. One breath. It didn't matter if you got the shackle wired or not. There was no up. When your breath was done, no up.

You could let go or hold on, no difference. No up. No brightness getting brighter. You got dumber and dumber in the dark.

He was caught tighter and tighter in this thought, motionless but shot by thought to the end of his breath.

At last he was released. He felt how tight he'd got. His body was twisted hard as rope. He let his shoulders go loose, and he must have moved his feet, because Elsie pushed them away in her sleep.

He wasn't scared. He wasn't calm, but he wasn't scared anymore. He let his feet slide off the sofa onto the floor, got up, and put a log at the back of the coals. It was still dark at the window.

He no longer thought he'd brought that despair on himself by thinking big. Now it occurred to him he hadn't been scared enough when the wave came through the window into *Spartina*'s wheelhouse. He hadn't been scared enough, he hadn't been thankful enough. All right, he could see that.

But he was goddamned if he was going to go on being scared, not for one black wave of thought that might be true, might not be. He had other thoughts; they might be true too. One picture of himself turning into minerals in the dark wasn't necessarily all there was to it.

He took up what he'd been thinking when he'd left off. He started off warily. He thought of the other people around the salt ponds, the salt marsh, up in the houses in the hills. Take Elsie for one. Now, there was someone as unlike him, as unlikely to be connected to him, as he could imagine. By comparison, Miss Perry's connection to him and his family made sense. And yet it turned out he didn't just know about Elsie, he felt her feelings way beyond what she told him, beyond their rushes at each other. He could trace other people in her. She talked about how she was scared of becoming like Miss Perry, as if Miss Perry's spinsterhood could overtake her like a flood of sterilizing salt up into the fields above the marsh. But Elsie stuck to her, took in the good Miss Perry as much as she could, kept out the salt.

Elsie had her pricks of jealousy against her sister, against her sister's beauty, against all the cultivation it took to tend the blossoms of her sister's life. Elsie stuck to her too, imitated her, was working on her own blossoming in a beach-rose way, a wilder imitation of her sister's flowering.

And then there was Mary Scanlon, now at home in Elsie's house. Dick remembered how he'd laughed at the idea of the two of them under one roof—he'd said they'd take the paint off anyone who dared to come in. There was Mary making the place a nest while Elsie was in exile. Elsie complained about Mary's getting sentimental and holy, but Dick knew she was grateful for every twig and piece of down Mary moved into the nest.

For all Elsie had explained just now about why she'd stopped him from making love to her—she had good reasons, but he'd felt her blood come up too, reasons wouldn't have been enough—one thing Elsie didn't say was she'd taken on more virtue from these three women friends in her recent solitude than she ever had before. He felt them in her, forces as real as those that made her face fuller, her hair glossier. He felt her need of these forces, he felt them balancing her in little ways. Better than anything he could do for her. Just as well, then.

But it sure as hell was Elsie who'd got his blood up until he was as helpless and fierce as he'd been the first time. Maybe more helpless and wanting. But then it was Elsie, Elsie right here, who'd turned him away with a finger. Good. Good.

So what would he be for her? Not part of her. Let all the forces in his life run heavy, keep him set. Let Elsie be. Let whatever longings he might have turn into letting her be, as outside him as the salt marsh, let her be herself the way the salt marsh was the salt marsh for all that flowed in and out. His mind swelled that thought—the way the sea was the sea for all the winds across her, for all the pull of the moon and the sun, for all the spinning of the earth under her, for all that sent her rocking from one edge to the other, sliding up sounds and bays, eating at shores, slithering into salt creeks and marshes. . . .

He saw how small they were, Elsie and him in this little room. Nothing like the sea. Two dots you couldn't find in the real sea. Just enough life in them to keep paddling so they could keep drifting with the little colony of dots that'd spawned them.

He was exhausted now. He sat down by Elsie's feet. He worked his way carefully onto his end of the sofa. He could just see the lump of her by the light of the fire, he could just make out the purple afghan. A day at sea and now this night. He was back in his tired body all right. Just a few stray notions between him and sleep . . .

He'd have to tell May he saw Elsie. He could do that, Elsie had managed him so he could do that.

Elsie's forearm slid onto his feet, felt warm.

He'd get home as tuckered out as he'd been when he brought *Spartina* in after the hurricane. And on account of about as much foolishness on his part. When he'd got back that time he'd been able to tell May to be glad of *Spartina;* he didn't see what he was going to tell her to be glad of this time ... Elsie gave me back? Better not go into it all.

He pulled the blanket up to his neck.

The sun would wake him through the sea-side window—enough time before Tran and Tony began to worry, enough time to fix the antenna and get back out to haul the rest of the pots, enough time to get home.

Now he lay down feeling he had enough. He closed his eyes and saw the marsh, the salt pond at high water, brimming up into the spartina. He felt his easy breath on his fingers. Enough time would flood and ebb in him, bringing in and carrying out. ...

He opened his eyes. The log he'd laid had some salt in it—now it was aflame, there was a green sizzle to it, like the Northern Lights, like phosphorescence in the sea.

He closed his eyes again. It didn't matter that he didn't have more to want. It felt like part of his present that it was in him and in the nature of things for him to take in more, give out more before his breath ran out.

He could forget everything he'd thought here, this night, in the middle of his life. Let it ebb, and it would flow back. He felt like the salt marsh, the salt pond at high water, brimming.